BODIES IN THE TIBER

AN ANCIENT ROME POLITICAL THRILLER

THE SERTORIUS SCROLL BOOK
BOOK THREE

VINCENT B. DAVIS II

THIRTEENTH PRESS

For my cousin Addison.

Addi, this book and everything I will ever write is dedicated to you and your sweet heart.

We miss you so much.

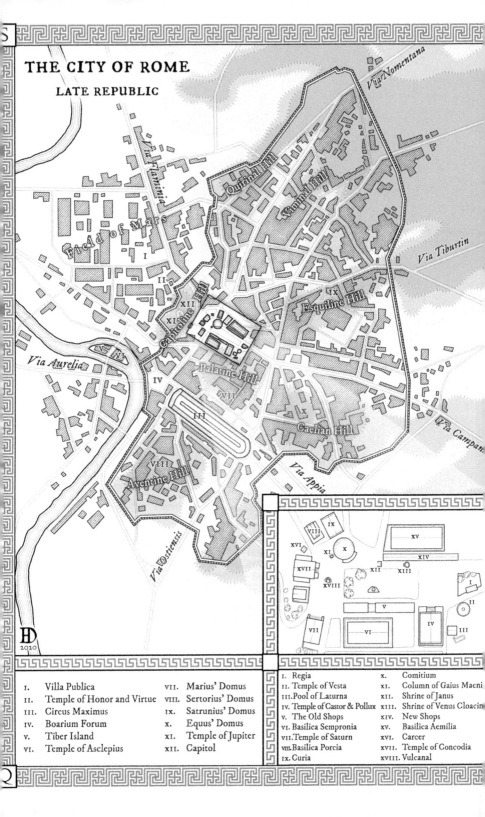

THE CITY OF ROME

LATE REPUBLIC

I.	Villa Publica	VII.	Marius' Domus
II.	Temple of Honor and Virtue	VIII.	Sertorius' Domus
III.	Circus Maximus	IX.	Satrunius' Domus
IV.	Boarium Forum	X.	Equus' Domus
V.	Tiber Island	XI.	Temple of Jupiter
VI.	Temple of Asclepius	XII.	Capitol

I.	Regia	X.	Comitium
II.	Temple of Vesta	XI.	Column of Gaius Maeni
III.	Pool of Laturna	XII.	Shrine of Janus
IV.	Temple of Castor & Pollux	XIII.	Shrine of Venus Cloacin
V.	The Old Shops	XIV.	New Shops
VI.	Basilica Sempronia	XV.	Basilica Aemilia
VII.	Temple of Saturn	XVI.	Carcer
VIII.	Basilica Porcia	XVII.	Temple of Concodia
IX.	Curia	XVIII.	Vulcanal

READING ORDER

KEEP
CALM
AND
JOIN THE
LEGION

To enhance your reading experience, Join The Legion to receive free downloadable companion materials like:

- High-resolution maps
- Family trees
- Free eBooks
- Glossary
- And more!

**This story is based on a
real man and real events**

I'm sitting beside a bubbling spring. The sun is just beginning to set, casting a marigold hue over the ripples in the water, but the frogs are already croaking from their lily pads. Children are giggling in the village behind me, playing with a dog.

My wife prepared a cup of warm honey water before I left our thatched-roof Iberian hut. She would have come with me if I asked, but she knows how much I enjoy stealing a few moments to myself to write these scrolls.

We've lived in this village for three weeks now. We'll be moving on soon, along with my men, but I've tried to savor my time here as much as the stress of commanding a revolution allows me. The villagers, after some resistance, have finally begun calling me by my first name. The men here bring their families to me, pride shining in their eyes as they introduce their firstborn, their brides, or their baby girls. I tell them they should be proud. They've accomplished the only thing in this life that really matters, and I encourage them to take that responsibility seriously.

As much as they admire me, I believe they visit most often to play with my pet fawn, Diana. Currently, she is nestled up beside me, her head in my lap, undisturbed by my writing on this parchment. Her legs just gave a gentle kick. It must be a dream of running alongside my legionaries in the meadow. She's become our most loyal camp follower, and occasionally, I jest that I plan on promoting her to legate.

Her pure-white coat is covered in dirt. We've spent the afternoon training with the men. It's her favorite thing to do. But we won't be doing that tomorrow.

For tomorrow, the men and I will be going to war.

My enemy approaches. My scouts say they're half a day's

march away. And I won't let them come closer and endanger these people, so I must sally forth to meet them.

This enemy is not made up of barbarian hordes, bloodthirsty pirates, or rebellious Macedonians. No, this army is led by the men I once sat beside in the senate house. The men on the front lines have probably served alongside me in some previous campaign or other.

Tomorrow we will be fighting Romans.

How has it come to this, you may ask? I ask myself the same question. Romans killing Romans? There was a time when the thought would have been absurd. But for as long as I can remember, it's all the Republic has known. How has it come to this? I'm certain the seeds were sown long before I ever entered this earth, but in my own experience, there is one moment in time that I recall as the catalyst from which so much death, loss, and tragedy has been born.

The 654th year from the founding of Rome. We had just returned from a victory over Rome's greatest enemy since Hannibal. At one point, the Cimbri and Teutones promised certain annihilation of the entire Republic and all we hold sacred. Yet Rome was victorious. We had conquered. And as far as a man could look into the corners of our Republic, as far as a man could see into the future, Rome was finally safe. There were no major wars to be waged. Our borders were protected. We boasted friendly relations with tribes and nations throughout the known world. In the summer of 654, Rome reigned supreme.

And yet, this was when the Republic began to die. The events that caused it I will here describe.

I've been writing these scrolls for over a year now and storing them carefully in a cedarwood box my mother gave me that same summer. My desire has always been that one day you, reader, will discover these scrolls. I hope the glory of what Rome was will burn in your heart. I pray it will encourage you to fight for freedom. To resist tyrants. To sacrifice what you must for the safety and future of what you love, and who you love.

It's a rather foolish endeavor, I must admit. Either I will be victorious and restore freedom and glory to our Republic, or I will be defeated and everything I've ever written will be burned with my corpse.

Still, I believe I will continue writing these scrolls as long as the gods see fit to allow me to continue my fight.

I hope, at least, that I'll be able to finish this set of scrolls. For these may be the most important yet.

They will reveal how we got here: Romans killing Romans.

May the goddess Diana keep you and sustain you. May you walk with her through green fields and quiet valleys. Beside bubbling streams. Until it is *your* time to fight.

Quintus Sertorius
679 ab urbe condita

SCROLL I

TWO DAYS AFTER THE IDES OF AUGUST, 654 AB
URBE CONDITA

THE MEN WERE RESTLESS, but restless was better than terrified. After all we'd endured, it wasn't so bad to be simply impatient.

We had been camping in the Field of Mars outside the boundaries of Rome since the ides of August, and the day of Marius's Triumph was finally upon us. Surprisingly, the men still made it to muster each morning but idled away their days playing knucklebones and convincing passersby to take love letters into the city.

The other officers and I generally let them have their fun. Mutiny didn't seem possible, but it was always a concern when fifty thousand legionaries were forced to sit and wait, spit-shining their armor, while the senate debated whether their victory was worthy of a parade.

Luckily, in this case, there was little cause for debate. By all accounts, we had saved the Republic. The delay was simply a matter of procedure.

After tending to some rather dull provisioning paperwork that evening, I made my way across the camp to Marius's tent, passing by the soldiers congregating around their tents and sharing wineskins among them and singing impromptu lyrics about the victory at Vercellae. They did their best, but it's hard to encapsulate the glory of a battle in which Rome single-handedly annihilated an enemy like the Cimbri.

As I passed by, one of my lower-ranking legionaries snorted some bile and hawked it near my feet.

"Soldier!" He froze at attention like he had caught sight of Medusa, his eyes fixed on the sky to avoid my gaze.

"Sir?"

"What was that?" I pointed to the glob of saliva on the dirt between us.

"I spit, sir." His comrades snickered behind him.

"You spit where?"

"On the ground."

"On what ground?" I put a finger into the chain of his lorica hamata.

"The Field of Mars."

"That's right. The Field of Mars. Pick it up."

Finally, he broke his gaze and met mine.

"Pick it up, sir?"

"That's right. Better men than you or I have trained and died here. Show them respect. Scoop it up and put it in your satchel."

He hesitated, his face reddening like a peach as his *contubernium* giggled behind him. As he bent to retrieve his spit, I turned on my heels. They burst into laughter, and I tried not to do the same. Something to keep the men on their toes, aye? This wasn't my first time performing the same routine.

Before I entered Marius's tent, I could hear laughter pouring out.

"Tribune Sertorius! How good of you to join us," Marius said as I pulled back the leather flap and adjusted my eye to the torchlight. The general had never been in better spirits. And who could blame him? Recently elected to another consulship, and about to celebrate a Triumph before the whole Republic, he was at the pinnacle of Roman prestige. One might say he had even surpassed the glory of his own hero, Scipio Aemilianus, or perhaps even the great Africanus himself.

"Good evening, gentlemen." I nodded to the officers gathered. In the back, I spotted Equus propped up on a table, swirling a cup of wine in his hand. He gave me a wink, and I deciphered it to mean the men were already good and drunk. Men can develop this kind of unspoken communication when on campaign together for so long.

"Would you have some wine? We're celebrating." Marius gestured to his massive slave Volsenio, who hurried to offer me a cup.

"I guess that answers my question, then," I said, accepting the cup gratefully. "I was going to ask how the meeting with the senate went."

"I just returned from the Temple of Bellona this hour. We're to Triumph tomorrow."

I raised my cup, and the others did the same. But the grin on Marius's face revealed there was something more. How could he have been refused a Triumph after defeating the Cimbri and Teutones? He could hardly be surprised that the senate acquiesced, even taking into account their disdain for him. No, his glee was springing from a different source.

"And?"

The officers chuckled, and all eyes fell on the general as he straightened his shoulders and tilted his head back in a grand fashion.

"I have received a new title: the Third Founder of Rome."

I sat in a backless chair and gave Marius a look of consternation.

"Is that right? And who bestows this title upon you?"

"The senate and people of Rome! Passed in legislation this very morning. And if I am to be immortalized with the gods of Mount Olympus, then you are my acolytes!" He wrapped an arm around Equus's neck and ruffled his hair.

"The Third Founder of Rome" was quite a title, but I wasn't sure it was equivalent to a god. Perhaps it was greater.

"We really have those nobles on their knees now!" Marius laughed and drained the rest of his wine. "Tomorrow will be a day to remember."

"So we Triumph tomorrow?" I said.

"Correct. All of Rome will praise their heroes," Marius replied. Everyone in the room swelled with pride, but certainly none more than the general himself. "Where's the slave of yours? What was it again, Apollodorus?"

"Apollonius. Freedman now. I've sent him into the city to help my family find a place to stay." My stomach turned when I thought of it. Apollonius had never met my wife or mother. He knew Arrea, of course, but it would be difficult to find them—despite the instructions I provided—with so many people flocking to the city.

"Yes, yes." Marius had stopped listening about the moment he'd asked the question. "He did give you that letter I wrote?"

"He did. I read every word," I replied as the others analyzed the general with sideways glances. He had written to me another long exhortation about his foray into the political arena. I was beginning to find this curious, and wondered if he had the time to write the others also, but their eyes revealed the answer.

"I think that letter will be informative to you, as was the last. Let's just leave it at that for now." He gave me a wink.

"Well, if we're triumphing tomorrow, perhaps we should stop drinking." I offered my cup to Volsenio, who filled it up with a smile rather than taking it from me.

"Nonsense. I've never heard of a triumphator showing up without a hangover."

I was certain that wasn't true, but I accepted the cup regardless.

"We really are at the peak of the world, men. If only Manius Aquillius and your friend Hirtuleius were here to celebrate with us."

I nodded sadly. Lucius had departed with Marius's co-consul to squash the slave uprising in Sicily. I could hardly imagine my oldest friend without a sword in hand by that point. When the commission was offered, Lucius was one of the first to volunteer.

"I wish it were so."

"Well, perhaps they will have a Triumph of their own. But tonight, we celebrate. To Marius's mules!" We laughed and drained our cups.

The next morning, I made for the stables. I would have the great honor of riding on horseback with the other officers behind Marius's four-horsed chariot. There was a buzz throughout the camp, like a field of insect activity. The men had been brash leading up to the Triumph, but now that the day had arrived for all eyes to be upon us, they were nervous.

"Do you need help ensuring your saddle is on properly?" I asked Equus as I gave Sura a pet on the snout.

"I do not, thank you. I'm a much better rider than I was at the beginning of our campaign. And I have always been much better than Lucius," Equus said, blinking the sleep from his eyes. "Were you able to rest any last night?"

Sura's tail swished as I adjusted her bridle.

"No more or less than any other night," I replied. He was one of the few I had confided in about my reoccurring nightmares. They had started after the end of the campaign when the noise began to die down. Equus implored me to wake him up when such nights occurred. I was hesitant to stir a man from restful slumber, even more so since I valued good sleep now that I was routinely denied it. But I occasionally took him up on the offer when I wanted to give Apollonius a break from my late-night intrusions.

"Oh, the impervious Tribune Sertorius." He rolled his eyes. "Not nervous at all about today, then?"

"About the Triumph? Why would I be?"

He considered it for a moment, then shrugged.

"I don't know. What if you trip up the stairs to the Temple of Jupiter?"

"I'm much more nervous to see my family." I took a fine-bristled comb to Sura's neck, the dust flying off in a manner that was oddly satisfying.

"Ah. That's a different story." Equus tried to adjust the reins of his horse, which fought him by stepping away. "Calm down, you Harpy. So, nervous to see them. Why?" He struggled with the horse but stole glances at me over his shoulder.

I considered the question and realized I didn't really know the answer. It had been a long time, and it felt even longer. My mother would love and guide me no matter what. But I wondered if she would even recognize me. However, Arrea and Volesa were another matter entirely. Arrea, because I still loved her but couldn't have her. Volesa, because I barely knew my wife, and she openly resented me for not dying with my brother, Titus. And Gavius, my son by adoption... Well, I doubted he would even remember me.

"Sertorius?" Equus asked. "What worries you? Are they critical of you? Dreadfully boring dinner company? What?"

"I'm just concerned they'll be disappointed in the company I keep." I shot him a wink, which I realized was much less effective from a man with only one eye.

"By Bellona. That's it? I'll be on my best behavior if you decide to introduce me. Besides, Lucius isn't here to make us look bad."

We hurried into formation as the sun was rising behind us, only to wait in position for hours. The centurions and *optiones* would take no risk that their men were not in proper order. They inspected every piece of armor for dints and scratches, every chin for a stray hair.

Luckily, Equus positioned his horse next to mine, so we could converse quietly without disturbing the inspections.

"Have you heard the ballad they prepared for Marius?" he said.

"I haven't. Any good? I can't imagine the men being talented songwriters."

He shook his head and exhaled through puffed cheeks.

"One of the worst things I've ever heard. Bawdy enough to make a temple prostitute blush. Offensive enough that old Marius might actually get his feelings hurt."

It was tradition to sing songs mocking the general during a Triumph. In theory, it was to ensure that the general did not become overly prideful on a day he was being hailed as a god. In reality, however, it was a time for the men to shout aloud what they usually said in whispers.

"That bad?"

"I wouldn't repeat it to my mother. She's a delicate woman, mind you, but the point remains. The thickness of Marius's pubic hair is a reoccurring theme." I let my head fall back and laughed. It was nice to have Equus here on such a day. When my mind drifted to seeing my family again, my extremities grew numb. "And you know how sensitive he is! I told a few of them to tone it down a bit, and they threatened to add a line about the inadequacy of my masculine appendages."

Cornu sounded, and the line began to move in front of us.

"Here we go." I breathed deeply and tried to slow my heart.

"Entering the city as heroes," Equus replied, but I could barely hear him over the thunder of fifty thousand legionaries stomping behind us.

I eased Sura into a trot and kept a calming hand on the nape of her neck. If she was anything like me, the marching soldiers reminded her of the battlefield. She was deaf, remember, but the rumble of the ground was enough.

We had barely stepped out of the Field of Mars before we were surrounded by well-wishing citizens.

"Hail!" they shouted.

"Rome's heroes!"

They showered us with flower petals and seeds of grain in thanksgiving as we passed under the triumphal arch, reserved in its use only for days such as this.

And there it was: the Eternal City. Granted, it had been some time since I'd left to join the legion, but she was entirely unrecognizable. There wasn't an insula, temple, or state building that wasn't covered in garlands. Men and women clung to every column and rafter, children perched on their shoulders for the best view. The streets—usually covered in dirt and horseshit—were swept to perfection. I was surprised to find that the stone path almost glistened white in the morning sun.

The cries rose as Marius passed. The crowds swayed like a retreating current to catch a glimpse of him and follow him into the heart of the city.

He was rigid and straight-backed, his balding head held high, and wearing purple robes embroidered with gold. He extended a laurel branch to the heavens, greeting the thousands he had saved. A slave stood behind him on the chariot waving a bell in one hand to ward off the evil eye. With the other, he held a laurel crown just a few inches above the general's head, symbolic that he was the closest thing to a king that Rome would ever allow, if only just for this day.

We continued along the *Via Sacra*, and somehow the crowds continued to grow. Their shouts of praise, so grateful to have been liberated from the terror of the Cimbri and Teutones, rose to such great heights that it drowned out even the stamping of the horses and the legionaries. The collective Roman voice coalesced and formed an almost-tangible presence. It was in the air. You could feel it on your skin, taste it.

Then, a shiver shot down my spine. A scream, a violent scream, coming from the hordes. I darted my gaze around the crowds, searching for the cause. To my bewilderment, no one else seemed to be concerned.

I felt a hand on my leg. It was Equus, who had closed the gap between us. He shook his head.

"It's the battlefield," he said. Peering around again, I realized I had only imagined it. I gave him a nod of appreciation. Only a man I had served with for so long would have even noticed.

I tried to force a smile again, and raised my hand to the crowds, doing all that I could to stop it from trembling.

But my breath caught in my throat, labored and short. My heart beat violently beneath my lorica. I resisted the uncontrollable impulse to flex my legs. I decided the pace of the procession was far too slow, desiring to make it out of the crowd as quickly as possible. The mob seemed to encroach, almost at Sura's haunches now.

I scanned their faces, unable to lock on to just one. Passing them by, I continued to glance over my shoulder to see if I had, as I imagined, seen the hooded men from Massilia or bearded Cimbri warriors spread out in waiting.

Thankfully, we soon arrived at our destination: the Forum. Marius's chariot wheeled to the right, and the officers and soldiers followed. Now, for the first time, we passed by what had led the procession. First, we passed by the war booty. Ox-drawn wagons filled with chests, three abreast, overflowing with gold and silver jewelry and religious ornaments, most of which the Cimbri had stolen themselves from other Gallic and Celtiberian tribes. Then came the statues, lifted high on the back of carts, held fast by taut ropes. I expected to find them depicting the strange gods of the Cimbri, but most of them were of the Greek Olympians. These, too, the Cimbri had absconded with from the temples of southern Gallic cities.

Then, we saw what the gatherers had been so enamored with. A procession of torchbearers, flag wavers, and musicians surrounded by the magisterial lictors. The people stood in awe of them, and only Marius stole their attention.

Following that, we passed the most detestable sight I had laid eye on since the battlefield at Vercellae. And to be certain, it forced my mind to return there for a moment.

The prisoners cowered shoulder to shoulder, shackled at their ankles and wrists. Their clothing was torn, some of them naked and bone thin. Their skin burned bright red from their first exposure to sunlight in so long. A unit of *evocati* whipped them from behind to ensure they kept pace, but it was the unleashed fury of the people that doled out the most punishment. Rather than grain and roses, the prisoners were showered with stones and piss pots from the nearby launderers. Even Marius was unable to steal the people's attention from this.

Many of these enraged citizens had lost husbands, sons, fathers, or brothers in the war against the Cimbri. Unable or unwilling to join the legion themselves, this is how they fought back and avenged the fallen.

At the prisoners' helm was the captive king, Teutobod, who in that moment was certainly regretting surrender. He was adorned in his royal regalia, for one last day, but by now, he was also covered in shit and his own blood.

It was quite a nauseating sight, to be honest. The memory of them shouting out that they would rape our wives upon their arrival in Rome kept it from being overly so, though.

We halted at the north end of the Forum square, and Marius leapt gracefully from his chariot and strode to the top of the Rostra.

He raised his arms in exultation to the city, who hailed him as imperator for the first time. He seemed to be shouting, but it took some time before the cheering subsided enough to hear him.

"Citizens of Rome!" His was the only voice commanding enough to have tamed the raving crowds. Finally, they gave way. "What a glorious day! A glorious day! For now, all the world *knows* what will become of them if they threaten the safety and might of Rome!" He gestured to the Cimbri and Teutone

captives. After waiting for the crowds to quiet again, he continued, "Rome is victorious. And not just because of Marius—"

Here they interrupted again, with shouts of, "Marius the
humble!"

"It was not just because of Marius! We also have need to offer
appreciation to the noble Catulus." He gestured to the other
commanding general, who had remained in his chariot beneath
the Rostra. The people clapped in moderate appreciation, but it
was clear who they attributed this victory to. I believe they
cheered as much for Marius's magnanimity as they did for Catulus's accomplishments. "And we must also offer thanks to some
of Rome's heroes who have served under me with distinction
and honor beyond comparison."

Here was an opportunity to applaud some noble's son, I
thought, a chance for Marius to earn goodwill from the senate as
he returned to Rome.

"Tribune Quintus Sertorius, come forward!"

My eye widened, and I ran it through my mind again to
ensure I'd heard it properly.

"Go!" Equus slapped my shoulder with a smile. He knew me
well enough to know I didn't desire this. What was Marius
doing?

"Quintus Sertorius, join me!"

A lower-ranking mule arrived at my side, took Sura's reins,
and offered me a hand down from her back. My knees nearly
buckled when I touched the ground.

The crowd ignited when they saw me. I kept my gaze fixed
on the ground before me and took each step carefully, now
fearing that Equus's comment about tripping might have been
prophetic.

Two legionaries helped me up the tufa steps to the Rostra. I
nearly fell over as my gaze shifted across the sprawling Forum
of Rome, bodies packed in as far as the eye could see. The
crowds continued to shout their praise, although I was aware
that they didn't know what or who they were even cheering for.

"Quintus Sertorius, who has already been honored for his bravery in scaling the walls at Burdigala, must now receive further appreciation from the Roman people," Marius began.

Two attendants appeared on either side of me, taking my arms within their own and clasping two golden armillae around my wrists.

"Quintus Sertorius has embodied the noble virtues every Roman should aspire to. He single-handedly infiltrated the Cimbri camp and helped free hundreds of Roman prisoners!"

The story was overly exaggerated, as you know, but the people gesticulated wildly, unaware. I kept my gaze down, aware that my family was somewhere out there. I felt ashamed. They did not need to know this, even if it were a fabricated retelling. I had not been privy to Marius's intentions to share this, since he had been quite clear that this was a secret mission.

A tinge of guilt rushed through me as I felt the gaze of the Cimbri captives, some of whom I may have interacted with.

"This gift Rome offers you, Tribune. Golden wrist plates, which depict your heroic actions in Gaul!" I looked down to find that the armillae indeed had finely crafted etchings depicting my flight with the captives from the Cimbri camp. There wasn't a bronze obol of truth to any of it, but the craftsmen had been careful to remove one of my eyes. "Rome is in your debt, Quintus Sertorius."

I was ushered from the Rostra, legs like kneaded dough, as Marius continued to offer other praises.

His speech continued on for some time, the general droning on about Roman might and the prosperity that could now follow the Cimbri terror.

I didn't take in a word of it. My vision swam, my stomach churned. I felt like I was in a dream. And perhaps I was. My nightly visions were just as vivid, but of a decidedly more horrific nature, so I decided that this was indeed real, despite how absurd it all seemed.

The crowd fell silent. I looked up from the side of the Rostra to appraise the situation. Silence in so large a gathering of people was haunting. Then the sound of wagon wheels on the stone filled the Forum. Teutobod, king of the Teutones, was wheeled to the foot of the Rostra, forced to meet the eyes of his victor. His eyes were wild like a wounded boar's. He spoke in his own language, and I'm certain I was the only Roman to understand it.

"Eat shit and die, you Roman cocks!" he shouted, or so I believed, his voice hoarse from lack of fluid.

The signal was given, and the bottom of the cart fell through. His shackled legs dropped, and his neck yanked up, restrained by a thick rope of animal hair. He thrashed wildly, as much as he could while bound the way he was. His eyes bulged, and his tongue flailed to and fro as he gasped for air. Above me, the general lowered his head, in respect for his defeated foe. When the king mercifully fell silent in death, Marius raised his head to the roar of thousands, louder now than ever before. The legionaries bashed their swords against their shields.

It was over. The two men had gone into battle, and the one who'd lifted his head was he who had won.

Before I could really come to my senses, I found myself joining the other officers as we followed the triumphator up the slope of the Capitoline to the Temple of Jupiter, followed by carts of gold to be offered to the god who had secured our victory.

The path narrowed as we approached the temple, guards struggling on either side of us to hold back the adoring crowd from a stampede. Marius ascended the steps first, pausing beneath the massive statue of Jupiter on his four-horsed chariot —much like the one Marius had just ridden into Rome—at the crest of the temple.

A beautiful black bull was led out by his nose ring to the center of the steps. Garlands adorned his head, and his eyes reflected the commotion all around him with a calm abandon. He neither resisted nor struggled. He was complicit in the sacrifice to Jupiter.

The *flamen dialis* led the offering, placing his long ceremonial knife at the bull's throat. With one clean cut, the beast collapsed, the thud echoing throughout, along with a single bellow to rival Theseus's Minotaur. Seemed like a waste of a good bull to me. And was it really Jupiter's victory? Some food for the returned veterans seemed a more fitting sacrifice for Rome, but tradition does have its place, I'll admit.

With the auspices now being taken and the feast being prepared, I broke away. First, because I was anxious to get to a less crowded area. Second, although I was nervous to see my family, there was nothing to delay it any longer.

"Where are you going?" Equus grabbed my arm as I turned to leave.

"My family will be waiting on me, *amicus*. I'll see you soon." I extended a handshake.

"You just don't want them to meet me." He shook his head as if saddened. "I guess I can't blame you, now that you're a hero."

"You're worse than a woman, Equus." I gave him a smile and a playful pat on the shoulder. "I'll introduce you soon."

He shrugged and gestured to the celebration around him. The people were going mad now, the whole of Rome swirling in wine, song, and dance.

"We're home now, brother. We've won. Try to enjoy yourself."

I hurried to the designated meeting point, the steps of the Temple of Castor and Pollux on the far side of the Forum. I realized as I pushed through the rampant crowd that my family was unlikely to know the location of the temple in the first place, let alone with so many packed in around us. I wasn't even certain I could find it with so many pressing in all around me.

When I made it to the steps, I found a pocket of open space to catch my breath. I hadn't realized until then that I was drenched head to toe in sweat. The armor hid the stains, but it would do nothing about the smell. Some way to greet your family after so long.

"Quintus?"

It was a familiar voice, one that pierced through the ruckus around us.

"Mother?" I shouted, lifting my head to find her through the crowds.

"Here!" When I spotted her, I broke into a sprint up the stairs. They were in sight now, and nothing could keep me from them. I was more grateful to see them than I had imagined.

"Dear Mother." I wrapped her in my arms as snot and tears fell on my shoulders.

"How dare you! You didn't write. You didn't write! You went into the enemy camp?" She pulled away to look at me as if to ensure I was really the boy she remembered before pulling me back into her embrace. "Oh, my boy, you're home!"

"I'm home, Mother."

She refused to release me, but I looked over her shoulders. Apollonius, smiling in that all-knowing way he usually did. Gavius, a foot taller at least since I had last seen him, his eyes wide with the shock of so much activity around us. Then Arrea.

Gods...her beauty was painful. The breath was driven from my lungs, the strength in my hands evaporated at the sight of her.

"Mother," I whispered after the embrace lingered for too long, and she released me. "My son." I knelt before the boy. Apollonius patted me on the shoulder plate and stepped away to allow us a moment.

Gavius studied my scarred face with trepidation and suspicion. He reached up and took hold of Arrea's hand.

Perhaps it was my helmet, or the scarlet plume atop it. I removed the straps and placed it at my feet.

"Will you not embrace me?" I gulped.

"Gavius, greet your father like we've practiced." Arrea's voice enveloped me and slowed my heart like the sound of trickling water in a peaceful spring.

Gavius finally lowered his head and took a knee.

"Here, now." I reached under his arms and pulled him to me.

He didn't resist, but he didn't embrace me either. "How I've missed you," I said, although, in truth, I hardly remembered him. He was nothing like the toddler I remembered. Nearly eight now, I could hardly recognize him. He did have his father's eyes, though, and that curly hair. I could never deny he was family.

"Arrea." I stood to my feet and met her eyes. I resisted the impulse to follow her name with "my love," as I so often referred to her when we were together in Gaul.

She lowered her head, as a slave does before her master.

"Arrea, embrace me." Rather forward, I'll admit. But I had waited a very long time to feel her skin against mine. And I was tired of being patient.

She leaned in to hug me, restrained and distant at first, but then fell into my arms, fitting like a sword in a scabbard, the way she always did.

The smell of her hair made my knees weak. So familiar.

I lingered until I realized it was becoming inappropriate.

"Where is my wife?" I asked.

No one replied. Everyone averted their eyes, except Apollonius, whose gaze expressed anguish.

"Where is Volesa?" I asked again, not taking their meaning.

Mother wiped away the last of her tears and reached for my hand.

"We should talk."

We settled in at an old wooden table in the room we had rented on the Quirinal Hill, and they told me what happened.

"She wasn't well, Quintus."

"She wasn't sick," I replied.

Mother refused to release my hand.

"She wouldn't eat. She wouldn't sleep. She was sick, and the best Greek doctors in Nursia couldn't figure out why." She leaned in closer. "But we did, Quintus."

I stood from the table abruptly, startling them.

"Tell me again. How did she do this?"

"She put arsenic in her wine," Mother said. Arrea distracted Gavius in the back of the room and whispered softly in his ears.

Your brother would blame you.

The voice rang crisp in my ears, as real as the walls around me.

"I don't understand. Her husband dies, and she decides to leave her child an orphan?" I asked, incredulous.

"He is not an orphan," Mother replied sternly. Arrea's glare proved she agreed.

"You know what I meant."

Your brother hates you more than he hates the barbarians that killed him.

I slammed the table to silence the voice.

"I need some wine."

Arrea led Gavius by hand to the door, under the guise of getting some fresh air. They had never been to Rome on a public holiday, if they thought they'd find fresh air out there. But I knew why they were really leaving.

"My son. There is nothing to be done of it now."

I drained a cup of wine, wincing at the poor quality.

"I'm grieved. Grieved deeply. And now I'm twice dishonored: first to marry another man's wife, and then to have lost her."

"You cannot possibly be so selfish?" Mother asked, genuine perplexity covering her face.

"Selfish?"

"To concern yourself with your own honor after Volesa dies?"

"What else is there but honor?" I said, even though I didn't believe it. It was the kind of thing Titus might have said, and for that reason, it brought me a twisted satisfaction to be so stubborn.

"I cannot talk to you when you're like this." She stood and turned her back to me. "We have waited so long for you to return to us, Quintus."

I wiped wine from my upper lip and exhaled. My mother could move me to shame as easily as a shepherd leads his sheep to green pastures.

"I apologize, Mother. I'm not myself. I was expecting a joyous reunion as well. I hadn't prepared for Volesa to be…" I couldn't finish the sentence.

I wasn't quite sure why I was so disturbed. I had never known her as a lover. I hadn't known her at all for quite some time. But she was a soft thing in a harsh world, and I was sad she was gone.

More than anything, it was that nagging voice in the back of my head that bothered me.

Titus wouldn't have let this happen. Your father wouldn't have let this happen.

"I've not quite returned yet, Mother," I said, my voice weak.

"Your father said something similar when he returned from his first campaign. Give it time."

When I feared I would be moved to tears, I stood and stretched.

"This armor is chafing me awfully."

The boy I was when I'd first donned the colors was dead. He'd died the moment I took a life, or perhaps when I'd first watched a friend take his last breath. A soldier had taken his place. But now that I must remove my helmet once again, back home, who was I? The boy was gone, the soldier must retire. All that was left was a shadow.

I unbuckled my helm and set it by my bended knees. I ran

my fingers through the plume, then opened up the chest before me. It was made of cedarwood, with silver plating on the sides. If you're reading this, I imagine you're familiar with it, as this is the box I'm storing these scrolls in. Those men etched into the side are my father and my brother. I would imagine it's the only portrait of them on Gaia's earth.

My mother had it crafted while I was gone for this very purpose: to house my armor until it was time again that I should have need of it.

"May that time never come," she said before leaving my room at the inn.

I leaned to the side and pulled the lorica over my head, allowing the chain to collapse on the floor. I felt weightless without it.

I ran the leather straps of the lorica through my hands, and remembered all the times I had scrubbed the blood off them.

"Is there anything you need?" Arrea entered and leaned against the doorframe.

I peered over my shoulder but couldn't meet her gaze.

I was aware that my scarlet tunic clung to damp flesh, with pools of black cloth beneath my arms, but there was nothing I could do to hide it.

She patiently awaited my answer as she walked across the floor and placed a hand on my shoulder, nothing more. But that gave me the strength I needed to fold the chain mail and place it within the trunk. I laid my sword and belt atop it. Then the helmet, careful to place it in such a way that didn't ruffle the plume.

"Show me where my armor ends and where my skin begins."

SCROLL II

I SPENT the majority of two days sleeping. It was as if a flood of energy had escaped my body and all that remained was a shell. I could barely stand. For the first time in so long, I could shut down self-preservation, I could quiet the voice that tried to calm me before battle or soothe my ailing conscience for taking a young man's life. Every time I considered getting up, I thought about the responsibilities that awaited me, or thought of Volesa, and then tucked myself back in. I wasn't ready to face it all yet.

Mother and Arrea were gracious. They didn't wake me very often, and were careful to remain quiet while I was sleeping, for our room at the inn was small and the wood creaked.

Apollonius entertained them with stories and read them poetry. Gavius didn't seem to mind my absence.

It wasn't until the third day that Mother woke me.

A beam of light poured in, so I pulled a pillow over my head to block it.

"Quintus?"

"What time is it?"

"Sixth hour. You have a visitor." She spoke softly, but it irritated me nonetheless. I knew I should rise. Any Roman of *dignitas* wouldn't sleep past the sunrise. But the warmth of the bed drew me in. The weakness of my legs compelled me to not move them, even an inch.

"Is it Equus? Tell him we'll have dinner tonight."

"I don't believe that's his name."

I threw off the covers and wrapped a belt around my waist. Who could be disturbing us? Who knew about our rented room on the Quirinal? And who would care to know?

The man at the door was unmistakable. There was no one else like Marius's slave Volsenio. He must have ducked to walk through the doorway.

"What a surprise." I shook his hand, and he smiled as if it were just a friendly visit. But I remained a bit on edge. Marius's most important attendant didn't make social calls.

"Marius was disappointed that you didn't join him in celebration after the Triumph."

"I didn't know I was invited." I gestured for Arrea to fetch him a cup of wine.

"He said it was implied."

"I'm not sure how. I assumed he would want to spend some time with his wife."

"He places his men before all. And he places you before most of them."

I blushed a bit, but shook my head, knowing it was pure flattery.

"Regardless, I discovered that my wife passed away during the campaign. I had to begin the period of mourning."

Volsenio looked contrite. "The consul and I both would have offered our condolences if we had known. He would have wanted to visit you to offer you his sympathies himself."

"I'm unsure what I've done to deserve such affection... although I return it. He just has many officers." I realized how rude I was being. I blamed it on the sleep, but wasn't about to tell a man like Volsenio that I had just stirred from slumber at this hour. "Please, sit." I gestured to the table as Apollonius rose and offered him the chair.

"I will, thank you. If only briefly."

"Volsenio, how have you found me? I mean, *why* have you found me?" I asked as I joined him at the table, a touch irritated that he hadn't made his purpose known.

"I've been asking for you for days. Tribune Cinna Equus was the only one who knew where you'd be staying."

"That doesn't tell me why."

"Marius himself wanted to talk to you, but after the delay, he says I must relay the information. Marius wishes to be consul again."

I laughed, then became sullen. Laughed, then straightened face. I couldn't tell if he was joking. Volsenio wasn't known for his humor, though.

"Why? He is consul now. He is at the height of his power. The people love him fiercely. What more could he want?" I didn't mention the heinous illegality of running for another consulship.

"Marius doesn't believe it's the height of his power."

"Oh, spare me, Volsenio!" I spit. "How can a man like that really believe in a prophecy from a blind Syrian priest?" It was the prophecy Marius held close to his heart, one he dwelled on constantly. The prophecy that he would be consul seven times.

Two times was illegal. Seven was a monarchy.

"It's more than prophecy." Volsenio didn't react to my words at all.

"Volsenio." I leaned across the table and met his eyes. "Rome was willing to follow the man because of the barbarian crisis. Now the Cimbri are being strangled in our *carcer*, and the Teutones are rotting on the plains of Aquae Sextiae. They will not tolerate a tyrant when he has nothing left to save them from."

Volsenio and I had grown familiar during campaign, so I

knew it wouldn't bother him if I was forward in my response. I did realize I was being a bit aggressive as I heard the others squirming behind me.

"He does have something to save them from."

"What, Macedonians? Lusitanians?"

"From the nobles."

"Oh, now I see clearly. That's why he wrote me that letter."

Volsenio's face registered confusion, so I didn't mention it further.

"Consul Marius has disbanded his men as any good man would—"

"As any law-abiding citizen would," I corrected him.

He exhaled but didn't reveal frustration.

"He will still need the support of the legions to win the election. And you."

I laughed openly now, not intentionally mocking Volsenio but instead the message that he brought. I couldn't believe what I was hearing. I recalled all the things the Caepiones said about Marius, and suddenly they felt believable, and that wounded me.

"Why would he need us? He has the love of the people."

"His opposition will not come from the people but from within the senate house."

I turned from him and raised my voice. "Roman armies are not tools to be used by politicians for personal gain!"

"I will not try to convince you." He finished his wine and stood.

"And I will not bring swords to the senate house." I turned and met his gaze.

"Marius doesn't want you to bring swords to the senate house. He wants you to be a senator."

I tried to formulate a response, but couldn't.

"I must go. The consul needs your answer within three days or the censors won't be able to add you to the senatorial rolls." He bent and kissed my mother's hand, and nodded a farewell to me, knowing full well he had stunned me.

The smell of fresh baked bread and stale wine filled the tavern.

"It's preposterous. Me, a senator! Too young, too poor, too inexperienced..." I tossed a few coins to the servant for a bowl of olives as my family laughed at me.

"And why not? This is the kind of opportunity you've longed for!" Apollonius replied. They were all merry with excitement and found my consternation amusing.

"You can help our village, Quintus," Mother said, the only one seeming to notice my irritation.

"And how much will I be able to do? If I gain entry from Marius's patronage alone, I'll be too busy following orders like I did on the battlefield to do anything on my own."

"Perhaps. But this is only the beginning! You have a long career ahead of you," my mother replied.

I pushed the wooden bowl of olives between us, and peered out into the street where a Greek tutor was teaching a handful of young boys, none of whom appeared to be listening.

"No, no. It's illegal, for one. I'm not old enough, I've never been a quaestor..." My voice trailed off as I exhausted my list of excuses. "One day, perhaps. But there are procedures in politics for a reason! I'm not ready."

"And yet Marius opens the door for you," Arrea said before popping an olive in her mouth.

"He must have a reason behind this." I turned and leaned on the tavern bar, shaking my head.

"What if his reason is that he wants to add good men to the senate, my dear son?" Mother placed a hand on my arm and met my eye. I wanted to tell her how naive it sounded but couldn't bring myself to do so. I felt certain Marius had an agenda. He always did. But perhaps they were right. What if I could do more good being a senator than anything else? How could I refuse? And what would I go on to do instead? Breed horses?

After Arausio and Vercellae, that didn't seem possible.

I took the rest of my lunch in silence, allowing the others to make jests about how fine I'd look in a broad-striped toga.

"Quintus, why don't we head back up to our room and you can pray to the ancestral gods? They can help you," Mother said.

"I don't want to wake them from their eternal slumber for something foolish like this. It made more sense for me to accept Marius's covert mission than to accept this."

Mother broke away from the tavern and gestured for us to follow. She wasn't to be denied, my mother.

When we arrived back up in the room, she lit incense on the makeshift altar the inn provided in each room, and pointed for me to kneel.

Apollonius provided a pillow for my knees so that I wasn't able to refuse.

I exhaled deeply, the only way I could make my resistance known, and kneeled before the altar. Mother sat beside me and wafted the smoke toward us with both hands.

I peered behind me at Apollonius and Arrea, who watched us, to my irritation. We Romans might have looked a bit odd to those foreigners in that moment.

"Here." Mother extended a bull-scrotum-leather pouch into my hands.

"What's this?"

"Look inside."

Within were tiny effigies. I could see that one was my father. Another was Titus. Beside them was my bulla, the amulet each Roman boy receives at his birth and gives up on his day of manhood.

"Why are you giving me this?"

"My son, I knew that you wouldn't be returning to Nursia. Even before today. The gods have destined you for greater things. Your bulla should remain within your home, at the altar of your household gods. And your father and brother should be with you wherever you go." I could say nothing, so she continued. "Pray to them."

She stood and left me alone.

The incense burned in my nostrils, the sting familiar from my youth when my father would gather the entire family each morning for a prayer just like this.

It had been a long time.

Brother, forgive me. Your wife has joined you in the afterlife. And it is my fault.

I was surprised that this was the first thing I would say. But I was unsure how they would greet me now.

Father, I live only to make you proud. Give me restraint when I am angry. Give me temperance when I am tempted to drink too much. I am none of the things you were. Impart your strength on me.

I realized my knuckles were white, palms clutched around the effigies.

Speak to me, please. Give me guidance for the days ahead.

I heard no voices, I guess I never did.

"Uncle Quintus."

I turned to find Gavius behind me. It was the first time I had heard his voice since arriving in Rome.

"Call him father as you've been taught to do." Arrea placed a hand on his back and wagged a finger at him.

"Yes, Gavius?"

"Mother used to say a boy could catch a fish in Rome. She said my father would catch fish when he visited here."

I felt uncomfortable addressing him. I didn't know how to do so properly.

"That's right. The Tiber has many fish just the right size for a boy like you to bring in."

"Could we go? Now?"

I looked to see if Arrea, Apollonius, or Mother had put him up to it. It didn't appear that they had.

"Certainly. Let's fetch a meal for the family, shall we?"

Perhaps it would do me some good to clear my mind before formulating how I would refuse Marius.

My mother stopped me before we departed. She leaned in and whispered, "I believe I shall be gone by the time you return. It will be easier on the boy."

I looked at her, perplexed.

"Already heading back home?"

"It is time."

"Are you taking Arrea with you?"

She smiled, all-knowingly, and shook her head.

"No. I think you need the company more than I do. Besides, I have Lucius's brother, Aius, waiting for me at home. He's been an excellent helper."

"Well, do take my horse, Sura, with you. I'd rather have her grazing our fields than stuck here in the stables."

I thought about extending a long embrace, but so as not to arouse Gavius's suspicions, I gave her a quick kiss on the cheek.

"Goodbye, Mother." I turned to Gavius. "Ready to go?"

He charged to the door without another word.

With a rented bamboo pole and a wicker fish cage to store our catches in, Gavius and I settled in on the bank of the river Tiber. I tested the weight of the horsehair line and adjusted the hook, pretending like I knew what I was doing.

The truth was I hadn't fished in years, and the last time I'd gone, my father had baited the hook for me, which gives you an indication of how distant that memory was. Damned if I would let Gavius know it, though. I was just pleased he was speaking to me, let alone wanting to spend time with me.

"Are you ready, young Neptune? We're going to bring back a feast." I ruffled his hair and watched him to see if that was acceptable. He didn't seem to mind.

I knew about as much of children as I did of fishing. I was the youngest in our family, save a little girl who didn't make it out of infancy, so I never had much experience in rearing children. Lucius's brother, Aius, had often been around during my youth, but my time with him typically consisted of practical jokes and occasionally letting him in on some game his brother and I were playing.

I didn't know the first thing about being a father.

"What kind of fish will we catch?"

I hesitated to answer, not wanting to spoil the moment by saying that we might catch nothing.

"Big ones. Small ones. Every catch counts." That was about as descriptive as I could be, as I didn't have a clue about the different types of fish in the Tiber.

He scrunched his nose as I set the worm on the hook, the poor critter wiggling in agony as I lowered it into the water, a cork on top to indicate when a fish had taken hold.

"Did my father ever go fishing?" He set the rod between his legs and scooped up a handful of grass and began splitting the blades in two.

"You better keep both hands on that rod, in case a beast from the depths takes the bait." He smiled and hastened to comply. I thought about correcting him, reminding him that I was now his father. I did not. "He did. Titus and I often went with your grandfather Proculus. We didn't fish for fun, though. We had to catch something or we didn't eat."

He looked at me with serious eyes.

"We are not fishing just for fun, are we?"

"No. That's right. We have women to feed, after all." I patted his shoulder, and to my relief, he giggled.

Perhaps we could still make this work. Perhaps I could be a fraction of the father my own was. Perhaps I could raise this child, even without Volesa.

"I overheard Grandmother say Momma didn't like you," he said, wiggling the pole to ensure everything was still attached properly.

"That's not true. She didn't mean it like that... Your mother was just...very sad."

"Of course *you* would say that."

At first, my pride was a bit injured, but I couldn't help but see his father in him. And somehow that pleased me.

I scrutinized the waters, trying to spot some sign of movement. There was none. For all I knew, there hadn't been a fish near that bank for a thousand years. How was one to tell?

Nothing was stirring, and I could see Gavius was already losing interest, so I decided to distract him.

"Look here, Gavius." I took out the leather pouch my mother had given me, and I reached in to grab the contents. "These are the effigies of our house. This is your father. This one, your grandfather. And this one represents our ancestors, all the men who came before us." I handed them to him one at a time.

He lingered especially on his father's, turning it each way and admiring the tiny details.

"It's not what I imagined he looked like."

"Well, he didn't really look like that, I suppose. But it suggests his features. A strong jaw, long nose...curly hair like yours."

"You don't have hair like mine," he said without turning to me. He had clearly already been wondering about that. He was right, after all. Titus had inherited the fair hair of my father's family; I, the dark hair and skin tone of my mother's.

"No. But you have my eyes. All the men of the Sertorii have them."

He analyzed me for a moment, and didn't confirm or deny

the claim. Neither did he mention that I, in fact, only had one eye to his two.

"What else do the Sertorii have?"

I considered it. There didn't seem to be many physical traits we all shared. My brother, tall and broad; my father, slight and short; myself, somewhere in between. My uncle was fatter than the three of us combined, and if I remembered correctly, my grandfather had a nose twice the length of mine and moles dotting his face.

"For one thing, we're stubborn. A trait I can already see you've inherited," I said, the joke lost to him. "The Sertorii are always devout in their faith, and are loyal servants of the Republic. We've all fought for Rome when it's been our time."

"What else?"

I thought that was a rather satisfactory answer myself, but Gavius was unsatisfied.

"Keep your eyes on that cork, Gavius, or you'll lose the rod." I stalled. "Good with horses. Talented riders. It's been our trade for generations. Adequate hunters, although your father never had the patience for it, a claim he most certainly would have denied." The thought of my brother warmed me and saddened me at the same time. "More than anything, Gavius, the Sertorii are good men. More than anything, we are *good*."

"Are you a good man?" He turned to me, without hesitation, and looked in my eye. He asked with genuine interest. He didn't have an answer in mind.

I took the pole from him and applied a fresh worm.

Was I? I considered it for longer than Gavius would have liked, but he patiently awaited my reply, refusing to move on until I answered him.

Who was I now, after everything? Who was *I*? What makes me *me*? My family name? It was hard to rest on that when all the other men were dead. My experience, then? My actions? My values?

"I was a good man, Gavius. I was. Perhaps too good at times."

"Can you be too good?"

I smiled and shook my head.

"You cannot be too good, Gavius, no. But I was foolish. So stubborn in my pursuit of virtue, naive in the ways of the world. Sometimes I irritated your father to his wit's end. Foolish and tiresome, he called me."

"But not anymore?" His brow furrowed.

I couldn't answer, and I scratched at my face to hide the quivering of my lips. How could a boy understand all that I had been through? All that war had asked me to do? How could he understand what it meant to take a man's life? How could my nephew appreciate the gravity of giving a command that resulted in the death of those under your leadership? If only he had known the young man who'd stood up to Gnaeus and Quintus Caepio in their own home. *That* was a good man.

It wasn't my actions that condemned me. Everything I had done was for the good of the Republic, and the safety of my family. It was how my actions had changed me. It was that I didn't know what I stood for anymore.

Would I stand up to Gnaeus Caepio now? Perhaps the Republic was saved because of it, but I had betrayed thousands of barbarians whom I trained, ate, and drank with to their deaths or enslavement. What more would I do for the Republic if adequately convinced of its necessity?

"I will be, my son. I will be again. It may just take some time."

He had lost interest in my brooding as much as he had lost interest in fishing, and the answer didn't appear adequate for him.

"It'll be getting dark soon. And the waters put off a cold that can freeze off a man's toes. We should head back to the inn," I said, staring at the sun's reflection stretched out on the water before us like an orange column.

"But we have nothing to feed our women."

That was a line straight from Titus if I'd ever heard one. "We can stop by the Forum Boarium on the way home and buy a few fish. I'll tell them you brought them in all by yourself." He turned to me with the righteous indignation of a child.

"That's dishonest," he said. I paused, stinging from the rebuttal. Then his face lightened into a smile. "We'll have to get a very big one. Arrea will be so proud of me."

"We'll bring home the biggest one in the market," I said, also with a yearning for Arrea's affection.

SCROLL III

THE FISH we brought home wasn't very convincing. We couldn't have brought that thing in without a harpoon, the way the rich fished. But Arrea and Apollonius were good enough to play along, and Gavius didn't even seem to mind much that his grandmother Rhea had left for home. Perhaps it hadn't set in that he would be living under my roof from that point forward, wherever that may be.

After Arrea had settled Gavius into slumber, the three adults sat around the table with cups of wine, still picking tiny bits of fish bone from our teeth.

My head was already swimming from the drink, but I did my best to not reveal this, as I could tell they were partaking far slower.

"Were you able to think any more about Marius's proposal?" Arrea asked in a hushed tone.

"Gods." I gulped. "I had completely forgotten."

"Perhaps that's a good thing. Nothing makes better decisions than a clear mind," Apollonius said, tapping his chin.

"No, I believe I need to dwell on it a bit further." Unwittingly, I was reaching for the amphora of wine.

"I don't quite understand your reticence, Quintus," Arrea said. Her voice sounded so distant. Whether it was or not, I interpreted it as devoid of love, but there was no time to analyze her words.

"Perhaps you should become the senator, then," I replied.

"Simply explain it to us, Quintus. All those nights we huddled in Gallic tents, you whispered to me of a desire to change Rome for the better, to leave a legacy."

The words bit at my pride because I remembered them but not the sentiment with which they were spoken.

"I don't know what I want anymore," I replied. I started to continue, but Apollonius stopped me.

"No, I think we need to rest here for a moment. What is it that you want, Quintus Sertorius?"

Her question irritated me, and I didn't know why. How would they like to answer such abstract questions? Then I became agitated with myself, because the answer shouldn't be so elusive in the first place.

"I don't know."

"You must know. Just say it. Without thinking or judgment, just say it."

"I would hurt bad people. I would find those who…harm women. Or children. Or animals. I would make them fight someone who could retaliate."

Arrea seemed a bit concerned by my response. I realized it was the wine talking, but Apollonius was nodding his head.

"You wish to protect the weak. Those who cannot protect themselves," Apollonius said.

"Yes," I said, thankful for the assistance.

"What else? What else makes your heart burn like Vesta's flame?" Apollonius asked. Arrea's cocked eyebrow revealed she didn't catch the reference, but she listened intently for the response regardless.

"The rich. Those greedy, fat old men who gorge themselves on delicacies while the people starve." Perhaps it was Marius's most recent letter that echoed in my mind then, or the memory of Gnaeus Caepio and his cronies. Either way, I didn't recall dwelling on this much.

"You wish to protect the weak once again, Sertorius. A noble calling if I've ever heard one. Do you not believe you can do so more effectively from the senate house than from Nursia?" Apollonius said.

The old philosopher had outwitted me once again.

The effects of the wine really seemed to set in at that moment, and I struggled to fix my vision on the table before me. Still, I found myself reaching for the red-figure clay amphora.

"Perhaps we should allow clearer minds to make this decision?" Apollonius said, reaching over and placing his soft hands atop my own.

I returned as defiant a look as I could muster.

"I've helped conquer two nations, the newsreaders call me a hero, and now I am to be lectured by a freedman?" He returned the glare until we both burst into laughter. I relinquished the amphora and leaned back in my chair. "If I do this, I will never be simply Quintus Sertorius again."

You aren't Quintus Sertorius anymore, already, the voice in my head whispered.

But I will be again, an entirely new voice replied.

"Senator Sertorius, they shall call you. And the name will go down in the annals of history as a defender of the weak," Arrea said with a furtive smile.

"And shouldn't I be able to raise a cup to the beginning of our good fortune?" I posed to Apollonius, looking for his permission.

At length, he nodded and scooted the amphora in my direction.

"Here's to wherever the gods and my ancestors lead me next." I lifted my cup and drained every last drop.

It wasn't difficult to find Marius's home once I reached his neighborhood on the Palatine. Graffiti covered the walls, as if directing the entire city toward it. "MARIVS VICTOR," "IMP. MARIVS," and "MARIVS EST TRIVMPHATOR" were painted in bold white paint on every corner, a vulgar drawing of Marius as Priapus a few times as well.

Two eagles with wings spread perched to hold the door ring between their beaks. Marius must have had it handcrafted, and to good purpose, for no one would have mistaken this domus as anyone's but his.

I rapped the ring three times and stepped back, feeling anxious like I had when I first approached the domus of Gnaeus Caepio, but for very different reasons.

A short, bovine-faced man answered the door.

"State your business."

"My name is Quintus Sertorius. I am here to see your *dominus*."

He sized me up, and I returned the gesture, I noticed, to my amusement, that he was adorned in a soldier's tunic.

He smacked his gums and considered it for a moment.

"I'll see you to the atrium. But the *dominus* remains detained with dinner guests."

I stepped inside behind the portly man, but wondered if this might be a good excuse to leave.

"I can go, then. Perhaps I can return tomorrow."

"No." He stopped his forward march and turned sharply. "The *dominus* will want to know why you've visited."

Perhaps Marius hadn't made the members of his household privy to his offer.

The porter pointed at the ground before the impluvium, directing where I was to stand like a soldier in formation. He snapped his fingers, and two female slaves began to untie my sandals and wash my feet with lavender-scented water, an urban tradition I always found uncomfortable, if necessary, because of the filth in the streets.

"I'll fetch the *domina*." The porter turned and waddled off, pausing to prepare himself before climbing the stairs to the ladies' portion of the home.

I was rather hoping to avoid Marius's wife, Julia, if it were possible. First, striking beauty always left me absent proper articulation, and second, the last time she had seen me, I had been a member of the Caepio household. Would she not think me a traitor? Perhaps she knew how persuasive her husband could be, though.

"Quintus Sertorius, what joy!" Julia said, descending the steps with the gentle assistance of a slave girl. I wondered if she actually remembered who I was, but the smile on her face nearly convinced me.

"My lady." I bowed and accepted her delicate hand when she approached.

I tried to avoid eye contact. Aside from her beauty, she had Marius's commanding, powerful eyes. The kind that could convince a man to go to war, if she wanted them to.

"By Juno, you've changed," she said, appraising me.

"I have?" I looked down and analyzed my dress. I owned no fancy clothing, but certainly, I could have done better than this. My feet, despite being freshly washed and dried, were still atrocious, covered in calluses from campaign.

"You were a young man the last time I saw you."

"What am I now?" I laughed, but she did not.

"A man."

I lowered my head to hide the blushing of my cheeks.

"I was sorry to hear about your sister Ilia. I only met her the one time, but she was a lovely woman."

Julia looked down and ran the hem of her teal sleeves through her fingers.

"Yes, she was. At least we're rid of my pig-spawned brother-in-law," she said. Julia was referring to Sulla, who she obviously shared Marius's disdain for.

I wasn't quite able to formulate a response to that, so I remained silent until she lifted her gaze.

"I'll see you to the triclinium."

"Your porter said the consul was detained with dinner guests. I could certainly return tomorrow." I inched away and hoped she would give her permission.

"Nonsense! He's been expecting you. There isn't a man in Rome who would refuse entry to the Hero of the North!"

Gods, I hoped that title would fade away. It was more of a myth than Scylla and Charybdis.

She saw me to the dining hall but refused to step in herself.

She offered me her hand to kiss once more and then turned to leave, moving as gracefully as if she levitated like a butterfly.

"Quintus Sertorius, by the gods, I've wondered when you would visit me!" Marius said, standing with a jug of wine in lifted hand, only to stumble back to his couch.

"Sir." I stopped before the circle of couches and offered a salute to my general. Marius's guests snickered around him, but the man himself nodded and returned the gesture.

"Join us." He gestured to the lone empty couch. I wondered if he had left it open for me, but perhaps that was vain to even imagine.

"I did not mean to interrupt, Consul. I can return t—"

"No. I insist."

I followed instructions and walked across the floor to the open couch, knowing all eyes were on me. Volsenio appeared at my side with a cup of wine, which I gratefully accepted. He wore a wicked, all-knowing smile that suggested he never doubted I would come.

"I'd like to introduce you to this congregation of heroes." Marius gestured to the room.

I looked up for the first time and met their collective gaze. They did not appear heroes to me.

"This is Gaius Saufeius." Marius gestured to the first man to my right.

He raised his cup and slurred, "How do you do?" He was a weasel of a man, I could see that from the start. He had a scrunched face pocked with acne scars and stray hairs. There was a wisp of a mustache above his lips that fluttered as he breathed heavily through his nose. Short and frail-bodied, he was the antithesis of the kind of men I had come to know under the Eagle.

I hoped this would not be my lot moving forward with Marius.

"Here is Lucius Equitius, the son of Tiberius Gracchus."

The man rose to his feet and bowed grandly. I nearly spit out my drink. I had just finished reading Marius's retelling of the infamous tribune Tiberius. How this man could have been his progeny was beyond me.

"Son of Tiberius Gracchus? Why do you not share his name?" I asked. Rather abrupt, and perhaps rude, I was already losing respect for the men surrounding my general.

"My mother was a whore, you see, so I'm illegitimate. But the blood of revolutionaries flows through my veins," Equitius said, unconcerned and unoffended.

He was short, even for a Roman, and almost as thin as Saufeius. There was a deep dimple in his chin, his hair came to a pointed widow's peak, and he had the making of a unibrow. Tiberius, a charming and handsome man by all accounts, must have made love to a goat to produce such a man.

"Gaius Glaucia, praetor," the next man said without waiting to be introduced. I knew I had seen him before. I probably stared for longer than I ought before I nodded a greeting. But that smile was unmistakable. I had indeed met him. On the Aventine Hill. Where I was to deliver a bribe for votes in the consular election.

And it was he who had refused me. Well, he had certainly improved his station.

"Greetings, Praetor." What the others lacked in height and size, Glaucia made up. He was built like a gladiator, and had the deep voice to match it, with eyes that revealed his ceaseless appraisal of everything around him.

"Lucius Saturninus, tribune of plebs. It's a pleasure to meet you, Sertorius." This last man was the only one to stride across the floor and shake my hand. I hurried to stand.

"Ave, Tribune." I shook his hand, and found it firmer than expected. His cloth was turquoise and trimmed with gold, not too dissimilar from the triumphal robes Marius had worn a few days prior. But somehow, and I don't know how one can manage to do so, he didn't appear vain in them. Saufeius had a ring on nearly every finger and a gold chain around his neck—a more vulgar creature there never was—but Saturninus, although richly adorned, seemed to belong in that cloth.

"Consul Marius has told us a great deal about you. We're pleased to have you here." Saturninus spoke for the rest of them, which I found interesting.

He had a head full of curly hair, pronounced cheekbones, with a deep dimple on one side, apparently the result of his perpetually half-cocked smile.

"I'm honored to be here," I replied, slightly less disingenuous than if I had uttered those words before Saturninus had introduced himself.

"These are the men I've told you about." Marius gestured to Saturninus and Glaucia, although I'm fairly certain he had never mentioned them. "They were the magistrates who helped us get land for my African veterans. Now they plan to do the same for the men who served under me in Gaul."

"A noble calling." I gave them both a nod. "I'll sacrifice that you are successful. My brothers need good land."

"We want more than the sacrifice of a few dead birds, Sertorius. We want you to join us." Marius straightened on his couch and leaned toward me like a bird dog on point.

"I'm not certain I would be of any use in passing legislation, Consul."

"So you have not come to accept my offer?" Marius asked, and I could see that famous temper pulsing in the vein on his neck.

"Well...no... I just... I'm not old enough."

"You aren't from Rome, or a noble family, so we have no record of your birth. Perhaps we've simply forgotten when you were born? With those scars, you can pass for a much older man," Glaucia replied without pause.

"I don't have enough wealth to register as a senator."

"Don't let that concern you." Marius sat beside me on the couch. "I'll secure you a loan. I've already arranged it. At the best rates in the city, I'm certain."

At the mention of a loan, my stomach churned, and I don't think it was the wine I was drinking too quickly. It was a generous offer, however.

"But I've never even been a quaestor. How can I be a senator without first being a quaestor?"

"Sertorius, you've just been recognized as a hero before all of Rome," Marius said, squeezing my shoulder. "If the censors try to block your enrollment in the senate over technical prattle like that, there will be riots in the streets."

"We can ensure that if necessary," Glaucia said confidently.

The purpose of my military recognition became painfully clear. I hated the gold around my wrists even more than before. I was so deflated for a moment that I almost stood to leave, but then remembered my conversation with Apollonius and Arrea.

"What would be expected of me?" The question seemed to give them pause, and it offered me a chance to collect my thoughts. "If I may, I'll remind you that I left the tutelage of the Caepiones because I refused to compromise my values."

"Oh, those Caepiones are sons of whores!" Saufeius was shouting as soon as I mentioned the name.

"Saufeius," Marius said, in a meeker voice than I might have expected.

"I don't have reason to insult their mothers, but I share no love for them either," I said.

"The point remains. I will not be a voice for something I don't believe in."

"Then do not speak, brother. Your presence is all that is required." Glaucia smiled. He didn't seem like a bad sort of fellow, but he had a look in his eye that indicated he might have enjoyed harming insects or small animals as a child.

"Speak plainly." I was beginning to feel uncomfortable, and could feel myself on the urge of saying something I ought not to.

Marius rose to his feet and approached me, maintaining form despite his inebriation.

"You may vote as you wish, and speak on what you wish. I ask only that you sit with me in the senate house. That you represent our veterans. That you present a united front with me, the patron of those veterans. Go where I go, eat where I eat, sit where I sit. That is all I require of you." He placed a hand on my shoulder. "You and I have been doing that for a few years now. Couldn't be so bad, nay?" Marius smirked.

"A one-eyed, scarred veteran garners empathy from the people. And your physical toughness will keep the senate honest," Saturninus said as pleasantly as if we were farmers discussing the crops.

I didn't care for the idea of being paraded about. I'd had enough of that during the Triumph. But I did want to see the veterans receive land. I knew, as much as anyone else, how much they deserved it.

Beyond that, Marius had never given me a reason to doubt him. How could I refuse?

I looked at each man in turn, and they seemed comfortable in allowing the silence to grow until I summoned the courage to speak.

"I will never have to speak for something I don't believe in?" I asked.

"Never," Marius replied.

But the others said nothing.

SCROLL IV

TWO DAYS AFTER THE KALENDS OF SEPTEMBER,
654 AB URBE CONDITA

I FOLLOWED instructions and arrived at the Basilica Sempronia
the following market day just after sunrise. Here, I was to meet a
man by the name of Gaius Cocles to secure my loan.

The September air was cool and crisp that morning, the kind
that leaves you somewhere between a chill and a sweat after you
traverse the hills of the city long enough. The sun glistened on
the top of marble basilicae of the Forum, and citizens of all
trades and wealth classes were busying their way around the
building for whatever dream or business venture they were set
upon.

Apollonius had joined me, under the direction of being a
notetaker, if one was required. In truth, I simply wanted the
company. We waited in a long line, and I wondered the whole
time if Marius would have ushered me to the front if he were
here himself. I was in no rush, however. After I received this
loan, I would be purchasing a home in the city. Like everything
else, Marius had orchestrated its purchase. I wasn't thrilled
about living on the Aventine, and was much less enthusiastic

about furnishing the place. But with my new property, along with my ancestral home, I would have enough assets to register as a senator of Rome. The process was underway now. And there was no going back. The Rubicon had been crossed, so to speak.

"Number forty-two, number forty-two up," the clerk shouted disinterestedly.

"I'm here for a loan, sir." I approached the bench. I followed this with, "On orders of Gaius Marius," when he failed to look up.

"The *argentarius* Cocles will see you now." He gestured to a small cubby behind himself, not at all affected by the consul's name.

"My name is Quintus Sertorius. I've been sent to collect a loan from you."

The pudgy man was too busy scribbling on the document before him to respond. He passed one leaf of papyrus after another to the slave behind him until he had exhausted the pile.

"Yes, step forward." Cocles spit some bile on the stone between his feet and prepared a new document for us. "Four hundred thousand sestertii." He let his head back and whispered, "On Gaia's earth."

"That is the requested sum," Apollonius said from behind me, placing a hand on my shoulder.

He snapped his fingers in rapid succession until more scrolls were placed before him.

"The organizer of this loan will be your cosigner. If you cannot pay, he will," the *argentarius* said, scratching at his balding head, apparently perplexed by the figures before him.

"I will pay it," I said, feeling Apollonius grip tighten on my shoulder.

Cocles leaned back and slouched in his chair before taking a bite of meat that had apparently been sitting on his desk for some time.

"I genuinely doubt that," he managed to say with his mouth full. People like him made me miss serving. Where the insubordinate could be punished accordingly. Where your enemy always looked you in the eye, so you could kill him honestly.

I was getting the impression that everyone in the city just liked to mumble insults under their breath.

"You doubt that I'll be able to pay?"

He lifted both of his hands in mock self-defense.

"I'm sure you're a *very* resourceful man. But I'm not certain how someone that looks like *that* could ever hope to repay four hundred thousand sestertii." He pointed at my chest with the blunt end of his stylus.

"Why give me the loan, then?"

"Oh, your benefactor is good for the coin. I just pity you, if he ever has to cover your debt."

I shook my head. "Just tell me where to sign, *argentarius*."

"Here. Here. And here. You do know how to sign your name?"

"My friend can write in many languages, actually," Apollonius replied before I could with the jovial smile of a grandfather.

"Done." I passed the documents across the desk.

"Enjoy your new endeavors. You now own more than the vast majority of Rome put together."

I turned away.

"Hey, Legionary." He pointed his stylus at me. "You tell the consul my debt to him is now paid. I owe him no more favors."

The home I purchased had three bedrooms. There was a tablinum where I could write and store volumes of my favorite philosophers and poets. The atrium was broad, with enough room to host a dozen visitors' cloaks. An impluvium marked the end of it, with wilting lilies bobbing in the shallow water. There was a triclinium with three couches the former owners hadn't taken with them. A kitchen the size of a closet, which remained perpetually warm from the stove. The peristylum was overgrown and unkempt, but this brought me more joy than any other part of the house. Arrea's eyes lit up when she saw it. She said she had always dreamed of tending a garden, raising birds.

But the home felt empty.

I'm not sure how, but Arrea had a natural eye for deals in the marketplace. With what coin I had left over for interior trappings, Arrea purchased enough furniture to fill the home.

But none of it was really mine. And the home still felt empty.

Someone else had lived here, and perhaps died here. Other children had run, and laughed, and played here. Perhaps two slaves had fallen in love here, stealing kisses by the columns of the peristylium when their masters weren't looking.

None of my ancestral busts lined the walls, and my father's worn leather chair wasn't in the tablinum, nor his collection of underlined scrolls.

This was someone else's life and someone else's home. But I wasn't going to let anyone see my disappointment. Not Gavius, Arrea, or even Apollonius. Our first day in this domus would be a joyous occasion, one to mark the beginning of a wonderful and new epoch in the life of the Sertorii.

When my knees felt weak, when I felt fear and regret and hate for having to live in this domus miles away from my true home, I took a sip of the wine Arrea had purchased for our inaugural day. And I busied myself with carrying in the furniture as it arrived on carts throughout the day, stumbling and pretending that it was Gavius who was really bearing the weight.

And the wine was necessary, because my next task would be difficult. The domus came with a dozen slaves, all mine now.

How was one to address a group of slaves already living in a domus he just purchased? "I am your overlord now, you will eat when I allow you and piss when it's convenient for me. Wash my feet, feed me, and maybe I'll let you live." I suppose it gener-

ally went something like that. Or rather, most slaveholders probably didn't address their slaves at all.

I thought of releasing them. The first objection was that it was
illegal to release twelve slaves at once. The second was that part
of the property value that would allow me to run for the senate
were those slaves. My last objection was that I simply needed
them. I didn't know the first thing about running a home. An
urban domus was nothing like the ancestral home of my youth.
Nothing. These slaves were far more adapted to this lifestyle
than I was.

But my father would have been disappointed if I hadn't
addressed them properly. Perhaps it was my upbringing.
Perhaps it was the wine. But I was determined that expectations
be laid out clearly from the outset, so I had them gather in the
peristylium.

"My name is Quintus Sertorius, son of Proculus Sertorius.
My mother's name is Rhea. I was raised a horse trainer." As I
spoke, I felt a few of them shifting and perhaps chuckling. I was
trying to compose myself, but knew the effect of the wine was
beginning to show. I assumed they were laughing, more than
anything, at the fact that I felt I had to justify myself to them.

They were healthy, well fed, and well kept. That made me
happy, even if I assumed it made them more insubordinate.

"I purchased this home so that I may run for senate. I do this
because I have people that rely on me. First, my family. I will do
whatever I can to provide for them. Second, my people. Once, I
would have called only the Nursians my people, but now I call
all of Rome mine. And I will serve them. Finally, my brothers,
whom I served with. They need an advocate, and I will do my
best to be that. Any questions?" I asked.

For whatever reason, I had anticipated that they might
respond. They did not. I guess they weren't used to being given
the opportunity. They were slaves, after all.

"This is Arrea." I pleaded with her to move forward, even
though she was uncomfortable doing so. "She was a slave, and

now she is free, and the woman I love." I knew it was the wine talking, but I wanted her to know, and I wanted the rest of them to know too. "And this is Apollonius. He will be the real master of this house, and he is my dearest friend. I purchased him once, as a slave. But I've freed him. And I will free all of you, too, when I am able, and if you so desire. In the meantime, you can live as you ought. Worship the gods you serve. You can marry under my roof and I will give you my blessing. You may have children. I will be good to you, and I ask only in return that you be good to this one... Gavius, come here, boy."

He reluctantly approached and let me pull him to my side. I nearly stumbled from the wine, but recovered myself. "This is my son. Born of my brother, who died in combat, and Volesa, his mother, who has followed him of her own accord. And now Gavius is mine. He will be treated with the respect any child is owed or I will know the reason why."

I dismissed them, and each one sauntered off. I might have expected a thank-you or a clap on the shoulder for such leniency, but I was offered none. The slaves disappeared, to whatever chores or occupations, I did not know. Apollonius and Arrea returned to preparing the home, and Gavius hurried to follow them.

And I was left alone. I knew the wine had fully set in by now, and I felt ashamed of it. I had held it in until now, despite drinking a great deal since I returned to Rome, but I knew something was bound to break. I took that jug of ceremonial wine to my new office and continued to drink. I resigned myself to my fate.

I sat in the leather chair Arrea had secured for me, and pondered existence. I surveyed the room with a false sense of grandeur only wine can conjure, and considered all the things I might accomplish here. My mind swayed between this loftiness and the fear that I was a complete imposter. This carried on until the sun had set and the slaves had ceased their scurrying about.

There was a moment of clarity for me when I looked up and

realized how long I had been sitting there, alone. Drinking. I stood and stumbled into the nearest bedroom.

Here Arrea was asleep, a single strand of moonlight pouring in from the windowpane above her.

I stepped to the side of the bed and squatted beside her. She was asleep. I swept a strand of hair from her forehead. Gods, there had never been a creature made more beautifully.

I crawled in bed beside her and struggled to pull the blankets up around us both.

"I've waited so long for this, Arrea, my love," I said, pulling her waist into mine.

"Quintus," she said, stirring from her sleep.

"I've missed your touch. I've missed you, Arrea." I leaned in closer for a kiss. But she resisted before my lips touched hers.

"Quintus!" She pushed back against my chest.

I froze like a criminal caught by the city watch.

"Arrea…"

"You don't get to… no! You don't just get to come back!" she shot back, shaking the sleep from her eyes. I stared, mouth open, shocked and appalled by her reaction.

"I don't get to what?"

"You don't just get to come back after all this time! You don't just get to have me again after you leave me. Get out of this bedroom!"

I sat up in the bed, head swimming, trying to understand what I was hearing. Perhaps it was that same sense of false grandeur that made me believe she had missed me all this time the way I had missed her. Perhaps I thought, selfishly and foolishly, that now that Volesa was gone, things could return to the way they were.

I was the *paterfamilias*. I could have her if I wanted. I didn't have to ask permission. But that's not how I wanted her. I wanted her to desire me in return.

"Arrea, I love you."

"We never loved each other, Quintus. We didn't even know

each other! We huddled in fear in the Gallic forests because we had no other option. But we're strangers now. We didn't even know each other, Quintus."

I stared back, trying to fix the blurred vision of my one eye. In my stupor, I considered it, and wondered if she was right. Had I ever loved her? Did I even really know her? Or was she just what I needed to get through the darkest time of my life? No. I did. I must have. I had always loved her, even before I saved her. Even before she saved me.

"No. No. I do love you. And I want you tonight." She slapped hard against my chest with both palms.

"Get out! You were married to another. You left for nearly two years! I do not know you. You are a good man, Quintus, and you saved me. For that, I thank you. But *get out!*"

I complied. I returned to my tablinum confused, disappointed, and with a plethora of other emotions I can't articulate properly.

The worst thing a legionary can find upon his return is that his love has been unfaithful. That happened more often than one might expect from a city that boasts of their patriotism and noble citizenry. I can't claim to understand that pain, but returning to your woman saying she doesn't love you isn't much better.

Sometime that night, I scribbled something on a piece of the new parchment Arrea had purchased for the home. I am ashamed of it, to be certain, but I've found it in my records since, so I will share it for the edification of all readers:

I apparently do not love those I fought for. And I didn't truly hate those I fought.

I used to see something delicious—now I just see a dead bird, roasted.

I used to see glory and honor. Now just a bloody field. Charred bodies and voided bowels.

I used to see making love. Now just friction and cloudy fluid.

This only do I still love: Wine. That warmth in the belly. The sweet release from the tragedy of existence she gives me. She never broke my heart.

Her only do I love.

I woke up the next morning in my tablinum, facedown on my desk.

SCROLL V

MY PROPERTY SECURED, my next objective was to meet with the censors at the Villa Publica to be enrolled in the senate. One of those censors was a man you may remember, Metellus Numidicus. A devout friend of the Caepiones, he was an enemy of Marius, and that naturally made him antagonistic toward me.

I had been dreading this meeting, but it was still preferable to staying at home. I had no idea how to approach Arrea about the happenings of the previous evening. I was still trying to piece together everything that was said. I'm not certain she mentioned anything to the others, but I felt that everyone observed me with suspicious eyes, or with pity. I couldn't even bear to address Apollonius.

The Villa Publica was bustling when I arrived, citizens from all over the city reporting in for the five-year census. Fortunately, I and the rest of the senatorial candidates were allowed to skip the line.

Numidicus audibly groaned when he saw me.

"I heard about Marius's little conspiracy to get you into the senate. I prayed it was just a villainous rumor," he said, glaring at me.

"Unfortunately, it was no tale, Censor."

"Not yet a quaestor, not old enough, not enough wealth... What other laws will Marius break now that he is the Third Founder of Rome?" Numidicus snarled, the poison dripping from his lips.

"I wasn't born to a great family, like your son was. Otherwise, no one would even notice the laws, would they? Unfortunately, I had to earn my respect by defeating Rome's enemies on the battlefield." I met his gaze and refused to break it, which seemed to disturb him more than anything.

But I am certain he had already discussed this moment with his political allies, if my time with the Caepiones taught me anything. And they must have collectively agreed it would have done more harm than good for Numidicus to try to block my entry. I was the Hero of the North, after all.

Without another word, he passed me my first senatorial robe and a pair of red slippers that appeared too small. Then he shooed me away like a fly.

Since I was already on the Field of Mars, I decided to visit Marius at the construction site of the temple he was building. I hadn't seen it yet, but the city was buzzing with rumors of its grandeur. Apparently, Marius and his previous co-commander, Catulus, were in a battle to see who could build a greater temple to commemorate their mutual victory.

"Sertorius, my boy," Marius said when I arrived without taking his hungry eyes off the building before him.

Only the shell of the temple was yet risen, marble columns

being stacked in perfect order with cranes and the shouts of slave masters.

"Can you see it, Sertorius? It will be the greatest temple on the Field of Mars. A temple to Victory and Honor. This will inspire legionaries for generations. Can you see it? You cannot." He looked disappointed, and walked to the side for a different viewpoint.

"It is marvelous, Consul. That much I can see, even with my one good eye," I jested, but he did not laugh. He was consumed with the vision before him.

"They are constructing a stream that will run before the temple, just here. A bubbling brook, and a bridge across it. Two statues flanking the entrance like a permanent watch, and the bounty of our victory lining the walls to commemorate Rome's salvation."

Finally, he turned to me and noticed the toga and slippers in my hand.

"So you've seen old Numidicus. How much did he fuss?"

"Like an old woman, Consul."

"Ha! As I expected." He clasped his hands behind his back and walked a few paces. "Already, they're bending knee. We have never had more control of the senatorial order, Sertorius." I was unsure what he meant by "we," if it was in a collective sense, or if I were somehow already part of his political regime.

A young boy ran to Marius and clung to his leg. "Tata, Tata! Granius says I cannot feed the pigeons."

"And I told you to listen to him, didn't I?" Marius said, tempering his frustration.

A slightly older boy came and relieved Marius of the child. "If you finish your bread, you can give them the scraps," he said. "Young warriors must feed themselves before they spread their bounty."

"What wisdom?" Marius said. "Sertorius, I would like you to meet my sons. This is Publius Granius, my wife's from a former marriage."

"How do you do, Senator?" The older boy extended a hand, formally and without affectations.

"It's a pleasure, Granius," I said, still reeling a bit from being called "senator" for the first time.

"And this is my son with Julia, Marius the younger." The young boy hid behind his stepbrother and eyed me with suspicion.

"It's a pleasure to meet you, young Marius." I kneeled to his level, which made him turn away bashfully. Perhaps it was just his size, but I felt he was a bit too old for such behavior, and Consul Marius shuffled in a way that revealed he felt the same.

"Granius, if you'll give us just a moment," Marius requested with a nod. Granius led the child away without any questions. "Tomorrow is your first meeting with the senate."

"Tomorrow? I...well, I have to..."

"You're enrolled now, Sertorius. And it's your duty to attend unless you are out of the city." He smiled. "You'll have to experience that drab affair sooner or later. And tomorrow should be harmless, so you have nothing to fear. After the elections, that may change."

"Consul, I was just hoping to... I don't know. I was wanting to perhaps read up on rules and regulations. I'm not sure I'm prepared," I said, pleading.

"There's really only one thing you need to know about in politics: the parties. There are the Populares and the Optimates. The Populares run for the rights and authority of the people, and they use the tribunes as their base of power. The Optimates stand for the nobility, and their bulwark is the senate. Then, of course, there are the moderates who play to both sides and usually antagonize both."

"Which are you?" I said.

"The people would say I'm a Populare."

"Are you?" I asked.

He only smiled in response.

"Sertorius, anything you read will be defunct by the time you arrive in the curia. Senatorial procedure changes too quickly to learn by manuals. Just do as I do. And you'll be fine."

"Will I have to speak?" I hadn't suffered from my stutter in several years, but I could almost feel it materializing in the back of my throat at the thought.

Marius laughed, but then stopped abruptly, embarrassed for me.

"No, my boy. Not at all. Those old Boni would howl you down from the rafters if you tried."

If he was attempting to make me feel any better, he was failing. But at least I wouldn't have to speak. Not yet, at least.

"I will be there tomorrow," I said, resigning myself to fate.

"I want you to arrive at my domus at sunrise. We will make the walk together to solidify our political relationship. Nothing could be more beneficial for you on the first day of your political career." He turned his gaze again to the temple columns.

"And what's the benefit for you?"

He turned to me and shook his head. "Sertorius, must you always imagine that I have a sword in hand?"

Before the sun or the slaves had begun to stir the next day, Arrea and I were awake. I had enlisted her to help me don my senator's toga for the first time. I stood with my arms out as she wrapped the folds around me in the way my mother had taught her.

A bronze mirror was positioned before me, and I wondered who it was that was staring back at me. The past few years had certainly changed my appearance.

"I've been having nightmares," I confided in her.

"I know you have. One of the slave girls said your sheets have been drenched in sweat."

SCROLL V | 63

"I'll take them to the launderer myself."

"That wasn't the point..." She shook her head and returned her focus to the complicated cloth.

"I'm sorry I upset you a few nights ago," I said, my heart racing even as the words escaped my mouth.

"You did not upset me...you frightened me."

"You seemed upset."

"Well, I wasn't," she said with finality.

"How could you be frightened of me, Arrea? I would never hurt you." That she would even consider it stole my breath. Felt like I'd taken a Cimbri shield to the chest.

"I know you wouldn't. It's just been so long, Quintus. You are different now. Your demeanor is different. You speak differently. I don't like how you drink."

"You think I would hurt you because I drink a little wine?"

"My master used to come into my room at night when he would drink. That's when he was the worst." I fell silent as she tucked one of the folds under my arm. "Almost finished, I think."

"Why are you staying here, Arrea? You know you don't have to."

"And where would I go, Quintus?" She avoided conflict when she could, but I could hear the anger rising in her voice.

"I have some coin left over from the purchase. You can take it and buy a home for yourself somewhere outside of the city for the same price you'd pay for a loft here."

"I'm not going to leave Gavius."

"Arrea, do you really believe we never loved each other?" She did not reply, so I lowered my arms and turned to her.

"Quintus, you're going to be late if we don't get this toga on properly."

"Arrea. Just answer me."

She exhaled and rubbed at her temples.

"I've never felt for anyone what I felt for you. Perhaps I just told myself that we never loved each other to help get through those nights... Do you know what that felt like, Quintus? I lay there each and every night, drying my tears on your pillow, wondering if you were alive or dead. You didn't write, news was grim...and even if you returned, I knew you were Volesa's. Not mine. And then to hear that you went to that camp to go spying like some..." She clutched her chest and tried to steady her breath, reliving the experience of when she'd first heard it.

"Or perhaps we just needed each other to survive in Gaul. Right?" I stepped down from the stool and turned from her.

"Quintus, that isn't fair."

"It is what you said, isn't it?" I asked, my voice rising despite my effort to stay calm.

"How can you be so obtuse? Can you not see what this has been like for me?"

"Can you not see what it was like for me? Out there, alone, wondering if each breath was my last, knowing I would never hold you again if I were discovered or fell in combat. Knowing I was married to another, one who despised me. And then, to come home and hear you say..." I paused and gritted my teeth. "I'll finish preparing myself."

"I'm nearly finished. Please." She gestured for me to return to position.

"I need to pray to the household gods," I said without budging. When she realized I wasn't going to relent, she exited, leaving me there alone.

The incense of the altar to the household gods was still smoldering from the night prior, but I had no intention of praying this morning. I spent twice as long finishing the toga as it might have taken if I had allowed Arrea to help me, but it gave me enough time to dry my eyes and calm my thoughts as best as I could.

I would need a clear head for my first day in the senate.

Marius's doorstep was bustling like the Villa Publica with all sorts of visitors. Senators, veterans, magistrates, citizens, and, of course, Marius's lictors were all gathered there.

I didn't quite know what to do with myself, so I waited alongside them, a bit taken aback by the spectacle. Was this what happened every time the consul attended a senate meeting?

When Marius exited his home, everyone erupted in applause. He lifted his youngest son high over his shoulders and kissed him on the cheek before passing him off to his wife, offering her a modicum of affection as well. Granius and another young man stood close by, as well as a girl not much older than myself, which I presumed to be his illegitimate daughter, Maria, from Spain. They each, in turn, offered him their blessings before he made his way to the front of the procession.

He was craning his head about, and I wondered if he was looking for me. I hurried to his side, and he seemed relieved to find me.

"Ah, I was wondering if you might have a difficult time waking without a bugle to assist you." He took my hand.

"It would've helped."

Marius gave a slight gesture to those behind him, almost like a commander gives to a column of soldiers, and we moved forward, his lictors clearing the way.

"Is there anything I need to know, Consul?" I was anxious to the point of sickness but did my best to maintain a straight face.

He thought about it for so long, I wondered if he hadn't heard me.

"Only speak when spoken to. Always look a man in the eye when he shakes your hand. Never show weakness, or they'll devour you. When I clap, clap. When I stomp, stomp. And do so with conviction." Since I wasn't able to speak during a senate meeting, I assumed my clapping and stomping would be the only way I could show support. Marius said I wouldn't have to speak for anything I didn't support, but never said anything about stomping.

After we had been walking for some time, I stole a glance at the others in Marius's retinue. There were several unfamiliar faces in the lot, and I didn't identify any of Marius's dinner guests from our last meeting.

"Consul, where are the gentlemen I met at your dinner party?"

Marius kept his eyes forward, waving magnanimously to the citizens who cheered as we passed.

"It isn't appropriate that the full extent of our collaboration and cooperation be known, not yet. Like a game of *latrunculi*, revealing your stratagem too early can lead to defeat." That was the only explanation he offered.

When we arrived in the Forum, Marius and I made for the *senaculum* across from the curia where the other senators had gathered. The consul's retinue parted with us for the first time, but they remained close by to have a view of the senatorial proceedings of the day if anything interesting were to happen.

Several men approached to introduce themselves to Marius—perhaps not for the first time—anxious that he should remember them if he were elected as consul once more, as was expected. He, in turn, introduced them to me. I was too preoccupied that morning to remember any of those I met, but I do recall that they were quite appalled to find a man like myself standing with the elite waiting for entry into the curia.

As the sun reached its crest, the *flamen dialis* opened the doors to the curia, announcing favorable omens for the day, and the senators began their march into the senate house. I began following them, but Marius grabbed my arm.

"We never want to enter first. We want to enter when all eyes can witness our entry," he whispered. That sounded like the opposite of what *I* wanted, but what *we* wanted was obviously now taking precedence.

I then saw Saturninus and Glaucia as they passed by with nothing but a smile and nod, remaining side by side their entire ascent up the steps to the curia.

"Now we may enter. Fix your eyes forward, on the dais at the head of the room. Do not scan the faces of the senators. You are indifferent to all of them. Let them know it."

The curia stood much higher when one ascended its steps than it ever did when viewing it from a distance. Perhaps the other senators took it for granted, but I was keenly aware of the fact that I was about to partake in something that so few throughout the annals of history ever had.

The senate hall was surprisingly dark for midmorning, despite the massive windows that allowed natural light in from the east. Since the senate house was considered a religious building in its essence, it was not permitted for fire to burn within those walls, and one could tell.

A thin layer of dust seemed to cover everything within the curia; I could see this even from the doorway.

At the threshold of the room, Marius stepped out in front of me, like an actor about to take the stage. He straightened himself and lifted his chin like he had during his Triumph, then strode the floor as slowly and confidently as any man could muster.

I did my best to match his example.

There were so many senators already present and seated that I was thankful for Marius's advice. I couldn't have scanned their faces if I had wanted to. My military training encouraged me to do so, but I resisted the impulse and kept my eye forward. They all moved independently of one another but also somehow in unison, and I could feel the eyes of each fixed on us as we entered.

Marius stepped away from me to shake the hand of the *princeps senatus*, Marcus Scaurus, who had called the meeting. I assumed I wasn't meant to follow.

Reality sank in, and I realized how much my hands were shaking. I looked quickly for a seat. There was an open chair at the foot of the left benches, and I made straight for it.

Before I could sit down, I felt a firm grip on my arm. It was Marius.

"Those are the tribunes' chairs. We sit on the benches."

I heard laughter around the room, and lowered my gaze. Marius sat on the front bench and directed me to sit behind him.

I stole a glance at the benches across from us, and everywhere there seemed to be pockets of senators leaning over to whisper to one another, their eyes locked on me.

I became keenly aware of my eye patch, and it suddenly irritated my skin more than it had in months.

Scaurus took to the center of the curia and prepared to begin the day, but it seemed Marius and I were not the last to enter, after all. Marius's former pupil Sulla had outlasted him. Perhaps he had learned the trick from the consul himself.

Sulla strode across the floor, appearing even more unconcerned with those around him than Marius had. He demonstrated this by stopping to look at each and every man he passed, sizing them up, like a judge in the Forum.

He stopped at the end of the senate house and locked eyes with Marius, who leaned forward in anticipation. I knew that the two of them had always sat together previously. After a dramatic pause, Sulla turned on his heels and made his way to the benches opposite Marius where he was greeted by the ranks of the Optimates with vigorous handshakes and back slaps.

Marius never broke his gaze.

"Conscript Fathers, shall we begin," Scaurus said.

I don't recall much of the meeting. My primary focus was to sit as quietly and inconspicuously as possible. The only time I was required to react at all was when Marius was called upon to stand and officially announce his bid for the upcoming consular elections. When he concluded, I stood with the rest of the men on the left side of the curia in vigorous applause.

Saturninus, from the tribune's chair I nearly sat in, led the cheering.

The right side of the room did not stir at all. They watched silently. With so many of Marius's supporters watching closely from outside the curia's open doors, they felt unable to offer a rebuttal.

But the look of distaste on Sulla's face spoke for all of them.

It was Marius's turn to look displeased when his oldest rival, Numidicus, stood and announced his bid for consulship.

"I have been consul before, my brothers, but I will run again. If Marius can run for the sixth time, then Numidicus can certainly run for his second." It wasn't the wittiest insult, but the nobles on the right erupted into exaggerated laughter to ensure the point landed.

"That's *Consul* Marius," the general whispered, but I don't believe anyone else could hear it over the applause.

All of this seemed to be expected, however. The electoral campaigning had been going on for some time, apparently. Even as others stood to announce their bid for praetor, aedile, or quaestor, both sides seemed to be relatively unperturbed.

That was until the bid for tribune was announced.

Each man took his turn, standing and offering a few trite and tired phrases about the Roman commonwealth and what he would do during his term of office. The majority of them were as bland and noncommittal as possible. Even when Saturninus spoke, the right offered few objections aside from rolled eyes and hisses.

It was the final man to speak who sounded the alarm. Perhaps it was just a sign of my ignorance, but at the time, I couldn't begin to understand why.

"I, Gaius Nonius, will stand for tribune of plebs." He was a thin and insignificant-looking man, not much older than myself. The only thing that distinguished him from the others was that he'd stood from the right, while the other tribune candidates had stood from the left.

The room erupted, the shouts echoing throughout the curia and across the high ceilings.

My eye darted about, trying to make sense of the upheaval. Marius, below me, was shouting just as violently as the others, and his voice carried as powerfully as it had on the battlefield. I stomped with the others, as I was instructed, but didn't have the first clue what it was all about.

"Senators, please!" Marcus Scaurus howled from the floor. "Does anyone have a legitimate objection to this man's bid for the tribuneship?" Everyone fell silent. "Then there is nothing more to be said on the matter. The people will decide. The election for consulship and praetor will take place four days after the kalends of December. The election of the tribunes will take place on the nones of December."

I hurriedly followed Marius out of the building. He did not wait to be the last to leave. We headed straight back for the *senaculum* where Marius stood and waited for his friends to rally around him like when he ordered drill formations in the field.

"What was all that about, Consul?" I asked as we waited.

"I will explain everything in due time," he replied. He was visibly angry, with bulging veins and a heaving chest, but I assumed it wasn't because of my questions.

"Marius, I didn't know," Saturninus said as he approached, taking Marius's hand within his own and kissing him on either cheek.

"Of course, you didn't. None of us did; otherwise, we wouldn't be in this mess."

Glaucia, Saufeius, and Equitius approached soon after.

"What are we to do now?" Saufeius asked in his nasal voice.

Marius grumbled something and shook his head.

"Well, we aren't going to determine that standing here. Let's discuss it over dinner. I need some damn wine." He began to depart but then turned to shake my hand. "You did excellent today, Sertorius. See that you are well fed and rested. The next few weeks may be difficult."

What was that supposed to mean? Regardless, I felt it wasn't appropriate to ask. I released his hand and watched as he walked away with Saturninus and the others.

As I entered my home, I felt something akin to the experience after battle when all the tumult stops and every sense you have dulls to exhaustion.

"Thank you," I told the slave girls who removed my slippers and washed my feet before I made straight for the peristylium where I assumed Arrea was.

She was feeding the birds and humming along to match their song.

I leaned against a column and listened, squeezing my eye shut to stall the headache that was coming on, until she turned and caught sight of me.

"How was your first day?"

"Can you help me undress?" I asked. She could have replied that we had slaves for that, but she nodded instead.

Neither of us mentioned that morning.

"Did everyone play nicely in the senate meeting?" she asked when the silence became uncomfortable, carefully pulling each fold from around my shoulders.

"As nicely as they ever do, I'd assume." I spun when she bade me to so she could pull the fabric under my arm. "I'm just not sure I'm meant for all this, Arrea."

"How can you tell after one day?" she asked.

"Good question." I plopped down on a bench beside the shrubbery when she finished, passing my toga off to a slave for it to be hung up for the next day. "I feel like every drop of life was sucked out of me, like it got left in that place."

"New ventures often leave us with that feeling," Apollonius

said, appearing alongside Gavius at the entryway. "They don't remain that way, though," Apollonius concluded.

"Greet your father, Gavius." Arrea waved him forward.

"Hello, *amicus*." I ruffled his hair and he half hugged me. "Most of the senators were even older than you, Apollonius," I said with a smile.

"We should all be praying for the Republic, then, since they'll all be dying soon." Apollonius sat down beside me.

"Would you like a cup of wine?" one of the slaves asked me.

"Yes. Wait, no. I'm fine," I said, and she bowed and took her leave. "I think I'm still hungover from the last time," I whispered to Apollonius as Arrea picked up Gavius to look at the birds.

"You've been drinking more wine than usual, my friend," he said without judgment.

"I picked up the habit in the Cimbri camp. It was the only thing that could calm me down...and it's all they ever did. Guess I got used to it." I rubbed at my eye and pondered my time behind enemy lines, still trying to see the curious experience for what it was. "Does it bother you?" I asked, feeling cornered. Perhaps I was upsetting everyone with my drinking, and I felt the need to defend myself if that were the case.

"I just like seeing you at your best, Quintus. With the light in your eye. Tragedy has beset our path since we've walked it together. But that shall not always be the case. Brighter days are ahead, but we won't be able to experience them if our vision remains shadowed by the darkness of the past."

"That's doubly true for a one-eyed man," I jested, but did listen to what he said. "I am not mourning anymore. I am not brooding. Arrea, I want you to listen to this too." I waited until both of them met my eye. "I am not sulking anymore. I am not dwelling on the past. I hardly have the time or energy to do so, with so much focus on the future. I left the war where it was, at the behest of a wise centurion. I've been drinking more for fear of the future than regret of the past. And I'll overcome the fear, right? With your help." I nodded until they did the same. I wondered if it was totally true, but I wanted to believe it.

But what could they expect? I was home now, but hadn't part of me died with my brothers? Or when I'd shed my true self to become a barbarian? I think it must have. There was no wallowing in that. No self-pity. Just a recalculation of what remained, as I've said before.

"We will always be there to help you, Quintus." Apollonius patted my shoulder, and Arrea nodded along as Gavius extended a bread crumb to one of our pigeons.

"I've no doubt. Let's have a meal, shall we?" I said.

SCROLL VI

NONES OF DECEMBER, 654 AB URBE CONDITA

MARIUS WON the election by a wide margin. He was the Third Founder of Rome, after all; how could he be denied another consulship? The surprise came with the defeat of Numidicus. Nothing solidified Marius's power more than this victory. The general had backed an Optimate named Lucius Valerius Flacchus as his co-consul, and he also won. Flacchus was a nobleman, to be certain, but he was an agreeable man Marius knew he could control.

Everyone knew this. Even before the day was over, some were calling it "the year of the consulships of Gaius and Marius." This was as close to absolute power as a Roman could get.

Glaucia won his bid for praetorship and Saufeius was elected as quaestor. Most of the city had probably heard the rumors about their connection to Marius by this time, but they had done well keeping up the appearance of being nothing more than friendly acquaintances.

The real question now was about the election of tribune. If Saturninus were to be successful, Marius would have an ally in every major magistracy within the Republic. The potential for what he could do was limitless. I simply hoped he meant to use the power for good, and I did believe that, in my heart.

We met at Marius's five days from the ides of December. I walked the streets to get there while the sun was still rising, but there was already a sense of festivity in the air. There was a mass migration toward the Forum, everyone anxious to arrive first and acquire good placement for the elections. The election of tribunes was always held in a Plebeian Assembly, mind you, where the urban poor had as much say as anybody, and they seemed to know it. This was their day. The time each year when their word was law, when they could effect change at the highest level, and the elite had no power to stop them.

For that reason, I asked Marius when we began our march what the cause for frustration was.

"Because the Optimates have put forward a candidate of their own. This Gaius Nonius is a nobody, but he is just a tool for Numidicus's ilk. He'll do as they say and ruin everything we have planned."

"But, Consul, the people control this vote. Why would they vote for someone who will obstruct their will?" I asked.

Marius kept his eyes forward.

"The Optimates wouldn't have put the man forward if they weren't confident he would win, Sertorius. That means they have plebs in their coin purse. Many of the people are gullible enough to believe they can still vote for Saturninus and earn a bit of coin to cast a random vote for this Nonius as well. Ten tribunes are elected each year, so why wouldn't they?"

We continued our ascent as the crowds grew larger and larger. The Forum was bustling like the day of Marius's

Triumph, each man attempting to get as close to the *comitium* as possible, every tradesman and street performer there to take advantage of the crowd.

"Better stay close or we're likely to get lost," Granius said, inching towards his stepfather.

"And believe me, my boy, we don't want to get separated on a day like this," said Marius.

We went as far as we could, but we had to stop back near the Pool of Curtius, not able to push any farther. We were attending as private citizens today, of course, since magistrates and senators weren't allowed to attend in any official capacity.

"Citizens of Rome!" the presiding tribune began.

It just so happened to be Saturninus.

The fact that he was also a candidate seemed lost on everyone, for the crowds continued to roar for some time before he could continue. "Today is a glorious day. Once more, the future of Rome is in your hands, the people of Rome!" I covered my ears to drown out the noise. "I present to you the candidates for the office of plebeian tribune." They lined up behind him, and when each tribune-elect had found his place on the stairs of the *comitium*, Saturninus joined them. "Under the good auspices of Jupiter Capitolinus, let the voting begin!"

People pushed past us toward the voting pens. The smell of perspiration was thick despite the bitter cold in the air.

"Good day, citizens!" came a brusque voice. Turning, we found Gaius Glaucia standing a head taller than the crowd surging past him.

"Well, if it isn't Rome's newest praetor." Marius embraced him familiarly.

"Hard to say that when I was praetor last year too." He shrugged. "What do you think? They seemed pleased." He gestured to the people.

"They should be. A glorious day for Rome, indeed, as our friend concluded." Marius nodded.

"And a friend who is about to be victorious." Glaucia turned to me and winked.

"And we're certain of that?" I asked.

Glaucia nodded confidently and coughed in his hand.

"Caught a cold. Yes, I'm certain. I was a renowned gambler back on the Aventine in my youth, you know. I learned to only play games I could win. And those are the only kind you can afford to play in politics, or you'll go bankrupt."

I leaned in closer to hear him over the tumult.

"Bankrupt?"

"Politics is quite an expensive venture. Something you might discover yourself in time." He leaned in closer still. "But not when you win."

We waited as patiently as one can in a thick crowd while the bitter winds yielded to a warm sun. It was nearly midday before the votes were tallied.

We were far enough away by this point, having gradually been pushed back to the columns of the old shops, that we had to wait for word of each vote to be relayed back to us.

"One thing's for sure. My Aventine is voting for Saturninus. Not one man of the hill will vote against him, I've made sure of it," Glaucia said to Marius. That was a bold statement—a seventh of Rome at least.

We cheered each time we heard a vote in our favor. At first, I feigned it. Eventually, I found myself cheering for the man as much as anyone else. I remembered our dinner conversation, after all. These men wanted to give land to our veterans. What if they were corrupt? What if they were ambitious? If they would help my brothers, if they would pass measures to benefit the people, then why would I not rejoice? I had a dialogue with myself a few times as the votes were being read, but it was of no purpose. I cheered each time regardless, with renewed vigor with each announced vote.

But we all groaned when Nonius received a positive vote.

"Glaucia, you told me this was taken care of. If he wins,

everything we've fought for..." I heard Marius say as the crowds around us hollered in response to the vote.

Glaucia pacified him with a hand on the shoulder.

"Consul, he cannot win. They've purchased votes, and we've purchased more. He will not win." Some things might have changed for Gaius Glaucia, but apparently his affinity for tampering with elections had not. I recalled something from Marius's letter, the words of Tiberius Gracchus... He said that the people weren't crying out for clean elections but for food and land and clean water. At least that was enough justification to help stall me from overthinking.

It wasn't long before Saturninus's victory was secured. The general, Glaucia, and I were jubilant, as was everyone else, but we weren't surprised. The surprise was that Nonius was making up ground, and he appeared a victor as well.

"Glaucia," Marius said, breathing through flared nostrils like a bull when another vote for Nonius was announced.

"Consul, he will not win." Glaucia feigned a smile as best he could, but he was becoming impatient as well, and perhaps fearful.

Then the crowd started shouting. Not the entire crowd, just a portion of it in the distance, close to the Rostra. I craned my neck to get a view, but could only see the body of people swaying like a violent current.

"What is happening?" I asked Marius as if he would know. He didn't reply but strained to see the cause of the commotion as well.

The shouts became wails.

"What is happening?" I cried to anyone listening.

I reached for my sword, instinctively, which of course wasn't there.

When I looked up again, a group of hooded men in tight formation was ascending the steps of the Rostra. Lifted swords glimmered in the sunlight. The tribune-elects were jumping over the edge like sailors on a breached ship.

But Nonius was too late. I caught sight of him as he was swallowed up by glistening swords.

The crowd panicked, people trampling over those next to them, twice as frantic to get away as they had been to draw near.

"Father!" Granius grabbed Marius by the shoulders and helped him get low.

"Run!" Marius shouted, and we joined the chaos and were swept away into the current.

I stole one glance over my shoulder as the hooded men gathered around the bloody, obviously dead body of Nonius, stabbing gladius after gladius into the carcass for good measure. Blood pooled at the edge of the Rostra and dripped off the edge. Nonius's starched white toga was torn to bits and soaked black.

Rome would never be the same again.

SCROLL VII

NONES OF DECEMBER, 654 AB URBE CONDITA

I WAS IMMEDIATELY SEPARATED from Marius. The crowds storming past us were vicious, leaving the weak on the ground to be trampled. I stuck to buildings and side streets, keeping my head low and scanning the mob for more attackers. In the ensuing chaos, I almost lost my sense of direction, but I followed the Via Sacra as closely as I could to the neighborhoods of the Palatine, where my general's home was. I felt it was my duty to ensure he was safe before anything else, even at my own peril. What would history say of Rome's newest senator if his consul should fall as soon as he was appointed?

When I arrived at Marius's domus, I burst through the door without knocking. Two slaves pulled knives on me as I entered but quickly exhaled with relief and sheathed them when they saw my face.

Marius was leaning up against a column in the atrium, a hand resting on the shoulder of his stepson, Granius.

"Thank you, my boy," he was saying to him. When he turned to see me, his eyebrows furrowed in confusion.

"Sertorius, what are you doing here?"

"I had to make sure you were safe, Consul." I strode over to him.

"Ah yes. I am safe, thanks to Granius here."

"I am sorry I lost you out there." I scanned him to ensure he was not injured. Aside from messy hair and a disheveled toga, there were no signs of distress.

"Who could blame you? One dagger in the Forum, and the whole mob went mad. They wouldn't last one day on the battlefield, would they?" he asked, accepting a cup of honey water and a stool from Volsenio.

"There was more than one. And I believe those were gladii, Consul, not daggers."

He gulped hastily and shrugged.

"You should return to your home and make sure your family is safe. Often looting and burning follow such occasions."

"Has there been an occasion like this before? A tribune-elect murdered during an election?"

He thought about it for a while and shook his head.

"No. Well, there was the one I wrote to you about. Tiberius Gracchus." Marius passed off the cup for it to be refilled as another slave cooled his forehead with a damp scented towel.

"But Nonius was attempting no political coup. And the senate wouldn't butcher their own candidate, so someone else must have been behind this. Who might have been responsible?" I stepped closer to him.

He stared at the floor and seemed to be searching his mind for any clues or hints.

"It could have been any number of people. You know how the people are about their politics. Perhaps they're tired of puppet tribunes that vote against their will," he said. I waited for some time, but he refused to meet my eye. So I said what I needed to regardless.

"Consul, those men moved in tight formation. They used gladii. Were they soldiers?"

He looked up at me and met my eyes for the first time, perhaps offended.

"How should I know? Although, it would make sense... They want to receive their land, after all. Perhaps they heard rumor that this Nonius would vote against them."

"Did you order it to happen?" I asked without hesitation.

He stood and locked eyes with mine.

"No. Our legionaries are sovereign citizens now and can do as they please." He inched closer to me, waiting for me to make another remark. "If they were soldiers—and I'm not saying they were—then it would make sense that they would have killed Nonius. Don't you agree?"

"I love my brothers, Consul, dearly. But they are not typically well informed on politics."

"Then perhaps it's time they become educated." He spun on his heels and ascended the steps to his chambers. Behind me, the porter opened the door for me to leave.

"What has happened?" Arrea shouted when I entered our home.

"Bar the doors," I told my door guard.

"Quintus, are you hurt?" she asked.

"I'm fine."

"We've heard a great tumult, Quintus," Apollonius said, a bit more restrained than Arrea but clearly disturbed.

"There was an assassination at the election." I didn't know how else to say it, but felt sorry when I saw the look on little Gavius's face. "I said bar those doors. Fetch wood from the kitchen furnace if need be."

"What do we need to do?" Arrea asked, sobering like a legionary when she heard the news.

"I need all of you to go to your rooms and shut the door. Gavius, stay with Arrea tonight."

"Are we in danger?" one of the female slaves asked.

"No. No, I don't believe so." I pondered it, and believed this was true, but I wasn't taking any risks with my family. "Go and bring me my gladius," I directed her.

"Quintus, if we aren't in danger, why do you need a sword?" Arrea asked, calmly bringing Gavius to her side. The look in her eyes betrayed fear, though.

"I'm standing watch. It's what a soldier does. But there is no cause for alarm," I replied, fastening my sword belt that the slave girl had retrieved around my waist. This caused Apollonius to chuckle, for good reason. I probably wasn't making sense to them, but I was having a difficult time explaining the situation when faced with so many questions. I was still trying to make sense of everything myself. They all stood by, waiting for something more. "Go. All of you. Go and pray to your gods, and then go to sleep. I will see you in the morning."

The slaves dispersed at once, and at length, Arrea and Gavius complied as well. I grabbed a chair from my tablinum and brought it to the atrium, where I positioned it just before the door.

I installed myself there, with nothing but my sword and a jug of wine, eye locked on the door before me.

There was no concern if those men were legionaries. They wouldn't be coming after me. But I almost hoped they would. I would put them all down if necessary. Murdering a tribune-elect... Had anyone ever violated something more sacred than a sanctioned election before?

I heard breathing behind me.

"Apollonius. You too. Go to bed."

"I think not, my friend."

He stepped forward from the shadows and put a hand on my shoulder.

"I'll need you at full strength tomorrow," I replied. I couldn't think of a reason to justify that, but fortunately, he didn't ask.

"The Roman watch is always two guards at a time, is it not?"

"We have two. Me and her." I gestured to the gladius on my hip. "Get some rest."

"Perhaps I can read you some Zeno?" he asked.

"Not tonight, dear friend. Perhaps tomorrow."

He stood long enough to run through a dozen potential rebuttals, but nothing satisfactory came to mind, so at length, he nodded.

"Good night, Quintus."

When he departed, and I was all alone, I poured my first drink. I sipped and ran my fingers over the scabbard of my sword, never taking my eye off the door.

It was silent for the rest of the night. Even the dogs ceased their barking, as if all living things could sense what had happened, or what was about to happen.

I did not attend the reelection the following day. My excuse for this was that Marius had given me no express orders for where and when to meet. The real reason was that I was awake, sitting before my door, until well after the sun rose. I stumbled to bed about the time Marius's retinue would have been gathering once more outside his domus.

Regardless, it was of no consequence. The election was as standard as any could be. The ballots were recast and the votes tallied once again. Saturninus was a clear victor once more. And of all the other nine elected, there wasn't a single man among them with known affiliations with the Optimates.

Whether they had orchestrated the assassination or not, no one stood to gain more from it than Marius, Saturninus, and

Glaucia. Though, some might have said that the name Sertorius belonged on that list. There might have even been whispers that Rome's newest senator had something to do with his old comrades butchering a man who was openly hostile to his party's aims. But, of course, you know me better than that by now. There was no call for such things.

Not yet, at least.

SCROLL VIII

FOUR DAYS AFTER THE IDES OF JANUARY, 655 AB
URBE CONDITA

THERE WAS a brief calm before the storm as the entire
Republic awaited the opening senate session of the year. The
winter weather was bad enough that the senate did not
meet for nearly a fortnight, or, at least, that was the
reasoning.

I wasn't going to complain. It gave Apollonius and me some
time to debate philosophy, something we had wanted to do since
we first met at Massilia. It also allowed me to spend more time
with Gavius, something I needed to do if I was to earn his
affections.

But all good things must come to an end, I suppose. It was
the beginning of January when Volsenio arrived at my door.

"Come in, *amicus*, you must be freezing," I said as my porter
ushered him in and took his cloak.

"This weather is not meant for Numidians, I vow that." He
embraced me.

"It's not meant for anyone, my friend. My slaves tell me
Rome hasn't seen a winter like this in years."

"Perhaps it is a portent from the gods?" he asked inquisitively.

"And what do you think they are warning us about?" I asked, not smiling along with him.

"If I had to guess...to not venture out without a coat." He slapped my shoulder.

"Can I offer you a cup of wine?" I ushered him into the atrium, away from the freezing air seeping in beneath the door.

"Actually, no. If you haven't anything more pressing to attend to, I've come to fetch you."

"Oh?" I asked, deflating. I had hoped to read through some interesting passages in Plato's *Republic* with Apollonius that afternoon, but that wasn't a sufficient reason to deny Marius.

"The consul has someone he would very much like you to meet."

"May I ask who?" I gestured for a slave to gather my warmest cloak, knowing the answer wouldn't alter the fact that I would have to go.

"Someone noble and powerful..." He tapped his lip and considered it. "Although, he does drool and shit himself."

He burst into laughter when he saw my consternation.

"A babe. Marius's nephew."

"Nicely done, Volsenio. For a moment, I thought he was going to introduce me to one of the senatorial elite."

I wrapped up in a cloak, already knowing it wouldn't be warm enough to keep out the cold that awaited us. Perhaps city life was making me soft.

"They are at Marius's home, if you'll follow me," Volsenio said, raising his voice a little higher than usual to overcome the whistling of the wind.

The cold turned the usually muddy streets to frozen slush, and the stone roads and buildings we passed were covered in a thin sheet of snow.

"This must be a special visit for Marius's nephew to brave such a storm," I said, pulling the hood to my forehead.

"The consul's brother-in-law has been away governing one of Marius's new cities, Cercina, I think they call it. He just arrived back in the city, and it's the first time Marius and the *domina* have met the child," he replied, his teeth chattering as he did so.

I thought it was rather odd that I would be invited on such an occasion, but I wasn't going to mention it.

After Volsenio's words set in, I nearly turned around. Brother-in-law.

"And which brother-in-law is this?"

"Gaius Caesar."

If you remember from my first set of scrolls, the man had been one of Marius's closest allies when I first met him. It was the other brother, Sextus, who had betrayed Marius and Maximus. His machinations had nearly led to the death of my friend Lucius, and he played an instrumental role in the tragic loss at Arausio.

"And will Sextus Caesar be in attendance?"

Volsenio stopped in his tracks and returned a pensive glance.

"No. The consul made it clear the man wasn't to set foot inside his home." I nodded, a bit relieved. "Just a bit farther."

When we arrived, the warmth greeted us before the porter could. There must have been a hearth burning inside.

"Look, he has his grandfather's eyebrows. Don't you see it?" I heard a female voice say, presumably Julia's.

"Well, that hair definitely belongs to the Caesars. Look how thick!" another said.

These doting voices poured out from the triclinium as we entered.

The slaves bent to wash my feet, but I shook my head.

"I'm afraid if you took off my shoes right now, my toes might just come off with them." I did reluctantly allow them to take my cloak.

I followed Volsenio into the dining room to see a crowd hovering over the child. They didn't even notice us at first.

"What about those feet, though? They're so...big. Where

could he have gotten those from?" Marius asked, analyzing both the child's and his brother-in-law's feet in half seriousness.

"You all seem to forget the boy has a mother. My father's feet were longer than my forearms," Aurelia said, to the laughter of all.

"*Dominus*," Volsenio said, cutting them short, and causing all eyes to fall upon us.

"Senator Sertorius! I'm pleased you could join us. Come." Marius gestured for me to come closer, and the group parted. At the center, rather than Aurelia holding the child, sat the tribune Saturninus with the swaddled infant in his arms.

"Look upon a future consul, brother. This is Gaius Julius Caesar, the fifth of his name," Saturninus said, folding back a piece of cloth from the child's face.

"Isn't he noble?" Marius asked, patting my back and peering over my shoulder.

"He is." In truth, I saw nothing that designated a noble lineage in the child, but the sight of a healthy infant was always a welcome one, especially after witnessing so much death on the battlefield.

"There are many Marius's in this boy," the consul said with a grin.

The child began to stir, reaching out and clenching his hands.

"Oh, he's hungry. Please, I should feed him," Aurelia said as Saturninus gently passed the babe into her arms. She was the image of beauty itself, with a thin shawl over her head, her hair down in thick curls. She needed no makeup to present herself; it was actually in her service that she did not. She was a life giver, and there was nothing that could add to her splendor with that child in her arms.

"I'm certain we have a nursing slave who could do that for you, Aurelia." Julia gestured, taking the consul's hand in her own.

"No, that's quite alright. Gaius and I have decided to do this the old Roman way. He'll draw strength from my ancestors."

Aurelia departed, and most of the women followed to share in the moment.

"Congratulations, my boy. He is as healthy as an ox." Marius clasped his brother-in-law's forearm. Gaius looked the same as I remembered him from the day of his wedding nearly six years prior, except that his eyes were pink rimmed and tired, presumably from the child (or perhaps his administration of Marius's new colony).

"The gods have truly blessed us," he said.

Saturninus stepped closer to the center of our congregation and said, "We have to ensure that the Rome this boy is reared in is not the one we live in now. Strife, anarchy, poverty, lawlessness… Rome's children deserve better."

"Well said, Tribune," Gaius Caesar said, speaking for everyone.

"And we hope that you'll join us in making it so, now that you've returned," Marius said.

Gaius Caesar opened his mouth, but the response died in his throat. He shook his head and tried to talk with his hands but couldn't find the right words.

"Consul, things are just different now," he finally summoned up.

"So different that you can't help us create a better Rome?" Marius asked. Some of the others gathered departed, deciding that watching a Roman matron breastfeed was somehow less uncomfortable than this.

"Of course I will always do my part to—"

"By the gods, Gaius, I have missed you at my side! Will you not join us?" Marius seemed utterly perplexed by his brother-in-law's hesitance.

"Can we talk of this later?" he asked. But when nothing was said, he continued, "I have my wife's family to consider. You know the Aurelii Cottae oppose you."

"So you oppose me as well?"

"Never, Marius. Never. But you knew what it would be like

when I married her." Gaius Caesar locked eyes with the consul, and I'm certain if they weren't so close, there would have been something said about the tone of his voice.

"Gaius, you could be a bridge between the two parties," Saturninus said quietly. "You can simply express that you know our hearts, and that what we do is for the good of Rome. And if there is a bridge built between us, you can ensure it doesn't burn."

Gaius Caesar slowly turned his head to the tribune and considered his response carefully. For a moment, I believed he was about to respond negatively—something in his eyes perhaps.

But instead, he said, "I will always do that."

"Oh, look at him!" came a voice, along with a great deal of cooing. The babe was placed now on a rug in the center of the dining couches, and was giggling and tugging at his own feet. "He's discovered those big feet." Julia laughed, and tickled him with a long fingernail.

Content with Gaius's answer, we all migrated toward the child, which left me with a few moments to consider why I had been invited. Was I supposed to be part of Gaius's interrogation? There were plenty of others gathered at Marius's, but my requested presence felt odd.

Before I could sort things out in my mind, Marius appeared at my side.

"The senate will be meeting on the nones."

"It will?" I asked, careful to not let him see my disappointment. I guess Plato would have to wait. "In this weather? Who called the meeting?" Even most of the old breed of Romans didn't want to travel more than they had to in this bitter cold. The thought of standing in the open *senaculum* for half an hour while the sun came up was painful.

"Glaucia."

"And he has that power?"

"Anyone with a curule chair can order a meeting of the senate, including the urban praetor."

"And he doesn't intend to wait for the snows to melt?"

Marius turned to me, surprised, as we halted before the giggling baby as if he were a shrine.

"Are you really that concerned with the weather, Senator? A man from Nursia like yourself? Or am I missing something?"

"I am not concerned about it, Consul. I will be there one way or the other. But some of our...older members in the senate have fragile constitutions. I imagine many of them won't be able to make it."

"Oh, they're able. If they decide to remain on their fat arses by the warmth of the hearths, then that's their choice. But the senate will always meet when it is summoned. And perhaps we can make that work to our advantage, if we're careful to arrive in full force." He made a fist, like he did when we would discuss strategy before a battle.

"Any particular reason why Glaucia is summoning the meeting?"

Marius shrugged. "We'll have to see tomorrow."

I grabbed him by the elbow and pulled him as gently (and respectfully) as I could from the crowd.

"Consul, I have given up everything to serve with you. I am following your leadership, and I respond to your beck and call at all times. And I do not like to be kept in the shadows. Please, General, I beg you. Do not keep secrets from me."

He began to respond but quickly stopped himself. He didn't seem upset. His brows furrowed and then he began to shake his head.

"You're right. My boy, you are right." He placed a hand on my shoulder. "From now on, if you are involved in something, I will make sure you have all the information you require." Now he led me back to the group. "You know I have not hidden anything from you intentionally. I've tried to protect you. That is all."

"Like what happened to Nonius?" I asked sternly but without accusation.

He breathed heavily through his nostrils and put a finger against my chest.

"That will not be mentioned again. I had nothing to do with that." He turned to ensure no one had seen his momentary flash of rage. He forced a smile across his face, and gestured to the child. "Let's celebrate the future, Senator, and all that it may bring."

SCROLL IX

NONES OF JANUARY, 655 AB URBE CONDITA

Jupiter, god of the storm, graced us that morning with a sheet of freezing rain. Even Marius, as resilient as he was, had a hard time making it to the *senaculum* that morning. Luckily, everyone was just as overwhelmed as we were, so it didn't take long for the auspices to be taken and the doors to open. Criers were sent out to gather the senators from their homes, but most of them returned with no senators to show for it.

We poured into the curia, most of us loathing the fact that no fires could burn within those walls, as it was nearly as cold as outside. Needless to say, we didn't worry about being the last to enter on this day.

And this time, I knew where to sit.

Glaucia placed his curule chair on the dais and prepared to begin the meeting, waiting a few more moments to see who would join us.

I peered around the room. It didn't take long to notice how skewed the attendance was. The benches on the left of the room were filled to capacity. The attendance of senators on the right was sparse, and they were spread out.

Numidicus sat beside a few of his colleagues and scanned the room, the look in his eye something akin to that of prey sensing a predator.

"Senators, good morning. I commend all of you on attending on such a day," Glaucia began. "If this meeting could have waited any longer—"

"It could have waited," a few voices grumbled, cutting Glaucia off.

He smiled and stepped down to face them directly.

"I would much prefer to be wrapped up in a blanket beside my loving wife, just as many of you would," Glaucia continued. "But matters of the state must be attended to, even when it is inconvenient or uncomfortable. I trust that you all agree?" Playing to their pride, he silenced them all. "There has been proposed legislation, which was posted to the Rostra yesterday. Now we must discuss it."

Startled looks were exchanged by the senators on the right.

"We've seen no legislation," a young aedile by the name of Lucius Crassus said.

"It was posted, I assure you." Glaucia was about to continue when Numidicus rose to his feet.

"I sent out a slave last evening as the sun set! He returned saying there was nothing posted, Praetor!" Numidicus's son, whom they called Metellus Pius, tugged at his sleeve. Senators were quite careful to maintain proper protocol around who spoke, and when, in the senate house. Unless, of course, they felt threatened by a man they did not respect. Pius seemed aware of the hypocrisy and tried to silence his father as respectfully as he could.

"I never said it was posted before sundown. We still need to address it, nay?" Glaucia shrugged and returned to his curule chair. "The tribune passing this measure is Lucius Saturninus. You may have the floor." He nodded to his companion.

Marius watched intently. I had no idea what was happening.

"Conscript fathers, how good of you to join us." There was a hushed laughter as he gestured to the half-empty room. "It has come to my attention that there is a problem with our Republic." He tapped a finger to his lip and summoned the most concerned look he could muster. "It's a pervasive thing. Something that strikes at the very heart of Rome and all that we stand for. I have made it my place—no, my mission—to eradicate this issue at its source."

He took his time speaking, choosing each word carefully. There was even a slight stutter to his voice, which caused everyone to listen a bit more intently, to take him a bit more seriously. It was a stutter born of passion, not of nerves.

"We were once a city-state. A village full of sheepherders and farmers. We were—"

"Oh, spare us the history lesson, Tribune! *Our* families were there," a young Optimate named Cato Salonianus interrupted, standing from his bench. Beside him sat Sulla, who seemed less disturbed than others on his side of the curia. When Cato reclaimed his seat, Sulla whispered something in his ear.

Saturninus seemed more shocked that Cato didn't continue his rant than at the initial outburst. "I've no doubt. If I were to believe the lot of you, I'd think my own ancestors were still buggering sheep at the time. However, we must remember that this Republic was not formed by city dwellers alone but by honorable men of every cloth." He paused and shrugged his toga a bit higher on his shoulder. Something in his stance changed, and I could see he was coming to his point. "But Rome is no longer a city-state. She is a Republic with territory spanning from the Pillars of Hercules to Africa and Asia."

"Get on with it," Cato grumbled, and Sulla whispered in his ear again.

I was beginning to become frustrated with their interruptions. They were being antagonistic for the sake of it, nothing more. Saturninus had said nothing out of line as far as I could tell.

"We are unable to manage all those faraway provinces from

this old, sacred building. So we appoint governors. Men of prae-
torian rank, like the good Glaucia here, govern these provinces
for us. With absolute authority."

One of the Optimates beside Sulla stood and hurried from
the building. I felt certain he was going to check on the proposed
legislation and see if he could return with news before Saturninus concluded his speech.

"What are you proposing? To take away the power of our
governors?" An old aristocrat from the right stood. As it
happened, it was Gaius Caesar's father-in-law, Aurelius Cotta,
with his famous stutter and bloated old body.

"Never." Saturninus seemed offended by the implication.
"But these men act with absolute impunity. No repercussions.
And most of Rome's magistrates are noble and honorable men,
so they need no fear of reprisal to keep them honest. Some,
however, need checks and balances." He paused. "Yet, if a
lawsuit is brought against him by the province he has appropri-
ated, who is it that judges him? His friends. That's hardly a fair
trial, Senators."

Not just one man but every man from the right stood. Deafening shouts carried throughout the high walls of the curia,
curses and left-handed pointing. I was still attempting to piece
together what might come next, but the Optimates could
certainly sense it.

The Optimate from the right burst back into the curia,
panting from exertion. "He plans to give the extortion courts
back to the equestrians!" The wealthy middle-class equestrians
once held the rights over the courts. It was something that
pleased my father, but even as a child, I could remember him
telling me about the trouble it caused. The nobility believed the
courts were an ancestral right. To have the courts given back to
the equestrians was sure to stir up anger.

The tumult continued, louder now.

"Yes. Yes, I do," Saturninus said proudly.

He took a few steps closer to them, turning his back to the

Populares and moderates on the left, who he knew were supporting him with stomping feet and clapping hands.

Glaucia reclined in his curule chair and watched the spectacle with satisfaction.

"The law has already spoken!" some shouted.

"We own the courts!"

"Who better to judge?" others asked, all on their feet, fury on their lips.

"Yes, and who was it that passed the legislation giving authority of the courts to you fine noblemen? If I recall correctly, it was a man known more for his infamy in battle than his public policy. A man by the name of Quintus Caepio. And, tell me, where is he now? Has he not been—" Saturninus's voice was drowned out by the shouts. He did not wait to continue but raised his voice all the louder. "So I move that the law courts be returned to their rightful owners, the equestrians, who will judge the evils perpetrated by this august body with fairness and justice!"

Glaucia jumped to his feet and hurried to the floor.

"Senators, Senators, please!" His booming voice was still barely audible.

The shouts continued on, half of the senate house refusing to cede the floor to a man they knew was Saturninus's political ally. But eventually, with so few of them there to continue the ruckus, they had to relent.

"We need to put this to a vote so I can go home, by Jupiter." Glaucia shook his head in mock disappointment at the outbursts. "Who will oppose the motion?"

"I," Numidicus said, standing in grand fashion, even if he knew it was a lost cause.

"Very well. We'll now begin the vote."

Everyone around me began to stand up, and I hurried to do the same, even before I knew what was happening. I hurried along with the rest to stand behind the tribunes' chairs, where alone Saturninus stood along among the ten, feeling the weight of support behind him.

"In turn," Glaucia said, pointing to the Populare closest to him.

"Lucius Saturninus *adsentior*," the first said, followed by many more.

I startled when I realized it was my turn.

"Lucius Saturninus *adsentior*!" I shouted like I was sounding off in formation.

When those behind Saturninus were nearly finished voting, Glaucia stopped the proceedings with a flick of the wrist.

"A majority has been met. The legislation proposed by Lucius Appuleius Saturninus has passed a vote of the senate. It will now be voted on in an assembly of the people. You are all dismissed."

Across the curia, Numidicus continued to stand, eyes glazed over, contemplating how this could have happened. There were no more shouts or jeers. Nothing more could be done. They remained silent, stunned.

"Go, in the name of Jupiter Capitolinus, and bring peace, prosperity, and glory to Rome!" the *flamen dialis* said, lifting his arms, but by that point, no one was listening.

I was sure many senators would be regretting their decision to stay in bed that morning.

We didn't bother going to the *senaculum*. Marius followed Saturninus to the Basilica Porcia, and I followed Marius, passing by a statue of the river god Tiberinus.

The god's face was of unspeakable agony as the basin in his lap poured nearly frozen water into the pool beneath him.

"Magnificent, Saturninus!" Marius embraced him with the same enthusiasm he did his legionaries.

"It was due time," he said. "Come, let's go to my quarters here. I'll have drinks prepared for the occasion."

"Consul, can you explain to me the implications of what just happened?" I asked as we followed the triumphant tribune.

The smile wasn't completely wiped off his face by the question, but I could tell he was irritated.

"You heard the man. The patricians have no business judging their own in court. Partisan allegiances will always outweigh justice in such moments, so bad men go free."

"Why was it important that we did this on a day no one was attending?"

"Well, some attended, as you could see," Marius said, proud of his supporters. "But the Optimates wouldn't have allowed such a thing to pass. Saturninus would have pushed this through to the assembly of the people if need be, but having the stamp of approval from the senate lends the bill a certain...credibility."

"Would no one really vote for justice if it were against their party's interests?" I asked, naively, I'll admit, but hoping there was something more.

"Our side did, Sertorius. Those men we stood with would have voted for this measure regardless of who it helped or who it hurt," Marius replied.

"I have a hard time believing it's that simple," I said, but Marius didn't hear me, or pretended not to. By that time, we were arriving at the tribune's headquarters, and plenty of wine was already being poured for all.

A cup was passed to me quickly by a few slaves who hurried to fill the cups of others, the purple fluid spilling over the sides as it filled to the brim.

"To the protection of our people and the glory of our Republic!" Saturninus lifted his cup, and we all did the same.

"Don't you expect there to be some retaliation?" one senator asked.

"Of course they will retaliate! With rumors, insults, and slander. Nothing more. A vote was passed, and we were victorious. Now it is in the hands of the people. They cannot even say we broke custom." Saturninus laughed, finally letting his guard down, no longer needing to put on a show.

Everyone laughed with him, even me.

The servants hurried throughout the room to refill cups whether they were empty or not. Everyone stood facing the tribune, who leaned on his desk calmly and told stories about how he had prepared for the day, with a few jokes thrown in for good measure.

I found it odd that Marius wasn't the focus of the room. I had never witnessed such an occasion. But the consul didn't seem to mind.

After the storytelling had carried on for some time, and the wine had begun to warm our bellies, I decided to approach the tribune myself. I thought well enough of the fellow. I appreciated his demeanor, if nothing else. I remained uncertain if his politics were my own, but then again, I wasn't quite sure what his politics were. And I wasn't certain what mine were either.

I inched my way through the gathered senators to the tribune's side. I anticipated a wait and having to fight for the man's attention. But when he saw me, he cut himself off midconversation.

"Senator Sertorius, tell me, how was your first senate meeting?" he asked.

"This was my second, Tribune, and it was…interesting." I leaned against his desk, determined not to stumble or sway.

"A meeting of the senate is many things, I have found, but uninteresting is not one of them," he replied, to the laughter of those eavesdropping.

"Congratulations on your measure today, Tribune," I said, changing the subject.

He paused for a moment, studying me and sipping from his cup before he responded.

"Thank you, Senator. If it weren't for your support and the support of those like you, the bill would have failed." His face sobered. He seemed to become more reserved.

"Could you tell me something, Tribune?" I asked. I wasn't drunk by any means, but my head was swimming.

"Anything."

"What was the benefit in giving the law courts to the equestrians?" I held up my cup for it to be refilled, anxious that I should drink again to calm my nerves as he formulated his response.

"My friend." He placed a hand on my shoulder and squared himself to face me. "We need the support of the equestrians. We already have the love of the people and the support of our veterans... Now we need the equestrians. They will shout our names in the street when this is passed. And they will vote for us. The only relevant party in the Republic we won't have the support of are the nobles. And that is just the cost of waging politics."

He spoke as evenly and honestly as I imagined he would to any man. No games, no secrets. He spoke with a careful sincerity that never encouraged him to break eye contact. Political maneuvering was quite opposed to the teachings of men like Zeno that I had been reared on. Scheming would have seemed unmanly to the philosopher. But honesty was a virtue I would always understand. And that was most certainly the most honest answer I had received since receiving my senator's toga and red slippers.

"And the people won't be displeased with this?" I asked, simply to continue the conversation.

Saturninus shrugged.

"They care not. The people are concerned with themselves and the welfare of their own people. Who judges the law courts is irrelevant to them." A smile split his face. "Although, they do love seeing the patricians squirm. So perhaps they'll love us all the more for it." He began to turn to others to continue from where he had left off, but I interrupted.

"Do you hate the Optimates?" I asked.

As he considered the question, his brows furrowed and his face became serious.

"Politically or personally?"

"Personally."

"Oh yes. By the gods, yes. I hate the lot of them. With the fires of Vesta," he replied with an even smile.

"You do?" I was taken aback by his answer.

"I was the grain monitor of Ostia once. A respectable position, and one I had worked diligently for. When I received that commission, it was the happiest day of my life. I felt I had made my forefathers proud, sheepherders though they may have been. And my wife, well, she was as thrilled as I. She was a quaestor's wife. I could afford to buy her things for the first time in my life. But that wasn't really what mattered to her. She wanted the prestige, and that position affords it to both of us."

The smile on his face evaporated, and for the first time, he broke eye contact. He looked down at the stone beneath us and exhaled deeply.

"But that was taken from me. After achieving the position through hard work and dedication to the Republic, that was taken from me. A special commission met and stole the commission from me, and gave it to the now 'Father of the Senate' Marcus Scaurus," he continued, saying the name with derision. "Do not forget it was less than a fortnight later that your friend Hirtuleius and the consul-elect Mallius Maximus were attacked on the road to Ostia."

I had not forgotten. Nor would I ever.

"I do know this. I didn't know that you had been stripped of your position, though... And you hate the Optimates for this?" I asked.

I felt my heartbeat quicken when I thought of my friend's account of the attack, which I've related in my first set of scrolls.

He smiled sadly and took a sip of his drink.

"My wife left me afterward. Her brother, Cato Salonianus, believed I wasn't influential or important enough to provide for her. She was married off to a patrician who might better take care of her. When he died in battle, I thought perhaps our love could be rekindled. But then Cato had her married to Lucius Sulla."

He crossed his arms and shook his head at the memory. And for the first time, I saw intoxication on his face, but perhaps it was my imagination, borne of my own stupor, which was growing like a weed.

"And so you hate the Optimates because you believe they took your woman?" I asked, feeling the room quiet around me. I feared I had spoken out of turn, but Saturninus didn't seem to notice. Having experienced rejection so recently myself, I would have understood. But I wanted to believe his aims were more noble than that.

"I hate them for many reasons. I hate them for what they stole from me. I hate them for what I lost as a result. But more than anything, Sertorius"—here, he leaned in and took me by the hand to ensure I was listening properly—"I hate them because they're all liars. They're pretenders. Not one breath has escaped their lungs that benefited the Republic...just themselves. And their friends. And their wives. And spoiled children. I hate them because they are all the things that make Rome weak." He watched my reaction intently. "Does that answer your question?"

"Yes, it does, Tribune."

"Another drink!" He turned from me quickly but waited for everyone's cup to be refilled before he proposed his toast: "To what has happened today, and what is about to happen next!"

SCROLL X

Saturninus's bill was passed in the assembly of the people without resistance. The first blow had been struck. The first, but not the last, as the entire city seemed to take a collective inhale in anticipation of what Marius and his allies would do next.

I've hesitated to include this among my scrolls, but here I have another piece from Lucius Cornelius Sulla. I'm assuming most of you have access to this already, but it describes the events that immediately proceeded from Saturninus's law courts legislation. And I would rather not have to do so myself.

LUCIUS CORNELIUS SULLA, FEBRUARY 655 AB URBE CONDITA

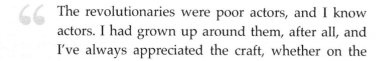 The revolutionaries were poor actors, and I know actors. I had grown up around them, after all, and I've always appreciated the craft, whether on the

stage or in political life. But Marius and his associates had no talent for acting. We all knew what they were up to.

The conversation had never begun as "how do we bring more justice to corrupt governors," but rather as "how do we secure a larger body of voters."

We all knew that from the moment Saturninus took the floor. And if any of us had seen that legislation posted, we would have certainly rallied every old, feeble senator in the city to stand against them.

We could see what was happening, yes, but we could only sit and wonder what aims those men had been conspiring for on dark nights, and what they had planned for us next.

The good men were in a panic after Saturninus's bill was passed by the people. We knew degenerate politicians like Glaucia would use the law courts as a weapon of intimidation and threat against good Roman magistrates across the Republic. And with the equestrians supporting them, along with their stranglehold over the common rabble, they were becoming a real threat to the established order.

Fortunately, there were men like myself who were apt enough to prepare. The old breed, men like Marcus Scaurus, Metellus Numidicus, and Aurelius Cotta, were too out of touch with the times to do anything about it. So I made the connections I needed to.

After returning from the northern campaign, I made a most beneficial union to one of Rome's most illustrious families. I married the sister of Cato Salonianus, and thereafter, the two of us were inseparable. My new bride was slightly dishonored by a previous marriage to the reprobate Saturninus, but it was worth it for me to see the tears in his eyes when Porcia and I passed him by in the street.

Cato was young and enthusiastic for our cause, a man whose heart was always after defending the Roman constitution. He wasn't nearly as much fun as I'd like, never partaking in much wine and detesting the company of actors and poets, but I understood that, for now, such things would have to wait. When power and authority were mine, I could do as I pleased and surround myself with those that humored me. Until then, I would have to play the game along with the rest of them.

So Cato and his companions became mine. I made connections with the aedile Scaevola, who was even more dull than Cato but played his part well. Through him, I became engaged with his friend and co-aedile, Lucius Crassus, one of the finest orators I've ever seen. Through them, I became acquainted with Pompeius, who, perhaps more than any of them, shared my view of the world. The five of us were determined to form the bulwark of defenses against the demagogues and their aims. We made preparations, but there was nothing we could do but wait.

And fortunately, we did not have to wait long before the popular party made their next move.

The meeting was called by Marius, the

presiding consul. It was under the pretense of a general meeting of the senate, but we were not going to make the same mistake we made before. Everyone showed up this time.

"Senators, we have something important to discuss today. The war against the slaves in Sicily is nearly at an end, as my dear friend and now son-in-law, Manius Aquillius, has sent word of his impending victory over the remnant of the slave army. That being said, the time for the harvest is upon us, and something must be done to address the grain shortage."

It always caused a general cringe in the senate house when Marius spoke. It was easy to forget just how uncouth he was when you saw him addressing plebs on the street or commanding his men in the field. But within the curia, it was clear how inept and incapable he was at addressing his intellectual betters.

I leaned over to Cato and whispered, "They're going to address the grain dole."

He looked at me with horror and then back to the bumbling consul.

"They cannot do that. The law has spoken plainly about increasing the grain dole. The corpses of the Gracchi brothers still attest to this at the bottom of the Tiber," Crassus said in a hushed voice.

I stared intently at Saturninus from across the senate floor. He waited patiently on the edge of his chair for his moment to speak once more.

"Precedence and law have never stopped revolutionaries before, comrade," I said in a whisper.

"I apologize for not posting my proposed remedy to this situation sooner,"

Saturninus said. "I am a night owl by nature, and due to my unwavering determination to only propose legislation that benefits every facet of the Roman Republic, I often wait until the last minute to ensure it is properly drafted."

There were groans and grunts of derision, but the tribune was not the least bit disturbed. I believe a grin even spread across his face.

"Something must be done, gentlemen," he continued, his words having a sobering effect on the room. "The harvest is upon us indeed, and our people have never been hungrier." Agreement sounded from the hordes gathered outside the curia. "I propose that the grain dole be—"

He was cut off by shouts of derision from our benches before he could finish.

"Lowered to five-sixth of an as so that our people may eat and be strong enough to serve this great Republic!" he concluded when he could make himself heard. But everyone had stopped listening the moment he'd mentioned the grain dole. Every senator, on both sides, was on his feet. The one side with thunderous applause; ours, with incredulous cries.

"Senators!" Marius stomped and shouted until he had the floor. He had no talent for commanding a room like this, and it would take a more articulate man than Marius to calm the curia that day. "We must put the matter to a vote. Before that, we will hear your response." The Father of the Senate, Marcus Scaurus, was generally the first to respond. In his day, he might have retaliated with clubs rather than words, but he was aging and losing the energy for such things.

He took the center of the curia, legs shaking

from his advanced age, as Marius returned to his seat. His voice was already hoarse from shouting, and his hands were trembling with repressed anger.

"We can see what this is. We all know what you are doing, Tribune. You as well, Praetor. And Consul," Scaurus said. Marius ignored the allegation, but Glaucia smiled and straightened his spine in response. "There has never been a more flagrant abuse of magistratical power in the history of the Republic. To gain for yourselves the support of the people, you would bankrupt the state. To sell grain for double that price would still be selling it below cost. Our coffers cannot survive under such circumstances! How will we fund our military? Our construction and infrastructure? Our religion?"

"We have no need to secure the love of the people," Marius interjected, rather foolishly. He should have never acquiesced to the fact that a "we" existed where the three of them were concerned. Of course, the entire city knew about their little triumvirate, but to acknowledge its existence proved that Marius was still lacking an understanding of his political ABC's.

"If you did not fear losing the people's support, you wouldn't be proposing this measure!" Scaurus responded without pause, pointing an outstretched hand at the consul. "Which makes me fearful of the aims you have in mind for the remainder of your terms in office. What do you have planned that you need to further grasp at the people's support? What sinister and wicked aims do these men have that they fear they might lose it in the first place, since the consul has already admitted that they have it?"

"This is not a place for speculation, Senator, but for addressing a piece of legislation," Saturninus responded coolly, unaffected by the accusations leveled in his direction.

Scaurus inhaled deeply.

"I have said what I needed to say. This will empty our coffers. It will bankrupt this state. It cannot happen. It must not happen." He returned to his bench, to the support of his followers and sycophants. If it were I to address this bill, I would have come with far more pointed accusations and rebuttals. I would have called for their arrest without hesitation, and I could have found the constitutional grounds for it later. But I couldn't speak. Neither myself, Cato, or Pompeius had ever held a curule chair, so we wouldn't be recognized. We were pedarii, only able to vote with our feet. And the revolutionaries were fortunate that was the case.

The rest of the former magistrates were now given the opportunity to speak. Most of them said the same things. On Marius's side of the senate house, they claimed again and again that the people were going hungry. They used inflammatory rhetoric to provoke the cries of those listening outside the senate house, as if those shrieks lent credence to their words. The good men all responded with the same arguments—bankruptcy and accusations.

Rutilius Rufus, Marius's old comrade, was the only one of the whole lot to respond with anything meaningful. He was a moderate by all accounts and did his best to sit as close to the center of the curia as possible, but on this, he was staunchly in our camp. He offered no insults to the character or dignitas of the tribune or his compatriots, but instead mentioned exact figures for the grain dole bill that explained how ruinous it would become if it remained in place for even two years.

"You've all said your piece. Now, it is time the matter be put to a vote."

We all stood and moved to the man we supported. The right stood behind Scaurus, the left behind Saturninus.

"Marcus Scaurus adsentior."

"Lucius Saturninus adsentior."

The voting began. But even at full capacity, it was apparent we were outnumbered. The moderates must have been frightened by the howling mob outside in the comitium.

"I veto the motion! I use my tribune's veto on the motion!" A lone tribune ran to the center of the room. The good men took a collective exhale, but I wasn't so sure. The tribune's veto was generally reserved to protect the rights of the mob, but at least one of the ten could see good sense. With that one word, "veto," the whole proceedings were to be shut down.

The Populares shot off into a rabid tirade, not remembering what it was like to be politically outwitted. Marius, slack-jawed, looked to his own tribune for answers. All eyes, in fact, fell on Saturninus for his response.

He moved deliberately from his chair to the vetoing tribune, and stepped in front of him.

"Shall we continue?"

Murmurs of confusion rose throughout the curia.

"A veto has been offered. The vote is closed," the flamen dialis said in his pitiful, frail old voice.

"On the contrary. When a tribune works against the will of the people, his acts are nullified. Recent history has proven that. And this is the will of the people, is it not?" Saturninus strode to the open doors and lifted his arms as the mob cried out in response. "Let us continue."

Appalled senators jumped down the benches and darted to assault him. His supporters jumped to their feet and rallied around him, repulsing the assailants. Saturninus simply turned from them, hands clenched behind his back. Both sections emptied as more and more rushed to the fray.

The plebs stormed the doors, the guards barely able to restrain them from entry.

I leaned back and watched with amusement. The enraged faces of old prigs like Numidicus. The stunned, heartbroken look of that one-eyed "war hero." The glee in Glaucia's eyes, like a child viewing his first gladiatorial bout. The scrapping, punching, clawing of the dusty old men. And finally, Marius, who stood by and watched it all.

SCROLL XI

IDES OF FEBRUARY, 655 AB URBE CONDITA

THE SENATE wisely decided to not reconvene for the next few days. The meeting was ended by the outbreak of violence, and it would have likely continued if we'd returned to the curia too soon. Both sides needed time to lick their wounds, come up with a plan, and let cooler heads prevail.

I assumed Saturninus would be putting the motion to a vote in the assemblies, since he already knew what would happen if he presented it to the senate house. And this would likely make matters all the worse. This was, in part, what Tiberius Gracchus was assassinated for, if you remember. So Saturninus was wise not to do anything immediately. Everyone was still reeling from too many punches to the head.

I received a letter that morning from Gaius Glaucia, an invitation to join him at the hot baths on the Esquiline Hill after lunch. It was rather formal for a social call, but it was the first time he had reached out to me directly, so I was determined to comply, more curious than anything.

I'd have bet that there wasn't a man my age in Rome who had spent less time in the public baths than myself. So I was apt to watch others and do as they did so I didn't commit any more social mistakes.

I undressed in the changing rooms, handing my toga off to a beautiful Syrian girl who placed it in a numbered box. I entered the *caldarium* and tried to make out the faces through the steam rising from the gently churning waters.

A bright beam of light poured in from a hole in the ceiling above us, cutting through the steam like a knife. Small figures of Hercules as Atlas held up columns around the room, and depictions of winged phalluses lined the walls above them.

"Senator Sertorius, I'm so relieved that you've joined me." Glaucia bobbed over toward me and gestured for me to enter. "I know it's a bit of a break of custom to meet in the hot rooms, but it's much too cool out for the frigidarium, is it not?"

"I am thankful for the heat, certainly." I stifled a wince as I put my foot in the water. It was remarkable that they could heat the basins beneath the baths when the aqueducts were nearly frozen.

"A few others may join us shortly. The consul is in the gymnasium presently. Pleasant, nay?"

"It is," I said, settling into the water when it reached my chest, my eye taking in the delight of the brightly painted stucco above us.

Glaucia bounced around on bended knees as carelessly as if it were a public holiday, flicking the water with his fingers.

"This weather. It's really something, isn't it? It beats the sweltering heat of Sextilius, that's for sure. But, I mean, which god is taking a shit break and forgot to warm the sun? Apollo, I guess?" He rambled as if talking to himself. But, to my surprise, he waited for a response.

"Oh yes. It's been quite cold."

"And the winds. I'd say Zephyr is pissed, if I believed in the gods."

"Praetor, if you don't mind...why have you invited me here?" I asked rather abruptly. I didn't have anything in particular to do that afternoon, but anything seemed preferable to sitting in boiling water with ten naked men discussing the weather.

He didn't seem perturbed by my directness.

"Social visit, that's all. We've been around one another these past months but haven't had a chance to really meet. I'd rather like to get to know the Hero of the North," he said with apparent sincerity.

"I'd like to get to know him as well. He sounds fascinating. If you ever meet him, let me know," I replied. Glaucia let out a laugh and lifted his hand from the water with a splash to slap my shoulder.

"Very good. Your humility is one of my favorite things about you, Sertorius. It's quite evident." He seemed to sober for a moment. "But you must be careful not to let *everyone* see it. Others may seek to take advantage of you before you realize your true potential."

"Who do you speak of?" I asked. There were only three men who had taken an active interest in my career thus far, and one of them was bobbing in the water beside me.

"No one in particular." He plugged his nose and dipped under the water for a moment. "I just mean you need to admit to your qualities," he said upon reemerging. "The stuff about you. What's in your guts. Don't discredit it."

"I know who I am, Praetor. Otherwise, I wouldn't have agreed to become a senator."

He shrugged. "I think you'll be hard-pressed to find anyone who will believe that." He gave me a wink. "But I will try."

Disgruntled shouts and equal laughter came from some dice players in the corner.

"You are not just a scarecrow for the old nobles, Senator. You could be greater than both Saturninus and me one day. Perhaps even greater than Marius." He tapped his nose.

"I have no desire for that kind of power. The burden isn't

worth the bounty." I leaned up on the edge of the pool and lifted my arms out to cool off.

"Much good you could do with that kind of power, if I had to guess." He stopped and looked up rather abruptly. Then a smile split across his face. "If it isn't Rome's baldest senator! Join us." He swam back in the water and gestured for the short, barrel-chested man behind me to enter.

"Oh, bugger off, Glaucia. I've more hair than you will at my age." The man winced at the warmth of the water as he settled in beside me.

"Sertorius, this is Lucius Cornelius Cinna. Rome's next praetor, if I were to place a wager."

I hope I didn't reveal my shock. I guess he did have the same reddish complexion and clay-colored hair as my good friend Equus, but they didn't appear much like father and son. He looked at me through squinted eyes and offered a hand.

"How do you do?"

"I served with your son in Gaul. He's a dear friend of mine," I said, accepting his hand gratefully.

He pulled it away and slapped his forehead.

"Of course! Sertorius. Oh, I've heard many tales of the mighty Sertorius from my boy. You and that Hirtius fellow."

"Hirtuleius, yes. The three of us were inseparable during the campaign."

"From my days in the legion, that usually only means one thing." Glaucia shot me a wink.

Cinna wagged a finger at him. "You be careful now, Praetor. You're lucky I know you jest."

I'll admit I was a bit surprised by Equus's father. My friend had always talked of him with a reverential admiration, as if he were a giant among men. He seemed rather unimpressive to me, although with an undeniable rugged handsomeness. Beads of sweat were already dripping from his forehead, and his breath seemed labored from the steam.

"Cinna here owns a farm out in Campania. Not a latifundium

but a real farm. Legend has it he tills the earth himself," Glaucia said with a poorly concealed smirk.

"As every true Roman should."

"And for the hair he's losing on his head, he's making up for it with this beard." He leaned forward and tugged at the auburn curls on Cinna's chin before the man slapped his hand away. "Some say it's unbecoming of a senator to grow a beard."

"Well, they do not know their history, then. The Romans of old all grew out their beards," Cinna said, quick to reply.

"And you'd do anything to link yourself with them, wouldn't you? We all act out our parts."

"Damn you, Glaucia. Are we dictating a biography or am I going to get some rest?" he said, at least with some humor.

Suddenly, the water splashed all around us as the bathers jumped to their feet.

We turned to find Marius at the entryway, chest heaving and drenched in sweat from his exercise.

"Never mind me, citizens. We're all the same in here, right? We all smell like shit if we don't bathe," he said, proud of himself and the laughter he received in response. He pointed to us. "I'll be back in a moment. Going to take a dip in the cold pools."

"The consul is in rare form," Cinna noted.

"Why shouldn't he be? The people's assembly will vote on our bill next moon, and we're guaranteed victory," Glaucia responded.

"It's guaranteed?" I asked, as I had previously. I was curious to see if Glaucia would admit to voter tampering in new company.

There was only a brief flash of irritation before his smile returned.

"It's the *people*'s assembly. The *people*'s. Of course, they'll vote on something that will see their bellies filled. Don't worry, my boy, you'll learn."

Marius returned presently and jumped in beside us, sending the water cascading over the edges.

"Afternoon, boys," he said with a toothy grin before shaking each of our hands. "Some well-watered wine, I think." He snapped his fingers, and a Cilician slave boy in a linen towel brought us each a cup. Marius materialized a few *sestertii* from the towel he just dropped and slapped them at the foot of the boy.

The consul gulped eagerly, then slowly sank into the water and rested his head against the ledge. "Gods, that's good." When he at last finished a deep exhale, he looked at me from the corners of his eyes. "A bit surprised to find you here, Sertorius. Glaucia, you did not tell me he was coming."

"I'd wager there are a great many citizens in Rome you don't know the location of, Consul," Glaucia said with a single cocked eyebrow.

"Plotting to betray me?" Marius asked before dipping his face halfway in the water.

"The plan's already laid out, sir," I replied, causing him to laugh through his nose and bubbles to erupt at the surface. He slapped my back, pleased at the joke.

"I'm glad you're all here regardless, plotting or not." He made his way between Cinna and me and balanced himself on the ledge, forcing all of us to focus our attention on him.

"We have a problem with the voters."

"You know, I rather prefer to begin these discussions with something redundant and meaningless... How about the weather?" Glaucia jested.

"That's why you'd make a poor soldier, Glaucia. Firm and direct. Right, Sertorius?" He nudged me with his elbow.

"Correct, sir."

"There's a rabble-rouser among the people who is causing quite a stir," Marius said, getting straight to it.

"And who is this man?" Cinna asked, sipping his wine slowly.

"Some prole on the Caelian. The people look to him as some sort of leader," Marius replied.

"A collegium head, perhaps?" Glaucia asked, suddenly more interested.

"That's it. Head of the baker's guild or something like that."

"That can't be it. Wouldn't have enough influence." Cinna looked up and scratched at the beard on his chin.

"Damn it, would you two let me finish?" Marius waited for silence. "This man, they call him Aufedius, has been going about convincing the people that if the grain bill is passed, the granaries will all go dry by July."

"He must be head of the baker's guild, then. He knows with free-flowing grain, he'll be inundated with work. Must be a lazy bastard," Glaucia said.

"Never mind all that. His intentions and reasons are irrelevant to me. It's the poisonous lies he's spreading that are of concern." Marius lowered his voice a bit, cognizant that it had been rising unintentionally throughout the conversation. "What are we to do about it? The man has many friends in the Forum Boarium, and they're spreading the slander to every pleb shopping for his dinner."

Glaucia thought about it for a moment.

"Sertorius, you must have several veteran associates in the city. Perhaps they could be persuaded to go and talk to the man for a few coins." All eyes turned to me.

"He won't be part of something like that, Glaucia." Marius shook his head.

"I would, if the cause were just," I said, surprising everyone, including myself. "But is this not free speech, gentlemen? Is this not the bedrock of any Republic, of a liberated existence?" I asked. I was quite pleased with the response, even if it sounded painfully contrived and naive. For me, though, it was the truth. And I hoped they would see that. Then again, the wine was setting in.

"Do you hear this, boys? This is Rome's next great orator. A defender of liberty!" Marius clapped my shoulder and pulled me in to kiss my head.

For once, Glaucia was entirely unamused.

"Should free speech be allowed even when it fuels a tyrannical system of government that is predicated on the oppression of the ill born and feebleminded?" There was not a jot of humor in his tone. He had never spoken so eloquently, or without any form of pageantry.

I declined to respond.

"Perhaps there is another way of dealing with him?" Cinna chimed in. We all turned to him and waited as he sipped his wine, taking his time. "We could have a few individuals research the man. Due diligence. Perhaps the man has a few habits he wouldn't like his disciples to know about? Perhaps he lies with boys, or he has a bastard child..."

"Not a bad idea." Marius raised an eyebrow and nodded his head. "We can silence the man with accusations as well as we can with swords," Marius said.

"I'm grieved, Consul." Glaucia placed both hands on his chest. "I hope none of you thought I was suggesting *harming* the man. There's no cause for violence. I was simply suggesting a few burly young men like Sertorius here could make a show of force. Most men are far braver when surrounded by like-minded individuals than when they are staring down their enemy. Surely, you all must know this from the battlefield."

"We know your heart, Praetor. Regardless, I'm inclined to agree with Cinna," Marius said.

"I am too. A better plan by half. Wish I had thought of it myself." Glaucia tapped his forehead and winked at Cinna.

"Glaucia, can you have one of your men look into this Aufedius for us?" the consul asked.

"Absolutely. I'll have every beggar in the city keep their eyes and ears open."

"Six days, men. Six days until the vote. We all know how important this bill is. Everything...everything rides on it. We want to rule Rome, don't we, gentlemen? We want to change it for the better? Well, it all begins here." Marius's eyes were as focused and serious as I had ever seen them. Content that we had all received the message, he relaxed. "Let's dry off and get dressed, boys. We have a Republic to run."

SCROLL XII

TWO DAYS AFTER IDES OF FEBRUARY, 655 AB URBE
CONDITA

"*Dominus*! *Dominus*!" the shouts came. All the soldiers of the
northern campaign had learned to sleep lightly, so I was on my
feet before I woke up. For a moment, I thought I was being
summoned to the walls for a Teutone attack.

"What is it?" I asked, hurrying to place my eye patch on.

"A man is at the door." The head slave of my house was out
of breath from simply running to fetch me. It was obvious from
his size that he had been taking a few extra sweet cakes from the
kitchen, but his former master seemed to overlook it, and I did
as well.

"So...who is it?" I asked, quite irritated, as I wrapped a belt
around my tunic.

"He wouldn't say...but he said he needed words with you
immediately. I've not seen him before, *dominus*."

"Go and fetch us some bread and olives. We'll have breakfast," I suggested to calm us both. But, in truth, my heart and
mind were already racing at the possibilities. I reached into my

trunk for my sword but thought better of it. Instead, I grabbed my dagger and concealed it with a strap on my ankle.

The entrance was left open, the frightened porter standing in the doorway, as if he could have managed to defend the place if necessary.

I pushed past him and prepared for the confrontation. Rather than the white robes of a senator, I found the scarlet cloak of a soldier.

"Lucius!" I shouted as he erupted in laughter at the look on my face.

"My brother, how good it is to see you!" He embraced me firmly. It seemed that every time I saw him, he'd developed muscles where none had been previously.

"Did you really have to go and frighten my lads like that?" I asked.

"Well worth it to see that look in your eye. You must have been expecting trouble." His eyes lit up, expecting to hear the latest news.

"Come in, brother. Let's get warm. I want to hear everything about your campaign." I ushered him in through the halls.

"Not much to say, really. Fighting slaves is a rather tedious task. Not much glory to be had. No joy can be found in such a war. But...all for the safety of the Repub—" His voice trailed off as his eyes scanned the mosaics on the walls. He seemed impressed by the size of the halls. "Quintus Sertorius. What a home you now have."

"I've been blessed beyond comprehension," I said, showing him into the triclinium.

"By which god? I'll be certain to sacrifice more pigeons to him."

"By Marius. He prefers the sacrifice of salutes and undivided attention."

The head slave brought us a bowl of olives and some leftover bread from dinner the previous evening. Lucius accepted it but didn't immediately dig in the way he used to.

"I'd actually like to see the general if I have the time. Well, if he has the time."

"Why would you not have enough time? The campaign is over, nay? Or, otherwise, why would you be here?"

He sipped at his water and pensively popped an olive into his mouth.

"It's over. But I'm not planning on staying long. I'm hoping to join up with the boys heading east to fight the Cilician pirates," he said nervously, as if he hoped for my permission.

"So soon? Why don't you stay in the city for a while? I have a spare room."

He considered it for a moment, then shook his head slowly. "Unfortunately, I fear I've no talent for peacetime. I've learned nothing but how to soldier."

"There's hardly anything peaceful about it. Haven't you heard about what's been happening?" I asked.

He stopped cold and looked at me with hungry eyes. "Tell me." Fighting for so long can leave a man wondering about the state of the Republic for which he fights.

"The general has some new allies. Saturninus and Glaucia are chief among them, a tribune and a praetor. And the three of them have been raging against the senate since the moment they took office."

"Ha!" Lucius clapped his hands together. "That's what I like to hear. Giving one to those old bastards."

"I'm a senator now too, Lucius," I said coyly, reminding him what I had shared with him in my letters.

"Yes, but I'm sure your cloth of senator isn't the type they're fighting against." Perhaps Lucius was more well informed than I thought.

"You should have seen it. They proposed a piece of grain dole legislation last week, and the whole place went mad. Half the three hundred senators were on their feet, punching and clawing in the center of the curia."

He cackled at the thought of it.

"I'd have paid to see that. More entertaining than any gladiatorial bout."

"But it's a disgrace. We can't hope to organize the state with our senators behaving like that," I replied seriously. But then a grin spread across my face from Lucius's contagious laughter. "It was rather humorous."

Lucius bit off a massive piece of bread and, with his mouth full, said, "Come on. Let's go have a drink."

"So early?" I asked.

"Yes, yes! I have limited time here, remember."

"I have wine here, you madman."

"I want to go out and see these citizens I fight for!" he said, picking the last of the bread from his teeth. "Besides, someone special is joining us."

I already knew who he meant.

"Equus."

"That's right. And the little fellow will be quite irritable when we arrive late." He waved for me to follow him to the door.

"He deserves it for all those times we were punished for his tardiness at muster," I said.

Lucius flipped a coin to the porter.

"Sorry for the fright, lad." He winked as we exited.

Lucius was the one constant in my life then. Perhaps my mother also, but she had not endured what the two of us had gone through together. His presence felt like home. He was the cornerstone upon which a temple is built, and I could feel my spirits rising with each moment, and the thoughts of sharing a drink with both him and Equus elevated them even more.

"I'll tell you, *amicus*, the real reason I want to go to a tavern is because...well, I haven't seen a real woman in what feels like a lifetime." Lucius laughed, revealing the truth of his statement by staring wide-eyed at the matrons passing us by.

"When you're wearing that cloak, you're expected to conduct yourself as a soldier, Lucius," I jested.

"You've been away from camp too long if you think the legionaries have any modicum of restraint."

We made for the Caelian Hill, where Equus currently resided and the tavern Lucius wanted to visit was located.

"What'll it be, boys? Good price for soldiers!" the portly old proprietor shouted as we entered. His hair was greasy enough to stand up on its own in thick locks that appeared unintentional.

"Three of whatever's fanciest!" Lucius shouted, tossing his coin purse on an open table in front of us.

"I thought you weren't going to show, you bastard." Equus appeared from the shadows and embraced Lucius warmly. When he turned to me, he pretended to be shocked. "Well, this is quite a surprise. This is a rather unseemly establishment for a senator, isn't it?"

"What about a senator's son?" I asked, kissing his cheek.

"Well, considering most of the other senators' sons are entrenched in debt and have three illegitimate children by my age, I'd say I'm doing fair by modern standards."

"Sit, friends, sit." Lucius gestured to the table as if it were within his own home. "By Mars, it's good to see you boys again." He leaned over to squeeze both of our shoulders. When the man arrived with our wine, Lucius tipped him heavily, as soldiers are inclined to do when they have money from a campaign they haven't been able to spend. "Sweet, sweet nectar of the gods," Lucius said in a feigned delirium after his first sip.

"What gods do you serve, then? Priapus?" Equus winced at his first sip. "It could use some more spice."

"You've both forgotten the pig's piss they serve in camp. I took a few cups from Aquillius's tent, and it still doesn't compare to real Roman wine."

"How was the campaign, by the way?" Equus asked. Lucius sobered and stared off at the table for a moment. He shrugged and pretended whatever thoughts he was having weren't bothering him.

"They're all the same, aren't they? A lot of marching, waiting, and hard fighting. It's over now, and that's what matters." He summed things up quickly, anxious to move on. Equus wasn't the most discerning fellow, though.

"I heard tell that men in Rome are willing to pay double for a rebellious slave once captured. Presumably for the sport of trying to break them. Did the legions bring any back?" Equus asked.

Now Lucius couldn't feign joviality, even if he wanted to.

He gulped hard.

"No. We had intended to, but…they took their own lives."

"All of them?" Equus asked, raising his eyebrows just a tad.

Lucius nodded. "The smell was the most remarkable part." His eyes glazed over for a moment before he looked up with a smile again. "Let's discuss happier matters, comrades. Campaign talk is dreary and generally boring."

We settled into the silence for a moment, all of us thinking of something to bring up.

"You remember that odd fellow? What was his name? Opiter. That's it. He was always digging through the garbage for bits of food." Equus laughed at the thought.

We both nodded along with him, remembering the man clearly.

"And asking everyone for their leftovers. Strange man," Lucius added.

"And skinny as a pilum too," I said.

Lucius took a gulp of his wine when the laughter died and said, "Well, here's something. Now that the general has made Sertorius a senator, perhaps he'll make the two of us senators as well?"

"Perhaps I should be able to grow a beard first," Equus suggested.

"If you're waiting on that, I'm not sure you'll ever enter public life."

"Do you remember when you showed up to formation half shaved, Equus?" I slapped him in the ribs as Lucius cackled.

"I never understood why formation needed to be so damned early. I never had time to read my morning meditations before all that marching and standing about."

"I'd hate to see what you'd be like as a general. You'd have the men reading poetry and contemplating existence rather than swinging swords," Lucius said.

"I wouldn't rush to public life, friends. It's more tedious than swordplay," I interjected.

"More tedious than shining every link in your lorica? Or marching in tune to a tone-deaf bugler?" Equus asked.

"I'm inclined to say it is, I'm afraid."

"Come on, Quintus, it can't be that bad." Lucius rolled his eyes.

"What is it specifically that makes it so?" Equus asked, genuinely interested in the answer, as he would almost certainly become a senator himself in time.

"Let me think. You have to wear that bloody broad-striped toga everywhere you go, at least when you aren't sneaking away to meet old friends at unsavory taverns. You can't speak in the senate house, not until you've been praetor. You just speak with your feet, stomping along with the rest like a donkey. You have to listen to the long-winded speeches of every decrepit old man in the curia. Shall I continue?" I took a sip of wine.

"Surely, seeing the spectacle of Consul Marius manhandling those decrepit old men makes it worth it, though?" Equus asked.

"I wouldn't say that's the case, even if the plebs claim it in the streets. It's his two companions, this Saturninus and Glaucia, who do most of the manhandling. And to tell you the truth, they're the ones who are really taking an interest in my career more than the general. I feel they're the only ones who aren't hiding something from me." I shook my head, surprised at what I was saying but believing it nonetheless.

"That's a hefty allegation, Quintus Sertorius. Why would Marius hide anything from you?" Equus asked.

"More drinks, boys? Second round half price," the proprietor addressed the table, smiling to reveal mostly missing teeth and a few golden ones.

"Keep them coming," Lucius said, "especially if the third round is quarter price."

"I'm not sure what the general's purpose is. But he's singularly focused. He can hardly discuss anything but matters of public policy. And when questioned, he declines to answer with anything substantial," I continued when our drinks were filled.

"Can you blame him? He likely doesn't want to overwhelm you so soon," Lucius said, ever the general's defender.

"It's like he's afraid I'll see what's really going on. Like I'll run away or neglect my duties the moment I see the Republic for what she is."

"And will you? The way you ran from the Caepiones?" Equus asked. Perhaps I would have been offended, but there was no malicious intent in his question.

"No. I don't need to be sheltered any longer. I've fought for a long time, brothers, and now I need to understand what it is I fought for, no matter how vile." They seemed content with the answer. They knew as well as anyone how naive I had always been. But as Marius said of our soldiers, it was time I became educated, if it was for the good of the Republic. "Either of you have nightmares?" I asked before considering it.

"By Bellona, I thought I was the only one. Every night," Lucius said. I knew he wouldn't have admitted to it if he hadn't been draining the warm wine so quickly.

"You have trouble sleeping, Quintus?" Equus asked.

"Sometimes. I wake with a fright, only to realize I've spent the entire night fighting a battle. Burdigala, Aquae Sextiae, Vercellae…Arausio."

"What happens in them? The true events or something more?" As a dedicated student of philosophy, Equus was interested in the interpretation of dreams.

"It varies from night to night. Most of the time, I'm searching through the ranks to find someone. I don't know who, but I know I have to find them."

"And do you? Find them, I mean."

I shook my head. "Sometimes I find a man buried underneath shields. The way I found my friend Bear, if you remember. But it's never him underneath, or whomever I'm looking for." I looked away and wondered if I should continue. Wine has a habit of forcing the answer. "Sometimes it's Gavius I find."

Both of them winced.

"Most of the time, I just draw my sword and the blade falls right from the hilt when the enemy arrives. That, or I've forgotten to dress for battle and I'm out there in the formation as naked as a blue Celt," Lucius said, trying to lighten the conversation.

"What about you, Equus? Any troubling dreams of late?" I asked.

He considered it but shook his head.

"No. I sleep as soundly as a babe, I'm afraid. Your dreams sound far more interesting, however."

We discussed more mundane matters.

Lucius discussed possible service opportunities. Equus updated us on the latest chariot races at the Circus Maximus and bragged about the hefty sum of earnings he'd made off them.

At one point, an Egyptian girl came and sat on Lucius's lap without his invitation.

She wrapped her arms around his neck and locked her lips on his ear.

"Come on. Bargain for soldier," she said with a thick accent.

From the smile on Equus's face, I wondered if he'd somehow put her up to it.

Lucius looked at us like a cornered animal.

I laughed. "Go on. If there's any time a man deserves a little bit of degeneracy, it's when he's on leave."

"No, thank you. I appreciate it, ma'am." He spoke like she was a Roman matron.

He smiled and rubbed at his neck, and his face colored like a Nursian turnip from the embarrassment.

"All that talk about women, Lucius, and here we are." I shook my head in mock disappointment.

"I just like to look." He winked and took a long drink.

By midday, we all had things to do. Lucius was due to report back in camp by seventh hour. Equus had a lesson in rhetoric planned with a Greek teacher. I needed to prepare for a dinner at the home of Gaius Saufeius, which I dreaded.

We parted ways, promising to do the same before Lucius departed. But even if he were only around for a few more weeks, I feared what things might be like at that time. Perhaps a drink with old friends wouldn't even be a possibility, or at least a safe one.

SCROLL XIII

THREE DAYS AFTER IDES OF FEBRUARY, 655 AB
URBE CONDITA

THE VOTE WAS three days away. Saturninus had invited me to
dinner that evening, but I had declined on the pretense of having
a cold.

I woke up early and sauntered through the house. I asked the
kitchen slaves if they were in need of anything. I laid out fresh
seeds for the birds. I cleaned my desk and placed my copies of
Zeno and Plato back where they belonged.

I knew what was coming soon, and I was intentional about
making every moment of calm last as long as it could.

"Morning, my boy," I said when Gavius appeared from his
room, phis blanket and rubbing at his eye.

"Why does Crito have to be so loud?" he grumbled. Our
head slave certainly had a voice that carried, at least when
addressing the other slaves.

"He has to keep this place in order, doesn't he? Unless you
think you're up for it?"

"If I were in charge, we would have a horse," he said, rather
pleased with the thought.

"And where would we stable him? In your bedroom?" I walked to him and gave him an unreciprocated embrace.

"Where's Arrea?" he asked.

"Something tells me she's in the peristylium. Would you like to go find her?" He started to walk that direction, so I followed. "We'll both go."

My new responsibilities had kept me from the house far more than I would have liked. And when I was there, I'll admit I was often selfishly predisposed with my own studies. I desired—no, needed—the escape, and since I was determined not to find it at the bottom of a cup, at least when the others were around, I found it in the scrolls I had inherited from my father, which my mother had sent me a few weeks prior.

But every time I saw my adopted son, it reminded me that perhaps the most important of all my responsibilities was being consistently neglected.

"What did I tell you? There she is," I said as we entered. She was perched up beside the garden fountains picking out debris that had fallen through the open ceiling.

"There's my sleepy boy." She dried her soft hands on her tunic and gave him a kiss on the cheek.

I remained back a few paces, and watched. If I had seen a vision of this previously, I would have thought all my desires had been realized.

"Your beauty is painful," I said, speaking to her in Gallic for the first time in a while.

She rolled her eyes and shook her head. "Then look away before it becomes unbearable," she replied, her Gallic much more refined.

"I still have the one good eye; I might as well use it," I said, stumbling over a few words I had forgotten.

"What silly noises," Gavius said, to our humor.

"We need to have candelabrum lit. It's too cold in here," Apollonius said, shivering as he entered.

"You old woman. It's warm out compared to the past few weeks," I teased him.

"It's almost as bad as it was in Gaul," he said, an obvious exaggeration, tucking his cloak under his bearded chin.

"What have we on the agenda for today?" I asked.

"Well, Gavius here will be receiving another lesson in mathematics," Apollonius said, and Gavius groaned and buried his head in Arrea's lap.

"And I will continue attempting to learn this 'weaving.' No matter how many of the girls try to help me, I find it more tedious than anything I was forced to do back home," Arrea added.

It saddened me that she still referred to Gaul as her home, although it was rather unrealistic for me to expect otherwise.

"I've an idea. Why don't we have a dinner tonight?" I asked, perking up at my own idea.

They looked at me like I was touched by the gods.

"Quintus, we tend to eat dinner. Every night, mostly," Arrea said with a raised brow.

"No, no. I mean a real dinner. A feast. Why don't I and little Gavius here head down to the Forum Boarium and fetch us a few delicacies?" I asked, watching his response carefully.

"Can Arrea come?"

"I must continue working on that basket I'm weaving for your toys. After it's finished, you'll have no more excuses for leaving them out," she said, noticing my disappointment from the corner of her eyes.

He debated whether or not he wanted to go.

"Well, I guess if you don't want to go, we can always just begin your math lesson?" I said.

"I'll get my cloak." He darted past me to his room.

"I'll prepare two lessons for tomorrow, young master!" Apollonius shouted after him.

"What are you going to get?" Arrea asked me.

"I haven't the slightest clue. Swine probably," I said as she tossed a handful of bird seeds at me, because both of us knew how much she despised it.

We departed at once before Apollonius cause chase down Gavius and convince him to come back. My young son was determined to walk by himself, a few steps from me, although I was often forced to stop and wait on him like a grazing horse, as he paused and inspected each stray animal we passed.

We came to the Temple of Hercules Victor and the construction of the Temple of Portunus, which marked the entry to the Forum Boarium, and swiftly found ourselves in an open piazza boarded by tall colonnades and throngs of bustling people. Stands, shakes, tents, and corals extended as far as the eye could see, and from the look on Gavius's face, he was quite taken aback by it all.

"See that bull statue in the center? If we get separated, you meet me there," I instructed, but he offered me no sign of acknowledgment.

Before we knew it, we were swept away in a moving current of bodies. Our three options were to continue moving forward, step off the path to inspect the offerings of the nearest booth, or be trampled.

A man cut in between the two of us, cursing in another language, two chickens flapping helplessly and clucking in his grasp.

"Let's try this." I picked Gavius up, and he reluctantly agreed, if only to get a better vantage of the Forum. He craned his head with intense curiosity to inspect the tin-roofed huts and the cattle we could hear and smell within.

"What about that one, Tata?" he asked. I swelled with pride. It was the first time he had referred to me affectionately as his father.

He pointed to a stand nearby with several massive pigs strung up by their heels, their open eyes staring back at us.

"Arrea doesn't like swine. Do you?" I asked.

"It doesn't look very tasty. Is it still alive?" He turned to me, intensely curious about the answer.

"I don't think so, lad. Let's hope not."

When we reached the center of the Forum, I stepped off the path, grateful to not be smothered on all sides for a moment.

The shop before us looked to be one of the more well kept in the Forum, and a bit larger as well, with a thatched roof over a permanent wooden structure.

The shopkeepers were yelling at one another.

"What in Ba'al's name do you want me to do about it, then? Huh? March to the Caelian and demand a refund myself?" the larger of the two shouted as he threw a bloody skinned carcass over his shoulder and slapped it on a hook.

"What you want?" the other asked when he noticed us.

"Lamb," I replied.

He pointed to a goat's severed head that sat on a display table, its eyes rolled back and its tongue hanging from the corner of its mouth.

"No. Lamb." I tried to enunciate more clearly. He pointed to a cage filled with little black rabbits in the back. "No..." I shook my head. Gavius reached out to touch the goat's tongue, so I stepped farther away. "Lamb."

"Lamb?" he asked, and I nodded vigorously to confirm. He snapped his fingers, and a few shirtless slaves took a slab of meat off a hook and began to prepare it.

The other butcher wasn't finished with his argument.

"You bitch at me like I can do something 'bout it. What can I do, eh? It wasn't my fault. He was the best man for the job when

I found him." Gobs of spit flew from his lips when he spoke, and he stared intently with two eyes that seemed to run away from one another.

"We have customers, Hanno," the other said, shaking his head at us to express his apologies. The two seemed to speak Latin well enough, so clearly they just hadn't been listening, or they were hard of hearing.

The slaves took a few moments preparing the meat, careful to not give us more than we needed. The silence became uncomfortable.

"Trouble in the Forum Boarium?" I asked as cheerfully as I could manage.

"Nothing that concerns you, citizen," the larger man said.

"Don't just talk to citi—" the shopkeeper began but then stopped to appraise me. "You a senator?" he asked, noticing the broad stripe of my toga.

"Yes, I am," I replied, anxious to hear his point. He turned and said something in the Numidian tongue over his shoulder, making me suspicious that their prices had just increased.

"Then you should know something." He threw a dirty towel over his shoulder and folded his arms. "We have a right bloody mess."

"Oh?" I asked, hoping he wasn't about to ask something of me that a man who only spoke with his feet couldn't do.

"It's that damned Aufedius!" the big one shouted. The shrewder of the two lifted a hand to quiet him, but I was already fixed on the name.

"Aufedius? Head of the baker's guide on the Caelian?" I remembered the name clearly. Marius's troublemaker.

The butcher chuckled silently. He clearly found me ignorant.

"Much more than that. He supplies us with what we need for our livestock. He owed me grain. And now he owes me money."

I set Gavius down and stepped closer to the table. Perhaps I was about to uncover some information that could be used against the man. Extortion had never been a trade I desired to enter, but I was already beaming at the thought of the praise I'd receive from Marius and the others if this proved successful.

"Aufedius is defaulting on his debts?"

Both of them stopped and looked at me with vehemence, but I'm not certain if it was Aufedius or myself who was the brunt of it.

"He has disappeared. And no one can find him."

"And the whole city falls apart. No one knows prices. No one knows who's in charge." The big man gesticulated wildly, accidentally backhanding the slab of meat, causing it to swing from side to side.

"Three hundred sestertii," the other said when the lamb was packaged and placed before me.

"Wait, Aufedius has disappeared? And now you can't get what you need for your livestock?"

I realized I asked a question they had already answered, but I wanted to be absolutely certain. I pulled a coin pouch from my belt and began sifting through it to keep them talking.

"Aufedius ran things...unofficially. Set the prices. Now no one knows who's in charge," the big man said, approaching the table between us.

"Will you shut your mouth, man?" The other slapped his towel against the table. He exhaled and appraised me again to determine what he should say next.

"Aufedius indeed set the prices. Now he's gone. But we bought from him directly. If you find the man, you tell him Maharbal is looking for him." He pointed at me with a cleaver. "If not, find a way to get things straightened out. Otherwise, this city will be in an uproar."

I tried to process this as I set the coins down and picked up the meat.

"Thank you, citizens. I'll see what I can do." Perhaps Glaucia's agents had been successful, so much so that the man had decided to go into hiding rather than have his secrets leaked. That, or something else had happened entirely.

We stepped away, and the two shopkeepers continued their argument.

SCROLL XIV

SIX DAYS AFTER IDES OF FEBRUARY, 655 AB URBE
CONDITA

I WOKE BEFORE THE SUN. Arrea did as well. And she helped me
don my toga. I didn't even have to ask.

We didn't talk much as she delicately placed each fold of the
toga. She could sense my apprehension. Today was the vote,
after all, and no one in the city knew what the day would bring.

Apollonius waited for me by the exit.

"May your gods be with you today, friend," he said,
accepting my hands.

"And yours with you. Watch over the house and keep this
place in good shape." I kissed his cheek.

"Gavius will be studying diligently until your return, I assure
you. And, Quintus," he said as the porter opened the door for
me, "I believe you have some guests."

I wondered for a moment what that was supposed to mean.
Apollonius wasn't a cryptic man by nature, but he enjoyed a
good riddle every now and then.

I turned onto the street and saw he was speaking plainly.

There were fifteen men lined up alongside the house.

"Patron," some of them said with a slight bow.

I certainly hadn't expected this. I had a difficult time catching my breath.

"Are you Nursians?" I asked. Some of them shook their heads, but not all. "Were you clients of my father's?" Most of them affirmed this. "I thank you all for making the journey here. I have not had the chance to meet some of you, but I plan to visit the Sabine cities when the time is available to me. In the meantime, know that I am ever your friend, and will always vote for your rights."

They clapped. I fell to the front of the line, and they followed suit, not their first time. It was mine, but they didn't seem to notice.

It felt a little bit like leading soldiers. And I had missed that feeling.

The air was still nippy, but it was filled with the humidity of spring's pending arrival. The sky above us was filled with gray clouds, and I feared showers might be upon us by midday. And I knew this wouldn't stop the vote either.

We made for Marius's home on the Palatine and joined with the hundreds of others who waited outside.

"Let's go feed our citizens, shall we?" the consul said, appearing in rare form. He was the image of energy and optimism itself, and why shouldn't he be, now that Aufedius was disposed of? "It's a blessing to see you here, Senator." He embraced me as everyone cheered the reunion of general and the Hero of the North. "And you've bought friends?"

"To vote with us."

"They may be of more use than that, if I know our enemy," he said. He was referring to the Optimates, or so I assumed, but found the term rather harsh for political opponents. I still had much to learn.

Marius led the way, shaking the hand of every citizen he could. The people cheered as we passed as if the consul had been the originator of the bill rather than Saturninus. Heads poked through the windows of insulae. Women extended their small children for a blessing from the Third Founder of Rome.

Citizens of every age and race followed us. Wrinkled old Romans with calloused hands and no teeth. Youthful Sicilian boys, too young for their first beards. Newlywed couples on hard times, bread makers, cloth dyers, Greeks and Gauls, freedmen and slaves. They hailed us as saviors, as if we were conquerors. It nearly brought a tear to my eye.

"Your bellies shall soon be filled, citizens!" Marius shouted, and they cheered all the more. "See how joyful they are, Sertorius? They already know they've won this day," he said to me directly, his words barely audible over the yelling of his supporters.

"And there is certainly cause for celebration when our citizens are fed," I said. But I analyzed the crowds with apprehension. Would the Optimates do nothing to stop us? Would they really allow this to happen so easily after the scuffle in the senate house? Perhaps they simply intended to repeal the legislation later, but something told me this was all too easy. I sensed a trap like I did when I saw cavalry reserves on the battlefield.

Arriving in the Forum, Marius's followers split off to join their tribes for the vote.

It's difficult to describe a mob without reflecting on the gathering that day. Every citizen in the city was present. The drunks had put down their wine. The beggars had dusted off their tunics. And every voice demanded to be heard.

I turned to my clients. "Thank you for today, citizens. You may join your tribe for the vote, and you can find me here afterward. I'll want to shake each man's hand to show my gratitude," I said as we were becoming hemmed in on all sides by the growing crowd.

One of them shook his head.

"They've announced the vote order. Quirina is going late. We'll stay with you until it is time, if that's permissible, patron," he replied. Gods, I had missed Nursians. I clenched my jaw to hide the smile, and nodded.

"Yes, that will be permissible."

Saturninus and the other tribunes took to the Rostra. A preliminary speech was given. The auspices were favorable. The voting was allowed to proceed.

We had barely finished shouting when another retinue, nearly twice as large as ours, formed a wedge through us.

A man shoved me from his path.

"Don't let them touch the senator!" one of my clients shouted, lunging at the man, but he was unable to reach him because of the crowds.

I analyzed the group, searching for some indication as to their purpose. Perhaps they belonged to one of the early voting tribes and were arriving late.

Then I caught sight of those unmistakable piercing blue eyes, and the coy smile to match them. Lucius Cornelius Sulla. He made direct eye contact, challenging me.

"Consul?" I shouted over the crowds.

"I see him." Marius nodded. "Sulla!" he shouted with hands cupped around his mouth. "What do you think you're doing?"

"Saving this Republic, old man!" Sulla shouted back carelessly.

"But he cannot vote! Right?" I asked.

"No, he cannot." Marius clenched his fists, and for a moment, I thought he was about to chase after his old protege.

Chaos ensued where Sulla and his companions had disappeared. The sound of voting urns being smashed echoed throughout the valley of the Forum.

A vision of Nonius's limp hand and a pool of blood on the Rostra flashed before my eye.

Marius attempted to move forward, but the crowds rushed against him, and Granius grabbed his arm.

"What has this Republic come to!" he shouted, struggling against the restraining grasps.

"Consul, what should I do?" I asked, waiting for the order. My clients waited patiently behind me to do the same.

He snorted like a caged bull and ran through the options in his head.

"We must not allow them to disrupt the vote. The vote must continue."

"Enough said, General." I turned to my clients. "Have any of you served in the legions?"

The majority of them raised their hands, apprehensive but not afraid.

"Good. Those of you who have not, stick close to someone who has. Three abreast, on me." I took the center, and they fell in line behind me. "If any of you have weapons, now is the time to brandish them. Harm no one unless it is absolutely necessary. No one dies this day. But we will ensure this vote proceeds. Understood?" They offered no rebuttal, so I led the way, forging a path through the crowd as best I could.

Young nobles and their clients were laying waste to the citizens nearing the voting booths. The people were tripping over themselves to get away, only to receive cracks of a club to their skulls.

"An illegal procedure! Go to your homes!" Cato shouted from the front, Sulla right alongside him. The latter watched everything around him with intense curiosity.

"Citizens!" I shouted, demanding their attention. Breathing heavily, they turned to see who defied them. "You will cease and desist immediately. This is a legally sanctioned vote of the Roman Republic. And you have no authority here."

"Legally sanctioned? Was a tribune's veto not offered? Was it not violence that halted the senate vote?" Sulla's associate Pompeius shouted, stepping toward me with a club as my clients gathered around me.

"You will not harm another citizen today," I said, every impulse in my body inclining me to grab the dagger I had strapped to my calf. But I did not.

"How about a senator, then?" one of them shouted as a few rushed me.

A big stupid oaf of a man lifted a broken table leg over his head and thrust it down at mine. I grabbed his wrist and kicked him in the shin as two of my men wrapped their arms around his shoulders and thrust elbows into his nose.

He hit the stone as others jumped over him.

Another swung his club. I blocked it with my forearm, the pain shivering up to my shoulder. I threw a punch at him as he recoiled and then quickly pulled him down to my ascending knee. Blood spewed back on the next man to take his place.

"Protect the senator!" some of my men shouted, and it was rallied by the citizens nearby.

"Protect the senator!" Weaponless, they jumped onto the backs of the Optimate hordes, raining down on them with strikes of the fist and elbows.

A man launched at me from my side, head-butting me with a crack. My vision faded for a moment, but I could feel his body beside me, so I flipped him over my hip and threw a few punches down until one of them landed.

I regained my posture and tried to see straight. A man stood in front of me. I jabbed at his nose. It landed, and the man's head shot back.

My vision slowly returned as I realized the man was Sulla himself.

He lifted a hand to his lips and dabbed at the blood, looking back and forth between it and the man who'd caused it.

His eyes shone with a fury I had never seen there before. He could find no humor in his own blood. For a moment, I feared he might lunge, but the citizens were arriving in full force, and his supporters were being overtaken.

"Retreat!" he shouted, turning and moving off with the rest of his men, never taking his eyes off me as he went.

Once new urns were brought out, the vote was allowed to carry on unimpeded. The legislation was passed unanimously, to the joyful tears of the people. Saturninus, Glaucia, and Marius were successful. And if they weren't universally adored by the people before, they certainly were now.

"If I could give you a military decoration for roughing up senators and their sycophants, I would do so without delay," Marius said when I saw him next, still beaming from his success.

"I did what I had to."

But I had little cause for celebration. I could think of nothing but that look in Sulla's eyes. That was the kind of hate that lasted a lifetime. One drop of blood, one split lip, and I knew for certain I had created an enemy.

SCROLL XV

NONES OF JUNE, 655 AB URBE CONDITA

MARIUS and his party had never been more loved by the people. But it was the name Saturninus that was scribbled in graffiti on every wall, the name whispered from the lips of every well-fed plebeian.

Sulla, Cato, and Pompeius were forced to answer for their actions in the senate house.

"Perhaps we were a tad overzealous, but we believed we were doing what we ought, after the tribune's veto was offered and disregarded," Sulla had responded. With the legislation now law, no one pressed the matter. And with Marius and his companions now at the height of their power, they felt no need to address it. The men suffered no consequences.

The winter quickly turned to spring, and the cool winds and gentle rains were quickly replaced by the heat of summer. Although most of my clients returned to Nursia after the vote, a few of them stayed in the city for a while to enjoy the grain dole, and so I began to host a morning levy to hear from them. For the first time, I felt like a real senator with the ability to affect change, at least on this small scale.

Hearing from these men each day, as well as tending to their needs and requests, took more time than I had anticipated. There was a great deal I needed to learn about managing a senator's life, and sometimes I wondered how men like Marius could fit it all in. It was all worth it, however, because the money from my clients was all that was sustaining me. Or, rather, all that allowed me to pay my new debtors.

Beyond these responsibilities, there was senate meeting after senate meeting, public holiday after public feast, and dinner party after play at the theater.

When the senate was recessed for the first week of June, I knew it was time that I did something with my family, something to repay them for their constant support and availability when I needed assistance.

And what was a man to do to show appreciation to his family? I could research the techniques of rhetoric or writing and still never learn how to articulate in spoken or written word my gratitude, so instead, I took them peach picking.

I had a carriage prepared to pick us up that morning, and from the look on Gavius's face, he must have thought we were royalty. As Arrea, Gavius, Apollonius, and I took our seats, I found the courage to reach over and take Arrea's hand. She didn't pull away, and I imagined for a moment that she ran her soft thumbs over my callused skin.

We took the Via Salaria north a bit and cut off near where the Aqua Marcia met the base of the hills near Austa. I had diligently conducted research in advance, and I found that this area had bountiful wild peaches free for the taking.

"Don't forget your basket, Gavius!" I shouted as he jumped from the carriage and took off for the nearest trees.

"I haven't seen him like this for a while." Arrea smiled and lifted a hand to block the morning sun.

"That's his father's fault. I've had him spending too much time learning from Apollonius and not enough time adventuring with his father." I offered them both a hand down from the carriage.

"The mind offers both its own adventures and its own vacations, once properly trained." Apollonius winced and grabbed at his knee when he jumped down.

"Careful, old man, or it'll pop out of place," I said.

"I'll show you a thing or two about fruit picking. You might best me in a wrestling bout, but I still contain a youthful energy for this sort of thing."

We followed Gavius to the tree, and as we walked, I took Arrea's hand again. At length, she interlaced her fingers with my own.

"Let me show you the trick, my boy," I said. "You have to inspect them first. We can't take just any old peach. If they aren't yet ripe for the plucking, it's better to leave them be so they can feed the next family that comes along." I placed the bucket at his feet.

"I like that one. Can you reach it?" He pointed up.

"I'm not sure, but I'd wager you can." I lifted him up, and he delicately popped the peach from its stem, only afterward inspecting it.

"It's bruised," he said, deflating.

"Not a problem. Nothing Arrea and the kitchen girls can't use to whip up a good paste." In truth, Arrea was an awful cook, but I lied whenever I could, and she was beginning to believe me.

"This tree is no good," he said. I set him back down, and he ran to the next.

"What? It's not a bad tree! Perhaps the worms just got to them first."

"That means it's no good, Tata!" he shouted and waved for us to follow.

"Nonsense! We can eat the worms too. Good for your muscles."

"Ew!" he shouted.

"Ew is right," Apollonius said, shaking his head.

"Now here is a peach, Gavius." While we had been talking, Arrea had been inspecting, and indeed had found the best of the bunch.

"Marvelous, into the basket it goes," I said.

"I want that one!" Gavius shouted.

"They're all yours, my boy, once we return home."

We continued our search while the sun warmed and the air thickened. Arrea and Gavius moved on ahead while Apollonius was determined to inspect each fruit on each tree, and I lingered with him.

"Are you enjoying yourself, my friend?" I asked.

"Very much so. I could use days like this more often."

"With weather like this, I'll make it a priority," I replied. But I sensed there was something else on his mind. "Are you certain you want to keep living under my roof, Apollonius? You know you don't have to. You owe me nothing you haven't already repaid in full."

He smiled and took a moment to respond, letting the last peach fall back into its place, still on the vine.

"I'm woefully underpaid, if that's what you're asking. But I'm happy." He chuckled.

"I sense something in you. Deception! You've sharpened my mind too much. Now, tell me."

He tried to continue his laughter, but sadness flooded his eyes.

"I think often of my little girl," he said in a voice that suddenly seemed exhausted. He did not mention her often, but I knew my dearest companion thought of the niece that was taken from him and sold into slavery constantly. "If I had even the slightest clue where to begin my search, I would go and find her. And I would spend every penny I've earned to bring her back." He looked up with shimmering eyes. "She should be picking peaches too."

I set down the basket, which was quickly becoming heavy with our bounty, and placed a hand on his shoulders.

"I will do everything in my power to free her."

He shook his head, unwilling to trust his hope.

"She could be anywhere now. Sold to some traveling merchant, or a farmer in some distant land... I hope he is not... they are not...cruel." He dabbed at his nose with a handkerchief.

"Apollonius, look at me." I lifted his chin until he met my one good eye. "I am a senator of the Roman Republic now. Perhaps I can find out things you wouldn't be able to otherwise. We will talk about this at length this evening upon our return. I have neglected to address this properly, and that is my own failure. I will remedy this with action soon, I vow to you."

Rather than happiness, his face flashed with fear and his gaze shifted to something behind me.

I turned as a hand reached my shoulder.

And there were those unmistakable ice-blue eyes, as vibrant as summer's first blueberry. I instinctively held out a hand to keep my family behind me.

"Sorry, I didn't mean to startle you." Sulla's lip had healed, and now it was curled into a smile.

"I just wasn't expecting to see anyone out here."

"Nor I. But how nice it is to see you outside of the curia, Senator." He laughed at himself and placed both hands on my shoulders, appraising me. "By Apollo, that will be difficult to get used to. I'm still inclined to call you 'tribune.' I always imagine you with that soldier's cloak, although the toga suits you fine too."

"Here for some peach picking?" I asked, looking for and finding no baskets.

"Yes, my wife, Porcia, is just that way." He pointed, but I could see no one.

"Did you know I would be here?" I asked directly.

He held up both hands in submission.

"Guilty as a naughty vestal. I heard you declined a dinner

invitation this evening to go hunting for fruit, and I assumed you would be here. I saw you from a distance and came running."

I couldn't formulate a response because I was too preoccupied trying to determine how he could have heard that.

So he continued, "I thought it best if we met under different circumstances than our last."

The last interaction I'd had with the senator had ended with my fist on his chin.

"I meant no disrespect, and have no quarrel with you. I did what I thought best in that moment."

He shook his head as if no apology were necessary, although I hadn't offered him one.

"You mistake my intent. You did as every good man should, as he believes the gods have guided him. I hold you at no fault for that." He plucked a peach from the tree nearest to him and took a bite, a single bead of juice dripping over his chin like the blood had a few months prior. He pointed at me while he chewed. "It'd been a while since I'd tasted my own blood. I rather enjoyed it."

"I prefer not to taste mine. Unless I have to." I turned to Apollonius and nodded for him to join Arrea and Gavius. Reluctantly, he agreed.

"You know, Senator Sertorius, there is something unique about you. A quality I much appreciate. It's something your current associates will not praise, because it's not something they prioritize in themselves. Do you know what it is?"

"What is it, Sulla?" I had already heard enough, and I felt I had feigned all the cordiality I could muster.

"Intelligence." He smacked his lips and cleaned his teeth with his tongue. "You're a clever man, Sertorius. Wise beyond your years. I might have put up a fuss if it were any other man your age entering the senate house, but I knew you're twice as clever as most of those half-its."

"I appreciate the compliments." I tried to determine if this was an adequate time to bid farewell, but he continued.

"Wisdom and intelligence are a hard thing to find among Rome's senatorial elite. We all benefitted from your ascension, not just Marius and his disciples. And I think you're wise and intelligent enough to see what's happening here, don't you?" he asked with squinted eyes, tossing the peach pit from hand to hand.

"Sulla, I'm not going to discuss politics with you or anyone else today. I am here to spend time with my family." I hoped he wouldn't ask many questions, as my little "family" was certainly the least orthodox of any man's in the senate.

"Oh, as am I. But as senators, we are a form of brothers, are we not? I don't want to talk politics, either, Sertorius. Policy, procedure, legislation…those are topics of discussion for drearier days than this. What I'm speaking of is more important than that. You're on a sinking ship. You must know that."

"And what makes you think that?"

"Just look at the men who came before them. What happened to them? Eventually, they will all be out of office, and then Saturninus, Glaucia, and Marius will all be held accountable for the illegality of their measures. There's no need for your career to be destroyed in the process." His eye contact was piercing.

"Is that a threat?"

"It's an observation, Sertorius. Some of my associates consider you to be a threat to the Republic just as they are. I've continued to vouch for you, time and again, but they will only listen to me for so long."

"Now I'm certain that was a threat." I stepped closer to him, looking up, as he was taller than myself.

"No. Marius may have helped you become a senator, but now that you are one, you have as much autonomy and freedom as any man in the curia. And I want you on my side. What's the saying? More men worship the rising sun than the setting one."

"And that must make you the rising sun, then?" I asked, balking at the man's arrogance.

He chuckled. "What I am is irrelevant. But Marius's sun is certainly setting, and there's no reason for it to set on you. You could join us, Senator."

"I have started this path. And I will follow where it leads."

He dropped the peach pit, and a fist took its place. His breathing intensified.

"You grieve me, Sertorius. You grieve me deeply. This is the second time I've approached you with an offer of friendship."

"With an offer of betrayal, actually," I corrected.

"No, friendship. And wise counsel. I'm afraid the offer won't be extended a third time."

"I have no quarrel with you, Sulla. Not unless you continue to violate sanctioned public assemblies. But I cannot betray Marius," I said as firmly as I could manage.

He dropped his eye contact, exhaled in acceptance, and shook his head.

"Then your fate is sealed with his. Good day, Senator." He turned on his heels and returned to a litter, in which he wasted no time departing.

After composing myself, I caught up with Arrea, Apollonius, and Gavius. But my heart was hardly in peach picking any longer. My mind was fixed on less enjoyable things.

SCROLL XVI

KALENDS OF JULY, 655 AB URBE CONDITA

ONE OF THE many responsibilities of a senator was attending the games. All senators were expected to go as often as they were possible to present a united front to the people. More practically speaking, each senator was expected to sit with his associates so that the populace could have an accurate look at the power dynamics that existed within the senate house.

I decided to skip the preliminary games. The weather was becoming unbearably hot, and I wasn't a fan of the gladiatorial games. I had attended various races since becoming a senator, but this would be my first time attending the arena without my father leading me by the hand to the stands.

When I arrived, there were designated guides waiting for senators like myself.

"Conscript Father! Conscript Father! Right this way, I'll show you up," several of them shouted. I approached the closest to me, a young man just a few years my junior, who wore old, dirty rags but had a thick gold chain around his neck.

"I'll see you right up," he said enthusiastically. "Have you taken a look at my tunic?" He gestured to the dried paint on his tunic as we ascended the steps, the crowds growing louder as we went. The image depicted a Thraex gladiator with a small round shield and a curved *sica* standing over his defeated foes.

"Is that one of today's combatants?" I asked rather disinterestedly.

"What? Of course, it is! That's the great Theophilus! Half the people attending are here to see him."

"Is that so? I'm not familiar with him."

"Not a fan of the games, eh? Well, prepare yourself for a spectacle. He's the greatest fighter we've seen in years." He turned and offered me a hand as we reached the steeper steps, as many of our order likely had a difficult time ascending to the senatorial balcony.

As we entered out into the glaring sun, I heard shouts of my name from the stands.

"Sertorius! Over here!"

"Senator Sertorius!"

After my eyes adjusted, I spotted Marius and his companions waving me over. I could already tell from their posture that they had been drinking. Fortunately, it appeared everyone else had been as well.

Several rows behind them was Sulla, who stood and lifted his cup of wine in my direction, a smirk on his face. I ignored him.

A posted lictor pulled back a rope and allowed me to enter, but the guide stepped into my path with his hand out. He bowed lowly and departed once he received his tip.

Along the front row sat Saturninus, with Marius on one side and Lucius Equitius on the other. Saufeius sat on Marius's other side, and beside him sat Cinna and Equus.

Equus lifted his cup and shot me a wink, apparently the only one who wasn't drunk. Fortunately, he had a spot reserved for me, so I hurried to scoot through the rows to meet him.

"Move aside, you bastards, this seat is for the Hero of the North!" Marius shouted, and they cleared a space between himself and Saturninus. I exhaled and shot Equus a look, who laughed and shrugged in response.

They all clapped my back forcefully as I sat down. Saturninus offered a handshake. Glaucia, who was sitting in the row behind me, clasped both hands on my shoulders and kissed the top of my head.

"Just in time for the real events to begin," Saturninus said.

"You must be a man who knows the games. Everything thus far has been dreadfully boring," Glaucia said. "The wine has made it bearable."

Gates on either side of the sands opened, and a gladiator entered it from either side, to the roar of the crowds.

"Four thousand sestertii on the Gaul," Lucius Equitius shouted to a man with a wax tablet close by, who quickly scribbled it down.

"How much is that so far today, Equitius?" Saturninus asked, only a tinge of judgment in his voice.

"I've lost count. I think I'm winning, though."

"Another fight?" Saufeius asked from the other side of me. "They're not nearly as interesting as the executions. Where's the sport in two men accepting their deaths? It's the running about and the look of terror that makes for the best entertainment." Everyone declined to respond.

The referee—an ex-gladiator himself, by the look of him—explained the rules of combat and then gestured for the two to proceed. They jumped into position, and the sound of clashing swords rang out.

"I often miss the days of old when the gladiators fought simply to honor the glorious dead, rather than for sport. Nowadays, there are so many rules," Cinna said, gesturing to the arena where the referee was halting combat to explain something to the two combatants.

"Oh, let them fight!" Equitius stood and shouted from the top of his lungs. Saturninus calmly took him by the hand and helped him back to his seat.

"Forgive me if my history is a little hazy, Cinna, but weren't those days long before your time?" Saturninus asked coyly when the crowds allowed him to be heard.

"It is quite possible to feel nostalgia for a time you've never known," Cinna replied, dabbing at the beads of sweat on his brow.

One of the gladiators thrust his shield up, connecting with the other's chest and face, sending his helmet cascading across the sands. Blood spewed from the Gaul's mouth as he hit the ground. The Thraex stood over him, sword at his jugular.

"Get up and fight! You coward!" Equitius yelled.

"That was anticlimactic," I heard Equus say.

Marius didn't seem to be interested one way or the other, more inclined to talk through the event with so many close associates nearby.

"Say, Tribune, would you mind sparing me a few thousand sestertii?" Equitius asked Saturninus, olive oil and wine stains on his toga.

"What? Oh. Yes. Certainly. I vouch for him." Saturninus nodded to the bookkeeper. I was still profoundly perplexed by their support for such a man.

"I'm going to win this next bout. I can feel it," Saufeius said.

As slaves assisted the defeated gladiator from the sands, a man replaced them at the center of the arena.

"Citizens of Rome! What a glorious day it has been, and the best is yet to come!" The engineer of that particular arena had done his job well, as the acoustics of the speaker's voice carried throughout. "It's now time to thank our editors, the aediles Lucius Crassus and Quintus Scaevola, who have sponsored these games to honor the wolf that suckled Romulus and Remus!"

The two men stood from their special balcony and waved to their adoring crowds.

"Oh, these games were to honor a wolf? I was under the

impression they were to honor Crassus and Scaevola," Saturninus said, staring out across the arena at the aediles.

"I'm surprised they spared the expense either way. Scaevola's
said to be the most miserly man in Rome," said Marius.

Glaucia leaned down in between us and said, "I've a friend
at the Basilica Sempronia. He helped draft Scaevola's last will
and testament recently. Said the man left *himself* as the only
heir."

"They must really be desperate if they'll spend this much to
have the people clap for them," Cinna added.

"Hard to imagine they dipped into their own coin purse to
fund this. I bet it came directly from old Numidicus, or someone
like him," Glaucia speculated.

The main event was beginning, it was easy to tell, as the next
gladiator who entered caused everyone to jump to their feet. The
shouts were deafening as the man raised his sword and shield to
the sky as if he were already the victor.

"This must be the Theophilus I've heard so much about," I
said, unsure if anyone could hear me.

"That's him. He fights as a Thraex, but he's actually a Mace-
donian, if I've heard right. They say he's a free man, actually—
volunteered to prove he can defeat the best Rome can throw at
him." Equitius leaned over Saturninus to me. I cringed at the
smell of stale wine on his breath.

"And can he?" I asked.

"Thus far. But eventually, Fortuna turns her back on every
man. She's a cruel mistress," Saturninus answered stoically.

The hero of the arena was introduced first, followed by his
opponent—a Numidian equipped with nothing but a loincloth
and a trident. After they both bowed to the sponsors, the clash
began.

"Theophilus hides behind that shield! Fight him like a man,
coward!" Marius jumped to his feet, showing his first bit of
interest in the games. Perhaps he was opposed to the man who
challenged Rome. Or, more likely, he had a vested financial

interest in the Numidian, who likely was a captive from his campaign in Africa.

A voice shouted from behind us, "There is nothing unmanly about using strategic advantage. How differently things might turn out for you if you didn't mistake idiocy for manliness." We all turned to find Sulla standing alone among his companions.

Marius's eyes filled with rage, and his fists clenched. For a moment, I thought he was going to bound up the steps through the rows of senators to assault the man, but Saturninus and Glaucia assuaged him.

"He's drunk, Consul. It's he who looks the fool," they said.

"I am a consul of Rome. A consul of Rome. He cannot speak to me that way," Marius said as they helped him back to his seat. He fixed his eyes forward, no longer concerned with the games, his jaw clenched. "Sertorius, I need you to do something for me," he said without breaking his gaze.

"What do you need, General?" I asked.

Theophilus taunted his prey as he dodged several trident lunges. He batted one away with his sword and thrust his shield into the Numidian's nose. He might have been able to strike a final blow while his foe recoiled, but instead, he encouraged the crowd to lift their voices.

"The next time the senate convenes, I need you to rally some men."

I was beginning to wonder if this was all I'd been made senator for. To stand at the front of a band of disgruntled veterans.

"Any particular reason?" I asked, even though it was inappropriate to question the consul.

"The next time we meet, I will be proposing that the veterans receive their land."

Saufeius whipped his head around with wide eyes.

"Marius!" he shouted with clenched teeth. Now here was someone who was forgetting his place. From Sulla, it was expected. From a friend? The disrespect was unimaginable.

To my surprise, Marius turned to him slowly, controlled.

"Quaestor, he is one of us."

"What if he says something? What if he tells his wife or children or slaves, and they run their mouths? Are all of *them* one of us too?" He was clearly drunk.

Marius exhaled and paused before responding. I was slack-jawed and dumbfounded. If a soldier had talked to the general like that, he would have received thirty lashes and a week in the brig.

"I vouch for him, Saufeius. And that is good enough for you."

"Hmph." Saufeius turned back to the games.

Marius returned his attention to me, and finally revealed the repressed anger he had barely been restraining.

"We will be announcing the land redistribution to our veterans. So we need them there."

"Is this procedural, General? I will do as you ask, I just want to understand," I said. He was still steaming from Saufeius, so he paid little mind to my questions.

"No. But if the Optimates are willing to lynch voters because we propose to give them grain at a reduced rate, what will they do when we threaten to take the land they've been drooling over and give it to the rough proles who fight for this country?"

"Surely, the senate must have *some* modicum of patriotism?" I asked. I didn't expect the land redistribution to be accepted full-heartedly by all, but I didn't anticipate the need for armed veterans at the senate house. Perhaps I was still more naive than I realized.

"Oh certainly." Marius nodded. "But they think the men have been paid a fair, if meager, wage. Exactly what they signed up for. They weren't promised land; therefore, they don't deserve it." Marius shook his head. "But they don't know what it was like. We do. Those men deserve land. And perhaps presenting the faces, and swords, of those who earned it will help convince our enemies."

Glaucia, who had apparently been listening the entire time, leaned forward and clarified, "And the senate is terrified of the power this will give us."

"What power could be gained by giving land to our veterans?" I asked.

"Voting power. Landowners can vote, and these men didn't previously own land. And they know who these men will vote for—the benefactors who gave them their homes," Saturninus said.

"Well, that, and having fifty thousand hardened veterans close by, must be frightening as well," Glaucia said with a grin. "If they behave too badly, Marius can stomp his feet, and legions will spring up all over Italy."

Marius glared at the both of them, whether for saying too much or for interrupting him, I was unsure.

"Can you gather some men, Sertorius?"

"I can. Perhaps Equus will help us."

"No need to involve him, unless you have to. I want the Cinnae to appear as moderate as possible. How many men can you gather?"

I considered asking for an explanation but decided against it.

"Perhaps twenty. I'm not sure where everyone is held up. How many do we need?"

"That will do it. Tell them to bring their swords, Sertorius."

I didn't like the sound of that, and wondered what else the consul had planned. I didn't have much time to consider it, however, as a finishing blow was struck on the sands. With two swift swipes of his sword, Theophilus hewed a scarlet X in the chest of his foe.

The Numidian hit the ground, his trident flying behind him.

A roar echoed throughout the arena as Theophilus stood over his fallen foe.

"Kill! Kill! Kill!" the crowds chanted.

The referee halted the execution and turned to Crassus and Scaevola for their declaration. They stood and looked around, trying to determine the desire of the crowd, as if it weren't clear.

The Numidian held up two fingers, asking for mercy. To be spared.

"Finally," Saufeius said.

Equitius moaned, low and long, as I'm assuming he'd bet on the Numidian for the greater return.

Scaevola gestured for Crassus to make the determination. He didn't deliberate. He thrust his thumb.

Theophiles nodded in compliance, then slammed his sword down on the Numidian's jugular, pinning him to the sand. A fountain of blood spewed from the wound as his limbs flailed and twitched until they fell limp.

"Decisive and swift. As all victors must be," Saturninus said with half-hearted applause.

SCROLL XVII

THREE DAYS AFTER KALENDS OF JULY, 655 AB URBE
CONDITA

IT WAS MORE difficult to find good men in the city than I had
anticipated. Most of Marius's soldiers were rural plebs in the
first place and had already returned to their villages. Those
within the city were either bunking in undisclosed dwellings or
had already left for another campaign as Lucius had.

Thirteen men arrived at my door that morning.

"Good morning, soldiers."

"Good morning, Tribune." They saluted me. The few who
had come seemed excited about gathering in a formation again,
or perhaps they were just intrigued by the secrecy.

"I would like to thank you all for gathering here today. I can
assure you that what you're doing today is as much a service to
Rome and your brothers as what you've done on the battlefield."

Their backs straightened.

"Opimius, you've been letting yourself go, I see." I gestured
to one of the men in the front row.

"Too many sweet rolls, Tribune," he said as the others
laughed.

"March with me. Maintain your ranks. Keep your swords sheathed. There will be no violence today, if I have anything to say about it. We need only to present a united front."

They nodded. I could tell from the pensive glances they shot me that they'd like more information about what it was that we were doing. But they were experienced veterans, and they knew better than to ask questions when information wasn't presented to them.

I gave the signal for a forward advance, a tinge of unexpected nostalgia passing through me like a current.

We passed the *via* we would have taken to Marius's domus. There was no sense in causing any kind of stir by having Marius's old mules arriving at his doorstep. Mine was much less conspicuous.

When we arrived at the Forum, Marius was already waiting for us at the *senaculum*. I could tell from a distance he was in rare form and ready to begin the day's meeting.

He smiled when he saw us and sprinted toward us in a way that would be unbefitting of any other consul than Marius.

I gave the signal for a halt, and the soldiers each snapped to attention and offered a salute. Marius beamed.

"Is this it, then?" he asked, craning his head to count them.

"It is, General. This is all I could manage to muster without asking for Equus to aid me."

He waved me to silence.

"Never mind that. This will do. Do you know why you are here, Legionaries?"

They didn't say anything, but a few shook their heads.

"I didn't feel it was my place to inform them without permission, General," I said. To that, he smiled.

"And you've come regardless. Good. You're all fine young men. And I thank each of you for joining me today."

"We will always serve you, General!" one of them shouted and stomped his feet. The others joined in. The gathered senators turned and watched us with wide, suspicious eyes.

"And I will always serve you." Marius bowed. "Today, I am proposing legislation to give the lands acquired in our campaign to Rome's veterans. Including yourselves."

Their jaws dropped, and they turned to each other with the joyful surprise of children.

"That's right. No one deserves that land except those who secured it. But we may face opposition." He stepped close to them and scanned each of their faces. "I need you men to reveal to those who oppose us just who they are opposing. I want them to see your faces as they leave, and know it's real men that they seek to deprive of homes, not just numbers. Understood?"

They nodded, eager to do as they were asked, and perhaps angry at the thought of some old noble trying to steal the promised land from them.

"Good. And if things get out of hand, I only ask that you make your presence felt. Violence won't be necessary. The threat of it should be enough."

Hands tightened around gladius hilts as they acknowledged the consul, and I hoped they would be disciplined enough to obey his orders, especially with so much on the line.

"Are you ready, Senator?" Marius asked. When I nodded, he led the way to the curia. "I want you to sit as close to me today as possible. Sit in the front row, even. If anyone has a problem with it, they'll address it with me. But I've no idea what this meeting will bring."

"Yes, Consul," I said, my heart racing. Would I be scrapping on the senate floors? Perhaps Sulla would like to land a blow of his own, if it came to that.

When we entered, no one turned to whisper about Marius. No one laughed at my eye or my scars. They sat stone-faced, frozen in anticipation like statues. I'm not sure if word had spread of our intentions, but those keen-nosed old noblemen must have smelled it in the air.

We took our seats, and I sat beside Marius as instructed. The last of the senators piled in behind us. Saturninus was one of the last to arrive, shaking the hand of every man he passed by, even those whose lips snarled as he approached. A few men turned their heads away from him and refused to accept. He simply shrugged and moved on to the next.

"Shall we begin, gentlemen?" Marius's co-consul, Valerius, began. He was the presiding consul that month, but as soon as he spoke, Marius was on his feet.

"Good morning, Senators," Marius began. Valerius took his seat. "Tribune Saturninus would like an opportunity to speak on a matter of legislation." He gestured to the tribune and sat back down.

"Consul Marius, I had intentions to speak on a few other matters, if I may," Valerius said sheepishly.

"Go ahead, then. You'll only be keeping the senators waiting to hear what the good tribune has to say."

Valerius considered it and then gave a feeble smile.

"My matters can wait. I cede the floor to Lucius Saturninus."

The tribune stood and bowed lowly, first to the presiding consul and then to the rest of the senate house.

"I thank you, Consul Valerius. I will try to keep my words as brief as possible." He turned to the men on the right side of the curia. "I know many of you hold a grudge against me. I know a great deal of the men in this sacred house opposed my grain dole legislation. And I hear you." He nodded and spoke as convincingly as any man could. "I understand your opposition. I hope that you'll agree, simply, that I've acted only in the best interest of the state."

He stopped and gave a few moments for anyone to speak up about this, but no one did. The senators simply shook their heads and narrowed their eyes.

"Regardless of your opinions of me or my past endeavors, I hope that today I can propose something that will please all Roman patriots—land for the brave soldiers who saved Rome from the northern menace!" he shouted as if he expected upheaval, but there was none.

"What land?" Aurelius Cotta asked through clenched teeth.

"The territories they secured for us, of course. Fertile bottom-land in Gaul and Northern Italy."

Now every senator was on his feet. This was the response Saturninus was waiting for. And from the smirk on his face, one had to assume he welcomed it with relish.

He turned back to us and let his head fall back with a laugh. Every hand on the right was pointing at him, every voice lifting curses.

He shook his head. "What times we live in."

Valerius looked stunned. Glaucia crossed his legs and leaned forward as if watching the climax of a play. Marius jumped to his feet and hurried to Saturninus's side.

"Wait! Wait!" he shouted until they heard him. "Before you tire yourself with your constant blathering, you should know that our Italian allies will be receiving land as well."

The volume increased twofold.

One lone voice rose above the rest.

"Marius, this is going too far, even for you! The illegality of giving land to Italians is unprecedented!" Numidicus cried out for justice.

"Treason! This is treason! We'll have you all tried and executed for this!" Lucius Cato was on his feet.

Some of the men on the left of the curia applauded Marius and Saturninus. A few stood and stomped their feet. But the majority sat silently, looking at their companions with blank faces.

"Giving land to noncitizens is treason, Marius. How can you deny it?" Marius's former associate Rutilius Rufus asked with wide, sad eyes. He was pleading with his old friend.

"That's *Consul* Marius to you, Rufus." Marius returned to his seat, but before sitting, he continued. "On the contrary, though. Land will only be given to citizens. Because all of our Italian veterans will be given citizenship for their service."

Senators jumped up and stormed the floor. I hurled myself

into the fray, holding out my arms to keep them back from the consul. A few flailing arms struck me in the neck and face, but I lowered my head and held them back as best I could, like a lone rock against the current.

"You willingly betray your own country! How could you do this?" Lucius Crassus asked, incredulous.

Marius, infuriated with the accusations, turned and jumped into the fray, pushing back some of the assailants himself. To even touch a consul could result in execution. But reason had escaped them.

It didn't hurt that Marius was twice as strong as the lot of them.

He grabbed a young Optimate by the neck and thrust the crown of his head into the man's face. The crack of his nose rang out as he flew back and hit the floor. Blood spewed immediately, and at the sight of it, most of his companions slowed their advance.

"Silence!" Marius roared like a lion of Carthage. "Once deafened by the noise of war, one can barely hear the soft voice of the law."

As if on command, our veterans lined up at the entrance of the curia. Every senator froze in their spot as if they'd seen Medusa and cast their gaze on the armed veterans.

The lictors posted at the entrance, certainly veterans themselves, did little to restrain them.

Marius cleared a path and pointed toward the veterans.

"Who will speak against them? Who will raise a voice against the men who have fought to allow you to speak it? Do you want to give the land back to the Gauls? You can go fight for it and claim it yourself if you so desire."

No one said a word. The curia was more silent than when it sat empty. Numidicus looked on as if seeing a terrible vision of the future. Sulla, for once, was just as stunned as those around him. There was no humor in his eyes and no smirk on his lips. Gaius Caesar buried his head in his hands, refusing to look upon the actions of his brother-in-law. Saturninus scanned faces and analyzed the reactions. Glaucia leaned back in his curule chair and lifted his chin high, like a player who'd just captured the king in a game of *latrunculi*.

"Who will speak against them?" Marius asked again, and not rhetorically. I'm not sure what they would have done, but Marius, Saturninus, and Glaucia seemed to wait in eager anticipation for one brave Optimate to raise his hand.

No one did.

"Magnificent," Saturninus said, wiping a single drop of blood from his cheek. "We shall put the matter to a vote in the assembly. Twenty-eight days hence, three market days from now, we will see how the people will reward her saviors. In the meantime, you men can formulate your defense. For your sakes, I'll pray you can come up with more suitable retaliations than your own greed."

He returned to his tribune's chair.

"Pontifex, say a prayer for our Republic and let's end matters for the day, shall we?" Marius said.

Valerius never addressed what he intended to speak on that day, but even if he had, I doubt anyone would have been able to listen.

SCROLL XVIII

ONE DAY BEFORE KALENDS OF AUGUST, 655 AB
URBE CONDITA

WE DIDN'T HAVE to summon veterans for the vote; they showed
up at my doorstep of their own accord. And there was far more
than thirteen.

The decision had been made in advance that we would
march to the Forum with the tribune himself, rather than Marius,
to show solidarity for the cause.

We met outside his home on the Esquiline Hill, which was
already surrounded by a massive gathering of supporters. Some
of these men might have been old veterans themselves, but
from the look of them, there were many rural citizens as well,
and perhaps some Italians who desired citizenship for their
people.

"We walk not just to the Forum today but into the annals of
history. Let us reclaim Rome for those who deserve it," Saturninus said before we set off. That was revolutionary rhetoric if any
had ever existed, but it was what the gatherers wanted to hear,
and they let him know it with roars of approval.

As we neared the Forum, more and more senators appeared,

moving in the opposite direction. I couldn't discern the cause, and from the look on Saturninus's face, he couldn't either.

As we neared the Temple of Vesta, Sulla strolled past us carelessly, his arm linked with Porcia's, his young wife.

I turned to whisper something to Saturninus but found that he had lagged behind. He was frozen in his place, knees bent slightly, his eyes fixed on Sulla.

"Tribune?" I asked, concerned as I saw him clutch his chest.

His skin twitched and he swallowed hard.

"Every time I doubt myself, I am reminded why I am doing all that I am." I realized his gaze was not on Sulla but on his bride. Saturninus's ex-wife. She did not spare him a passing glance.

I looked over his shoulder and saw the concerned eyes of Saturninus's followers.

"We should keep moving." I placed a hand on his back.

"Just a moment," he said. He spit up some bile and then straightened. "To glory."

He moved on with fresh vigor, and clenched fists.

When we arrived at the *comitium*, more and more citizens and senators were departing. A handful of augurs stood apart discussing among themselves.

"What is the meaning of this?" Saturninus demanded, holding up a hand to halt his followers.

An obese man in white robes, about the height of a child, turned to Saturninus, perturbed at his tone.

"The day has been declared inauspicious. The vote will be postponed."

"Inauspicious?" he asked, making sure he'd heard them correctly.

There was no scheme or political maneuvering we could have summoned up to overturn the will of the gods, or its interpretation.

"What signs have you seen, Augur?" he asked, reckless anger on the brim of erupting.

"The entrails give concerning signs, and thunder was heard this morning." The chief augur's flappy cheeks jiggled as he gesticulated.

Perhaps there *was* something in the entrails that caused concern. Perhaps someone had heard thunder that morning, although the skies were clear and bright. Or, perhaps more likely, the college of augurs was made up of men from the leading families who had a vested interest in the acquisition of fertile bottomland in Gaul and Northern Italy.

Saturninus said nothing at first. He stepped forward, towering over the fat little augur. He placed a tight grip on both of his shoulders. All of the augurs gasped and took a step back.

"You should be careful, Augur, lest thunder be followed by lightning."

The threat was received. They nodded along with open mouths until he released his grip and turned from them.

"No vote today, men. The Optimates bribed the college of augurs, if I had to guess. But it will not be postponed again, I can assure you," he said as his followers groaned and shook their heads. He made sure to say this loudly enough that the augurs behind him heard every word.

The retinue dispersed reluctantly.

"Tribune Saturninus, what can I do?" I asked, needing orders like I did on the battlefield.

He turned to me and considered it.

He took my hands within his own.

"Spend time with your family. Conduct yourself as a Roman citizen. And find out how the people feel. Consider it reconnaissance if you'd like, I know you have a talent for it. They wouldn't have worked so hard to postpone the vote unless they believed the voters can be swayed. We'll need to keep our finger on the people's pulse, nay?"

I was disappointed there wasn't more for me to do. But one way or the other, I would ensure my men got land.

FIVE DAYS AFTER THE KALENDS OF AUGUST, 655 AB URBE
CONDITA

The Optimates wasted no time. They made good use of the
additional fourteen days until the postponed voting day. They
immediately set out to sow dissension into the ranks of the
Populare supporters. *Contiones* were being held daily from the
Rostra, where ambitious young nobles sought to cast their lot in
with the senatorial party.

And it was effective. They specifically addressed the Italian
citizenship, played to the people's pride and greed, and ignited
their anger against having to share their most prized possession
with anyone else. To further infuriate the people, they often
addressed their living situations—holed up in cramped, hot,
dank apartments throughout the city while the Populares sought
to give homes and farmland to the Italians and rural plebs
without pause or consideration. And it worked. The graffiti that
so recently praised Marius and his supporters was quickly
covered up and replaced by new, less favorable depictions.

These public gatherings weren't without violence, though.
Soldiers or supporters of the bill often broke up the meetings,
whether at Saturninus's or Glaucia's behest, I do not know. Likewise, when senators who wanted to further entrench themselves
in our camp gave speeches in favor of the bill, or spoke of
applying real patriotism in legislation, they were often assaulted
by a drunken mob, pelted with horse shit or whatever else could
be found lying on the streets.

As the vote drew nearer, I was summoned to a dinner at
Gaius Saufeius's house. Eight days, one week, until the vote, and

the political landscape continued to shift to the opposition's favor.

I arrived late, but Saufeius still spent half a watch showing me his pond and describing at length the moray eels he had spent over a million sestertii to acquire.

I'm not sure who this was meant to impress, but it certainly wasn't me.

The inside of his domus was much the same. Every gaudy, overpriced trinket peddled in the Forum had found its way into Saufeius's house. It was difficult even to navigate to the triclinium for fear of bumping into the displays of silver cutlery and vials of purple dye.

"Are you finished with your tour, Saufeius? We need to begin," Marius said, sitting up on his couch.

"So soon? Perhaps we should wait on dinner?" Saufeius replied, his words slurred from wine.

"I love honeyed dormouse and savory flamingo tongue as much as any man in Rome, but I'm inclined to agree with the consul," Saturninus said, sober and serious.

"I won't be of any use until I get some food in my gullet, but you men go ahead," Equitius said, leaning back and propping himself up on a few pillows.

"Things are not good, gentlemen. My lictors had to fight off two plebs yesterday morning. They accused me of treason and lunged for an attack," Glaucia said, and I could tell from the banality of his tone that this wasn't one of his witty tales.

"How fickle can the people really be? Did they forget that we just fed the masses with endless grain?" Saufeius asked, gesturing for a slave to cool him down with a fan of peacock feathers.

"As fickle as you can imagine, Saufeius, you'll come to find. They forget what you've done for them the moment they see you doing something for someone else," Saturninus replied.

"It makes me think the Optimates are on to something." Equitius chuckled by himself.

"Perhaps we could lower the grain dole again? Fatten them up as a distraction?" Saufeius posed.

"How much lower can we price grain? It wouldn't work. The effect has already worn off. It would be clear what we were doing, even to the dullest minds in the Forum." Glaucia shook his head.

"What about staging gladiator games? Just redirect their passions away from politics entirely?" I made the rare attempt to offer input.

"Not a bad idea. But it would be nearly impossible to outdo the games put on my Crassus and Scaevola. Besides, we don't want to distract them, we need to earn back their trust." Marius gritted his teeth, clearly astonished that he would ever need to *earn* the love of the people.

"Even the equestrians have turned on us. They have their courts, and now they want our land," Glaucia said, taking a sip of wine.

"What are we to do, then, gentlemen? What are we to do? We've given the people and the equestrians everything they could possibly want. And now they cannot support us in this one thing..." Marius stood to his feet and stomped around the center of the couches.

"Perhaps we should have added a clause in either bill that required their support for all future endeavors," Equitius said half seriously. No one addressed it, because in hindsight, it wasn't helpful and the illegality of such a clause would have led to the bills being stricken down.

"Sertorius, I asked you to do your research. What do the people say? Are they really against us, or are those clamoring just a vocal minority?" Saturninus asked.

"Well..." I considered it. I had done as the tribune had asked. I'd spent most of my days perusing shops in the Forum with Gavius, Apollonius, and Arrea. We took time to watch plays in the theater and attended a few religious festivals. But my purpose was primarily to overhear all that I could. "I believe the majority of the city dwellers are against us."

"Who do they blame, Sertorius?" Marius asked, hands akimbo on his hips. It seemed like an irrelevant question to me, but perhaps it was simply that I didn't want to answer.

"Well...you, Consul."

"They blame me?" he asked. The room fell silent. "It was Saturninus who proposed the bill."

"It doesn't matter what the plebs cry in the street, Consul Marius, what matters is how they vote," Saturninus said, trying to redirect the conversation, but Marius was waiting on his answer.

"But...they're your soldiers, after all, Consul," I said.

"So. The people plan to vote against the land bill. I can't say we didn't anticipate some form of resistance," Glaucia said.

But Marius was steaming.

"And how do the veterans feel, Sertorius?" he asked.

"How do they feel, sir? They're excited to receive land. The Italians are thrilled to be called citizens."

"Who do they give credit to for this bill?" Marius breathed heavily through his nose. The muscles in his jaw twitched.

"Consul, really, that is irrelevant," Saturninus said, attempting to assuage him.

"Who? Answer me," Marius demanded.

"Saturninus," I said abruptly as he continued to push me. "He proposed the bill."

Marius exhaled like he had been struck in the chest.

"I could have proposed the damn thing, but I could have been blocked from holding an assembly of the people!" His brows furrowed, and he glared at me as if I were the one who gave credit to Saturninus.

"The veterans will always be loyal to you above all else, Consul. Just a few old fools in the street, that's all," Saufeius said, finally appreciating the tension in the room.

"I don't believe a damned word of it. The people and my

legionaries know who provides for them." He returned to his seat and crossed his arms, visibly disturbed.

"The way I see it," Glaucia began, trying to pull the conversation back to center, "the only way to pass this bill is with vast sums of money. Vast. Saufeius, can you take care of that?"

"Coin will be flowing in the streets, Praetor." He smiled, revealing stained purple teeth.

"The people can always appreciate gold. This will be an expenditure, though, gentlemen. Perhaps larger even than that of the election."

"Not a concern. The greedy little plebs will forget all about the Italians and the veterans once they have enough coin for a bit of wine and women," Saufeius reassured him.

"We need to ensure we have as many rural plebs in the city as possible," Saturninus added. "Dispatches should be sent to every village within three days' ride. We need to flood the streets with the families of Marius's mules."

"I can assist," I said. "The people in my homeland have only been citizens of Rome for a few hundred years, so we tend to sympathize with the Italians, and the ranks of the legions swell with Sabines."

"Very good. Consul, can you send representatives to your village, and the surrounding cities of Latium?" Saturninus asked.

At length, Marius nodded.

About the time we all forgot about our meal, the dormouse and flamingo arrived.

"You and the rest of the cooks will receive thirty lashes!" Saufeius barked. "You've embarrassed me. Next time, I'll feed you to my eels."

"Yes, *dominus*," the slaves replied, keeping their eyes down as they passed the food around.

Equitius was apparently the only one hungry, as he began shoving slivers of food in his already-full mouth while the rest of us picked at it delicately.

I wasn't sure how much my stomach could tolerate.

Marius threw his plate aside and stood abruptly.

"We have to pass this vote. I was elected for this purpose. If we… If I don't… If this vote doesn't pass, I'll burn down the whole fucking city," the consul shouted through gritted teeth.

Everyone cringed, but no one could find the courage to rebuke him.

"This meal's too fancy for me anyhow. I'll see myself out." He turned his back and stomped out of the room.

No one said anything until we heard the massive wooden doors of the entry shutting behind him.

"What on Gaia's earth got into him?" Equitius asked with wide eyes and a chuckle.

"He's concerned about this vote, Equitius. Along with the rest of us. Perhaps you should join us and begin to take this seriously," Saturninus said, glaring. Equitius smacked his gums loudly and shrugged.

"Perhaps in the future, Sertorius, only mention the people's love for him. And never again admit that the veterans applaud any man but their general," Glaucia said, leaning in my direction.

"Noted," I replied, and took a final bite of the over-spiced flamingo tongue. "I should be going."

"I've not shown you my Greek artwork yet. You said you wanted to see the statues from Apollo's temple in Corinth?" Saufeius whined. I believe what happened was that he had mentioned it, and I had nodded. I had no interest beforehand, and I certainly didn't now.

"I'm beginning to feel unwell."

As I made my way to leave, Saturninus stopped me.

"We need your people in the city, Senator. All of them. Our success or failure could very well depend on your support. Will you do all that is required?"

All eyes raised to me.

It was a fair question, but for the first time, I wondered if my loyalty was being questioned.

"I will."

After he took a moment to appraise my response, the tribune nodded.

"To the Republic, and our victory." Glaucia raised his cup in my direction as I turned to leave.

SCROLL XIX

NONES OF AUGUST, 655 AB URBE CONDITA

SHORTLY AFTER I nearly drowned as a child, I began to experience something very strange with my sleep. It happened rarely—very rarely, thank the gods—but I remember each time it happened. It's been years now, and I shudder at the thought still.

I would wake in the morning, unable to speak, move, or even blink. My heart would begin to race as panic crept in. Then a dark presence would materialize in the room, encompassing it. Footsteps would approach from all corners, a shadow would flicker along the wall. Hushed whispers, all jumbled together and not forming any words. I would feel whatever it was come close to my bedside, or my tent cot when I was on campaign. Was it Dis Pater? Was it Pluto come to bring me to the afterlife?

Sometimes whatever it was would crawl onto my chest, causing even my breath to cease. It was then that I realized it was Charon using a paddle to row on either side, and I was on the ferry on the river Styx.

I never told anyone about it. Not even Lucius, Apollonius, or my mother... I feared that the moment word of this spread, I would be feared as a man cursed by Apollo, or perhaps by all the gods on Mount Olympus. Any hopes of a political or military career would have been dashed. Who would follow a cursed man?

I thought I was having an episode that morning.

My eyes opened, and I saw a figure standing at the door. I could hear breath. I pretended to be asleep. I kept my eyes cracked just enough to see his movement.

I twitched my toes. They responded, so I was not asleep.

As slowly as I could, I moved my hand along the bed to the dagger I had beneath my pillow.

The figure stepped closer, dim light from the atrium silhouetting him but illuminating none of his features.

He paused at the foot of my bed. I tightened my grip around the dagger hilt.

"Stand at attention while I'm talking to you!"

I sprung from the bed with my dagger in hand. I poised to strike. But the shout was followed by my general's laughter.

I dropped the dagger and ran both hands through my hair, almost weeping with relief.

"Damn it, Consul," I managed to say from trembling lips. If it had been anyone other than Marius, they would have felt the full extent of my wrath.

"Ha! Sent you back to Gaul, didn't I?" He laughed so hard, he nearly choked.

I couldn't blame him for not knowing about my difficulty with sleep.

"I'm surprised my porter let you in without awaking me," I said, taking a seat on the edge of the bed and trying to calm my breath. If I was the kind of master who doled out lashes, the porter would have been receiving some.

"I demanded his silence and compliance! Slave or no, he wouldn't be denying the consul of Rome." He laughed again, reimagining the face I must have made. "Come on, get dressed. Let's have a cup of wine."

"This early? What time is it?" I peered through my bedroom window to find that it was still dark outside.

"Never mind that. There isn't a law against wine before breakfast, is there? I hope you have something sour. I'm getting tired of Falernian grape, I miss the swill we drank in camp."

I wrapped a belt around my tunic. I had to convince myself to leave the dagger behind. My heart was still racing, and I was fearful this was an illusion.

"What's happened?" Apollonius asked, rubbing his eyes as he met us in the atrium.

"Everything's fine, friend. Have someone bring us some wine and return to bed," I replied. His eyes shot open when he saw who was with me.

"Consul Marius, it's a pleasure," he said, reddening as he realized he was underdressed.

"Apollonius, have you still been putting men to sleep with your philosophical droning?" Marius smiled.

I could barely begin to understand the man. The last time I had seen him, he had stormed from a dinner party, cursing and threatening to burn the whole city down. Scarcely had I seen him discuss anything other than public policy since the moment we returned to Rome. And here I found him, before the sun had arisen, playing pranks, joking, smiling, and wanting wine.

"It's what I do best, Consul."

"I've been having trouble sleeping lately. Perhaps I could buy you from Sertorius here and you could read me some Plato each night?" He slapped Apollonius's back, not realizing how powerful he could be to a frail man like my friend.

"You'd be hard-pressed to purchase a free man," I said, reminding Marius that I had freed Apollonius.

"Every man has a price, nay?" he said. "Lovely home. I did well acquiring this for you. You're making all your payments, aren't you?"

I showed Marius into my tablinum, and naturally, he sat at the head of the room, my desk.

"Yes, I am." Fortunately, my new clients were keeping me afloat; otherwise, my answer might have been different.

"Good lad. I knew I was right to trust you." He flipped through a few papers on my desk, to what purpose, I did not know. I'm not sure he even knew.

Two cups of wine were brought in for us.

"Ahhh," he said with his first sip, tipping his head back and smacking his lips to savor the taste, "now this is the kind of filth *real* Romans drink."

I rather liked it. It was the most expensive wine I had ever purchased, but I didn't mention it.

"Do we have something planned for the day?" I asked, taking a seat before the desk where my guests typically sat. I couldn't imagine this was a social visit.

"Nothing in particular. Why? Have you got something for us to do?"

I stared at him for a moment, blinking and squeezing my hands. Was I really awake? None of this seemed to make sense. The man before me looked like Marius, but his presence felt entirely different.

"Nothing comes to mind, Consul."

"That your father?" he asked, gesturing to the bust in the corner of the room.

"Yes, it was. His name was Proculus, and he—"

He cut me off. "Say, Sertorius, what do you think about Saturninus and Glaucia?" For the first time since he had arrived, he met my gaze and stopped piddling around.

"I'm not sure what you mean, Consul. In what capacity?" Anything positive or negative I could say about them would obviously reflect on Marius as well, so I had to be careful. Aside from my time with Marius on campaign, his actions since we returned to Rome had been one and the same with Saturninus and Glaucia.

"Don't think about it so much. What do you think of them? You may speak plainly."

Was this some sort of test? Was my loyalty truly being questioned?

"They're good men, Consul. Perhaps a bit expedient for my taste, but they have the Republic's best interest at heart."

"Well, I'm beginning to think they are snakes. Two-faced as sure as Janus is." He drained his wine and snapped his fingers for more as if my slaves were his own. I wondered if I was being baited.

"Whatever would cause you to think that?" I asked.

"I have my reasons," he said without explaining himself further. "Don't you have similar concerns?"

I wasn't going to allow him to trap me if that was his purpose. I ran through the past few weeks in my mind, trying to determine either why I was being doubted or what would have caused the change in Marius's appraisal of his companions. I recollected nothing of substance.

"I've had no reason to believe that."

"Well, you're new to all this. You'll learn in time, if you stick with me. The two of them can't be trusted," he said. I was careful in formulating my response, but Marius continued before I had a chance to speak. "They were necessary tools to get my legislation passed. That's all. The whole damned lot of them. Especially that little worm Saufeius; if he were not a quaestor with access to the public treasury, I would have snapped his neck the first time he stepped foot into my house."

Well, that explained their tolerance of such a man. But it didn't explain why Marius was speaking so recklessly. A threat against the life of a quaestor could mean persecution and exile. Did he trust that I wouldn't say anything, or did he simply believe himself to be untouchable.

"I'm no fan of Saufeius," I said, unable to speak further.

"And Equitius...claiming to be the son of Tiberius Gracchus. Ha! An imposter if there ever was one. I've grown tired of their company, Sertorius."

"You do not believe he is the son of Tiberius?" I asked. I

thought it was relatively obvious to anyone with discerning eyes, but Marius had thus far given me no indication of his disbelief.

"I've more chance of being Tiberius's son than he does. And if I had a name like Gracchus, I would already be ruling Rome," he said, his words quicker and more emotional than they typically were. He was a six-time consul of Rome. If he wasn't ruling Rome now, what did he have in mind?

"I found it hard to believe myself," I said, accepting another cup of wine to calm my nerves.

"But it's Saturninus and Glaucia that cannot be trusted." He pointed a finger at me as if offering a warning.

"Consul, please speak plainly. Why can't we trust our allies?"

"Allies in pursuit of certain legislation only. They have no love lost for me. I can see how they look at us. I can hear how they speak of us when our backs are turned." Marius used "us" as if we were one and the same. For all my political ignorance, I had always had a perceptive eye for duplicity. And I had no reason to suspect that Glaucia or Saturninus had ever spoken poorly of me.

"They've only spoken of the great Marius in admiration and respect when I've been around, Consul," I reassured him. He smiled and shook his head.

"*When you are around.* That's it. They know you're loyal to me. But they are just loyal to one another. They're as close as man and wife, or closer even. There's no room for another in their monogamous commitment."

Was it really jealousy that brought Marius there that morning? I searched for something deeper, but Marius was not a multidimensional man. Not in my appraisal, at least.

He continued. "Everyone else is just a tool for them to use," he said, echoing what he had just referred to them as. "Saufeius and his money, Equitius and his forged legacy…me and my legions. But we are not tools to be used, are we? By anyone?"

"No, sir."

"You're damned right. It is Marius who commands the legions. It's Marius who is consul. We bow to no one. Right?"

"Correct, General," I said, fearing what he was getting at.

"We need them for now. Until we get this bill passed, at least. But there may be a time soon when we have to abandon them. I hope you aren't overly attached. We might need to forge more useful alliances. Do you understand this?"

"I understand, sir," I said, assuming that the least I said the better. If Marius could change his mind this quickly, perhaps it would return to form just as fast.

"Senators! Senators!" a voice carried in through the halls. "Senators!"

"Expecting visitors?" Marius asked me, and I imagined there was suspicion in his eyes.

"Not at all. Let me see what is afoot." I stood and hurried to the door.

"Senators of Rome! The senate is convening in the Temple of Concord! The senate is convening in the Temple of Concord!" the crier shouted, both hands cupped around his mouth.

"And who is calling the meeting of the senate?" Marius asked, apparently having followed me to the exit.

"Tribune Lucius Saturninus," the crier said before moving down the line and continuing his shouts.

The consul appeared to be as surprised as I was. He grunted and his lip began to curl.

"See? They cannot be trusted."

We crammed into the Temple of Concord as best we could. It was a far larger building than the curia, but the seating was limited. I stood behind the consul, along with Cinna.

Glaucia gave us a nod of the head but remained at a safe

distance, keeping up the guise of indifference we had been maintaining since our party formed. I'm certain that, at this particular instance, Marius would have liked to ask him what this was all about.

We waited for quite a while, baking in the heat of the enclosed temple. We were waiting on none other than the tribune himself, who had called the meeting.

"By Juno, just get on with it," the Pontifex Maximus Ahenobarbus bellowed, dabbing at the sweat of his brow.

Sulla, Cato, and Pompeius were whispering to each other and giggling like schoolboys. They must have smelled blood in the water. Perhaps the tribune was calling the sudden meeting to repeal his own legislation. Perhaps he was so ashamed, he had decided not to attend at all.

"Blessed Mother Concord, we pray your blessing covers this holy place today, and that you guide our leaders in peace, as Mars does in war." As the priest began his prayer, Saturninus strolled through the entrance.

He had a wax tablet in one hand and a stylus in the other. He didn't look up. He didn't seem to notice the body of senators around him at all.

He paced in our direction, still working diligently on the tablet.

"Consul," he whispered with a nod of the head.

"You did not tell me we were calling a meeting of the senate, Saturninus. What is the meaning of this?"

He closed the tablet and buckled it. He lifted it and waited for a senator I had never seen before to take it from his hand and hurry to the exit.

"I had an idea." He tapped his forehead and smiled.

The priest continued, "We ask that you offer wisdom among—"

"How has it come to this?" Saturninus's voice roared, drowning out the recitation of the priest like a violent wave over a boat. "How has it come to this?"

"You interrupt a sacred prayer, Tribune!" Cato was on his feet, no longer giggling.

"And you interrupt a tribune! Speak again while I have the floor, and I'll have you arrested and thrown in the *carcer*." Saturninus approached Cato's bench, daring him to make a move. Cato remained frozen until Sulla pulled him back to his seat.

"I ask again—how has it come to this? Rome's oldest and most sacred law holds that conquered lands be handed over to the authority of the assembly, and yet the Republic has been afflicted by your insatiable greed, and that of your fathers, for so long that we consider upholding the law a matter of debate. The very fact that this legislation is met with vehemence is a sign of the times."

He turned his back to them and let the silence linger over the temple like nightfall. The priest, still stunned, slowly retreated to the shadows and stood beside the statue of Concordia.

Saturninus still did not speak. He was giving them a chance to retaliate. He knew they were seething. We all did. He had struck a chord. He'd slandered their heritage. He'd called them lawbreakers, the worst insult they could imagine. Their anger was visceral, I felt it in the air. But no one said a word.

"I have just this moment added a clause to my bill. And, if it necessary, I say again: conquered land has always been distributed based on the assembly's vote—"

"It was not conquered land! It was retrieved land. It was ours before the war, we simply reclaimed it from the invaders!" Pompeius shouted, his face beet red.

Sulla stared at him with wide eyes. He was perceptive enough to notice this was not the time or the place.

"Guards!" Saturninus roared, and without delay, armed men rushed into the temple. "See this man arrested!"

Pompeius's eyes flickered as he considered retaliating, but when no one stood to his aid, he went willingly.

"I have been reasonable with you. I have been kind and

generous to you all. But no longer. Do I speak out of turn? Do I interrupt our brave consuls, or do I interject when our good Father of the Senate speaks? No."

The sound of the crowd gasping echoed through the temple as Pompeius was led to the nearby *carcer*. I wondered if Saturninus had called for the meeting to be held here for this very reason, as the *carcer* was right outside the doors.

"This clause is a simple one; even the dullest of you will be able to comprehend it. If the law states that conquered land be distributed by the people, and we as the senate live to serve the people, then we must agree to uphold this law. At all costs. No matter the outcome."

He scanned the faces of men on either side to ensure they listened. To make sure there was absolute silence.

"Regardless of how the people vote, all of us will be compelled to march to the senate house and swear an oath of fealty to this law."

No one spoke. No one cried out against him. Not a noble in the room cursed him or pointed with their left hand.

"Even if the people vote against me, *I* will swear this oath. Because *I* uphold the law. *I* respect our traditions. And as long as I am tribune, I will ensure you all do the same."

He turned on his heels and strode from the temple.

We remained silent where we stood. I had been too stunned by Saturninus's uncharacteristic display to survey the room around me. For the first time, I looked at Marius and realized he was just as perplexed and slack-jawed as the rest of us.

The only man in the senate house who seemed to have his wits about him was Gaius Glaucia, who leaned back in his curule chair, crossed his legs, and waited patiently for someone to speak.

"Finish your prayer, priest. While you're at it, offer the closing prayer as well," Glaucia said.

The frightened old man crept from the shadows, glancing at

either side of the room to see if he would be met with any more resistance.

He continued the recitation, the words even more potent and ironic now: "And we pray that you bless us with unity and a singular devotion to the glory and honor of the Roman Republic."

SCROLL XX

EIGHT DAYS AFTER IDES OF AUGUST, 655 AB URBE
CONDITA

THE ROSTRA, which was so recently swarmed with ambitious
senators, now remained empty. Tension was in the air as sure as
the humidity; you could see it on every pleb's face in the street.
Word had spread. Pompeius was seen being locked away in the
carcer. Even after he was released, the entire city was buzzing
about it.

Rome was uncertain. The court legislation and the grain dole
bill were nearly guaranteed to pass as soon as they were
announced to the public. There was no such indication now.

The vote was four days away, eight days after the ides of
August. It was the day of the Vulcanalia, a celebratory holiday
most Romans waited for all year. All the fish caught that day
were brought to the Forum, where they were burned in a
massive firepit on the Volcanal to appease the god's wrath, and
to prevent him from devouring the city in flames.

It was well attended, to be certain. But whereas the citizens
usually drank, danced, and sang around the fire, now they jour-

neyed to the pyre, somber, as if wondering if their sacrifice would actually be accepted.

"It's too hot for that fire," Gavius said, already sleepy and rubbing his eyes. Waves of heat carried through the crowd like the Tyrrhenian's current carrying flakes of white ash with it.

"I'm inclined to agree," Apollonius said as I led the way through the crowd, holding on to Arrea's hand as she held on to Gavius's.

"Move out me way!" a rough man shouted over the rumble of wagon wheels, whipping the two oxen that led it. The putrid smell of fish followed.

"This is a strange festival. I can't pretend to understand why your gods would want roasted fish. That could feed the whole city for a month," Arrea said, half seriously, half in jest.

"Because if we don't appease the god, he'll burn us all alive, you ignorant bitch," came a voice from the crowd.

I paused in my steps and jerked my head around to find the culprit.

"It's fine, Quintus. Just ignore it," Arrea pleaded, pushing past me to take the lead.

"You heard me. She's a stupid bitch." The pleb was drunk. His tunic was covered in wine stains, but somehow he still managed to reek of piss.

"You cannot speak to my woman in that tone," I said as calmly as I could. I could feel Gavius's eyes on me, or I wouldn't have been talking.

"What are you going to do about it, city dweller?" the man asked, attempting and failing to focus his vision on me.

I released Arrea's hand and moved forward. It didn't take long. The drunk man faded into the crowd without pause.

"Let's keep moving," Apollonius suggested.

"It's the rural citizens. They're not used to the festivals. And they're making the most of it," I said, rejoining them.

I was trying to convince myself not to turn around and find

the man when I spotted Marius at the foot of the Capitoline, the fire before him glowing orange on his face.

He was biting at the nail of his thumb and staring intently into the flames, noticing nothing of the havoc around him.

"Come, let me introduce you to the consul," I said to Arrea.

"Please, Quintus, I'm not proper." She gestured to her dress.

"Nonsense. I want him to meet my son too."

I led the way, pushing through a few congregations of plebs to get there.

"Do you know what I am wondering, Sertorius?" he said when I arrived, sparing any introductions as if he had expected my arrival.

"I don't, Consul," I said, gesturing to Gavius and Arrea so I could introduce them.

He didn't seem to notice.

"That's my old friend Rutilius Rufus over there. I am wondering if I should go talk to him." He pointed to a man barely visible on the other side of the firepit.

"I... Well...why wouldn't you?" I said, embarrassed and feeling awkward as Arrea and Gavius stood by waiting for an introduction.

"I accused him of treason, if you recall. I thought it was he who betrayed me. It wasn't. And I shall not go begging for forgiveness."

"Perhaps it's best to just—"

"But he could be useful. He is a wise man, even as my junior. His counsel could be valuable," Marius said, spitting a fragment of nail from his lip.

"Then, why don't you go talk to him?" I said, giving up any attempt to claim his attention.

"What if he refuses my hand? I will be twice dishonored."

I was still irritable from the man who'd insulted Arrea. So I threw caution into Zephyr's wind.

"Rufus. Senator Rufus!" I shouted.

"Damn it, Sertorius," Marius cursed under his breath.

The man searched until he found me, and I waved him over.

"Senator. Consul," he said with a respectful, unemotional nod as he arrived. "Can I help you?"

"No," Marius said, poorly attempting to hide his discomfort.

Rufus analyzed both our faces. I said nothing to help Marius.

"Well, you called my name for something."

"I wanted to have dinner with you," Marius grumbled under his breath.

"What?"

"I'd like to dine with you. I'm extending an offer."

"We can. If you would make your purpose known."

"By the gods, Rufus! I'm extending my hand. Can we break bread and share wine, or not?" Marius pursed his lips.

Rufus hid it well, but his eyes smiled. He must have known Marius well.

"Let's. I'm hosting a symposium tomorrow evening. Perhaps we could invite Gaius Julius. And Norbanus has returned from campaign. I'm sure he'd be overjoyed to see you."

"Overjoyed to drink free wine, if he's still the same man I remember," Marius said bashfully, only laughing after Rufus did the same.

"I look forward to our reunion. Senator Sertorius, I'd be honored for you to come as well. When shall I expect you?"

"Before the sun sets. I'll need to get some good sleep." Marius seemed to offer conditions for no other reason than to do so, but Rufus accepted it in stride. The fact that Marius was willing to visit Rufus's rather than the other way around showed just how desperately he wanted to reconcile with the man.

"Marvelous. I'll be counting down the hours." Rufus offered a curt bow and left us.

"If you embarrass me like that again, Sertorius, I'll—" He could think of nothing to say. I smiled, convinced that I had done nothing wrong. He knew it too, regardless of whether he would admit it or not. "I'll see you at my domus tomorrow. Be on time."

He turned to leave. Gavius and Arrea never did receive their introduction.

I arrived at Marius's well before the appointed time. I knew where Rufus's home was, as it was on the crest of the Palatine Hill and overlooked the Forum in such a way that most of the city knew its location. But I wasn't about to arrive alone. My excuse, if I needed to offer one, was to show my solidarity with Marius, but in truth, I simply didn't know how one was supposed to behave at a symposium. I had never attended one, as that wasn't the sort of dinner gathering one hosted in Nursia. I needed someone to imitate, and I hoped Marius was more comfortable in that environment. Even as I arrived, I doubted it.

His curule chair was placed on a platform hoisted by several burly slaves, and beside it sat a more decorative chair for his wife. He didn't tend to go about the city in this manner, but he wasn't going to let his hosts forget who he was.

"Let's go, then," Marius said, and the slaves lifted them higher and took the first step in unison. I walked beside them. I could tell he was nervous, either that or dreading the evening, from the look in his eyes. He reached over and took Julia's hand in his own, and I could see his knuckles were white around hers.

When we arrived, the chief lictor hailed Marius's arrival, to the gentle applause of everyone within. I knew the company Rufus kept, and I couldn't imagine they were fans of Marius's politics. But having a consul—especially one like Marius—at a dinner party meant there'd be juicy gossip and the expectation of entertainment, so they clapped regardless.

"Greetings, Consul," Rufus said, greeting us at the door. "I'm so pleased you've arrived."

"I appreciate the invitation," he replied. "You remember my wife, Julia?" he asked.

"But of course. Beautiful as ever." He bent and kissed her hand.

"You flatter me, Rufus." Julia laughed, obviously far more comfortable in this environment than her husband.

We were ushered in through the atrium and greeted by the sweet smells one might expect to find in a meadow. Garlands, myrtle, and mistletoe were draped across every wall, laurels placed on the heads of every statue.

Every man and woman in attendance wore togas as brightly colored as the mosaics on the wall: purple, azure, ochre, and emerald greens, all fringed with gold hemming. I realized I was the only man present in his senatorial toga, it being the only kind I owned after I discarded my equestrian ones. That was a social blunder I wouldn't make again.

Rufus showed us into his triclinium, and everyone already reclined there stood to their feet.

"Applause for our consul is in order!" Rufus said, more cheerful than one would find him in the senate house. The women were especially overdressed. I imagined how Arrea would have fit in here. She would have found them gaudy and their makeup overdone, I decided.

"Thank you," Marius said with a few nods to those around the room. I couldn't tell if he was uncomfortable with the praise, or if he was disappointed that there wasn't more.

"This couch is for the lovely Julia, and for you, the seat of honor," Rufus said, gesturing to the couch directly to the right of his own.

I couldn't understand why he was being so kind. As I understood it, the break between the two had been difficult and irreparable. Perhaps it was Rufus's stoic leanings that allowed him to forgive so easily. Or perhaps there was something he wanted from the consul.

"Senator, you will be here. I assumed you would want to sit

beside fellow soldiers. Perhaps you can regale us with tales of your time in the north," Rufus said, ushering me to my couch. I looked around and wondered who would be sitting beside me.

I didn't have to wait long.

The Caesar brothers entered, to the applause of the room.

Gaius Julius, holding on to the hand of his young wife, Aurelia, and Sextus Caesar, holding on to his cup of wine.

I cringed when I saw the latter. He bowed low as if the cheers were for him rather than the happy couple.

I took a peek at Marius. He turned his back to the entrance and locked eyes with his wife, who smiled and tried to calm him. The fact that he would be in the same room with Sextus Caesar told me something. Was our situation with Saturninus and Glaucia really so desperate?

"If it isn't Rome's newest senator," Sextus Caesar said as he approached. My knuckles tightened around the leather of my couch. I clenched my jaw. "No greeting for your former brother-in-arms?" he asked with a chuckle as he stumbled to his own couch. He scooted it closer to mine, his wine spilling a bit as he did so. "The last time we saw each other, I was your superior. You were not yet the Hero of the North…and you had both of your eyes. Oh, how fickle Fortuna can be." He struggled to lift the cup to his lips.

"Do not mistake my attendance for complicity with all Rufus's guests, Sextus. I am not your friend," I replied, my best effort to shut the man up.

"More fool you, then. I'm much more entertaining as a friend." He shrugged, unconcerned.

Three young girls dressed as nymphs of Aphrodite entered the room and made for the corner. Two sat on a low bench and began to pluck on a harp. The other hummed a soft tune, a ballad telling of Achilles's love for Patroclus, if I remembered correctly. The murmuring in the room died down until the next guest arrived.

"Who's ready for some drink?" Norbanus shouted upon entry, raising his arms up like a victorious gladiator.

I hadn't known the man personally, but Lucius had told me a great deal about him. I respected him for one reason or another. He was a degenerate by all accounts, but there was no guile about the man. He was the same before Marius as he was when addressing a slave—specifically, an unabashedly drunk and a loyal friend.

He made jokes at the expense of a few attendees, to the humor of all, until he locked eyes with his old friend Marius.

He wagged his finger at him in mock admonishment.

"Two weeks I've been back in Rome, and I haven't received an invitation from you."

Marius smiled for the first time that evening, and embraced his old friend.

"I didn't know an invitation was necessary. I've waited by my front door for you each morning."

"He was probably too drunk to find it!" Sextus Caesar shouted. Marius's eyes lit with fury for a moment until Norbanus reclaimed his attention.

"To tell the truth, I've hardly left the brothel. It's tiresome work chasing down pirates. I felt I deserved a reward."

"So the campaign against the pirates is over, then?" I asked, anxious to hear that my friend Lucius would be returning soon.

"That's correct. Their bodies litter the seas. I've returned early to lobby for a Triumph." Norbanus patted Marius's shoulder and approached me. "You must be the Hero of the North?"

A few of the others laughed. I did not.

"Quintus Sertorius. Pleasure to meet you." I extended a hand, but he embraced me, spilling wine over my shoulder as he kissed my cheek.

"If I were to have received such a commission, perhaps I could have been a hero? Nothing glorious about crushing slaves in Sicily or hunting down pirates in Cilicia."

"It's hard to be courageous when you're hungover, Norbanus," Gaius Caesar said as he reclined on a pillow beside his wife.

"There's truth in that." Norbanus laughed.

"If only Sertorius could have been a hero before Arausio, rather than after," Sextus Caesar said to himself, but loudly enough for me to hear.

If you don't recall, Arausio was a battle in which Sextus and I both participated, the same battle where some ninety thousand Romans were butchered. Sextus made it safely away on his horse; I jumped into a river.

I glared in his direction, but once again, Norbanus intervened.

"Arausio...that battle made me famous and rich. If Caepio had been any harder to persecute, perhaps I'd still be living on the Aventine," Norbanus said. I had heard about the treason trial; apparently, it was Norbanus who'd led the persecution.

"And if my client hadn't been so flagrantly guilty, I would have bested you," spoke a voice from the entryway. We turned to find the aedile Lucius Crassus entering, arm locked with his wife's. He smiled wide as he approached, and embraced a man who apparently was once his enemy upon the courts.

"He disappeared before the verdict, so I guess that made us both successful, nay?" Norbanus patted Crassus's back with familiarity.

I didn't mention that I was the cause of that, for good reason. After Marius discovered that his son-in-law Maximus had mysteriously died, he planned to have Caepio murdered. Already under trial for treason, I sent Caepio a letter of warning, and he escaped to exile. If anyone present knew about that letter, I'm certain I wouldn't have walked out of that symposium alive.

"That's the best part about not being in command. No one brought a trial against me," Sextus said with a wink.

If it had been up to me, Sextus Caesar would have been the first to take the stand.

The crescendo of the music reached its height, and captured our attention. All the guests found their place as dancing girls in sheer tunics entered the center of the room, ribbons in hand.

As the performance began, the individual cups of wine were collected from the attendees, and one massive goblet with a depiction of Bacchus was brought out and passed around. Flute players joined the lyrists and singer, and a Greek girl took to the center and began reciting poetry.

Rufus's guests looked entranced, enjoying every moment of the spectacle. Everyone except Marius. When the goblet reached him, he drank far more than his share, and passed it on with a bead of purple wine dripping down his chin. He burped into his arm, and his feet began to tap impatiently.

I had always liked poetry, for the most part, and music had always had the ability to move me deeply. But I couldn't figure out for the life of me what the poet was talking about. I drank more than my fair share of the wine when it was my turn as well, and deflated when I had to pass it on to Sextus.

The performance concluded to heartfelt applause. A few of the women dabbed at their eyes, careful that the dark paint around their eyes wasn't running.

"What a marvelous reading, Rufus," Julia said, nestling up to her husband.

"Thank you, Eudorus," Rufus said. The poet bowed and stepped away as the music continued quietly. "Norbanus, why don't you recall the bravery of your mission against the pirates? Any grand tales to tell?"

Norbanus puckered his lips and considered it.

"I could tell you about the ships we roasted with fire, or the two hundred ringleaders we crucified near Salamis. But it's all rather dull stuff, if I'm being honest. Perhaps I can show you something I've brought back with me instead?" He pulled out a leather pouch from his belt and revealed a plate with herb in the center. "It's hemp. Bought it from an Egyptian merchant. They say it allows you to commune with the gods."

The others laughed, giddy with anticipation.

"I shall not partake, but by all means, enjoy yourselves," Rufus said.

He lit the herb and inhaled the smoke deeply through a hollow stick.

"Who's next?" he asked. Sextus Caesar hurried to take the plate, and a few of the women around the room joined in as well. Crassus and Scaevola, the two aediles, looked mortified as their wives knelt beside the plate. They were married to one another's sisters, so they probably felt less capable of reprimanding them than they would've otherwise.

Marius kept his grip tight on Julia's knee, ensuring she didn't join. I doubt she would have regardless. The consul looked mortified, and she seemed to notice.

"Perhaps the women could leave so we can talk some damned business before our heads are too hazy to do so," Marius said abruptly, his voice carrying like it did on the battle-field. It was forceful enough that the musicians stopped midtune.

Everyone looked to Rufus, obviously uncomfortable.

"I was unaware we were talking business tonight. I thought you simply wanted to dine with me?" Rufus asked. Disappointed perhaps, but not surprised, as he and the others obviously knew Marius well.

Marius didn't respond. Rufus eventually nodded to his wife.

"Come, ladies, and let me show you our terrace," she said, leading the way.

"What would you like to discuss, Consul?" Rufus said, hiding his irritation as best he could.

Marius remained silent until the musicians and poets took the hint and departed as well.

Our host Rufus, Marius, the Caesar brothers, Norbanus, and the two aediles, Crassus and Scaevola, were all that remained. And what an odd congregation it was. Norbanus and Crassus had once been rivals in the court. Gaius Caesar was the son-in-law to one of the leading Optimates, and hadn't supported his brother-in-law Marius since the day of his betrothal. Rufus and the aediles had adamantly opposed everything Marius had done since he'd come into office. Sextus Caesar had betrayed Marius several years before, and Marius had blamed his true friend Rufus, to the destruction of their alliance.

And now Marius demanded they talk "business," whatever that meant.

As we waited for Marius to address the topics he had in mind, I wondered if even the consul knew what he would like to say. If I had to guess, he would have liked to demand their allegiance and support, but even he knew that would be unacceptable.

"We've been asked to swear an oath of allegiance to the land redistribution bill. What are we to do?" he said, at length.

"'We'? What do you mean 'we'? You're in league with those reprobates, are you not?" Scaevola said, not without malicious intent.

Marius glared in his direction.

"I had nothing to do with that clause."

"I'm sure you'll understand why that's hard to believe, since you've been their ally and supporter since the moment you took office," Crassus said, a bit more contained than his friend.

"I wouldn't be here if it were my design, Aedile," Marius replied, already losing his patience. It had been a long time since he was in a situation where it was acceptable for him to be questioned.

"Well, that may be. But why would we believe you are here to do anything but report back to them everything we say? That Glaucia...that fool...is the excrement of the senate house, if you ask me," Crassus said, a snarl developing on his lips.

"You'll find no argument from me. They are not my friends." Marius met the eyes of every man in the room to ensure they believed him.

I'm glad I wasn't asked for my opinion, because I *did* consider them friends, at least to some degree.

"You lost our support the moment you helped them take the law courts from us," Crassus said, speaking for them all.

Rufus watched passively but listened to everything carefully. Sextus plucked at a bowl of grapes, disinterested. Norbanus seemed bored out of his wits.

"What do I care about the damned courts? I needed support for my land bill, and they alone were willing to offer it. I had to offer support to them as well."

"When did you ever arrive at my doorstep asking for support? I don't recall such an event. They were my soldiers too, Consul. I trained them," Rufus finally said, his voice gentle enough to avoid provoking the consul's wrath.

"I am the consul of Rome. I don't go begging at doorsteps."

"You had friends, Marius, who would have supported you. Myself chief among them. But the moment you opened the doors to those men, you began alienating yourself from us," Norbanus said, speaking up for the first time, apparently listening closer than I had imagined.

"That's *Consul* Marius to you!" Marius was on his feet.

To my dismay, Norbanus jumped to his feet as well.

"You might be my consul out there, but you're my damned brother in here, and I'll speak to you as such!" Norbanus shouted, his voice the only in the room to rival Marius's. For a moment, I believed he had gone too far. But Marius reclaimed his seat, and so did his old friend. "I've wanted to help you. Gaius Caesar would have supported you. Rufus here, despite past difficulties, would have been the first to your aid. But with each passing month, we found less and less invitations to your home. Your inner circle excluded us. You did not join us at the baths. What were we to do?" he pleaded, and I believe the hurt in his voice was genuine. I did steal a glance at Gaius Caesar, and he seemed less certain if he'd be willing to support Marius again. Fortunately, Marius didn't notice.

"The past is the past. I cannot repair the vase once broken."

"Here, here!" Sextus said, raising a cup he had inexplicably acquired.

For a moment, I feared the conversation would be taken off course by Marius's hatred for the man, but if he expected them to forgive him, he must do the same. He wouldn't ask for their forgiveness either, so the best path forward was to simply mention it no more.

"Even now, the good men of the senate house would accept you, if you would renounce Glaucia, Saturninus, and their lot," Crassus said. He and Scaevola were staunchly in the Optimate camp, but at just forty years old, they were part of a younger generation that was desired to remain moderate, at least in the people's eye. I wondered if the old breed like Marcus Scaurus or Aurelius Cotta would ever welcome Marius into their camp. I'm certain Numidicus wouldn't.

Regardless, Marius hid the delight on his face as best he could. He straightened with pride, and nodded his head as if he were considering it.

The entire evening was beginning to make me sick.

"Consul Marius, for personal reasons alone, I should refuse to help you. In any manifestation. I shouldn't have allowed you into my home," Rufus began. His words were pointed and firm, but he spoke gently enough that Marius allowed him to continue. "I saved your life more than a few times in Numidia."

"By the balls of Mars!" Marius shouted, but the others laughed to make it appear a joke.

"We both know it. In Spain too. And you accused me of betrayal. I have ever been your friend. And even now, I would see you restored to good company. For the welfare of the Republic, we will do all we can to support you. Because you are the only one who can stop those Gorgons now." To my surprise, Marius nodded his head. This played to his pride, I assume. What about all that talk of ruling the Republic with the tribune and praetor? Had one clause announced without his permission really changed things so much?

I had half a mind to stand and say something, but I was aware that my career would be effectively ruined in that moment if I did so.

"What am I to do?" Marius asked, much out of character, and I began to wonder if the wine was causing him to act so strangely.

"You cannot swear the oath. Much of the senate house will follow your example either way. And the demagogues cannot persecute us all if we abstain," Scaevola said with finality.

"But it is my legislation, gentlemen. I want the veterans to receive their land, can't you see that?"

"Then do all you can to ensure they do. We will fight against that, I assure you, but you can still seek to give the land to the veterans while disavowing the illegality of this bill," Crassus said. I'm not sure I agreed with him. It sounded like political deception to me, but Marius was nodding along.

"Can you vow that I'll have the support of the other Optimates?" Marius asked, biting at his thumbnail again.

"We don't call ourselves that. But if you mean the good men of the senate, yes. I am certain," Scaevola said, speaking for all of them. I wasn't sure if he had the authority to do so from the look on Rufus's and Gaius Caesar's faces.

"Catulus, Marcus Scaurus, Aurelius Cotta...Numidicus?" Marius poised.

"You are the Third Founder of Rome, Marius! Even they would welcome you with open arms if you do what is right," Crassus said passionately, jumping to his feet.

Marius wasn't foolish enough to believe that. Was he? He couldn't.

But he remained on his couch, his feet tapping wildly.

Finally, he stood.

"I'll see what can be done. I must go."

"Hail Rome's consul, men!" Sextus Caesar lifted his cup, and for once, Marius didn't glare at him.

Marius exited, and I slipped out behind him, anxious to not be left behind for any questions they might direct at me.

After he had gathered Julia and woken the slaves who had fallen asleep beside his litter, he turned to me.

"Go and gather Saturninus and Glaucia. Tell them to meet at my house immediately."

"What?" I asked, stunned and perplexed by the enigmatic man before me. Was the whole evening a plot? "Are you going to report what they've said?"

"No…well, I don't know. But they'll be suspicious if I don't meet with them. Go."

Exhaustion washed over me like steam in the bathhouses. I couldn't stand the thought of another meeting like the one we'd just left.

I did as I was asked, and reported to the homes of Saturninus and Glaucia. But neither of them were home.

SCROLL XXI

THREE DAYS BEFORE KALENDS OF SEPTEMBER, 655
AB URBE CONDITA

I DRESSED BEFORE THE SUN. I was due at Marius's before first light,
but I stole a few minutes to visit Gavius's room. He was sound
asleep, with a clear conscience and nothing to be afraid of. I sat
on the edge of his bed, as carefully and quietly as I could. But he
did not stir. Children can sleep so soundly.

I combed my fingers through his hair and thought of what
Saturninus said of the babe Julius Caesar. I indeed hoped Rome
would be different by the time the children replaced us. I hoped
that Gavius wouldn't have to worry about where to lay his head
after he served his country in battle, if he ever decided to do so.
But I also hoped that land wouldn't have to be secured by civil
strife and gang violence.

Even then, such a wish seemed foolhardy.

But I would do what I could.

"Are you ready?" Arrea whispered from the doorway, her
slender figure illuminated like a goddess from the torchlight of
the hall.

I nodded in the affirmative and leaned over to kiss my son on the forehead.

"Bid me fortune."

"I'll pray to my gods and to yours today," she said, taking my hand.

I embraced her. She kissed my cheek.

As I turned to leave, she grabbed my wrist.

"Wait." She materialized my dagger from behind her back. She must have known I generally kept it strapped to my calf when I left home. And today was probably not the best time to forget it. I'd left it on purpose, though, because I feared I might actually have reason to use it. And I did not want to. "You should take this."

"Yes...I probably should." I relented and tied two leather straps around it and my calf.

"There's a smell in the air I don't care for, Quintus."

"That's probably the rural plebs," I tried to jest, but the concern in her eyes was unbroken.

"No. I want you to be careful today. As careful as you can be."

"I will return. I vow to you." I kissed her cheek, lingering as long as I could.

Unlike elections, votes for legislation were generally held in the Forum. The tribes voted one by one rather than simultaneously, so there didn't need to be as many gangways constructed, and the Forum could usually contain the population.

But on the morning of the land vote, there were rumors abounding that the location would be moved to the Field of Mars. Unable to substantiate the claims, Marius, myself, and our retinue moved on to the Forum. It was clear that the vote was still being held here, but we understood why the claims had been made. The mob was shoulder to shoulder as far back as the Regia. Never had the Forum been so flooded, even during Marius's Triumph, if it were possible.

There was a foreign element to the lot of them, and a massive gathering of soldiers as well, from all over Italy.

"Make way!" Marius's guard shouted, opening up a lane as best we could.

They parted reluctantly, but on either side, we were flanked by antagonistic voters. On the one side, veterans howled at us, obviously not noticing their commander behind the guards surrounding him. On the other, the urban plebs. One might think that a gathering of disgruntled, landless, grizzled old soldiers would be one of the most intimidating things a man could face in the Forum, but a drunken mob with clubs wasn't much better.

"Ay, who you voting for?" both shouted.

"You voting for the veterans, patriot?"

I broke off.

"Soldier! Stand at attention!" I shouted as I made a knife hand and placed it on the veteran's chest.

"Officers' afoot!" one of them shouted. Most of them straightened. Even drunk, they remembered the military training Marius had instilled in them.

"How I vote is my own damn business. As is everyone else's. Citizens don't answer to citizens. And that's what you are now—citizens—at least until you put on the Colors again. Understand?" I asked. They nodded in reply, but I could hear them begin again after I hurried to regather with Marius.

"Quite a display, Sertorius. Perhaps we should keep a lower profile for now," Marius said. I could tell by the milky hue of his face that he was nervous. Despite all the talk, I truly believe he had never anticipated his land reform would have attracted so many enemies among the people. Walking to the Forum that day, I'd have to say it was a form of identity crisis. If he wasn't "Marius, hero of the people," then who was he?

The closer we came to the *comitium*, where the voting would take place, the more and more outbursts we were exposed to.

"You want to take our land? Dirty cutthroats! Buy your own with the fortunes you took from the Cimbri!" some shouted.

"Pig spawns! To Hades with the whole damned legion!"

"If only the Cimbri were here to shut your mouths!" the veterans retaliated.

"Ungrateful half-men! We'll take your land and take your wives with us!"

The hordes rushed in, crashing against each other like waves on rock. Fists and clubs swung. Teeth and blood spewed in the air.

The guard and I rallied around Marius.

"This is disgraceful." The consul shook his head in disgust.

Ahead of us, I could see that the voting urns had been replaced by wicker baskets, presumably so they couldn't be broken as they had been during the grain dole vote. The regular voting *custodes* had been doubled, to ensure no one rushed the gangways. I doubted it would really be enough, if the mob set their mind to it.

Marius's guard continued to forge a path to the best of their ability, hands covering their faces to block the errant projectiles being hurled through the air. When we finally reached the roped-off section for senators near the comitia, we found those in attendance to be far fewer than expected for a measure so important. But who could blame them? Most were afraid of either the veterans or the mob, the Italians or the rural plebs. The brave ones simply might not have been able to make it through the crowds without a personal guard to make a path.

One way or the other, though, every senator was expected to meet in the senate house after the vote. The threat of exile loomed over any who dared to avoid attendance.

The few there gathered looked disheveled, their togas streaked with soot, their hair up in tuffs, their eyes wild with fear.

Some of them tried to address Marius, but not a word could be heard.

"People of Rome!" Saturninus began from the Rostra. Even with a voice as commanding as his, it took some time before he could be heard. When at last the crowds yielded to him, he was not greeted with cheers as he had been previously, but rather by silent anticipation. Saturninus's appearance was just as disheveled as the others, his toga pulled low over his shoulder and a bloody split in his lip. I could see that his knuckles were bruised and smeared with scarlet as well. He had never been a stranger to violence when it was called for. And sometimes when it wasn't.

"Today is the day. We will put this matter to a vote and then put it behind us. One way or another, this legislation will pass into law, and we will be able to return to peace and harmony. The fate of our Republic depends on it."

The people half-heartedly lifted up applause, but the frustrations they felt for those who disagreed with them in attendance was apparent. I'm not certain they would be prepared to let it all go if the vote didn't proceed to their liking.

"The voting order has been decided by lot. The tribe of Esquilina has been decreed by Fortuna to vote first!" he said to shouts from a particular gathering to the right of the *comitium*. The Esquilina was an urban tribe that most definitely would be voting against the bill.

The leading men of the tribe ascended the gangway in a hurry. They took no time to deliberate. How they would vote had been decided far in advance.

"You know, when I was a tribune myself, I passed a law that narrowed those gangways," Marius said, leaning close enough so that I could feel his breath on my ear.

"Is that so?"

"It was to ensure that voters couldn't be bribed or intimidated by the *custodes*. Such a thing could actually have been useful on a day like today."

"You don't regret it, do you?" I asked, but he had already turned from me and returned his attention to the voting tribe on the gangways above us.

They were handed a wax tablet with simply two letters scratched onto it. *V* to vote for the law, and *A* to oppose it, indicating "as things are."

They marked one way or the other and hurried to place their vote within the covered wicker basket.

"Stellatina votes next!"

One by one, the thirty-five tribes voted. The violence was subsided for the most part. There was nothing to be done now but wait for the votes to be tallied and read out.

Saturninus took to the center of the Rostra, and an ominous silence fell over the entire Forum. No one laughed, shouted, or even coughed.

The August winds seemed to pick up, and gray clouds materialized that I hadn't noticed previously.

The tribune accepted the scroll and straightened to read it aloud. He paused, waited, drew out the moment. He gave no indication of the results.

When some of the crowds began to murmur, he crumpled up the scroll and stepped to the edge of the Rostra.

"Citizens of Rome. Your voice has been heard. The legislation has passed with eighteen votes to the affirmative, sixteen—"

The reading was drowned out. Saturninus didn't attempt to continue. He hurried down from the Rostra and into the ranks of his guard. And immediately crossed the *comitium* to the curia, where he expected us to follow.

"Rally around the consul!" I shouted as his retinue came as close to the senatorial seating area as was permitted.

I took Marius's arm within my own and led him into the protection of his ranks. I stole a glance at him and couldn't see any inkling that he was pleased by the outcome. There was nothing but shock in his eyes.

When we entered the curia, Saturninus alone stood on the

senate floor. Some of the other senators were already at their benches, nursing wounds and crying aloud about the various indignities they had endured on their way there.

"Consul Marius, I hope you are well pleased." Saturninus approached and gave an unreciprocated kiss on either cheek. He took Marius's hands within his own and tried to force eye contact.

"The veterans have their land," Marius said, but it sounded like more of a question.

"You look like you've seen Medusa. Bring the consul some water," he shouted to anyone listening. I showed Marius to his curule chair on the dais, where he was to sit as the presiding consul over this meeting.

When I turned to take my seat on the left side of the curia, Marius gave me such a look that I will never forget, like he was begging me not to leave his side.

It took some time, but eventually, the senate house was filled to the rafters. Not a man among the three hundred who wasn't present.

And never had Rome's senatorial order appeared less august. Their hair matted with dirt and horse shit, togas stained with blood or ripped right off as the senators tore their way to the senate house. Some labored to breathe. The companions of old men like Scaurus and Aurelius Cotta attended to them with care and attention to make sure they wouldn't keel over from exhaustion or effort.

"Thank you all for attending. The people have spoken. The vote has been passed. Eighteen tribes have indicated that they want the veterans to receive land," Saturninus said, standing alone on the senate floor.

"Not true! Sixteen tribes voted against it. Eighteen indicated nothing, except that they demand their payment in advance," Numidicus roared.

Saturninus turned to him with a jerk, head tilting like a bird spotting prey, eyes locked with the former consul's. He paused and allowed the entire senate to wonder whether he would call for the guards to arrest the man.

"A legally sanctioned vote has been passed. The legislation is now law. You can bemoan that all you like, but you will swear an oath to defend this law, as you did when you first donned that damned toga." He pointed a finger directly at Numidicus. "It is time. No sense in delaying it any further. We'll retire from this sacred house as soon as possible so you can begin your plotting against me and about how to repeal this bill. But this clause is in effect whether you like it or not. The man who does not defend this law with his every breath will be expelled from the senate and exiled from his country. Stand to your feet, Senators. Vote now." There was malice in his voice such that I had never heard before. No more quips or jokes at the senate's expense. The full extent of his hatred was on display, and there wasn't a man in the curia who didn't realize it.

The majority of the left stood tall the moment they were asked to. Some of the known moderates did as well, but others wavered. The Optimates remained tentatively in their seats.

But all eyes turned to Marius, who was alone upon the dais.

"What will it be, Consul?" Saturninus asked, not anticipating an answer either way. But the way he approached the dais, with his hands locked behind his back and his chin high, he seemed to be daring the consul, his old ally, to provoke him. Even with half the room remaining in their seats, Saturninus made it clear he would follow through on the clause.

Marius's mouth was open, and he was breathing heavily. He stared at the tile beneath his feet, beads of sweat materializing on his balding head and upper lip. He tapped his feet. He rubbed his hands together vigorously in his lap.

In that moment, I had no idea what he was going to do. I stole a glance at Rufus, who appeared apprehensive but had hope in his eyes.

"Consul?" Saturninus said again.

Every eye in the senate house was on him, but he didn't seem to notice.

Then he stood.

"In that this law is really valid, I will defend it. With my life."

The Optimates roared, Rufus, Crassus, and Scaevola the most surprised and furious among them. Marius kept his eyes on his red slippers.

Saturninus exhaled and shook his head at the cowardly answer, but the moderates all jumped to their feet to take the oath as well.

The Optimates were scrambling. They tried to whisper to each other for direction, but more and more of them stood to their feet. Eventually, the entire senate house was standing.

Saturninus smiled in ultimate Triumph.

"Repeat after me: I vow to uphold this law with my life."

"I vow to uphold this law with my life," the senate house repeated in unison, with many of them adding "in that the law is really valid," like Marius had.

Saturninus lifted his arms and gestured around the room, as if to say, *Was that really so hard?*

But then his eyes locked, his fists clenched, and the veins of his neck bulged. He charged across the senate house and nearly jumped into the ranks of the Optimates.

He spotted what I had not. One man, alone, seated among the senate benches. With his arms crossed.

"You will not swear the oath to defend this law?" Saturninus asked.

Metellus Numidicus lifted his chin high, his lips curling like the smell of death had just wafted past him. "I will not."

Saturninus paced back and forth and considered what should be done. He ran his fingers through his coiffed and oiled hair.

"I am giving you one last opportunity, Numidicus."

Metellus stood to his feet. For a moment, I thought the fear of exile had overcome him. Perhaps he decided he could swear the oath as Marius had without losing too much face.

"I will not swear your oath. And I will not defend this law." He extended his neck, gesturing for the tribune to attack him, if he was so bold. "I will repeal this illegal legislation the moment I am able. And you, you have earned yourself not a seat of power in this august body, as you think, but a cell. There—" He gestured in the direction of the *carcer*, our state prison, across the senate house. "You've left us with no option but to give you that which all tyrants deserve. A rope."

Saturninus remained planted where he stood. He considered it. He met the eyes of the ex-consul as if the two were trying to best the other in a game of will.

Then he spun on his heels and hurried to the exit.

A few of the Optimates laughed and clapped old Numidicus on the back.

"Off like a dog, with tucked tail!" one of them said, chuckling. But Numidicus stared out at the door, not yet ready to celebrate.

"People of Rome!" Saturninus's unmistakable voice carried into the sacred senate house.

Every senator in the place stood and stampeded to the door, trampling one another to get out.

"There is one member of the senate who refuses to uphold the Roman law. He has proven today that his first and only allegiance is to his political party, to his plutocratic friends. He denies the process of our sacred constitution, even when reason and law oppose him. Therefore, I banish Quintus Caecilius Metellus Numidicus from the senate and from Rome!" he cried, forgetting the calm demeanor usually expected of an orator. Some immediately roared out in resistance, while others cheered wildly, thrilled to see one of the nobles out on his arse. Many stormed the ascending steps to the curia. The lictors, even binding together, were barely enough to stop them.

We flooded around Saturninus and watched helplessly as blood was spilt. The senators turned on each other too. I turned from fray to fray and tried to spot Marius so that I could protect him. Over the mass of swarming senators, I spotted him still in his curule chair, head bowed and hands in his lap.

"Stop! Stop! I demand you stop!" Numidicus surged to the forefront beside the man who was expelling him.

At length, the people halted and turned to hear him. Some out of reverence, some out of curiosity.

"I will not permit such violence on my part. I'll be going. Before first light, I'll be gone from this city. For, in time, Rome will come to her senses and recall me. And if she should not, it is better that I not be here."

He descended the steps without further delay, and the crowds parted before him as if he were a high priest rather than a man exiled.

SCROLL XXII

FOUR DAYS AFTER IDES OF SEPTEMBER, 655 AB URBE CONDITA

I HAD NEVER CARED for Metellus Numidicus or his haughty nature. But one had to respect his stoic display as he walked to the capean gate. He was followed by wailing mourners as if it were his own funeral. Throughout it all, he was said to have shown no emotion or concern, keeping his head high in the manner he was accustomed to, above all and untouched by the world beneath him.

It was a quite brilliant response to being exiled. And the point was received. Some began to wonder if Saturninus had made a martyr out of the old noble.

Saturninus wisely faded from the speaker's platforms for a while. Still, he didn't take any extra precautions. He went everywhere with an armed cortege, but he led from the front, with no weapon himself. He still sat outside the Basilica Porcia with the other nine tribunes each day addressing the concerns of various citizens.

Marius, on the other hand, went everywhere surrounded by his lictors and clients to protect him.

Had there ever been a more successful politician than Lucius Saturninus? He had earned all the praise for his legislation, and none of the blame.

When Marius wasn't walking about under an armed guard, he remained at home in ill humor. I imagined that he probably invited Rufus and his companions over for a drink to explain himself but they didn't attend. He likely invited Saturninus and Glaucia too, but the break between them was nearly complete. He remained secluded, and was resentful of it. But no one was surprised after Marius took the oath, or about the fashion in which he did so. If he had been trying to appease both parties, he had failed miserably.

I found myself emulating my old general. I remained at home as well. I tried to seclude myself as much as possible. I tried desperately to make sense of everything. What was my part in all this? What was my blame? What was I to do now?

I had never had a stronger urge to drown out the excruciating nature of existence with wine than I had at this time. I did all I could to avoid exposing Arrea and Gavius to it, so I'd wait up late at night and sit in my tablinum drinking the cellars dry and trying to commune with my father through his emotionless statue on the wall.

Of course, it was partially my own doing, but I felt utterly isolated. I had alienated myself from my family for the past year to serve Marius and his allies, and now the foundation of that alliance was collapsing. I could not trust Marius. His behavior was becoming erratic and reckless. I could not support the expediency and violence with which Saturninus and Glaucia conducted themselves.

I didn't know what I was to do now. My brother would have known, if he were alive. But I didn't. I searched each night for the answer at the bottom of a jug of wine, but found it empty each time.

Fortunately for all parties involved, there was a necessary distraction coming upon us. A Triumph—a naval Triumph, to be specific. Marcus Antonius had returned from his campaign against the Cilician pirates, and with him was my old friend Hirtuleius.

I needed his counsel as much as ever, but not as badly as Rome needed a festival. It was time that their mourning over Metellus was put to an end. Debating about the outcome and happenings of the land vote was quickly becoming out of fashion.

And everyone—no matter his allegiances, wealth, or status—enjoyed a Triumph. A simple reminder that despite the weakness constantly on display within our city walls, that outside them Rome still reigned supreme, a pillar standing over all the world.

Gavius was apprehensive to attend the Triumph, as one might understand. It could be a touch overwhelming for a child, especially one not raised in the bustle of the city. He did take some comfort in that his father was going with him this time, and that he could ride on my shoulders if he pleased, and this warmed my heart.

We packed in along the Via Sacra and were lucky enough to find some seating at the foot of Castor's statue at his temple. I had written Lucius while he was camped outside the pomerium and told him to meet us there. There was no way of knowing if he had received it, but I hoped he'd arrive regardless.

As the preliminary processions began, I hoisted Gavius onto my shoulders and pointed out things for him to see.

"You see those men? Those are the captives taken from the campaign."

"They're bad men?" Gavius asked, and I could hear empathy in his voice as the hordes pelted them with dung and spit.

"They were pirates. Made their living by sacking small villages and sinking ships, by selling free men and women into slavery."

He didn't respond for a moment, but I felt his grip tighten around my shoulders.

"They're getting what they deserve, then," he said.

Arrea and Apollonius chatted about the performance of the musicians and dancers as I gave a few sestertii to a small foreign girl in return for a few handfuls of rose petals we could throw at the victorious legions as they passed. But first passed wagons filled with ornamental ship beaks from the conquered Cilicians, along with oars and painted wood from their biremes.

When the commander's chariot finally arrived, Gavius let out a gasp I could hear even over the crowd.

"That's the general, my boy. He is the man who defeated the pirates."

"He looks like a god!" Gavius shouted.

"Today he is one. He wears the purple robes of Neptune. See how his face is painted red?"

The victorious legions passed behind the chariot, waving their swords in perfect unison, singing a ballad of their battles over the shouts of the crowd.

"Is that what you were, Tata?" he asked.

"That's right. I was a legionary just like them." I felt an unexpected tinge of longing in that moment. A desire to be marching under the standard again, with brothers. Men I could trust and rely on unto death. "And your uncle Lucius is among them."

"I have an uncle? I thought you were my only uncle?" His question was so honest that I had to laugh.

"He's something like an uncle. And I'm not your uncle anymore, silly boy."

The people cheered wildly when the wagons full of booty were opened and put on display. Marius might have saved Rome from the greater threat, but he returned with not a quarter of the spoils Antonius had. A few designated legionaries climbed the wagons and lifted up handfuls of coin, letting the gold sift through their fingers.

"Our coffers will overflow!" some of the citizens roared, jubilant as if the coin would line their own pockets.

The real surprise was when Antonius took to the speaker's podium and addressed the people for the first time. He said a few words in honor of his soldiers, and specifically highlighted the wisdom of his officers and legates that had allowed for such a hasty and successful campaign. Then he turned to address the pirates.

"The triumphator is by law given power over life and death of his conquered foes. And it is custom that he has them executed. But I will spare your lives." The crowds gasped, and the captured Cilicians wept for joy, falling to their knees on the stone roads, their chains jingling as they praised him. "However, I damn you to a worse fate. You'll all be sent to the salt mines in Macedonia." How quickly their tears of joy became tears of agony cannot be overstated. "So that you may begin to repay the debt that you owe to the Republic for your years of banditry and theft." He lifted his right hand in a gesture that his word was law, and stepped down from the podium without further commentary.

Rome's newest slaves were led away, fighting and clawing against the chains around their ankles and the whips upon their backs, as Antonius ascended the Temple of Saturn for the sacrifice of a bull. The sacrifice was always the pinnacle of the Triumph, but the people were far more determined to usher out the pirates with a display of hatred than they were to listen to the recitations of an old priest.

We ascended a few steps of Castor's temple for the best vantage point, and looked out for Lucius. I thought I spotted him several times before I finally did, but then again, legionaries look nearly identical from a distance, even with an officer's crest.

It was Arrea who finally spotted him, my old friend passing through the crowds slowly, happily accepting a kiss on the cheek from many swooning Roman matrons.

"Lucius!" we all shouted until he spotted us. His eyes were wild with excitement by the time he found us.

"Citizens, what a glorious day!" He summoned up his best Marius impression as he embraced me with a kiss. "And if it isn't the prettiest girl in Rome. Venus herself." He embraced Arrea warmly.

"Cease and desist, you silly man." She blushed as Lucius turned his gaze to Apollonius.

"You're still alive, then?"

"The gods have kept me around so I can school you in the art of manners, young man." Apollonius offered a hand, but Lucius wrapped his burly arms around him instead.

It made me so happy to see us all together again.

"Gavius, greet your uncle as we've practiced." I gave Gavius a push forward as Lucius squatted to eye level.

"Thank you for your service to Rome, Uncle," he said bashfully.

"A handshake will do just fine." His massive sunbaked hands enveloped Gavius's tiny white ones, and then he ruffled the boy's hair. "I'm not sure about 'uncle,' though. Volesa always had a keen eye for me, I believe. Perhaps I'm the boy's real father?"

"Don't confuse Gavius any more than he already is!" I laughed. "My son, the first rule with Uncle Lucius is to not listen to a word he says. Understood?"

"Understood," Gavius replied, not perceiving the humor in our voices.

"So, what does Rome's returning hero have planned for such a day?" Apollonius asked.

"Wine. Song. A game of dice. We'll see where Bacchus takes me."

"Returning to our back-alley tavern, then?" I asked. Lucius shook his head vigorously.

"You heard Apollonius! I'm a returning *hero*. That's no establishment for heroes. Besides, the old shops are offering free drink for all soldiers today."

"Ha! There it is. That's what I was looking for. Well, lead the way, *amicus*," I said, but I saw the smiles evaporate on the faces of my family.

"I'm not feeling well, Quintus. The frenzy of these parades gets my head spinning." Arrea rubbed her hands together.

"I can see her home, friend," Apollonius said with an old man's smile.

"I can curtail my indulgence. I assure you." I reddened.

"That's not it, Quintus," Arrea replied, but I could hardly believe her.

"Surely, it's no place for a young lad like the young master here," Apollonius said, patting Gavius's back. "Besides, it will give the two of you some time to swap war stories."

"If you insist." I accepted that they wouldn't be swayed, and kissed each on the cheek. "Gavius, you'll protect Arrea and Apollonius on the way home, won't you?"

He nodded, accepting the commission like a centurion's order.

"Let's go, then," Lucius said, tainting me as always with his cheerful demeanor.

"I'd say we should go find Equus, but there's no chance in this madness," Lucius shouted over nearby laughter as we approached the old shops. "One for me and another for my friend here." He gestured to a slave who was rushing from man to man with an amphora filled to the brim and a few cups clutched beneath his arm.

"Free for you. He pays," the slave said, nodding to me.

"What? This man's the real soldier! The Hero of the North.

Ever heard of him?" Lucius objected as the man appraised me blankly. "Never mind, lad, I'll pay."

"I'll cover it, Lucius," I said, but my friend was already sifting through a thick coin purse and handing a few pieces of copper to the slave.

"To our reunion," Lucius said, passing a cup to me.

I had wanted Arrea and Apollonius to come with us, but now that I tasted the warmth of that wine, I was glad they hadn't. It quenched my thirst and abated the heat of the day, but I knew it was just the beginning.

Lucius immediately began regaling me with stories of sea battles and land assaults. He beamed when he spoke of his commander, Marcus Antonius.

"Now that's a real Roman. He'll make for a damned good consul, if I had to wager," he said.

"And will he run for consul?" I asked.

"He intends to. Or so I've heard."

"Well, if he can command the senate house the way he commands the fleet, he has my vote. We certainly need it," I said.

"So, tell me, Senator, how has Rome been treating you since I left?" Lucius asked.

There was no room for seating, so we squeezed in among other patrons and propped ourselves up alongside an old column.

"It's been a right mess, *amicus*. Certainly you've heard?"

"Only that old Numidicus got sent packing. That must have been quite the sight." Lucius chuckled as he tried to picture it. It occurred to me then that he had been gone for a very long time, on one campaign or another, and couldn't possibly understand the ramifications of this.

"It was one of the strangest things I've witnessed in Rome. To say the least. The man went without any sort of objections. Even his closest associates could do nothing but watch in surrendered silence. I think the retaliation is yet to come, though."

"It seems your boys have really backed them into a corner.

Perhaps the nobles have finally learned their place." Lucius took a sip. A few drinkers sauntered over to offer a word of appreciation to Lucius for his service to Rome.

"And where is that, comrade? Where is the nobles' place?" I asked. This sort of rhetoric was common in camp, so I'm not sure he realized how inflammatory a statement like that could be in the city.

"I don't know." Lucius shrugged, momentarily distracted by an attractive Greek girl across from us. "At the whim of the people."

"That's a dangerous place to be, and I'm not sure it's best for anyone involved."

Lucius turned to me with a furrowed brow.

"Surely from the letters you've written and the conversations we've shared, you stand for the rights of the people? I can't imagine you aligning yourself with those old prigs?"

"You have it right. I stand for the people, but"—I stalled by gulping at my wine and smacking my lips to savor the taste—"I've seen firsthand how fickle the people can be. How they only care for their own desires."

"Well, it's their desires that matter most, isn't it? The majority. The many over the few."

"The people's *desires* and the people's *needs* are not always reconcilable. And many aren't wise enough, or willing enough, to see what they truly need. The grain dole bill for example. Looking back, I see that the people pushed for the bill because of the immediate gain it brought them. But with some foresight, they might have sided with the nobles who opposed it."

Lucius puffed out his cheeks and shook his head. "You've lost me."

"The people choose expediency over long-term strategy, that's all I mean. There's a reason why democracies like the Athenians' never work. That's why we're a Republic, so elected men can make decisions for the betterment of the people and the state, over generations."

I could see he was starting to lose interest, but perhaps he simply wanted to avoid conflict. "I never did read Plato, despite your incessant pestering that I do so. Surely, the nobles vote for their own betterment rather than the people's, most of the time?"

I gestured for a refill of wine, and this time, I was quick to pay for it myself.

"That's true. It's not the system that's broken, though, it's the character of the nobles themselves."

"It will take more than a few legislative reforms to fix that, I'm afraid," he said as a drunken lady approached and gave him a kiss on the cheek.

"You're right about that. But it's the only thing that will work, I believe. Sound minds and clear consciences from those in the senate house. I'm not sure how else Rome can be saved."

He ignored his pandering fans for a moment and turned to me, completely vexed.

"Is Rome really in need of saving?" I took a drink and declined to respond. "Still having trouble with old bald head, then?" For all his reverence of Marius, he enjoyed a good jest at the general's expense, like the rest of the legionaries, just as long as the general wasn't around to hear it himself.

"He's changed, Lucius. Before my eye. He has become... He's been..." I couldn't articulate it properly. Even if I could, I'm not sure he would have understood. Lucius's was a simple loyalty, a special dispensation that soldiers have over politicians. "And his friends have pushed too far. They're committing—"

"Surely, you aren't talking about me?"

I turned to find the Praetor Glaucia directly behind me, his famous grin upon his lips. I wondered how long he had been there.

"Praetor, it's a pleasure."

"Always a pleasure when Rome is triumphant, right?" He gestured to a massive gathering of his clients behind him, who all roared their approval with lifted cups. "Another round for these two, on me," Glaucia shouted to the nearest slave. Lucius declined to mention his wine was free, but Glaucia probably already knew this.

"This is my friend Lucius Hirtuleius. We grew up together in Nursia and have served together ever since."

He leaned forward and shook Lucius's hand with both of his.

"What's next, Legionary, now that you're home? On to your next campaign, or perhaps you'll follow your friend's footsteps into Romulus's shithole?" Lucius looked perplexed, so Glaucia clarified: "Politics."

"Oh, not me." Lucius shook his head vigorously. "I'll spend a few days going where the wine takes me, and then to wherever Rome needs me most."

"Now that...that is a politician's answer," Glaucia said, amused with Lucius. He slurred his words as if he were drunk, but his eyes revealed he was more sober than he let on. "Would you mind if I stole your old friend for a moment?"

"By all means." Lucius gestured, not knowing what he was consenting to.

Glaucia took me by the shoulders and led me away a few paces.

"I've been wanting to talk with you," he said.

"You know where to find me." I shrugged and took a sip of wine.

"I don't, actually. Geography has never been my strong suit. I'm directionless outside the Aventine," he replied, but I had trouble believing him. "Our glorious consul has been acting strangely, has he not?"

The break between Marius and his former associates seemed to be real, but I had learned by then that politicians could be extraordinary actors. I wasn't going to be tricked into betrayal, if that was his cause.

"He's been concerned by recent events, to be certain."

Glaucia smiled, and the muscles in his jaw flexed.

"He looks at us with wild eyes, like we're painted Germans hiding behind bushes in an ambush set for him."

"If I'm to be honest, Praetor, one can hardly blame him. That stunt Saturninus pulled...with the clause and the exile—"

He cut me off. "We've done only as we set out to do. It's Marius who has changed course. It is Marius who has become squeamish."

"He believes he's been left out of the decision-making. He believes his wise counsel has been ignored."

"He said that, did he?" Glaucia's eyes widened.

"I'm not here to spread rumors, Praetor Glaucia. I offer only my interpretation, if it be of any use."

He nodded his head and clicked his tongue.

"Of course. Of course. But you must know that Saturninus and I have followed through on the stratagem we all laid out from the onset. Our consul has become jealous, and there's nothing more to it," Glaucia said.

He continued to perform as if he were drunk, but I had spent enough time around the inebriated to know these were calculated words.

"I don't think we can speculate about the consul's feelings."

At last, he rolled his eyes, losing his patience.

"I speak for Saturninus when I say that we hope we still have your support. We know you're Marius's man and all, but we hope that your prior service under him doesn't blind you to what needs to be done."

I looked over my shoulder to ensure Lucius was still there. If he'd made eye contact, I would have gestured for him to intervene, but, as always, he was in the midst of an innocuous conversation with a few strangers.

"I am not Marius's man, or Saturninus's, or Glaucia's. I will support whomever I believe is right. I don't swear oaths of fealty to men, only to Rome."

Glaucia seemed perplexed by the answer, and in response, he dropped the drunkenness charade. His eyes sobered, and they locked with mine.

"So, you will no longer support us?"

"I will do as I see fit. I believe in much of what the two of you have set out to do, but…the expediency with which you conduct yourselves… The violence it has caused… The widening gap it has created between the people, the equestrians, the senate…"

Rage flashed in his eyes, but it quickly abated. He was far too collected to give himself over to an argument when he could perceive my mind was made up.

"Well, if you won't support us, I'll have to look upon you as my enemy. You understand that, don't you?" he asked.

I looked down and shook my head. I was saddened to hear that, but I understood it. I had come to enjoy the praetor, and the tribune, too, for that matter, at least in some manifestation.

"I do. I wish it were not so."

"Saturninus and I would welcome you back into the fold with open arms if you should ever change your mind." He placed a hand on my shoulder, and the smile that materialized on his face didn't appear contrived.

"Praetor, I hope that one day soon the two of us can gather at the bathhouses or over dinner and enjoy each other's company without the need for plotting political machinations."

He extended a hand, which I accepted.

"If I should ever begin to believe in the gods, I shall sacrifice to it." He placed a hand on my neck and pulled me to him for a kiss on the cheek.

When he left, I returned to Lucius.

"Well, he was a cheerful fellow! If that's what all senators are like, it can't be that bad!" Lucius said, his eyelids drooping from the wine.

For the first time, I realized how my hands were shaking and my heart was beating.

"I'll take another." I gestured with a raised cup, rubbing at my temples with the other hand, wondering what I had just done.

SCROLL XXIII

TWO DAYS AFTER KALENDS OF OCTOBER, 655 AB
URBE CONDITA

I ATTENDED the meeting of the senate alone that morning. I
hadn't the time or the energy to congregate at Marius's, so I
reconvened with the others in the *senaculum*, and hoped I
wouldn't be drawn into any more conversations with my political allies. The consul, now reaching the last days of his consular
year, arrived late surrounded by a cortege of lictors and
bodyguards.

It appeared from the sullen look on his face that he and I
were the only two senators not pleased to be there that morning.
Everyone else busied about shaking hands and smiling. There
was an air of joviality and goodwill that surrounded us.

When the doors of the senate house were opened, I found the
senatorial benches crammed full. Everyone was in attendance. I
hadn't been aware ahead of time, but I began putting the pieces
together from bits of overheard discussions. Today would mark
the announcement of the candidates for the upcoming elections.

"Conscript Fathers, before we begin, let us welcome home
our triumphant general, Marcus Antonius," Father of the Senate

Scaurus began, and the house erupted into applause. Finally something everyone could agree on, both sides of the curia stood to their feet and clapped their hands. Marius was the last to stand, and his praise was lackluster. I could see the jealousy burning in his eyes.

This time last year, he had been the triumphant general. He stood alone at the pinnacle of fame and power. He alone the people loved; he alone the senate revered. And how quickly things had changed. Now he must share his position with Rome's darling of the day. And it was eating at him.

"That's enough," the consul said from his dais, cutting them off and gesturing for silence with two hands patting downward. "We have many matters to attend to."

As we began in dull order attending to various matters of public policy and procedure, it occurred to me that Marius was much less natural at leading from the dais than he was leading from a warhorse. He covered up for it when he had revolutionary aims and could turn the floor over to Saturninus, the superior speaker. Now, he groaned on about the taxation of certain provinces in Asia Minor, and the potential recall of the pro-praetor in Macedonia.

He knew that, as soon as procedural matters were put to bed, the bids for next year would be announced and his term as consul would be as good as over. His sixth term as consul, might I add. And from the look on his face, he had no intention of running again, mercifully.

"I cede the floor to Marcus Scaurus," Marius said when he finally retook his seat.

"The elections will be swiftly upon us. It is time once again to announce candidacies. By order of *cursus honorum*, we'll begin with quaestor."

Starting with the junior magistracies, each hopeful candidate rose to his feet and was allowed, in his turn, to give a short speech discussing why he was the man to support.

There was a great deal of laughter when Saturninus stood for quaestor.

"Will you be taking a step back, dear tribune? Perhaps that's wise," Scaurus asked, wiping a tear from his eye. Saturninus joined in the laughter at his own expense.

"I think not. I am announcing the bid of a dear friend of mine. Gaius Saufeius will be standing for quaestor once again, to continue the good work he set out to do for our state treasury." The bonhomie immediately ceased, and Saturninus retook his seat.

The plebeian tribune candidates stood next. Saturninus once again rose, slowly, as if for dramatic effect. The other men waited until he spoke. He gestured to each one in turn, but no one could find their voice.

"I announce another bid for a companion of mine." A wave of relief flooded through the curia. "Lucius Equitius. Many of you do not know his name, but I assure you that you shall. He is a faithful son of the Republic, and just as importantly, he is the rightful son of Tiberius Gracchus. And it is time he claims his legacy as a leader of the people." He turned to sit but hesitated. "Oh, and I also will be running for reelection as tribune of the people. I have no intentions of letting you noblemen drag me through the courts. Not yet, at least." He smiled and crossed his legs as he retook his seat. There was no need for a speech. He knew no one in the room, aside from his compatriots, would be supporting him. And they all knew what he stood for.

The candidates for praetor were much less divisive. Leery eyes watched Glaucia to see if he, too, would stand for reelection, but he remained in his seat and watched others with passive interest as several made claims about repealing all he had done in his year of office. Standing ovations were offered to every man who promised to give the law courts back to the patricians, or return the grain dole to full price. Glaucia smiled and nodded. Unsurprised.

And he remained that way until it was time for the consul-elects to stand. He joined Marcus Antonius and a few other esteemed noblemen. Every Optimate jumped up with outstretched hands and lifted cries.

"Are you all running for consul too?" Glaucia asked with raised brows.

Some of them returned to their seats; others continued roaring their disapproval. He nodded affirmingly to each of their pleas and waited his chance to speak.

"I, Gaius Glaucia, of the Aventine Hill, tribe of Collina, will be running for consul."

"No. No, that is illegal," Marius shouted as he took to the floor. Jaws dropped around the senate house, and everyone silenced in disbelief. "A man cannot be praetor and consul in consecutive years. You must first become pro-praetor and leave to govern your province."

Glaucia let his head fall back with a bellowing laugh. "Now I've seen it all! To be lectured on the legality of consecutive terms of office by a man who's been consul for six straight years is a bit like receiving instruction on the institution of marriage from a temple prostitute."

It's difficult to convey the response this quip received. The entire house shook with hysterics. Senators grabbed their knees and literally rocked with laughter, some grabbing at their sides and others tearing up.

Even the noblemen who just moments before had been cursing Glaucia joined in on the fun at Marius's expense. Sulla and his cronies found this particularly hilarious.

Marius tried to speak a few times, but he was drowned out. His gaze darted about wildly like he had discovered himself in a dream, naked in the Forum.

"I have been—" he began, but was silenced by fresh waves of hilarity spreading throughout the sacred house.

Mottling red spread across Marius's face, and he clenched his jaw. In defeat, he returned to his dais, and slumped. One would almost feel sorry for the man if men like Glaucia hadn't been born of his efforts.

The laughter continued, but I couldn't join in. Not for fear that Marius would see—even his closest companions and most loyal allies were guffawing all around him.

But because I knew it was all over. The break was complete. There was no going back now.

I didn't seek out Apollonius or Arrea when I returned home. In fact, I handed my toga off a slave at the door and walked as quietly as I could to my tablinum to avoid them, and shut the door behind me. What would my father do in this moment? I could hear his advice: "the best retreat for a man is within his own mind."

I sifted through some papers until I found a well-worn copy of Zeno and unraveled it on the table before me.

"Do you need anything, *dominus*?" one of the girls asked me.

"I would appreciate some wine, thank you," I said.

I read the words: *to be like a rock with the waves crashing around it. It stands unmoved and the raging of the sea falls still around it.* How fortunate, I thought, that the great philosopher Zeno wasn't forced to wade through politics. The waves were much fiercer and the sand beneath you less firm when you stood in the senate house.

I accepted the amphora of wine and poured a cup for myself. I tried to read on, but quickly gave up and placed the scroll back with the others.

I slumped in my chair. I drank my first cup with little water, and quickly, so that it might take the edge off. When I didn't feel the effects quickly enough, I poured another and did the same.

Perhaps Plato was the reading I needed today. I found some

of my favorite sections and began reading through the old lines as if I didn't have them memorized. I found Plato's *Republic* to be so irreconcilably different than the one I now helped run that I put it aside as quickly as Zeno.

Perhaps something comical? I had to search a bit further through my archives, but I found one of Terence's comedies. I poured another cup as I read the lines of *Eunuchus*, but none of the jokes seemed funny.

I gave up trying, my thoughts too innumerable and their contents too unpleasant to focus on anything else. I felt like Marius owed me answers. As to how this had all happened. As to what came next. As to what I was supposed to do now.

Clad in nothing but my tunic, and without an invitation, I strapped on my sandals and headed from Marius's domus. The sun was just beginning to descend over the hills in the west when I reached the Palatine, the effects of the wine beginning to set in.

Marius's doorman seemed surprised to see me.

"Is the *dominus* expecting you?" he asked.

"He probably should be," I said, stepping through the threshold without invitation. A few slaves bent to remove my sandals and wash my feet, but I moved past them.

I could hear Marius's voice coming from his peristylium.

"Damn it, Gaius, I don't care if you enjoy your studies or not. It's expected that you learn how to speak properly, and learn to speak you shall."

"I've tried talking with him, Father, but he won't listen. Archidemis says he's a terror to the other boys in class, distracting some and bullying the others," I heard Granius voice in response as I neared.

"I don't have the time or patience to deal with this. Gaius, listen to your brother as if he were me. Do you understand? If I hear of this again, you'll get the whip."

"You won't whip me, Father. Please don't say that," Marius's youngest replied. "Archidemis is an old fool, he drones on—" Gaius the younger halted midsentence when he spotted me.

Marius glanced over his shoulder and gave me a look whose meaning I couldn't discern.

"Out. Both of you."

"Good evening, Consul," I said as I entered. I could hear the contempt in my own voice and made a note that I'd have to be careful about how I proceeded. I wasn't even quite sure the purpose of my visit by the time I arrived, but I could feel myself on the brim of an outburst. I knew drinking as much wine as I had before leaving was foolish, but I found myself searching to see if Marius was already partaking so I could join him.

"I'm done with Saturninus and Glaucia. For good this time," he said, leaning his head back against a scarlet-painted marble column.

"That's convenient, since they've already exiled your worst enemy and given land to your veterans," I replied without thought.

Marius sprung to his feet and across the peristylium to me like a slinger's rock. "You'll mind your damn tone in this home, you ungrateful wretch!" he roared.

"I apologize," I said, looking down and doing the best to ignore the finger in my face.

After a moment, his posture relaxed and he patted my shoulder.

"No need. That's why I've always liked you, Sertorius. You're honest. You tell me the truth, not like these other sycophants that surround me for favor, speaking with honey lips and poisonous intentions." He recomposed himself.

"I spoke out of turn, Consul. I've not been in a good way."

"You either, eh?" He chuckled. "Volsenio, bring us some wine. I'm going to show you how a real Roman drinks." He gestured for me to sit beside him on an old wooden bench. He noticed me appraising it. "This was built from the wood of ships I brought back from my campaign against the Balearic sea people. Antonius squashes a few drunken pirates and thinks he's a general. Bah! The Balearics, now those bastards could fight." We both accepted a pewter cup of wine, and he clanked his against mine.

"We've got a real problem with our former associates," I said, taking a sip and relaxing instantly.

"That we do. And I don't know what is to be done. I can't be seen to openly oppose them, not yet, at least. I could lose support among the people and my veterans," he said as if he hadn't already.

"We've created a Hydra. If we cut off one head, another will grow to take its place."

He seemed disappointed that I didn't respond to his comment about the veterans. "Do you really think my men favor Saturninus over their old general now?"

The consul said he favored me because of my honesty, but it was impossible for me to be completely forthright about that. Recent events revealed how he would respond.

"Never. They wanted land, and he took point on acquiring it. That's all. Now that he has nothing left to give them, what will they look to him for? Do you think they care about who judges the courts or the grain dole of a city they never set foot in? When things settle down, they'll cast their gaze back on the man who has always supported them." I spoke to convince myself as much as Marius. It's true, they would always love Marius as their general. But they had heard about the pensive manner in which he'd vowed to protect their land bill, and they wouldn't be forgetting that soon.

He grinned like a child and nodded his head as if he had already known this.

"What do you suppose should be done about them? Go after them and hope that the people will see through the facade sooner than later? Or perhaps I should send a message that I am not to be trifled with?" he asked. He seemed to be anticipating a particular response, as he had to his previous question, but I wasn't sure what the desired answer was.

"If you do go after them, you'll certainly alienate some of your supporters. And you'll need support from somewhere. Who do you suppose will give it?"

He shrugged, but his smile faded as he considered it.

"Rufus will forgive me in time. He must know I was put in an impossible situation with that oath. On Jupiter's Black Stone, I had no other options."

Recalling the faces of Rufus and his compatriots when Marius stood to swear the oath, I doubted if they would ever be reconciled.

"Gaius Memmius, perhaps? He's a popular man, a devoted servant of the people. His followers are noticeably less vocal than those of Saturninus and Glaucia, but they're just as many. If he is elected as consul, he could protect and support you, and your name could lend weight to his cause."

Marius ignored my comment altogether. He stared into his fountain and his eyes glazed over.

"You know, if things get any worse, I may have to run for consul again myself. The people may ask me to restore order." He turned to me to appraise my response. Now it was my time to ignore him. "I won't run unless I'm asked," he said with an exhale.

"*Dominus.*" One of his slaves entered and kneeled before us.

"What is it?"

"I bring word from the Forum. The fake son of Tiberius Gracchus has been arrested on your orders."

Marius leaned back and crossed his arms.

"Good. That should send the message."

Perhaps, up until then, the Republic could have been saved. Marius could have assuaged his old friends and they could have been brought to reason with a show of goodwill and some compromising. But not after that. The fate of Rome had been sealed with the consul's stamp.

SCROLL XXIV

THREE DAYS AFTER KALENDS OF OCTOBER, 655 AB URBE CONDITA

I WOKE up trying to put the pieces of the last evening together. I was hungover. Well, hungover doesn't quite cover it. It was something more akin to dying, with a heartbeat that seemed to compensate for a hemorrhage.

The smell of poppy and oleander filled my nose, nauseating me, and I realized I had fallen asleep in a peristylium. I blinked the cobwebs from my eye and looked around, thankful that it was my own garden rather than Marius's. Then I remembered ambling home late the night before after an evening of drinking wine and swapping old war stories with the general.

"You're up. I hope there wasn't a meeting of the senate this morning. If so, you've missed it. It's nearly midday," Arrea said, feeding the birds.

"What? No...I don't think so," I replied. I searched my mind to recall if there had in fact been one or not.

"You look a fright. We were beginning to worry about you. We all stayed up until at least third hour to ensure you made it home safely, but I believe everyone was asleep by the time you returned."

"I'm sorry I kept you up." I sat up and leaned against a column, rubbing at my throbbing eye until stars streaked behind the lid.

She knelt beside me and plucked a twig from my hair.

"You're unwell, Quintus."

"I know that. All of this business with the senate...it has become untenable." I brushed off my tunic and accepted a cup of honey water from a slave who noticed the state I was in.

"No, it's more than that. You aren't the man I remember. I know you've done your best...but—"

"But what?"

She thought about it, and a sad smile split across her face. "I miss the man who rescued me in Gaul."

"I do too. I shall let you know if I find him."

She seemed displeased by the answer, exhaling through her nostrils and shaking her head.

"Arrea, I've been back a year now..." I took her hands in mine and bade her look at me. "Will I ever have your love again?"

She met my eyes. "The man I knew as Quintus Sertorius could have me. But you are not yourself."

I clenched my jaw in frustration. I couldn't blame her. How could the man waking up midday in his own garden be the same man who'd scaled the walls at Burdigala or saved a dozen prisoners in a war camp?

"How can I get that back, then?"

"I think you already know," she said, although I didn't. She rubbed her soft hand on my knee. "I think you should go see a priest."

"I'll sacrifice some spelt wheat and grapes at the household altar."

"No, Quintus, really. I think a priest might do you some

good. They say your Romans gods can offer healing, just like mine do."

"I thought you found the Roman gods silly?"

"Well, they certainly are, but I don't see a temple to Belenus around here, so you'll have to make do." She smiled, and despite my splitting headache, I found myself doing the same.

"If it will make you happy, I will visit a priest sometime."

"When?" she asked, head tilted. She already knew me too well. She was like an intelligence officer, the damned woman. She knew I wasn't going to go unless she pressed me.

"Today, of course. Otherwise, they might run out of birds to sacrifice."

She patted my leg and stood. "That's it. Make sure to wash first, you have a bead of dried drool across your cheek."

"You Harpy." I laughed, rubbing at my cheek to find she was telling the truth.

It had been a long time since I had visited a temple for anything other than a public festival or a meeting of the senate. I wasn't keen on the idea. The whole process was as monetized as a transaction in the Forum, and I didn't quite believe in the prophecies of goodwill that always resulted from the sacrifice of more expensive animals.

But if it would make Arrea happy, if it showed her I was trying to be the same person she remembered, I would do anything.

I avoided the major temples of the Forum. I had no interest in running into another senator, or some candidate-elect who was canvassing for his magistracies by a public display of piety. Instead, I made for the Temple of Asclepius by the river Tiber.

I halted before ascending the well-worn steps, attempting to summon up the courage—no, patience—for interacting with the priests. I appraised the dilapidated columns with chipping scarlet paint as I rehearsed my objections to inquiries for excessive spending.

Exhaling, I took the first step and allowed momentum to carry me the rest of the way. Before I reached the top, I was hit with a wave of nostalgia. When was the last time I'd stood here? It was when I'd come with Marcus Caepio, both of us not much more than boys. We'd talked to the begging veterans and those seeking a blessing from the god of healing. How different things had been. I wondered what had come of Rabirius, the friend I had made on those old stone steps, after I had earned for him and his friends a position on the *evocati*.

"Come in, my child," a voice carried from inside the temple along with the smell of burning incense and coals on candelabra.

As I entered, I spotted several parishioners on cots around the room, all praying fervently. Some were coughing; others were missing limbs or had boils on their flesh. One was bloated with dropsy.

"What can we do for you, my child?" the same voice rose from a priest by the altar of two intertwining snakes. He tended to the coals with a poker and wiped his hands on his toga before turning to me.

"I've come to make a sacrifice," I said, kneeling and bowing my head.

"And what is the purpose of this sacrifice?" I looked up to see kindness and concern in his eyes, as if he could feel my distress before saying a word about it. "Your eye?" he continued when I did not.

"No. It has healed very well."

"May I ask the cause?" He placed both of his hands over mine and beckoned me to stand.

"Slinger's rock in a battle."

"You have much to be thankful for. If it drove any deeper, you wouldn't be here to ask for healing, would you?"

"No, I suppose I wouldn't." The chants of the sick and afflicted around me seemed to increase in volume.

"Do you know much about the god you wish to commune with today?" he asked.

"I know that he heals the sick," I replied, although I had never seen a miraculous healing from those who attended this temple.

"He was a son of Apollo. History says he was the greatest doctor who ever lived. While he was alive, no man died. They say he could even bring the dead back to life."

Visions of my lost companions flashed before me: Titus, Flamen, Pontius, Bear, Scrofa, Marcellus... If Asclepius was this powerful, I wondered why he had abandoned us.

"And thus he angered his great uncle Pluto. He was robbing the underworld of its citizens, so the god of the death went to his brother Jupiter and demanded a solution. Jupiter then attempted to kill his own grandson, but Asclepius cheated death, and has forever remained as a constellation in our skies." He gestured to the heavens above us. I wondered what this history lesson could have to do with me and considered a polite way to say I'd like to pay him for a few chickens and leave. "When you look up to the stars in the sky, my child, remember always that there is healing available to you. Sometimes for wounds of the flesh and other times for wounds of the heart."

I looked up and met his gaze, his eyes slightly narrowed as if concentrated on something within me I couldn't see myself.

"How much for a chicken? Or will Asclepius require more?" I asked, removing the coin purse from my belt.

"I can see that something is troubling you, my child. And I can understand why when I see the senator's toga you're wearing. I will cover the cost. You may make a donation by the door if you wish to do so." He gestured to a man in the shadows of the room, and he pulled a chicken with a silly little laurel and a ceremonial cloak from its pin.

He allowed me to leave then, but I felt unable to move.

Perhaps I was just waiting for the catch, or maybe there was something I did actually want to say.

"How does one discern the will of the gods? For his life, I mean. How can one determine how to live well?"

He chuckled and rubbed a hand over the sunspots on his bald head.

"That's an interesting question, and one that can't be answered easily. Many priests in Rome will tell you that you can only determine this by the entrails of bulls or the flight of birds. I'm inclined to say most of us already know the will of the gods."

"All due respect, Pater, but that is unhelpful. I don't know the will of the gods. Otherwise, I wouldn't be here." He must have sensed I had something else to say, so he waited. "I'm not sure I even believe in the gods anymore, to be honest." I spoke quietly, ashamed. I expected an immediate tirade of appalled insults, but he nodded and placed his leathery old palm on my arm.

"Do not worry, young man. The existence of the gods is not predicated on your belief. They exist or do not exist independently of our thoughts, despite what the *flamen* of the Forum might tell you. And if the gods do exist, they could only want one thing, in my estimation. If they are just, they would desire us to be just. Selfless too, and honorable. If you want to discern the will of the gods for your life, look to the single action before you. If you're faced with a trial, what would they seek you to summon up in response? Courage, fortitude, patience, wisdom? If not these, then what? That is the will of the gods. To do as they compel with each day they allow us to remain here."

"That sounds like something Zeno might have said," I replied with a grin, finding myself far more comfortable than I had anticipated. He placed a finger to his lips and winked.

"Just because I'm a priest doesn't mean I don't know my philosophy. The gods desire strong minds, do they not?"

The cock was taken to the altar behind us, and a different priest recited a prayer as he placed the knife along its neck. It fell limp with a flow of blood that was drained into a bowl without so much as a cluck.

I nodded my appreciation, and I genuinely meant it. I wasn't offered specific direction, but the priest had affirmed what my father had always taught me so many years ago.

"One last question," I said, turning back to him. "Would you ever believe the prophecy of a Syrian priestess?" I asked. It had been quite some time since I'd considered my meeting with Marius's prophetess, Martha. But her claims on my life had remained at the back of my mind since I'd exited that tent.

He clicked his tongue and raised his eyebrows. "I'd imagine the gods have chosen even stranger ways to reveal their nature in the past. Why?"

"I was instructed to speak with one when I was on campaign... Never mind. It was probably rubbish. She said I would return home to my wife, and I would love her alone and always. It came to pass that she had taken her life before I even set foot in Italy."

He nodded as if he had discovered the answer I was looking for.

"Prophecies have a way of mystifying us until we can look on them with hindsight. One only has to consult an oracle or the Sibylline books to see that. Perhaps the priestess was right. Perhaps the wife she spoke of simply wasn't the one you believed you were returning to."

He stepped forward and placed a gentle hand on my forehead. He inhaled deeply and recited something under his breath.

"Go, my child. Your sacrifice has been received. The god of healing bless you."

He turned again to the serpentine altar and lifted his arms in prayer.

I placed my entire coin purse on a podium as I exited.

SCROLL XXV

IDES OF OCTOBER, 655 AB URBE CONDITA

ALTHOUGH THE PRIEST had improved my spirits, Rome itself wasn't improving in the slightest. Saturninus and Glaucia had bodies of citizens roving the streets everywhere "campaigning" for them, or rather threatening and intimidating to ensure their respective elections to tribune and consul.

Speeches were given from the Rostra, from the platforms outside of the Temple of Bellona and the Temple of Castor and Pollux, where all of the candidates for office staked their claims on the future of the Republic. The rhetoric was increasingly inflammatory, and to good effect. The one side swore they would repeal every piece of legislation passed that year, the other vowing to maintain it and to propose more of the same cloth.

And the people responded in kind. Brawls in the street became commonplace. Rumors of lynchings spread like a fire in the subura, and tattered bodies were certainly discovered in increasing volume, drenched in blood and morning dew. The causes of their deaths were rarely determined, but everyone believed political stance was the dagger that slew them, their opinions the noose around their necks. Some Republic that my brothers had fought for, that my brothers had died for.

It was in this climate that we attended a meeting of the senate on the ides of October to discuss the procedures of the upcoming elections. I remember the day clearly because I dictated the events to Apollonius the moment I returned home, and have reflected on that document many times since.

The consular elections had been repeatedly delayed since July, as they often were, to give the governors a chance to return from their provinces. Marius, who was a figurehead in delaying the votes, was simply trying to stall before another man was called consul, if I had to guess. That, or privately he hoped the people would ask him to run again and restore order to the Republic.

The meeting was held in the Temple of Castor, where seating was always more difficult to find. I found a spot beside Cinna and the consul's old friend Norbanus, who was finally attending the senate again. Marius generally gave me a nod to indicate where he'd like me to sit, but he was too busy glaring at his former associates. He was so preoccupied by the rebuke Glaucia had given him a month prior that he even forgot to sneer at Sulla the way he usually did.

"I've got a horrible toothache, I can hardly think for the damn thing throbbing so," Cinna said, kneading the flesh of his jaw.

"You know there's a dentist in the shops beneath this very temple. They could remove it as quickly as Pan," Norbanus leaned over me to add.

"And pay another to do what I can do myself? I think not. I'll take a dagger to it myself if I can fit the thing back there," Cinna replied.

Chatter at the start of a senate meeting was common, but I couldn't help but believe this was the kind of discussion that was born from nerves rather than a genuine interest in discussion. And who could blame them? I was nervous too, not for any particular reason but because the air was thick with unpleasant spirits. The only difference was I had a habit of clamming up like a Sicilian shellfish when I was uncomfortable.

The priest, clad in vibrant ceremonial robes, began his prayer. All parties of senators pretended to listen, but it wasn't difficult to see that their focus was elsewhere. The priest had hardly finished his recitation when Marcus Scaurus was on his feet.

"I thank you all for coming today," he said. "December is swiftly approaching, and we need to deliberate as to the procedure. It appears as though the consular elections will be delayed until the nones as well as the remaining elections, so we'll need to ensure we have everything planned in advance."

To me, and probably to everyone else, it seemed as if this was the kind of thing that could wait another month. As the only non-magistrate who had the capacity to call a meeting of the senate, the old noble Scaurus took advantage of this as often as he could find a reason to. And he was too senior and respected for anyone to fuss about it.

"The elections will have to take place on the Field of Mars— both elections, I mean. That requires no explanation. The Forum —no, even the capitol—will not have the capacity to maintain the expected number of voters," Scaurus's ally Aurelius Cotta stood to his feet and added.

"Very well. We'll vote on it to ensure every member of this august body feels the same, but I have no doubt you are right, good Cotta. Now, the question remains, which election shall come first?"

This was the sort of senatorial meeting that could put a man to sleep. Despite the anxiety surrounding us all, there were a few drooping eyes around the room, including the senator with the toothache beside me. Everyone was well awake when Marius stood from the dais.

"Before we move forward any further," he began, puffing out his chest and lifting his chin high, putting on airs of confidence and resolution I could tell weren't really present, "I think we need to discuss our candidates."

"That matter has already been settled, I believe, Consul," Saturninus said from the tribune's bench.

"I don't believe it has. It isn't settled until I say it's settled, right? I'm still consul of this place." He waited for a response, but no one offered anything. I could tell from the posture of the room that there were several waiting to respond if he said the wrong thing. "Gaius Glaucia was a praetor this year and cannot run for the next. I am putting forth a formal ban for his election."

I cringed. The popular party gasped, and Sulla and the Optimates offered sinister smiles. They no longer had to fight the Populares; we were devouring ourselves.

I lowered my head and closed my eyes but felt the full-bodied Glaucia stand from his curule chair across the room.

"And I shall ignore it." He retook his seat and crossed his legs, unconcerned.

"You cannot ignore it, Praetor."

"Oh, I certainly shall, or I'll spend my last two months as praetor preparing a lawsuit against you for corruption, greed, and treason! Your multiple consecutive stints as consul attest to that! It won't take a talented orator to reveal that to the judging equestrians."

The nobles were rocking in their seats and clapping. Cheering for neither party but certainly enjoying the spectacle.

"You threaten me in this house, and I'll have *you* tried for treason!" Marius roared, his composure evaporating before our eyes. He stormed to the foot of our benches and stretched out his left hand.

"I invite you to do so. But as a friend, one who has not forgotten the alliance we so recently shared, I implore you to not throw away the legacy you worked so diligently to build. I assure you, your name, tarnished as it is now, can only get worse with such ignorant pursuits."

"Gentlemen!" Saturninus shouted as he jumped to his feet,

lifting his sinewy arms and demanding the floor whether it was offered to him or not. Marius was steaming, too preoccupied with Glaucia's challenging glare to notice. "This is unnecessary and unproductive. There will be no trials for treason among two men who have fought so diligently to serve this glorious Republic."

"And for that matter, you shouldn't be permitted to run for office either." Marius's outstretched hand turned to the tribune. "Is there anything more illegal than creating a monopoly around the sacred position of people's tribune?" The Optimates bellowed their approval as men were wont to do during a play at the theater, rapturous with the destruction they were witnessing.

Saturninus smiled and stepped closer to Marius on the temple floor.

"I can think of a few men who have done this well, and for the good of the Republic. Tiberius Gracchus comes to mind, or have you forgotten how highly you praised the man in the confidence of our company?"

A collective gasp rose from the entire company. Popular party or not, to tie yourself to the Gracchi brothers was synonymous with treason. They had been killed and thrown in the Tiber for a reason, their names now only uttered in whispers. Saturninus was so entrenched, it was no surprise to hear him claim such a thing, but a Roman consul? If the senate could be convinced this was true, Marius could have faced a trial.

"You lying wretch. That's untrue. Take it back," Marius replied, stunned.

I lowered my head, fearful that someone might see the truth in my eye, for I was the only one who had received the letter from Marius about Tiberius Gracchus. He didn't explicitly offer his approval of the revolutionaries' actions or indicate he would follow in the man's footsteps, but the tone was accepting, at least to my appraisal.

"I'll not. You said it. It's true."

"How could any of us be surprised?" Cato Salonianus was on his feet. "The actions of all three of these reprobates before us have proven they are forged from the same ilk as the revolutionaries who have come before." Sulla no longer had to discourage his overzealous friend. Instead, he and the others applauded him. "If it were up to me, each and every one of you would be tried for treason! You'd end up in the *carcer* along with that wretched freedman you've bolstered as the son of the demagogue!"

"You'll have to wait awhile, dear Cato, for we will be elected again. I assure you." Saturninus adjusted his toga and smiled, welcoming more accusations.

Every senator in the temple jumped to their feet, shouting out in an indiscernible crescendo of curses. I alone remained in my seat. I slumped over and rubbed at my temples. The tumult continued for some time, no one ceding the floor to anyone else. There wasn't a man in the place who had thought of something other than this election and this moment for months, and everyone demanded to be heard.

I scratched under my eye patch and tried to drown out the noise. I did my best to summon up pleasant memories. Training horses on my father's farm, training with the legions on the Field of Mars, holding Arrea under a makeshift tent in the Gallic wilderness.

But it was the priest who entered my mind.

If you're faced with a trial, what would they seek you to summon up in response? Courage, fortitude, patience, wisdom? If not these, then what? That is the will of the gods. To do as they compel with each day they allow us to remain here.

I jumped to my feet before I could overthink it.

"I demand the floor!" I shouted. The roar of the senators continued, but they were beginning to lose steam. "I demand the floor! I demand the floor!"

"Conscript Fathers! This display is unbefitting. I ask that you retake your seats!" Marcus Scaurus shouted as loudly as his years would allow.

Several took their seats.

I did not.

"I demand the floor!"

"We need to put this matter to a vote! I move that Glaucia and Saturninus both be barred from candidacy!" Marius bellowed, but even with the voice of a commander, his words were drowned out.

"I demand the floor!" I repeated.

I didn't have the time or patience to consider Marius's claim, but, of course, he would have been unsuccessful. With the mob listening intently by the door, there wasn't a senator brave enough—at least now that Metellus was gone—who would have voted to bar these men from the elections. Especially not at Marius's behest, with the irony so thick.

"I demand the floor!"

Norbanus and Cinna, who had already taken their seats, were tugging at my toga.

"Sit down, lad," Cinna said.

"You can't do that, Sartorio," Norbanus said, shaking his head sadly and drastically misremembering my name.

I shrugged them way. I knew what the gods wanted me to do. My heart was pounding, my hands sweating, my mind surging. But I knew what the gods wanted me to do. I knew.

"I demand the floor!" I roared once more, but this time, the senators were quiet enough that the echo rang throughout the temple roof.

"Who do you think you are?" the old noble Catulus asked with a scowl.

I had met him briefly during the war against the Cimbri, but he must have forgotten. I looked in his eyes and tailored my response to him.

"Who am I? I'm the damn Hero of the North." A few others began to speak, but I cut them off. I learned to sound off under the standards of the legion, and I was stronger than the men trying to tug me back to my seat. "I demand the floor!"

"Say your piece, then!" Scaurus shouted, exasperated.

"You should all take a bow. Bow, all of you," I said, looking around at each senator throughout the temple. "Take a bow, for you're all marvelous actors. There has been no such performance throughout the theaters of the Forum for decades. Really, I beg you, take a bow." No one complied. "You stand and derail the men across from you. You claim to know the answers, as if some divine prophecy has presented you with the answer to this Republic's chronic illness. Yet I have yet to find a man among this august body who truly embodies all that is Rome, a man who knows how best to proceed from here."

"And we can assume that you are the one-eyed oracle who will show us the way?" Crassus shouted. Many on both sides of the temple belted out laughter, but I ignored them.

"Do I know the way forward? Not at all. I've attempted to analyze this from every angle, and there is no easy path. But the one thing I do know to be evidently true is that we *must* lay down our arms. We *must* stop the escalation before this goes further. It will take both sides of the curia, or this temple, to restore the Republic to its true glory. Reconciliation is the only means for progress."

"And what is a man to do when he feels personally insulted by the actions of another party? Where is the honor in reconciliation then? Should insult mean nothing now?" Pompeius, still stinging from being thrown in the *carcer*, stood to his feet, and Sulla nodded along as he spoke.

Surprisingly, in the silence, no one else howled for me to sit down. I wouldn't have, regardless.

"Both sides have legitimate cause to feel grievance. There isn't a senator in this place who does not feel he has cause for revenge. Let us take it some other time when the fate of our Republic is not at stake. Our constitution is fragile, Conscript Fathers, and so is the state. Let us move forward together, as best we can. Only unified can we address the issues thrust upon us by circumstance and foreign entities. Only unified can we reconcile the people to ourselves to create a wholistic state."

They waited for me to continue, but I had said all that I felt implored to, so I returned to my seat. There was mild applause in response.

When the meeting was concluded, several men moved past me. Norbanus and Cinna, who were closest to me and therefore the most complicit in my display, ran away like I had the plague. Marius exited the temple the moment the priest finished his prayer.

There were a select handful of gentlemen that came to me directly, though.

"I agreed with much of what you said today, Senator," one of them said, offering a handshake.

"I applaud your display today, Hero of the North," another said with a bit more humor but the same amount of consolidation.

The consul-elect Gaius Memmius was one man in particular who came to see me as I descended the temple steps.

"What you said today is what I have tried to say for so long yet have not ever been able to articulate as clearly." When he shook my hand, he did not take me by the wrist but by the bicep, to express his deep affection and trust of me.

"I thank you, Senator. I said nothing but what I felt I had to."

He closed his eyes and nodded all-knowingly.

"I know you did. Sertorius, I've been watching you since the moment you entered the senate house. Others may have protested you speaking the way you did today, but I've been waiting for you to do so for a year. You and men like you are the antidote to the plague Rome is infested with. Please..." He paused to consider how he would continue. "Do not let anything —be it the mob or the senate—keep you from speaking truth the way you did today."

"I will do my best, Senator," I replied, careful not to break eye contact with an honest man.

"At first, I did not approach you because you're Marius's man. Later, I did not because I believed you to be complicit with the actions of men like Saturninus and Glaucia... Now..." He tightened his grip around my arm. "Now I regret that. I will say this: if you've need of a friend in the *shithole of Romulus,* you need look no further. I would be honored to have your support, and support you in turn."

"Thank you, Senator," I replied honestly. There was much more I wanted to say, but I was too taken aback to find the words.

By the time I found my way home, the adrenaline that carried me through the senate meeting had evaporated. I ambled into the doors of my home and slumped against the wall as my slippers were removed and my feet were washed. Exhausted or not, my mind was singular.

The moment I was freed, I made for the peristylium. It was empty. I hurried to the kitchen and found it likewise. Then the triclinium, then my tablinum, both empty. I summoned up the courage and made for Arrea's room.

I pushed back the collapsing door and found her standing by a mirror in the corner, humming a tune and brushing her thick brown hair.

She spotted me in the reflection before her.

"Quintus?" She turned to me, lips split and comb dangling in the tangles of her locks.

I said nothing but moved forward.

Without thinking, I wrapped my arms around her waist and pulled her in, as close to me as another can be.

She remained rigid, like I was hugging a statue, for an indescribably prolonged moment.

Then she melted into me.

Without delay, without permission, I pulled away and pulled her toward my lips.

"I love you," I managed to say before plunging my lips back to hers.

She pulled away, her breath heavy. "I love you more."

SCROLL XXVI

IDES OF NOVEMBER, 655 AB URBE CONDITA

MID-NOVEMBER BROUGHT on the Plebeian Games. It was a time of celebration when drunken revelry was not only tolerated but encouraged. It was the perfect distraction for Rome's people, and the perfect excuse for more displays of public aggression. By the ides of November, the election was less than a month away, and although there were still speeches to be given and promises to be made on behalf of the candidates, it felt as if the die had already been cast. The parties stood in such stark opposition to one another, it seemed foolhardy to believe anyone could be swayed from one side to the other, especially after the hefty sums of bribery that were rumored to be swirling about the city.

But the games gave me an opportunity. I knew where Saturninus would be during the games, and for once, he wasn't likely to be surrounded by petitioning plebeians or a mob of guards.

And I wanted to talk with him.

I made my way to the Circus Maximus, dodging the horse-drawn carts of those hurrying to make it before the races were concluded. I knew from attending the games as a child that the tribunes, who sponsored the games, had their own booth to overlook the crowds. I wasn't technically supposed to have access, but the infamous tribune was the sort of gregarious fellow I believed would allow me entry if pressed.

And that was the case.

"Oh, do let him in. The senator is an old friend," Saturninus addressed the guard by the entrance, who reluctantly stepped aside and pulled back the rope to allow me to enter. "Come and sit by me. The next charioteers are said to be some of the finest the Blues and Greens have to offer. If I was a gambling man, this would be the race I'd be wagering on."

"And you're not? A betting man, I mean?" I asked, finding that my knees felt weak as I approached the tribune and took a seat.

"No. I certainly gamble in life but rarely on the games. I tend to only make calculated bets on events where I can guarantee the outcome."

"That explains a great deal," I said, waiting for an opportunity to deliver the rehearsed speech I had been preparing for weeks.

"Why have you come to see me, if I might ask?" Saturninus was unable to wait for a response, as the game's host shouted for the tribunes to stand. He and the nine other tribunes of the people jumped to their feet and basked in the love of the crowd. Saturninus continued to stand after the others sat, and I believe the volume of cheers only increased. "Go on," he said when he reclaimed his seat, an infectious smile spreading across his face.

"I want to talk to you about our current circumstances, and your role in it. I believe—"

"By the gods, Sertorius, I have missed you by my side." He interrupted me and slapped my shoulder. "Get this man a drink, won't someone? He's the Hero of the North, for Mars's sake."

A slave brought me a decorative chalice, and Saturninus lifted his own for a refill.

"To the people," he said, lifting his cup. I hesitated but obliged and lifted my own.

"To the people. Now, as I was saying—"

"You know, Sertorius, there is no one in Rome I would rather discuss politics with than you. I truly mean that, you understand? But I'd prefer it if we could wait until this race is concluded." He nodded to the racetrack where the participants were lining up. "The Blue team is expected to win by a large margin. Every gambler in the circus is wagering on it. But I'm pulling for Green. I do so enjoy watching the weak devour the strong—an upset—the unlikely victor."

"As you wish, Tribune," I consented, and resigned myself to watching the race.

Over the course of my time with Saturninus that past year, I had come to believe there were a great many events he could foresee before the rest of us. Outcomes he could anticipate when the most brilliant minds in Rome could not. Such as how the people would react to certain legislation, or how the senate would respond to increasingly revolutionary tactics. Perhaps he had a similar intuition on this day, for the champion of the Blue team scraped a barrier on his final lap, and his wheel went soaring into the lower stands. One of the champions of the Green team sped past him and crossed the finish line with time to spare.

Saturninus clapped along, pleased with the outcome, as many of the other tribunes groaned and questioned their slaves about how much they had just lost.

"Even a middling poet could turn that into an epic. This victory shall be carried down through the ages."

I analyzed the tribune and found myself utterly perplexed by him. How could a man appear so careless when half the world stood against him, when his failure would likely end in a trial and exile? How could the same man who harangued the most august body in the Republic—the man who had thrown senators into the *carcer* and a former consul into exile—sit so pleasantly and enjoy the races without concern for the future in which both he and the Republic hung in the balance?

There was something in the way he blinked that indicated he might have been indulging in wine more often than he normally did, something I could understand with the amount of pressure he was under. Otherwise, he was as cool as a breeze off the coast of Naples.

"I think I shall take my leave for the evening. I'll see you gentlemen for the finale tomorrow," Saturninus said.

"Tribune, I was rather hoping we could talk."

He turned and nodded his head. "Yes. Let's. Would you mind to walk home with me, Senator?"

I considered it but then signaled that I would.

He turned to the nearest slave. "We're going to take this amphora and the two cups, if that's permissible. It's a dreadfully long walk back to my domus. I shall compensate you threefold at first light." He tossed a few coins to tide him over in the meantime.

The slaves looked among themselves but said nothing, so Saturninus began his descent from the tribune's booth with the wine, and gestured for me to follow.

Outside the circus, hungry beggars swarmed us like a pack of angry bees. Saturninus wasn't disturbed. He took out a coin purse, emptied it into his hand, and then threw the coins up in the air, gold pieces raining down all around us.

"Have a drink and something to eat on the good tribune Saturninus!" he shouted as the beggars dove to the ground to scrounge up what they could. He turned to me and whispered, "Cheapest votes a man can purchase, if they can make it to the elections."

As the crowds of beggars rushed behind us, Saturninus's massive guard caught sight of him from across the way and hurried to him.

"Are we moving you to your domus, Tribune?" spoke one who appeared to be in charge.

"I think not actually." He turned to me and placed a hand on my shoulder. "Senator Sertorius will accompany me. You men are dismissed for the evening."

The rough man rubbed at an old scar on his forehead and considered it.

"Perhaps we can follow at a distance. It's unsafe for you to be walking alone."

"I'll not be alone. Nothing will befall me with the Hero of the North by my side. Will it, Senator?"

"I won't let anything happen to you as long as I can help it."

"See? You can protect me from my enemies, but Sertorius can protect me from my enemies *and* my friends. Thank you, Torquatus."

He brandished the last few coins he still had and passed them along.

"What is it you wish to discuss, my dear friend?" he asked as we set off on the Appian Way toward the Esquiline, a cup of full wine in his right hand and the amphora in the other.

"I wanted to discuss with you your actions before it's too late."

He leaned forward and peered into my cup.

"Let me refill you." He paused to pour wine to the brim. "So, what is it exactly that concerns you?"

I chuckled.

"Where to begin? There are a great many things."

"So, my actions are why you left my side? I did something to offend your sensibilities?" he asked, taking a sip and smacking his lips.

"I never left your side, Saturninus. I was never fully on it. I made it clear from the onset that I would not stand for what I disagree with."

He smiled sadly. "Well, that's disappointing to hear. I thought we were the closest of friends."

"We were… We are… I simply don't know how I can support your bid for tribune once again if you plan on continuing the violence into your next term of office."

He nodded as I spoke.

"The way I see it, I do not bring violence. That has never been my intention. I meet force with force. If my opposition would lay down their arms, I would order my followers to do the same."

"Someone has to do it first, Tribune. Someone has to take the first step toward restoring order in the Republic. I know your heart, Saturninus, and I beg you to do the right thing."

"You know my heart?" He seemed to dwell long on those words. "You know my heart."

"I believe I do. Yes. You're a good man, Saturninus. Of that, I have no doubt. But what you are doing... What you and Glaucia are doing... It could bring ruin to Rome."

He considered it and finally showed some opposition, but still with some understanding.

"I disagree, Senator. I believe Rome is already in ruin. When the governing body can no longer be controlled by policy, something more must be done. I've systematically—and legally—outmaneuvered them at every turn. So they've turned to aggression in order to stop me. You would advocate that I lie down and allow them to undo all that I've done?"

"No, but perhaps an act of reconciliation could save us from escalating bloodshed. You have that power, Saturninus, and I'm inclined to say you're the *only* man with that power."

He nodded his head and puckered his lips in consideration.

"I see. Again, I disagree. I don't believe there is anything I can do now to reconcile my followers with the senatorial order. My own people would believe me a traitor, and the nobles will always hate me for what I've done to them." He turned to me, his eyes fixed and face as stony as the death masks on a patrician's wall. "And I will always hate them for what they've done to me."

"For personal vengeance, you would destroy the Republic?"

We turned left before the Via Latina and continued our ascent to Saturninus's domus. He paused only to refill his wine and

gulped thankfully, for the heat of the afternoon was still oppres-
sive despite the nearing arrival of winter.

"When I was removed from my office as quaestor, and my
wife was stolen from me...everything changed in an instance.
You say you know my heart, but you did not know me then. I
still had dreams and aspirations, Senator; I always have. I looked
around this indulgent city, I gazed into the eyes of the corrupt
oligarchs, and I desired change. But I had all that I wanted in my
life. I dreamed of a family, of a son who would bear my name,
mourn my death, and carry the torch I lit in this life."

"Saturninus, that is still an option. There are eligible ladies
throughout the city who would rejoice at the prospect of a
marriage proposal, at carrying your heir."

He closed his eyes and slowly shook his head.

"I made a vow to one woman, Sertorius. And I've never
desired another. She may have forgotten that vow, but I have
not. I'll take no other wife. Besides, recent events make me
believe she'll be left a young widow." He chuckled.

"But, Tribune, if you would only—"

"May I continue?" His gaze pierced through me. Despite his
calm demeanor and persiflage, I could tell there was anger
boiling beneath the surface as sure as the cauldrons beneath the
bathhouses. And he wanted to be heard. I nodded my consent.
"When I lost her, I knew things would change. This life would
not offer me what I desired most, but with nothing to lose, I
could offer what was desired most from me. By the gods, by the
furies, by the people...I could do what others could not."

"There is still more to lose, Saturninus, I assure you," I said.

He continued as if he did not hear me.

"And I made a vow that one day I would be the most
powerful man in Rome. That one day, my statues would stand
tall across Italy and my face would be minted on currency
throughout the Republic. So that when the rich men Licinia
married would give her what she most desired, she would be
looking at me. I was determined to be the most powerful orator

in Rome so that I may even alter the way in which Romans speak. So that when her lover whispers to her each night, she might hear my voice in those words. I even wished that I would become so powerful in this life that, upon my heroic death, I might be immortalized and added to the gods on Mount Olympus. So that when she says her prayers each morning, even then, she would have to be with me."

We were nearing his domus then, and he drained his wine and swirled the amphora around to see how much remained.

"I did it all for her, you know?" he said, his words beginning to slur as he looked at me sidelong. Then he laughed. "No, that's not true. I did it for me." His house came into view, and he propped up on the door when we arrived. "I did it for the Republic." He sobered, straightened, and narrowed his eyes. He spoke in the past tense, which confused and concerned me, but I assumed it was the wine. "Understand?"

At length, I nodded.

"Is there really nothing I can say to talk you down from the ledge of this Tarpeian Rock you're creating for yourself?" These were the most hostile words I could have spoken to him, given that the Tarpeian Rock was reserved for traitors, but I was running out of options. My stomach was sinking and my chest tight. I was genuinely saddened by his resistance to reason.

"I'm afraid not, my friend."

"So you'll continue to bring violence and bloodshed into the Forum? You'll continue to bribe voters and pose threats against your rivals? You'll continue to push divisive legislation through with force and coercion?"

He poured the remainder of the wine, giving it a shake to ensure the last few drops found their way into his cup.

"I will."

"Then I am sorry, friend, but I must oppose you. In whatever capacity I am able."

He met my eye and nodded.

"I understand. I would have opposed me too, probably.

Perhaps when the nobles take everything from you, you will feel differently. I cannot be certain—and I hope I'm wrong—but I believe there will come a day when you will wear my toga. A day when you'll wish to better Rome and you'll have nothing left to lose, and you'll go after the oligarchy with every means at your disposal."

"I don't believe that is true," I replied more confidently than I really felt. As I said, Saturninus had a habit of being right in his predictions.

"As I've said, I hope I am wrong." He turned to the entrance of his home and hammered the door ring three times. "I'd invite you in for dinner and another drink, but I suppose you shall decline?"

"I would."

He set the empty amphora down by his feet and extended a hand. I accepted it.

"May Rome never corrupt you. May you always be the better man."

"Farewell, Tribune," I replied sadly.

He entered when the porter opened the door, and I turned to leave.

The two of us would never shake hands again.

SCROLL XXVII

KALENDS OF DECEMBER, 655 AB URBE CONDITA

"IT WILL BE FINE, Quintus. Don't be afraid," Arrea leaned in close and whispered in my ear. I pulled her in closer and smelled her hair. It had a calming effect on me—it always did—something like the effect of flower petals when enjoying a picnic in the field.

"I know it will be. I know," I recited to myself.

"You've been preparing for this day for so long, my young friend." Apollonius smiled and took my hand.

"And you've helped me do the preparing." I smiled at him, hoping to comfort the old man the way he comforted me, for I could see his hands were shaking. "Write down as much as you can. I'll want a record in case I'm called to account for what I say."

"I'll be watching you," Gavius said. I knelt and took his little hand in my own.

"I hope so, my son. Cheer for me, will you?"

"I am proud that you're my *tata*," he said, shifting like he was as nervous as I was.

Gaius Memmius descended the Rostra before us, the crowd still roaring its approval from every direction.

"That's my signal." I kissed them each and made my way across the *comitium*. I paused at the foot of the steps and spent a moment focused on controlling my breath.

I had prepared for this moment, hadn't I? I had bid my time and bit my tongue for over a year since I became a senator. And now it was time I address the people I served.

I placed one foot on the tufa limestone steps and let momentum carry me forward. I'd stood beneath the Rostra and watched an orator speak on many occasions, but never did I have a clue about how vast and expansive the view could be from there. The Temple of Castor lay in the distance, then the busy Via Sacra, and I could even see as far back as the Regia. Umbrella pines lined the roads, along with the carts of bread makers and the mats of snake handlers, priests walking in single file waving bells to ward off evil spirits. I must have been too busy staring at my feet to notice all this when I'd been hailed Hero of the North. An overcast shadowed most of the faces, but I could see thousands of eyes fixed on me in anticipation.

And everywhere in between, the Forum was filled with blank faces, waiting to hear what I had to say.

I tried to speak, but nothing came out at first but a moan low enough that thankfully no one could hear. I became aware of the growing silence.

I adjusted myself and straightened my toga, pretending I was waiting on silence, as I had seen great orators like Saturninus do on many occasions.

"Citizens of Rome! My name is Quintus Sertorius, born of Nursia, a Sabine. Tribe of Quirina. I am a senator of this Republic." Many in the crowd turned to one another and whispered. They were likely asking who on Gaia's earth I was. "Oftentimes, people have called me the Hero of the North." Apollonius's notes mention a pause for prolonged applause here. "I have not accepted the title for myself, however. I served faithfully in the north, as many of your brothers and fathers did, as some of you did. And I have yet to see a man serve under the standard who should not be hailed as a hero."

The crowds roared their approval and gestured for others around them to echo the cry. I nodded my head and felt a surge of energy pass through me as I had never experienced before, not even in battle.

"And for that reason, I stood to give land to our veterans. I would do so again, and I will always do so, to ensure that the men who serve us share in a small portion of the glory they've given us. We can truly never repay even a portion of what they deserve."

I knew many of those beneath the Rostra had voted against the bill, but even they chanted along with the others, "Rome! Rome! Rome!"

"In so doing, you know that I supported the tribune Lucius Saturninus and the praetor Gaius Glaucia. I considered them my friends. On many occasions, we dined together. We shared a cup. We laughed. I've met their families."

Some in the crowd anticipated that I was about to voice my support for the revolutionaries. Many cheered, but others booed.

I lifted my hands to indicate that I would like a chance to finish. At length, they complied.

"But I cannot support their measures now."

"Traitor! Traitor!" some in the crowds shouted, no doubt the same men who were lynching Populare antagonists in the streets.

"I have betrayed nothing," I said, addressing the faceless hecklers in the crowd. "I would welcome them into my home even still, if they would halt their forward march into oblivion. But I cannot support the violence they have brought upon this Republic. I cannot stand in defense of the division and civil strife that is growing over this eternal city daily like a foreboding cloud!"

Most of the crowd cheered, but I wasn't yet content.

"And many of you are the very individuals who have been

the purveyors of that violence. There are those who stand here before me today that have spilt the blood of his friends simply because they have differing opinions on the direction this Republic should proceed in. And I beg you—all of you—lay down your arms! Unclench your fists. This is no time for the Republic to devour its own children. Fighting in the north, I know how close we were to experiencing the death of our Republic. We cannot now inflict this destruction on ourselves!"

I had heard other orators say that well-timed tears could be useful when imploring the people to a certain course of action, but I felt myself stifling them as best I could. Despite my best efforts, water welled up in the corner of my eye.

"If we continue down this path, if we continue to follow divisive men who seek to tear our citizens apart rather than bring them together...this Republic will fall. The glory of our forefathers will be as a memory, as shrouded and covered by the sands of time as the once-great Troy. We will be a memory, a cautionary tale spread to the children of royal families in faraway nations so that they might not commit the same errors we have.

"But Rome was meant to be more!" I continued. "The gods have orchestrated our glory from the day Romulus and Remus were suckled by the wolf; from the moment Lucius Brutus overthrew the kings; from the day Scipio brought an end to Hannibal of Carthage; from the moment Gaius Marius saved us from sure butchery at the hands of the northern invaders!"

When I paused briefly, the silence of the crowd was nearly deafening. Were they listening intently, or were they losing interest? The only path forward was to continue, one way or the other.

"If my former companions are elected to the tribunate and the consulship, they will have a power unrivaled by an ambitious man in the annals of Rome. With Saturninus's control of the assembly and Glaucia's authority of consul, there is nothing we—you the people, or those in the senate house—can do to stop them."

"Traitor!"

"Saturninus is twice the man you are, cyclops!"

I approached the ledge of the Rostra, aligning myself with the two statues flanking it. Those cries gave me renewed resolve.

"You may call me what you like. But let me make this clear." I raised my hand as if taking an oath, and increased the volume of my voice like I was forced to do in battle. "Let no man say that I allowed personal allegiances to overcome the best interests of the state."

With the exception of a few hidden hecklers, the crowd erupted into applause.

I had to fight to make myself heard. "And that is the disease that is festering within the very heart of this Republic! We follow ambitious men, men with names and illustrious careers behind them, or the man with the loudest voice, the man who tells us what we want to hear!

"Our forefathers would be ashamed! Rome was built by the men who ruled justly, for the future of this great Republic rather than the expedient desires of today. We must vote for the man who is best for this position, and not for the man who offers us the most coin or threatens his opponents into silence!

"Therefore: I would like to endorse two men for consul. First, the returning imperator, Marcus Antonius!"

A wave of awe spread throughout the Forum. Some would have shouted out their disapproval but were too stunned to do so. I continued before they worked up the courage.

"Yes, he is a firm supporter of the nobility. And I, Quintus Sertorius, will always support the people! I stand with the common man, with the Romans in villages spread through Italy, with our veterans. But Marcus Antonius is the right man for consul. Next, I offer my public support to the man who just addressed you. Gaius Memmius has ever been a devoted servant of the people, but brings with him none of the violence and expediency of his peers. The two of these men stand opposed on many issues, but they are good men. Good men. I've inspected their character and determined that both men stand above the fray that has developed in this very Forum. Together, with sober minds and stout hearts, they can bring equanimity, peace, and prosperity to this Republic!"

Such an eruption of dismay overtook the crowd that I believed for a moment I had made a grave error. But the eyes of all gathered stared through me. I followed their gaze to the *carcer* in the distance and saw several men marching from it.

"Equitius is free! The son of Tiberius Gracchus is liberated!"

Saturninus, Glaucia, and their supporters were quickly approaching, Equitius hoisted up on their shoulders.

He was laughing, obviously exuberant at his freedom, until he locked eyes with me.

He lifted an arm and wagged his finger at me while his followers brandished daggers and pointed them toward me.

"You've been a naughty senator, Sertorius!" I heard his nasal little voice rise above the cheers. Someone must have rushed to the *carcer* to report my speech the minute it had left my lips.

They descended into the *comitium*, heading straight for me. I had nowhere to escape to.

I could almost see the blood of Nonius pooling up at my feet, and I wondered if mine would soon replace it.

"Protect the senator!"

"Protect the senator!"

Voices echoed, but I could hardly process them. It wasn't until several bodies clambered onto the stage that I realized a handful of citizens had come to my rescue.

They rallied around me and lifted their togas to guard their faces against Saturninus's hordes.

The revolutionaries halted at the steps of the Rostra, determining whether the cost of an attack on me was worth it.

Equitius was shouting for them to continue, still riding atop their lifted hands like he was on a litter. Glaucia glared at me with a tempting smile on his lips. Saturninus was not smiling, but he didn't break his gaze either.

"Come, then! Test your mob against the *true* sons of Rome!" I shouted over the shoulders of my protectors.

Eventually, Saturninus whispered something to Glaucia, who passed the message along to everyone else.

"We'll save you for another day, cyclops!" the fake son of Gracchus cupped his hands around his lips and shouted.

"I'll be waiting with anticipation, Equitius."

When they disappeared in the distance, I found that many in the crowd had scurried away the moment they'd sniffed violence in the air. The others who remained lifted their voices.

"Sertorius! Sertorius! Sertorius!"

When I descended, my family didn't offer me words of congratulations. They were too frightened by the near confrontation, so they clung to me like I was a rock in a storm instead.

I kissed each of them, more thankful for them than I had ever been. We began to make our way back home, and kept to the shadows and the back roads as best as possible until we arrived.

SCROLL XXVIII

NONES OF DECEMBER, 655 AB URBE CONDITA

AFTER I LOST my eye at Arausio, I was often afraid. It can be difficult to explain just how disorienting it is to lose half of your vision. Walking from tent to tent could be frightening. Objects appeared more distant than they were.

I developed a habit of blinking constantly. Lucius joked that I simply found Gaia's earth too beautiful and profound to behold. But in reality, I blinked because I was frightened of everything that lurked in the darkness where I could no longer see.

But I was not scared this day. My vision had not improved, my ability to see what that day might bring was even more hindered, but I was not afraid. Whatever the election would bring, I was prepared for it.

Rumors had spread like a fire in the subura after the brawl was nearly avoided at the Rostra. Equitius immediately promised to punish the men who had betrayed the cause when he was elected. He didn't have to say my name, for everyone to know whom he meant. Well, not only myself, but Marius also. He promised to use his power to drag us through the courts, and he said he had inside information about our corruption that he would use to see us exiled. Perhaps they were just rumors, but I knew Equitius well enough not to doubt them. Still, I was unafraid.

A lack of fear wasn't going to lead me to be careless, though. I followed sound advice and strapped a dagger to my calf, no longer concerned first with whether I might have to use it, and was joined by Lucius and a handful of other faithful veterans outside my domus.

"Ready to move, *amicus*?" Lucius said with his wide, goofy smile. He likely had no idea just how bad the day might become, nor would he have cared if he had known. He addressed each threat when it appeared, prayed to the gods, and sorted out whatever was left. I admired that and was resolved to become more like him.

"You're damned right I am. To glory," I said, remembering that Saturninus often said the same thing before marching to the assembly. I repeated it, but to me, it meant something much different.

The Field of Mars was sprawling when we arrived. Thank the gods we hadn't attempted to host the election in the Forum—we could have never squeezed that many citizens into the city. Thirty-five booths abreast, each with a gangway attached to it, were prepared for the vote, as if they were standing structures.

"The future of the Republic will be decided today, comrade," I said privately to Lucius.

"I believe I've heard that many times before, such as when Maximus was elected."

"The fate of Rome was decided that day also. But not like this."

The tribal assembly was hosted first. We would know before the sun reached its height whether Saturninus and his companion Equitius would be elected to the tribuneship, whether they would be immune to the consequences of their actions for the following year, and whether they would be able to come after their former associates like myself.

Saturninus wisely did not speak that morning but deferred to another tribune to host the election. There was nothing else left to be said. The whole Republic knew what platform he was running on and what would become of us all if he were to be elected along with Equitius. Some longed for it, others dreaded it, and some didn't care with new coin in their pockets. Regardless, no one was going to have their mind swayed today.

All thirty-five tribes were aligned and voted simultaneously. Mercifully, we would not have to wait as long as we did on a vote for legislation.

"Go, all of you. To your tribes. I can protect myself," I said to the clients and soldiers surrounding me.

"We think not, sir. We've discussed it, and we will remain by your side," one of them replied.

Lucius pulled back his cloak and revealed the gladius sheathed at his hip.

"Don't worry, gentlemen. Nothing will befall the senator while I stand by his side."

"We need as many votes as we can. Rome is in short supply of good men, and thankfully, that is what all of you are. Now go." After hesitating, they bowed dutifully and departed.

"I was lying. If a gang comes our way, we're both dead," Lucius whispered, elbowing me in the ribs until we both laughed.

The urns were collected and carried to the center of the recently constructed stage. The votes were counted and passed along for inspection and a recount.

"Citizens of Rome, you have spoken, and your voice has been heard. Your tribunes are as follows: Publius Furius, Sextus Titius"—cheers from their supporters carried throughout the Campus Martius until others silenced them impatiently—"Quintus Pompeius Rufus, Lucius Cato Salonianus…" These last two were the dear friends of Sulla. Any other time, I might have feared their election, but not today. "Lucius Saturninus, Lucius Equitius…"

Voices rose throughout the field, some in favor and some in horror. A gasp escaped those closest to me, and they turned in my direction with compassion and grief as if I had just received news of a terminal illness. I avoided their gaze but was surprised that I wasn't overwhelmed with grief of my own. I composed myself and again focused on my breath.

"Steel yourselves, gentlemen. We cannot be surprised when the corrupt profit from their corruption. We should only be surprised when the incorruptible thrive despite it," I calmed them, my voice shaky but my resolve as strong as ever.

I could no longer focus on the remainder of the announcement of the elected tribunes, but in reality, it did not matter. Perhaps Marius had installed a puppet or two of his own to check the efforts of the revolutionaries, but Saturninus and Equitius were tribunes. And they were resourceful enough to outwit the best intentions of any man in the senate house.

But the day was not over. The elections of the quaestors were held next, and Gaius Saufeius was once again elected to the position. The day was certainly against us, but there was another election to come. One battle at a time.

The voting booths were deconstructed and the stage cleared to accommodate the Centuriate Assembly. Ropes were strung up to replace the voting booths, and small windowless shacks were set up for voters to enter. Typically the Centuriate Assembly voted within a temple, but we hadn't the time. The December winds were already increasing, and the sun was periodically covered by dark clouds.

Once the construction was concluded, the election for consul could commence.

I spotted Marius and his co-consul, Valerius, taking to the stage, sitting in their consular chairs for the last time. Even from a great distance, I could imagine the sour look in Marius's eyes. I knew him well enough by then to know he was unwell today, especially after the news that his old protégé would have another year to exact vengeance at any perceived betrayals.

More than that, though, he had perhaps reached his final days as consul. I knew deep in his heart he longed to be hailed by the people again, begged to return to his position, and "save the Republic" once more. A bit of applause that afternoon would have properly sufficed, but no one even looked in his direction. His days as the Third Founder of Rome were all but behind him.

It did not help that if the day went poorly, his torch would be passed to a man who had insulted him publicly and who would likely seek to make Marius's first year back as a citizen arduous and unprofitable.

The candidates ascended the steps to the stage. Glaucia turned his back on Marius without so much as a nod or shake of the hand, as did the rest of the candidates. They each faced the crowds and waved to the pockets in the audience where they heard their names cheered.

The *flamen dialis* offered a prayer before the assembly and announced that auspices were favorable.

Perhaps the gods are not paying attention, then, I thought to myself, but I dared not speak it aloud.

The tribes broke up, and the people assembled themselves into their centuries. There were 193 of them in total; this type of voting always favored the nobles, the rich, the old, and the leisured. In theory, I shook my fist against the higher magistracies being voted on in such a rigged manner, but not today. Anyone voting against Glaucia was my ally, and the nobles certainly wouldn't be voting for him.

Consul Valerius began to read out the votes after the first of the centuries had cast them.

"Marcus Antonius as senior, Aulus Albinius as junior!" His shaky voice didn't carry well, but word was passed back through the crowds so that we heard just moments after the announcement. The first several votes were the same, Antonius and Albinius, to no one's surprise. There was never any doubt that the Optimates would vote for two of their own. The real question was how the people would vote.

"Gaius Glaucia as senior, Gaius Memmius as junior," a few of the popular centuries voted.

I tried to swallow but hadn't realized how dry my throat had become. All the moisture had seemed to migrate to my palms.

"Gaius Glaucia as senior, Attius Balbus as junior."

I shut my eye and tried to do the math in my head. When I reopened them, I could see Glaucia's white teeth shining behind a smile as he reached over and shook the hand of the latter candidate.

"Many more tribes to come, Quintus, never fear," Lucius said, but even he was beginning to shift uncomfortably.

Valerius was handed a few more tablets but took an extra look over them before he read them aloud.

"Marcus Antonius as senior, and Gaius Memmius as junior. Marcus Antonius as senior, and Gaius Memmius as junior!"

"Ha! Did you hear that?" Lucius grabbed my shoulder and slapped my chest. "That speech of yours got to a few centuries yet!" He shook me until I smiled.

"Perhaps good sense got to a few of them yet."

"Gaius Memmius as senior, Attius Balbus as junior."

The voting continued. Even among the more junior tribes, Marcus Antonius's name was the most frequent.

"Citizens of Rome! Your first consul has been nominated. Marcus Antonius, imperator of the Republican fleet, has been elected!" The crowds roared their approval.

"Now things will get interesting," I said, exhaling deeply and watching the faces of the candidates to see if I could get a sense of what was expected. No one seemed to be certain except for Glaucia, who continued to smile, wave, and shake hands. In fact, he was the first to congratulate Antonius, who accepted a handshake with the reticence of a man being approached by a leper.

"Attius Balbus as senior, and Gaius Memmius as junior," Valerius continued.

"That's rather unexpected," Lucius said with raised brows.

"Any vote that's not for Glaucia is a victory, in my opinion."

"I thought you were cheering for Memmius?" my simple friend asked.

"I like Memmius. But a haughty old noble like Balbus is less dangerous to the good of the people than Glaucia."

Lucius shrugged and returned his attention to the stage as Valerius shouted out the next vote: "Statilius Taurus as senior, Gaius Glaucia as junior."

Marius crossed his arms behind himself, his feet tapping violently enough that I thought I could hear the cry of the creaking wood over the mob.

"That Taurus fellow doesn't stand a chance. Why cast away a vote?" Lucius asked. I thought of a few ways to respond but was too nervous to do so. Glaucia and Memmius were as close as legionaries in a testudo. There was no indication that either man was taking the lead.

Memmius remained composed as best he could, but his skin had turned a shade of white. Glaucia, on the other hand, was hardly paying attention, chatting with the other candidates around him.

"Aulus Albinius as senior, Gaius Memmius as junior."

"How many is that? Are you keeping count?" Lucius asked.

"I believe I've lost it. What's your guess?" I replied.

"I've been relying on you. You're the one that can count!"

"Gaius Memmius as senior, Aulus Albinius as junior!"

The next three votes repeated this configuration.

"Your man's got to have the lead now, right? Memmius has to."

"I think so. I don't know," I said, rubbing at my temples. I could hear the blood thumping in my ears, my heart pumping in my chest as if I had just finished a thirty-mile forced march. A drink would have been welcome, but even if one were available, I wouldn't have accepted it. I had made a decision to drink less, for Arrea and Gavius, and whatever came next, I knew a sober mind would be necessary.

"Gaius Memmius as senior, Statilius Taurus as junior."

"I believe that Taurus fellow is making a comeback, don't you?" Lucius nudged me with his elbow, but I was far too consumed for laughter.

"Gaius Memmius as senior, Attius Balbus as junior."

"He has it, Quintus. I really think he has it," Lucius said, clutching my forearm, serious for the first time.

"Aulus Albinius as senior, Gaius Memmius as junior," Valerius read aloud, and reached for the next tablet.

There was something shifting in the distance, though, something I couldn't see but I could sense. Something like when you can feel a snake slithering in a tree when you're in a forest but cannot yet perceive its location.

"Ay!" I roared and pointed toward the stage. I set off running before I had considered it. Perhaps it was another vision like I'd had during Marius's Triumph, but Lucius was right behind me regardless.

The crowds shouted at us in consternation as we passed through them, but several heads turned to the foot of the stage as well.

Saturninus's hordes. Now that I was closer, I could spot those hooded thugs anywhere.

"There!" I roared, shoving citizens aside.

I turned to find Lucius's eyes wide with fear but his sword unsheathed and lifted above his head.

Cries sounded from across the field, and citizens began the same stampede they had upon Sulla's attack in the Forum.

"Stop those men!" Lucius bellowed behind me, but we were too far away to do anything.

The hooded men fought their way through the petty guard, storming the stage.

I could no longer see Glaucia.

Marius jumped from the stage and disappeared behind a throng of his guards.

Candidates cried out and bounded from the sides of the stage like they were aboard a burning ship.

Memmius did not, though.

"Stop those men!" Without halting, I reached down and brandished my dagger.

We had almost pushed our way to the front when Memmius was enveloped by the hooded men. Daggers and clubs were lifted high in the air, and a thud rang out, along with bloodcurdling cries from the center of the violence.

The assassins scattered as quickly as they had appeared, pouncing from the stage and disappearing in every direction.

"Stop! Stop those men!" I bounded up the steps, but the light was already fading from the consul-elect's eyes. "Memmius? Memmius! We need a doctor!" I roared, but there was no one in earshot who could hear, or anyone that would have listened if they were able. Total panic had ensued. There had never been a battlefield more chaotic.

"I'll hunt down every one of those bastards, Quintus, just say the word," Lucius said from behind me, sword still in hand and waiting for an assailant to test him.

"Memmius, can you hear me?" I asked again, but the answer was self-evident. His forehead was caved in, and blood shot out in spurts from several wounds to his torso and thighs.

His eyelids still blinked and twitched rapidly, but the eyes themselves were beginning to roll away, unwilling to look upon this vile earth any longer.

"Give the word, Quintus," Lucius repeated.

"No. We need to rally every good man we can find. Do you understand me? Every man armed, and with a shield if he has one. Meet me at the Temple of Castor."

"Where will you go?"

I looked again at the fallen consul. I had never seen a man mangled like that. The battlefield rarely produced such hatred.

I considered my answer, and sighed when I realized what it was. I had sworn allegiance to a man. Despite my differences with him, and even though I blamed him for a great deal of this, I needed to find Marius. If the general's life was in danger, I must protect him. I had sworn a sacred oath under the standards of the Ninth Legion. And I would do what I must.

"I'm going to find our general. He could be next."

Lucius, as much as anyone, knew how stubborn I could be. He would have likely tried to talk me out of it if he thought it possible.

"If I had to wager, *amicus*, I would say that you are next on their list, if anyone."

"I know you would encourage me to return home. But I cannot, not yet. This Republic is on the brink of destruction. I'll do as I must."

In a rare moment of solemnity, Lucius snapped to attention and saluted me before hurrying down the steps.

"Go with the protection of the gods, and all our ancestors."

SCROLL XXIX

NONES OF DECEMBER, 655 AB URBE CONDITA

I DIDN'T KNOW where to begin my search, but thankfully, I didn't have to search long.

"The senate is convening in the Temple of Honor and Victory! The senate is meeting in the Temple of Honor and Victory!" criers shout out, beginning to appear not but a few moments after I'd descended the stage.

I hurried to Marius's temple, which was still under construction. Fresh paint remained on the marble columns and stucco walls, but none of the senators seemed to mind, propping up against them to catch their breaths. Their togas were splattered with blood and dirt already.

Some were huddled in the corners nursing wounds. One or two were regurgitating from the exhaustion and effort. Everyone was shouting.

"Please, gentlemen, you must calm yourselves!" Marcus Scaurus's old-seeming voice echoed throughout the barren temple.

"Calm? Calm? How can we be calm? The Republic is under

siege from revolutionaries!" the newly elected tribune, Cato, roared.

"Such drama right now is unhelpful, Cato, really. I agree with the Father of the Senate. The mob butchered a candidate. Now those responsible will be executed. There is no siege," the pontifex Maximus Ahenobarbus said, dabbing at the sweat of his brow.

"A candidate for consul of the Republic has just been butchered before the whole of Rome! How can you be so callous?" Rutilius Rufus, usually stoic and moderate, shouted.

"Mind your tone, Rufus!"

The whole temple erupted again in shouts and cries for justice.

Consul Valerius sat surrounded by a few younger men who patted his back and tried to calm him. He stared at everyone around him with wide eyes.

Even Marius looked rattled. His eyes were glazed over, and he seemed to rock back and forth on the steps of the altar he was constructing. I had seen the man ride gallantly into battle. I had seen him come within an inch of losing his life and never so much as blink. I had never seen this look on his face.

"Can any of us be sure—can anyone be *certain*—that Gaius Memmius is dead?" Gaius Caesar asked, speaking up for once.

"I am. He took his last breath before my eye," I said, stepping farther into the temple.

Cato rushed to me with a finger pointed in my face.

"And you did nothing to stop it?" he snarled.

He might have just been elected, but he didn't take office until the following month. I grabbed him by the wrist and pulled his hand away from me.

"I ran from fifty yards back. There were many of you I spotted closer, tucking tail and running for your lives. What say you, Senators?" I asked, not finding the ability to restrain myself.

"So he is dead. And we know who is responsible. Justice

must be brought upon them. Swiftly and without mercy!" Sulla shouted.

"Just because Memmius was butchered doesn't mean that Glaucia and Saturninus ordered it. We cannot kill them without a trial," Norbanus said.

"The fact that you knew who I meant without saying their names proves my point! Look among you, gentlemen. Are there any senators not here among us except the demagogues themselves? Saturninus, Glaucia, and Saufeius. They are behind this, and they know it, or they would have come to this meeting," Sulla replied, his blue eyes shining with wrath, the only look that ever replaced his smile.

"They must be put down!" one of the senators roared.

"We must march against them at once!" another echoed.

"Calm yourselves, Conscript Fathers!" the newly augmented consul, Marcus Antonius, bellowed, his voice the only trained enough to command the senate in a time like this. "I want to put down the revolutionaries as much as any man here."

"I might add that I've warned you all about this," said the aedile Crassus as he glared daggers at the known Populares in the room—including myself and Marius.

Antonius continued, "But the last time the senate swore an ultimatum to put down a rebellion, the men killed were not holding office. Each of these renegades holds the *sancrosanctitas* of a tribune or the imperium of a praetor. If we butcher them without trial, eventually some ambitious young demagogue of the same cloth will come after us and drag each of us through the courts for murder! We need to capture them and put them on trial!"

"They can't persecute us all!"

"Damn the law in this case!"

Each man lifted his voice in an attempt to be heard. Each man except Marius, who remained with his head bowed.

"Senators!" A man rushed into the temple halls, slamming into my shoulder as he passed me.

He halted in the center and placed his hands on his knees. His breath was so labored, I feared he might die then and there.

"What is it? Out with it!" Scaurus ordered.

"I've come... I've come... The capitol." His face was scarlet like a soldier's cloak. He could hardly get the words out.

"Speak!" Ahenobarbus roared.

"Saturninus and Glaucia are taking over the capitol! They're freeing slaves and promising freedom to anyone who will fight."

The whole temple went silent. The only sound was the panting of the messenger, who finally collapsed to his knees.

"Get him some water," Scaurus said, his voice barely audible.

"Come now, this is blather! Rumors borne of terror and nothing more. Slaves? Really? Saturninus and Glaucia are rascals, to be certain, but to free slaves? Never!" Cinna said, breathing almost as heavily as the messenger.

"Can you attest to the truth of what you say, boy? You're certain?" old Aurelius Cotta asked. He had been around long enough to know what would come next if it were true.

"I can... I can... I did not hear them make the offer myself, but I can attest to the looting and pillaging. Fires have been set to the temples in the Forum. I've seen that myself."

A gasp escaped even the most hardened old patricians.

"Send water-bearers to put out the flames immediately!" Ahenobarbus shouted at a junior senator.

"Damn the old temples! We need to quash this rebellion before the whole of Rome burns down!" the tribune-elect Pompeius shouted, his companion Sulla nodding along in agreement.

"This changes things. If there is an active rebellion in the city, we cannot wait for a trial. The rebellion must be extinguished, slaves or no slaves," Antonius said, shaking his head as he considered the implications of what he was saying.

Metellus Pius, son of Numidicus, grabbed a blank scroll and made quite a display as he stomped over to a wood bench and hastily scribbled something. He rolled the scroll up and marched directly to Marius.

"Consul." Marius refused to look at him. "Marius!" Pius roared, and for a moment, we feared we might have another source of aggression on our hands. Slowly, the consul lifted his head, bloodshot eyes staring back at the son of his oldest enemy. "This is a *senatus ultimum*, one which I've no doubt we will all vote for. Now, I ask—no, implore—you to restore order to the Republic! Take up arms against your former associates and destroy this resistance you've helped build, and prove to this august body once and for all that you are not the debauched, traitorous coward we believe you to be!"

The senate froze like a congregation of statues, terrified of Marius's response. Pius was close enough to the consul to feel the warmth of his breath. Marius had only to stand up and swipe the document from his hand to push the man back in fear.

"With what army shall I repulse them? Are any of you brave enough to take up arms alongside me, to fight a gang of ruffians and freed slaves? Speak!" No one volunteered themselves, but each man looked with judgmental eyes at everyone around them. "I didn't think so. Then propose a fucking alternative."

"Consul, I have veterans gathering now at the Temple of Castor. Only give me the word and I'll rally with them and end this," I said.

"A man of action, thank the gods!" Cato roared, but I glared at him with my one eye in return. Marius's response was the only that mattered.

Cato's insult, or perhaps Pius's lashing out, had been enough to pick at Marius's pride.

"No. I am consul of this Republic, and I will defend it. I will lead a body of my own people who are brave enough to end this." He turned to his co-consul. "Gather some of the city guard and go guard the Quirinal Hill. You two"—he pointed to the two junior senators nursing the trembling consul—"haul him by the legs if you need to. But I'm not going to do this alone and be 'dragged through the courts' like Antonius prophesied."

He seemed to reconsider my proposal, though, and turned again with a different tone in his voice. Something more familiar flooded into his eyes. Command suited him well, and he seemed to straighten now that the room was bound to listen to him. He approached and spoke low enough so that every man might not hear. "Take your men and descend into the Cloaca Maxima. Exit near the Forum Boarium and ascend the steps near the Tarpeian Rock. I'm going to cut off water to the capitol, and you will flank them, barring their retreat. Understood?"

"Yes, Consul," I replied.

"And when they surrender, we will take them to a place where they can be held until a trial is possible."

Voices raised in protest, but Marius's drowned them out. "Quiet! I demand you! I am consul, I am given the *senatum ulti-matum*. I will handle this. Go home to your noble wives, recline on your couches, drink some wine, and read some poetry! Leave combat to those who understand it!"

Marius's rage had never been more evident. All those near him stepped back, and fortunately so, for I have no doubt he would have struck the nearest if someone offered a complaint.

"Go! Everyone, out of my temple!" I lingered to see if Marius had any other special instruction. But he cast his gaze on me with the same vehemence. "You too."

SCROLL XXX

NONES OF DECEMBER, 655 AB URBE CONDITA

THE CLOACA MAXIMA, the sewers of Rome. There was good reason to call it the greatest invention of the Roman Republic. It had allowed the city to flourish. Despite the filth of the streets we often complained about, there was not a city in the world that rivaled the cleanliness of Rome's streets.

But that didn't make the sewers smell better.

I charged first, followed by two dozen good men and my friend Lucius, through the wide, dark sewers. The waters of piss and shit came as high as our chests at some point.

"Oh gods, I don't think I can do this," one of them said behind me as several others vomited up the wine they chugged before our entry to steel their nerves.

"Many a man has told me that politics are the sewers of Romulus. Now I can tell them they're wrong," I said, to laughter and more puking. I did my best to keep spirits light. The men were prepared to defend their country, but they did not know what came next. None of us did. And ultimately, it was out of our hands. We were tasked with apprehending the revolutionaries, but there was no indication that they would give themselves up willingly.

"I hope we aren't planning an ambush. They'll be able to smell us from a mile away," Lucius said before dry heaving.

"One of you with a torch, on me." I gave the hand signal to those who could still see me.

"Here, sir," one of them said, hurrying to my side.

"Take point. I can't see a damn thing. Pick up the pace, men, pretend we're on a march in the beautiful fields of southern Gaul."

"I'd rather be marching in a Cimbri camp under yoke."

Another vomited.

"Did you just throw up in the sewers of Romulus?" one of the men asked, and then assumed his best Sertorius impression. *"Better men than you or I have shit here. Pick up that vomit and put it in your pocket!"*

We all belted out with laughter, including myself. It was a nice momentary relief, but not enough to distract us.

"Wait. Wait. Here it is, this is the exit," I said, spotting a ladder on the side of the shit-filled tunnels.

We began our ascent one by one, most of the men still hacking and gagging as they reached fresh air for the first time in half a watch.

Nighttime had descended sometime while we were underground.

"Quiet now. Cease your coughing." I lead the way to the Tarpeian stairs and began the ascent. Everyone had forgotten about the smell by the time we reached the top, for even the fittest among us were out of breath. Those were steep stairs, and there were a lot of them. The irony was not lost on me that the majority of men who ascended them were either being executed for treason or were carrying out the execution.

There was fighting somewhere in the darkness. The cries of the dying rose throughout the night sky, and I could see movement in the pale light from the burning fires in the distance.

"Retreat! Retreat!" rose the cries in the distance.

"That them?" Lucius asked.

"I think so," I whispered as I hunkered down behind some shrubbery and gestured for the others to do the same.

I watched as shrouded figures ascended into the Capitolium. I heard whistles blowing in the distance. Marius had reached the crest of the Capitoline Hill and must have been cutting off the waterlines as we spoke.

"What are your orders, Commander?" Lucius said, half serious. But I could tell he was as nervous as I was. I could tell by his eyes that my bighearted friend wanted nothing to do with murdering or even apprehending magistrates of the Republic. The thought alone was harder than killing a foreign enemy.

"Stay here." I stood.

"What?" Lucius's eyes shot open wide, glistening in the moonlight.

"Stay here. I'm going in alone."

"They'll kill you!"

"No. They will not. They will hear me because they have no other choice." I pulled out my dagger and extended it to Lucius. "Take this."

"I will not."

"Yes, you will. Unarmed, I will not be seen as a threat. Besides, with nothing but a dagger, I stand no chance of fighting them off."

"Quintus Sertorius, I—"

"Not another word. Follow me, and I'll have you tried for treason."

I shot him a wink as I turned for to the Capitolium.

The doors were shut and barred from the inside, but I wasn't going to enter without permission anyhow.

I straightened my shoulders and prepared myself. I closed my eye and thought of Arrea. I thought of Gavius. I thought of what death may feel like, what my last thought would be. I wondered what I would see if I was plunged with daggers or had my head staved in like Memmius. Was it only darkness that awaited us? Or would my father, brother, and fallen comrades be there to shake my hand upon the fields of Elysium?

I knocked on the door.

There was shouting within, and finally—after a few more raps against the massive wooden doors—it split open just enough for the moonlight to shine on the eyes of the man behind them.

"Who are you? State your name!"

"I am Senator Quintus Sertorius. And I am here to speak with Lucius Saturninus and Gaius Glaucia. I demand you let me enter."

"They aren't here."

The door shut again before more shouts, increasing in volume and in vehemence, rose from within.

I remained in position until the door opened, Saturninus himself on the other side.

They stepped aside from me to enter, then swiftly shut the door behind me.

Few of them still wore togas, and not a man among them wasn't bloodied.

Saturninus had a split forehead, and blood covered his face like a death mask, his eyes shining bright and alert like cornered prey behind it.

"What are we waiting for? Kill the bastard!" Equitius shouted.

I clasped my hands behind my back and glared at the little worm of a man.

"We should kill you, Sertorius. You betrayed me," Saturninus said. There was nothing in that moment that resembled the suave, charming, controlled young tribune I had come to know. Tears welled up in his eyes.

"I betrayed nothing. I never vowed an oath to defend your

revolutionary measures. I never consented to the murder of a consul-elect, or the tribune-elect Nonius, which I can now see you also orchestrated." I spoke with as little malice as I could manage. I kept my tone even. Calm and composed, like I was forced to do in the Cimbri camp. In both cases, saying the wrong thing could have resulted in my death.

No one spoke for a moment.

"You were my friend, Quintus Sertorius," Saturninus said, struggling to swallow. A single tear ripped from his eye and streaked down the dried bright-red blood on his face.

"And I hope that I still am. But friends listen to the wise counsel of their friends, and if any of you had listened to me, we would not be at this sad pass. I hope that you will listen to me now."

"What do you propose?" Glaucia's famous infectious smile was so removed from his face I knew it would never reappear, no matter the outcome.

"Lay down your arms. Walk out of this temple with me and place yourselves on the ground. You will be ushered by an armed guard to the curia and held there until it is time for a trial."

"What are we waiting for? I'm with Equitius! Let's kill this dog and burn down every temple in sight!" Saufeius's voice cracked with rage.

"You can guarantee us a fair trial?" Saturninus asked, his voice barely audible.

"The consul himself guarantees it," I replied.

"Sertorius, this is not what we intended. I intended none of this," Saturninus said as more tears streaked through the blood.

"What? This was your idea, coward! Sertorius, it was all him! Him and Glaucia, I hadn't anything to do with it!" Equitius grabbed my toga and implored me to look at him. Glaucia grabbed him by his shoulders and threw him on the ground.

"It was you, you little bastard!" Saufeius bellowed. "He said he would do what his father did not! Who was your father, you little rascal? A peasant or a slave! That's who!"

Equitius scrambled to his feet and threw a punch that connected with Saufeius's nose twice as powerfully as I believed it would from a man as puny as him.

I ignored the scuffle and turned to Glaucia and Saturninus.

"Your intentions are irrelevant. Marius has cut off your supply. You'll die of starvation or dehydration if you don't capitulate immediately."

Glaucia ran his fingers through his hair and groaned, with wide, wild eyes.

"Marius," Saturninus whispered, as if to himself. He dabbed at the snot on the tip of his nose as if he didn't notice the blood covering his face. He did his best to compose himself. "We have no other choice, Gaius," he said.

"We're dead. We're all dead." Glaucia fell to his knees and buried his face in his hands.

"We haven't a choice."

"I'm not going to die with these bastards. Sertorius, tell them, won't you? Tell them this was their idea!" Equitius bellowed as he tossed Saufeius aside and stood with a freshly swollen eye.

"Silence!" I roared, unable to maintain my composure. "If it were up to me, the both of you would be hanging from crosses by morning." I pointed to him and Saufeius, who dabbed at a bloody lip. "I give you all but one chance. Walk out with me right now, and you may yet live. Otherwise, you'll die here."

"Would you defend us?" Glaucia turned to me, shuffling to his feet.

"What?"

"In court. No one else will defend us. Would you?"

"I am not a lawyer," I replied.

Glaucia seemed to remember himself, and straightened his back.

"I told you once that you didn't understand your potential.

You gave a speech that nearly brought us down. And perhaps you could give a speech that could save our lives."

"Your lives are not mine to decide. But both of you have been fair and kind to me. I will speak the truth before the Roman people and the selected jury, and they will decide."

Saufeius stood and spit blood on the ground between us.

"Cowards, the lot of you. I'll not surrender. Damn the senate. And damn you, Quintus Sertorius." He uttered my name with the most incorrigible vehemence; it would have stunned me had it come from any other man.

"Then stay here and die."

I turned and walked from the building as the revolutionaries began shouting among one another.

"Wait! Wait!"

I continued facing forward but felt several men following me.

"Put yourselves in the dirt." When at last I turned, they were all there. Saturninus, Glaucia, Equitius, and even Saufeius, along with all their other supporters who had holed up within the Capitolium. "Put your noses in the dirt of the city you sought to burn down," I said. And even then, I felt it weighing heavily on me. If I had spoken those words to Glaucia or Saturninus a week prior, I might have been tried for insolence. And roles are not reversed quickly.

I felt sicker than I had in the Cloaca Maxima.

Lucius and my soldiers came charging forward, as did Marius and his men from the Forum below us.

"Don't move! Don't move!"

"Don't move an inch!"

I stepped away from them and lowered my head. I tried to conjure up thoughts of Arrea and Gavius. I tried to express my gratitude that I was still alive and could hold her or my child again, but nothing could enter my thoughts but the bloodied faces of my former associates.

When I looked up, Marius was standing before me. I didn't

know why, but his face made me sicker still. The way he stood with his head still high and his back still straight...

"Good work, Sertorius. Let's get these men to the curia."

"Give me a minute. Take them yourself, if you would," I said without restraint. He analyzed me long and hard, contemplating whether or not to rebuke me. He must have decided it wasn't the time. He moved on and rounded up the prisoners.

SCROLL XXXI

W HAT LITTLE I had in my belly was emptied onto the Capitoline. After I recomposed myself, I descended the hill to the Forum, passing by the Temple of Saturn. Slaves were hurling water at the last remaining embers there.

I saw the doors being barred and Marius's troops discussing among themselves what to do next. In the dim twilight, I spotted the consul himself offering some instructions.

Approaching, I felt all eyes turn to me. My toga was covered in the shit of the cloaca, but still, my mind was more tormented.

"They're locked up now. We'll have guards posted to block their exit. And when the time comes, they'll be put on trial. Tomorrow we'll meet with the senate and decide which of the lot of them should be taken to the *carcer*. Glaucia and Saturninus seem like obvious candidates," he said, his hands clenched behind his back.

I don't know why, but a tear welled up in my eye. I felt the impulse to hit him, or spit on him. I didn't, but instead, I said something I should not have.

"It's ironic, isn't it? That they're locked up within the same building where you schemed with them to overthrow the Republic? I find it ironic. It wouldn't take a great playwright to make a comedy of it."

He clenched and unclenched his jaw many times. He must have known I was one of the only allies he had left, for he didn't assault me with words or fists. He simply returned my glare with one of his own. I could see from his eyes that he was as wounded as anybody. But was it due to the loss of his friends or his own pride? I assumed the latter, and it made me angry.

"I'll stand watch tonight," I said.

"I think not. Your loyalty is in question." He turned his back to me.

"My loyalty? I was the one who risked my life to secure their surrender. I was the one who scrambled all over the Field of Mars to find you today to ensure your safety rather than returning to my home to protect my family. My loyalty?" I turned to the senate house, and those within. "Don't you dare talk to me about loyalty."

He snorted through his nostrils like a bull. I met his eyes and tempted him to leave me, to be all alone.

Then I remembered that I was alone too. In the back of my mind, I remembered Gaius Memmius's promise to support me. The chaos of the day had forced me to forget that his death was the cause of it.

Marius stared at me until his gaze softened.

"It's been a long day, Quintus Sertorius. Loyalty or no, you can guard the curia if you'd like. But I think you deserve some rest."

"I wasn't complicit with the things you all conspired for, Consul Marius. I despised it. My guts felt tied up in knots every time I consider it." I could feel my face contorting in pain. I tried to maintain a stoic demeanor, but I couldn't. There was much I wanted to say to the consul, but at least I could avoid saying all that. "I didn't agree with it, and that's why you routinely lied to me. Still, though, I helped these men get here. I did support them

302 | BODIES IN THE TIBER

for a time. And I will have trouble sleeping until this is all sorted out. I feel it's my duty to stand guard."

"Do as you please, then!" He flicked his wrist at me and then turned away.

Before he could get too far, footsteps were heard approaching. And a lot of them.

We turned to find a body of senators at least fifty strong approaching from the Argiletum.

"Good evening, Romans! What's the verdict?" one of them shouted. I wasn't certain, but the voice was familiar to me. I believed it belonged to Lucius Cornelius Sulla.

My anger got the best of me, and I rushed past Marius. I hoped they would say something that displeased me.

Before I reached them, Lucius and the other veterans were by my side.

"Who asks?"

"The senate and people of Rome, young man," the reply came, and then I was certain it was Sulla despite the darkness.

Marius, thankfully, approached before I could respond.

"The verdict? Consuls cannot pass verdicts on Roman lives. Nor can senators, even those as illustrious and talented as you, Sulla," he said.

"They can't? That's interesting. I was under the impression you were presented with a *senatus ultimum*. I thought you were given express orders to pass judgment." The senators around him nodded and acknowledged their agreement. As my eye adjusted, I spotted the newly elected tribunes, Cato and Rufus, among them.

"I don't take orders, I give them," Marius replied without pause.

"Correct me if I'm wrong, dear Cato, but I'm fairly certain that consuls *do* take orders from the senate. Do they not?"

"They do," Cato said, his pensive gaze cast on Marius.

"Especially when a decree such as this is offered. The consul must obey commands."

"Do not push me, Sulla. Enough blood has been shed this night," Marius said through clenched teeth.

"And the order, if I recall correctly, was to kill the rebels." The senators around Sulla sounded off their approval.

"Sulla, stand down. This is under control."

"Perhaps we'll have to take this into our own hands, if our consul's allegiance to his old companions overcomes his allegiance to justice?"

"That isn't your place, Sulla," I shouted, rushing forward, my men following me.

"And there he is. Hero of the North he may be, but he obviously isn't the hero of Rome. He said upon the Rostra that he wouldn't allow personal allegiance to overcome his allegiance to justice, but here we are."

"Consul, bring this to order." I turned to Marius and ground my teeth.

"Senators of Rome, over the past six hundred years, we've been called on many times to be the last line of defense of this Republic. I believe tonight is just the latest of such occasions."

"Consul!" I roared. Marius only glared back at them but said nothing.

"How about it, then, Senators? Shall we bring order to the Republic?" Sulla asked, turning back to Marius, his teeth shining in the flickering light of the dwindling fires.

"Marius, please," I pleaded. With the right words, he could stop them. I could not.

Every senator turned their gaze to Marius.

"Make it quick, then," he said.

"No!" I roared.

Sulla and his associates let out a cry and shot off to do their work.

"No! No!" I unsheathed my sword and ran in the direction of the nearest aggressor.

But arms linked around my own and pinned me in place.

"No, Sertorius, no!" a voice whispered in my ear. It was

Lucius's. "Touch one of them, and your life is over. You know that."

"No! Please, please, no!" I cried. But the restraints around me were too strong.

Some of the senators climbed the side of the curia and opened the windows at the top. Others threatened the guard until they stood aside, then strutted through the front door.

Cries carried on the December winds to the night sky. I could see nothing but what the moonlight revealed, namely senators atop the curia pelting those within with roof tiles.

The doors burst open again, and Glaucia stumbled forth covered in blood. What was left of his toga was as scarlet as the Roman standard.

He was crying out for justice as the senators set upon him.

He died in much the same way as Memmius had. Perhaps worse because he had not accepted his fate with nobility.

"No… No…" I struggled against my restrainers again, but they held fast.

"Lie still, sir. Please. Please."

I lowered my head, closed my eye, and wept openly.

When I opened it again, the senators had sauntered off.

Lucius and the others holding my arms let me go.

"No, no," I was still saying. I climbed my way up the curia steps to where Glaucia was strewn out. He was not breathing. His heart was not beating. His eyes were open, and they stared up at the statue of Vulcan, the god of flames.

I hurried inside, but Marius had already beaten me there.

He was slumped in the curule chair he was accustomed to sitting in, staring at the body of his former associate on the senate floor.

I hurried to Saturninus's side, but the tribune was already twitching.

"Saturninus," I said softly. His eyes moved to me, but only blood bubbled from his lips. "Tribune Saturninus," I said again.

His body began convulsing, his legs flailing.

"Tribune? Tribune?" I placed my hands on his knees. He looked at me as intently as any man ever had. There was something he wanted to say. He opened his mouth, and a moan escaped him, but nothing more.

A yelp escaped him, sounding like a dog when its tail has been stepped on.

"Saturninus, I'm here."

I thought he was going to try to speak again, but a steady flow of blood spilled out of either side of his lips. And then he fell still. I placed a hand on his chest. Neither lungs nor heart pumped.

"I promised him a fucking trial!" I shouted as I stood. "A trial!"

Marius remained slumped in his curule chair, his eyes empty and pink-rimmed as he stared at the broken body at his feet.

"I think I shall go east. I vowed a pilgrimage to Cylene years ago. Perhaps it's time I fulfilled it."

"I think that's wise, sir," I replied.

And I realized I hated him in that moment. As much as Quintus Caepio. As much as Gnaeus Caepio. As much as any ambitious man who cost his country more than words can articulate.

Because he had birthed all this as surely as a midwife. And after giving unlimited power to Glaucia and Saturninus, his jealousy bade him betray them and leave them to their own devices. Unchecked by reason.

I turned and walked out of the senate house, leaving the broken bodies of my old associates and the fallen consul behind me.

EPILOGUE

"I DON'T WANT to see them either, sweet boy, but it's important," I said, Gavius glued to my side as we approached the river Tiber.

"Why do we have to look at them, though?" he asked, burying his head in my chest.

"There are a few reasons, my son. First, because we need to show our respects for those who at one point did serve the Republic that keeps us free."

"Okay," he said, wiping his weary eyes with the heel of his palm.

"Also because these men are a cautionary tale. To the both of us. A tale that bids us not push too far or too fast, or tragedy could beset us on all paths." I did my best not to reveal the pain in my heart.

We had been waiting for hours. The line was long. Merchants took advantage of the occasion, offering any number of goods at an increased rate to the impatient members in the line.

"Wine? Wine! Good price, best quality!" one of them shouted when we were close enough to the river to see the bodies.

"Not today, citizen. Thank you," I said. I reached back and took Arrea's hand. She resented this even more than Gavius. Almost as much as I did.

"Come, family. Look upon Rome's fallen," I said. My voice cracked just a bit, but I hoped they hadn't noticed.

We reached the edge of the waters, and there upon the river-bank were the bodies of my former associates. Gaius Glaucia and Lucius Saturninus. There were many points where the bodies of other men like Saufeius and Equitius had washed up, but I had no interest in seeing them.

As if the two had deigned it themselves, though, Glaucia and Saturninus had washed up together.

The blood had drained from their bodies, their corpses pale as shades of Hades. But their eyes remained open. Saturninus's gaze was no less piercing in death than it had been in life. And his eyes seemed to follow me, still crying out for justice. For land for the veterans and cheap grain for the people.

As we arrived at the edge, I turned away and tried to stifle the bile collecting in my throat and the tears welling in my eyes. I felt Gavius looking directly at them, though, and I regained my composure and turned again.

"These were friends of mine, Gavius. They did some bad things. Don't follow their path. But remember them. Remember —" My voice caught in my throat.

Gavius turned and placed his tiny hands on either side of my face.

"I'll remember, Tata."

I kissed him on his cheek.

"If only we could charge a few denarii for entry to see their corpses, perhaps we could begin to earn back what these two demagogues stole from the city," a voice said from behind me. I didn't have to turn to realize who it was. I kissed Gavius again and passed him off to Arrea, who helped him to the ground and walked him closer to the riverbank.

"What did you say?" I asked.

"I said—" Sulla tried to continue.

"Have some respect for the dead, Sulla. Even those you killed yourself."

Sulla chuckled. "I'll not have respect for—" he tried to continue, but I cut him off.

"Enough. You conniving, sniveling little worm. You caused their deaths. The fact that you're here is disturbing enough. Don't continue to insult them."

He smiled and turned to me. Unlike the rest of those who quashed the rebellion on the nones of December, Sulla bore none of the injuries.

"Apollo save me, it appears that the one-eyed senator is—"

"Sulla, leave my presence before I open your stomach."

He accepted prolonged eyed contact, chuckled, and shook his head at my ignorance. Despite the fact that he was taller and broader than myself, he knew I could overpower him if it came to conflict, so he shrugged and moved away.

I turned back to Arrea and Gavius at the crest of the Tiber. Apollonius stood behind them; he alone perceptive enough to notice the trouble I might have just caused myself.

I waved him off. I had no time for more fear of the future. Those I had thought would protect my future—Saturninus, Glaucia, Marius, Memmius—were all either dead or otherwise gone. There was no one to tell me how to act or behave any longer. And even if telling Sulla to go bugger himself was dangerous, I was compelled to take the risk.

"Say goodbye to the fallen, Gavius," I said, taking his hand in my own. He freed himself and waved at the bloated bodies of my old friends.

"Goodbye," he said. I was on the verge of tears, so I swept my boy up into my arms and moved on, allowing the gawkers behind us to take our place.

When we returned, there was a line of gatherers at my door, extending down the street and disappearing beneath the hill.

"Hail," they said. The veterans present saluted me. Their eyes relayed sympathies. It wasn't time for my morning levy—no, they had come to pay their respects.

I nearly wept.

So much had happened. So much had gone wrong. In the process, I had made many enemies and lost so many friends. But in the end, I knew as long as I had their support, we would be just fine.

I released Arrea's hand and stepped toward them, shaking a few hands but unable to reach them all. I knew some kind of speech was required, even if they didn't expect it. I delayed as long as I could, trying to find the right words.

But they knew what had happened. Everyone did. And tales of my role in it all had surely spread by now too.

"My brothers…" I had to pause. "Thank you. Your presence here reveals something to me. I've had my suspicions, but now I am certain. Your being here proves that you are not simply my clients, but my friends."

They nodded along with me as I gestured for Arrea, Apollonius, and Gavius to join me at my side.

"My family and I are grateful for your presence, although I didn't anticipate it. I know from our private conversations that many of you had your doubts about Saturninus, Glaucia, and their regime. I'm sure there is more than a few amongst you that celebrated when news of their deaths greeted you. And I understand why.

"Yet you are here. That is no small matter to me. I've expressed my fear of Saturninus and Glaucia to some of you many times, but you all knew I didn't desire this. I did all I could to change the course of events, to save them… us from the brink of violence. In the end there was nothing I could do. They charted their course and were determined to finish it. Aside from divine intervention, I'm not convinced this could have turned out any other way. Those men, who were once my friends, were threatening chaos and destruction on the entire Republic. I will not attempt to defend their actions. All I will say is this: if any of us are to ever find our own bodies in the Tiber, let it be for what we believe in, as they did."

A few of them nodded in agreement, others tried to clap but it didn't catch on.

I turned to Apollonius.

"Sort them and send them in one by one."

"I'm afraid it will be long into the night before you could see all of them."

"That may be so. We'll have to cancel dinner, but let them know I will see them all if they are willing to wait."

I found my way to the tablinum and sat in my chair, finally free to weep in a moment's reprieve before the first guest was ushered in.

Most of them said the same thing. They offered their condolences, if I wanted them, and asked if anything was required of them now that peace had returned and the elections were rescheduled for the next auspicious day. Some of them actually inquired about my welfare... these were no ordinary clients.

I expressed my heartfelt gratitude and shook each hand until an unfamiliar face presented itself.

A young man, perhaps twenty or so, strode in and stood before the desk. He was wearing a simple blue-dyed tunic but radiated a certain nobility that wasn't typically present in the farmers and veterans who called themselves my clients.

"Good evening, amicus," I said, still trying to register a name. I tapped two fingers on the desk to signal for Apollonius to whisper his name in my ear. It was his role to remember the names and faces I forgot, but when I turned he shrugged his shoulders.

"It's good to see you, old friend." He stepped forward and took me by the forearm with a posture and formality that was undoubtably noble.

"What can I do for you?" I asked when I could find nothing else to say. He smiled and looked to his feet.

"Do you not know me, Sertorius?"

"I apologize, but I'm afraid I don't."

"Perhaps it would help if you held my hand and we ran through to the forum on some errand for my grandfather?"

I sprang to my feet.

"Marcus Caepio?" I asked, eye widening.

"The same, just a bit older, perhaps."

"I'll shake your hand again, then, if you'll accept." I placed both hands around his and kissed his cheek. "It's been so long. You stood beneath my shoulder the last time I saw you." Now I'd be lucky to reach his.

"That's what happens when you're away fighting in the legions! City life continues even if we believe it froze in time with a sight of medusa. I've just returned from my first year on campaign, actually."

"And until now I've continued to see you as a boy." Silence crept in. "It's so good to see you."

As the silence lingered I wondered why he had come. For those of you who don't remember, I left his family home in a not-so-pleasant manner, to put it mildly.

"You know we never blamed you for what happened?" He turned to me and made eye-contact, unperturbed that the other was missing. My words caught in my throat. "At least mother and I didn't. My family are a vicious brood. I know that."

"Well... I'll speak no ill of your family, but I am relieved to hear that. You know how I cared for you and Junia."

"She sends her regards by the way." He turned and closed the doors to the tablinum. His gait reminded me more of his grandfather than his father, but there was also something different entirely. "We know what you did for our family."

"I..."

"The letter, Sertorius. You saved my father's life, and perhaps mine as well. And my mother's. We will never forget that."

My heart began to race and panic began to creep in. Marius was no where within ear shot, of course, but the letter I sent to Quintus Caepio which warned of his impending assassination could put me on the general's list of foes if he were to know of it.

"Don't worry. We know that we can never mention it. And I vow to you that we haven't. We are safe and isolated on a Greek island which I'll not name. Whether he'll admit it or not, my father is actually happier than he's ever been. More time for poetry. He's even stopped brooding over the *glory* that was stolen from him and the gold of Tolosa, if you can imagine it."

"I'm pleased to hear that."

He finally seemed to appraise my apprehension. "Sertorius, I owe you a debt of gratitude. And I mean to repay it."

I searched his face, trying to recall the boy who played with toys beneath my feet all those years ago. There was only the faintest hint.

"You owe me nothing, Marcus."

"I disagree. But more than that, my associates have been watching you. Even the staunchest nobles in Rome have been impressed by your dauntless courage, or your persistent and at times tiresome—as they say—determination to follow your heart. Tales of your bravery on the night of the assassinations have been the topic of many dinner conversations. It revealed, if nothing else, that you were willing to put the safety of the Republic before your own personal allegiances. That means something to my circle."

I began to speak but he cut me off.

"I am here to extend an offer. One of my grandfather's proteges, Titus Didius, was just named governor of Macedonia. He needs good men to quash the rebellion, and your name is at the top of his list. He's too proud to come to you directly, of course, but I told him I'd be more than happy to visit an old friend."

"In what capacity?" I asked, suddenly scooting to the edge of my stool.

"Legate," he replied without hesitation.

I felt Apollonius gasp behind me. I did my best not to do the same.

"When does he leave?"

"The kalends of March. Until then, he needs officers training with the legions. They're raw recruits and need a veteran like yourself to help whip them into shape."

I gulped. I considered asking about compensation, as my debt was beginning to consume me, but I differed to my better judgement.

"Will I be able to pick my own staff?"

"Of course."

"What about my horse?"

"You can bring whatever steed you'd like. Bring two or three even, if it pleases you. You'll be making more than enough to feed them."

"And what about my family?" I asked.

He furrowed his brows and shrugged.

"You'll need a slave to assist with administration, to be certain. It's an egregious amount of paperwork, being a legate..." he droned in a way that finally reminded me of his father. "It's a war campaign, so I wouldn't advice bringing that boy of yours. Legates are known to bring their wives occasionally, especially while in winter quarters."

"Wives?" I asked.

"Yes. You are married are you not?"

"Not yet," I said, looking down at my desk.

"Listen, Didius wants you on this campaign. Badly. But he won't say it himself, and a delay in responding will likely insult him. Take a few days but—"

"I'll accept." Decisiveness was a rather new trait for me, but I liked how it felt.

He smiled, perhaps surprised.

"I'm thrilled to hear it. I'll let the proconsul know then. It was a joy, Sertorius. Perhaps we'll serve on the same battlefield one day." He leaned across my desk and kissed my cheek.

"I'll pray that it's so, if there are more battles to fight."

"There will always be more battles to fight."

There was only one thing left to do.

All that was to decide was the right time to do it. I consulted with Apollonius, Lucius, and Equus of course, but the only thing I cared about was that the sun was shining.

I wanted the light to shimmer with the tears in her eyes the way they did the first time I told her I loved her.

The location, however, was never up for consideration. It had to be in the garden. It's where she felt most at home, it's where she looked the most lovely.

Apollonius laid a path of bright flower petals from the atrium to my footsteps. He then waited at the door to take her by the hand and usher her to me.

All of our friends were gathered, but it was only her I could see as she entered.

I smiled in triumph. Her eyes were shining just as I had hoped.

"Arrea," I whispered.

The face she made then is forever encapsulated in my mind. A tear comes to my eye and a smile splits my lips as I remember it. Excitement, fear, confusion, nervousness, passion, pain, joy. That look, forever etched into my mind, expressed everything we had gone through, and everything we would go through together.

Her knees became weak, so she found her way to her favorite bench beside the garden flowers and the chirping birds. I sat beside her.

I didn't have much left that I hadn't given to my creditors. Whatever I did have though, I spent on that ring. I couldn't afford a gold one. An iron ring would have to do, but believe me I searched the treasure peddlers of the forum until I found the right one. I would have bought a gold ring if I could, but perhaps I preferred it this way. We didn't start with gold. Our story began with iron swords and mud-thatched huts. And yet we loved each other anyways.

"Quintus..."

"Arrea, I want you to be—" She cut me off, but in her tears all I could hear was 'politically ruinous'. "I don't care. Everything I've ever had was earned by the sweat of my brow and the speed of my sword arm. With your strength at my side, I will do so much more."

She squeezed her eyes shut and placed one hand on my face and grabbed my hand with the other.

"Quintus, I'm barren. I cannot give you a..." she managed to say, but now I cut her off.

"A child we have already." I gestured for Gavius to join us, itching at the rose-petal laurel around his head as he did so. "I will listen to anything you have to say, but I can promise you it won't change my mind. I want you to be my wife, Arrea."

She opened her mouth again, but rather than offer another objection she brought me to her lips. Those gathered clapped and roared like an assembly in the forum. With trembling hands, we managed to slip that iron ring onto her finger. And to this day, I'm not sure if it's ever come off.

This is not the beginning of my story and it also isn't the end. But perhaps it's the end of the beginning.

I wish I could tell you that this was the end of the bloodshed.

If only I could tell you that everyone put down their swords, pursued reconciliation despite how difficult it may be, and worked together to restore the Republic to the glory she once knew. Unfortunately, that would be a lie.

Since then, more Romans have killed more Romans. There was certainly more wars to be fought. More bodies have wound up in the Tiber.

In truth, the end of the story has already been written. Now all there is to do is to tell it.

Join the Legion to receive Vincent's spinoff series "The Marius Scrolls" for FREE! Just scan the QR code below.

GLOSSARY

- *Ab urbe condita—Roman phrase and dating system "from the founding of the city." The Ancient Romans believed Rome was founded in 753 BC, and therefore this year is AUC 1. As such, 107–106 BC would correspond to 647–648 AUC.*
- *Aedile—Magistrates who were tasked with maintaining and improving the city's infrastructure. There were four, elected annually: two plebeian aediles and two curule aediles.*
- *Agnomen—A form of nickname given to men for traits or accomplishments unique to them. Many conquering generals received agnomen to designate the nation they had conquered, such as Africanus, Macedonicus, and Numidicus.*
- *Amicus (f. Amica)—Latin for friend.*
- *Appian Way (via Appia)—the oldest and most important of Rome's roads, linking Italy with farther areas of Italy.*
- *Aqua Marcia—the most important of Rome's aqueducts at this time. Built in 144-140 B.C.*
- *Arausio—the location of a battle in which Rome suffered a great loss. Numbers were reported as high as 90,000 Roman casualties. Sertorius and Lucius Hirtuleius barely escaped*

with their lives, and Sertorius' brother Titus died upon the battlefield.

- *Argiletum*—a route leading direction to the Roman forum.
- *Asclepius*—The Greek god of medicine. There was a temple to Asclepius overlooking the Tiber River, and this is where Rabirius and many other wounded veterans congregate.
- *Augur*—A priest and official who interpreted the will of the gods by studying the flight of birds.
- *Auxiliary*—Legionaries without citizenship. At this time, most auxiliaries were of Italian origin, but later encompassed many different cultures.
- *Ave*—Latin for hail, or hello.
- *Basilica Porcia*—the first named basilica in Rome, built by Cato the Censor in 184 B.C., it was the home of the ten tribunes of the plebs.
- *Basilica Sempronia*—built in 170 B.C. by the father of Tiberius and Gaius Gracchus. It was a place often used for commerce.
- *Bellona*—The Roman goddess of war and the consort of Mars (see also **Mars**). She was also a favored patron goddess of the Roman legion.
- *Bona Dea*—"Good goddess." The term was occasionally used as an exclamation.
- *Boni*—Literally "good men." They were a political party prevalent in the Late Roman Republic. They desired to restrict the power of the popular assembly and the tribune of the plebs, while extending the power of the Senate. The title "Optimates" was more common at the time, but these aristocrats often referred to themselves favorably as the boni. They were natural enemies of the populares.
- *Caepiones*—A powerful aristocratic family, and the former patrons of Sertorius.
- *Caldarium*—hot bathes.

- *Carcer*—*a small prison, the only one in Rome. It typically held war captives awaiting execution or held those deemed as threats by those in political power.*
- *Centuriate Assembly*—*one of the three Roman assemblies. It met on the Field of Mars and elected the Consuls and Praetors. It could also pass laws and acted as a court of appeals in certain capital cases. It was based initially on 198 centuries, and was structured in a way that favored the rich over the poor, and the aged over the young.*
- *Centurion*—*An officer in the Roman legion. By the time Marius's reforms were ushered in, there were six in every cohort, one for every century. They typically led eighty to one hundred men. The most senior centurion in the legion was the "primus pilus," or first-spear centurion.*
- *Century*—*Roman tactical unit made of eighty to one hundred men.*
- *Cimbri*—*a tribe of northern invaders with uncertain origins that fought Rome for over a decade. Sertorius began his career by fighting them.*
- *Circus Maximus*—*a massive public stadium which hosted chariot races and other forms of entertainment. It's speculated that the stadium could have held as many as 150,000 spectators.*
- *Client*—*A man who pledged himself to a patron (see also* **patron***) in return for protection or favors.*
- *Cloaca Maxima*—*the massive sewer system beneath Rome.*
- *Cocina*—*Kitchen.*
- *Cohort*—*Roman tactical unit made of six centuries (see also* **century***), or 480–600 men. The introduction of the cohort as the standard tactical unit of the legion is attributed to Marius's reforms.*
- *Collegium(a)*—*Any association or body of men with something in common. Some functioned as guilds or social clubs, others were criminal in nature.*

- *Comitiatus (pl. Comitia)* — a public assembly that made decisions, held elections, and passed legislation or judicial verdicts.
- *Comitium* — a meeting area outside of the Curia Hostilia. The rosta speaking platform stood at its helm.
- *Consul* — The highest magistrate in the Roman Republic. Two were elected annually to a one-year term. The required age for entry was forty, although exceptions were occasionally (and hesitantly) made.
- *Contiones (pl. Contio)* — a public assembly that did not handle official matters. Discussions could be held on almost anything, and debates were a regular cause for a contiones to be called, but they did not pass legislation or pass down verdicts.
- *Contubernalis(es)* — A military cadet assigned to the commander specifically. They were generally considered officers, but held little authority.
- *Contubernium* — The smallest unit in the Roman legion. It was led by the decanus (see also **decanus**).
- *Curia* — The Senate House. The Curia Hostilia was built in the 7th century B.C. and held most of the senatorial meetings throughout the Republic, even in Sertorius' day.
- *Decanus* — "Chief of ten," he was in a position of authority over his contubernium, a group of eight to ten men who shared his tent.
- *Dis Pater* — god of the Roman underworld, at times subsumed by Plato or Hades.
- *Dignitas* — A word that represents a Roman man's reputation and his entitlement to respect. Dignitas correlated with personal achievements and honor.
- *Dis Pater* — The Roman god of death. He was often associated with fertility, wealth, and prosperity. His name was often shortened to Dis. He was nearly synonymous with the Roman god Pluto or the Greek god Hades.

- *Dominus(a)—Latin for "master." A term most often used by slaves when interacting with their owner, but it could also be used to convey reverence or submission by others.*
- *Domus- the type of home owned by the upper class and the wealthy in Ancient Rome.*
- *Equestrian—Sometimes considered the lesser of the two aristocratic classes (see also **patrician**) and other times considered the higher of the two lower-class citizens (see also **plebeian**). Those in the equestrian order had to maintain a certain amount of wealth or property, or otherwise would be removed from the class.*
- *Evocati—An honorary term given to soldiers who served out their terms and volunteered to serve again. Evocati were generally spared a large portion of common military duties.*
- *Faex—Latin for "shit."*
- *Falernian wine—The most renowned and sought-after wine in Rome at this time.*
- *Field of Mars—"Campus martius" in Latin. This was where armies trained and waited to deploy or to enter the city limits for a Triumph.*
- *Flamen Dialis—Priest of Jupiter Optimus Maximus.*
- *Forum—The teeming heart of Ancient Rome. There were many different forums, in various cities, but most commonly the Forum refers to the center of the city itself, where most political, public, and religious dealings took place.*
- *Gerrae—"Nonsense!" An exclamation.*
- *Gladius(i)—The standard short-sword used in the Roman legion.*
- *Gracchi—Tiberius and Gaius Gracchus were brothers who held the rank of tribune of the plebs at various times throughout the second century BC. They were political revolutionaries whose attempts at reforms eventually led to their murder (or in one case, forced suicide). Tiberius and Gaius were still fresh in the minds of Romans in Sertorius's*

day. The boni feared that another politician might rise in their image, and the populares were searching for Gracchi to rally around.

- Hastati—Common front line soldiers in the Roman legion. As a result of the Marian Reforms, by Sertorius's times, the term hastati was being phased out and would soon be obsolete.
- Imperator—A Roman commander with imperium (see also **imperium**). Typically, the commander would have to be given imperium by his men.
- Impluvium—A cistern or tank in the atrium of the domus that collects rainfall water from a hole in the ceiling above.
- Insula(e)—Apartment complexes. They varied in size and accommodations, but generally became less desirable the higher up the insula one went.
- Jupiter—The Roman king of the gods. He was the god of the sky and thunder. All political and military activity was sanctioned by Jupiter. He was often referred to as Jupiter Capitolinus for his role in leading the Roman state, or Jupiter Optimus Maximus (literally, "the best and greatest").
- Jupiter's Stone—A stone on which oaths were sworn.
- Kalends—The first day of the Ancient Roman month.
- Latrunculi— (lit. Game of Brigands) a popular board game of sorts played by the Romans. It shares similarities with games like chess or checkers.
- Legate—The senior-most officer in the Roman legion. A legate generally was in command of one legion and answered only to the general.
- Mars—The Roman god of war. He was the favored patron of many legionaries and commanders.
- Medicus—The field doctor for injured legionaries.
- Military tribune—Senior officer of the Roman legions. They were, in theory, elected by the popular assembly, and there were six assigned to every legion. By late second century

BC, however, it was not uncommon to see military tribunes appointed directly by the commander.

- *Nursia*—Sertorius' home, located in the Apennines mountains, and within the Sabine Tribes. It was famous for their turnips and little else until Sertorius came along.
- *October Horse*—A festival that took place on October 15th. An animal was sacrificed to Mars, which designated the end of the agricultural and military campaigning season.
- *Optimates*—(see **boni**).
- *Ostia*—Rome's port city, it lay at the mouth of the river Tiber.
- *Patron*—A person who offers protection and favors to his clients (see also **clients**), in favor of services of varying degrees.
- *Peristylum*—An open courtyard containing a garden within the Roman domus.
- *Pilum(a)*—The throwing javelin used by the Roman legion. Gaius Marius changed the design of the pilum in his reforms. Each legionary carried two, and typically launched them at the enemy to begin a conflict.
- *Plebeian*—Lower-born Roman citizens, commoners. Plebeians were born into their social class, so the term designated both wealth and ancestry. They typically had fewer assets and less land than equestrians, but more than the proletariat. Some, like the Metelli, were able to ascend to nobility and wealth despite their plebeian roots. These were known as "noble plebeians" and were not restricted from any power in the Roman political system.
- *Pontifex Maximus*—The highest priest in the College of Pontiffs. By Sertorius's time, the position had been highly politicized.
- *Pontiff*—A priest and member of the College of Pontiffs.
- *Popular assembly*—A legislative assembly that allowed plebeians to elect magistrates, try judicial cases, and pass laws.

- *Praetor*—The second-most senior magistrate in the Roman Republic. There were typically six elected annually, but some have speculated that there were eight elected annually by this time.
- *Prefect*—A high ranking military official in the Roman legion.
- *Princeps Senatus*—"Father of the Senate," or the first among fellow senators. It was an informal position, but came with immense respect and prestige.
- *Proconsul*—A Roman magistrate who had previously been a consul. Often, when a consul was in the midst of a military campaign at the end of his term, the Senate would appoint him as proconsul for the remainder of the war.
- *Publicani*—Those responsible for collective public revenue. They made their fortunes through this process. By Sertorius's time, the Senate and censors carefully scrutinized their activities, making it difficult for them to amass the wealth they intended.
- *Quaestor*—An elected public official and the junior-most member of the political course of offices. They served various purposes but often supervised the state treasury and performed audits. Quaestors were also used in the military and managed the finances of the legions on campaign.
- *Res Publica*—"Republic," the sacred word that encompassed everything Rome was at the time. More than just a political system, res publica represented Rome's authority and power. The Republic was founded in 509 BC, when Lucius Brutus and his fellow patriots overthrew the kings.
- *Rex sacrorum*—A senatorial priesthood, the "king of the sacred." Unlike the Pontifex Maximus, the rex sacrorum was barred from military and political life. In theory, he held the religious responsibility that was once reserved for the kings, while the consuls performed the military and political functions.

- *Rostra* — A speaking platform in the Forum made of the ships of conquered foes.
- *Salve* — Latin for hail, or hello.
- *Sancrosanctitas* — a level of religious protection offered to certain political figures and religious officials.
- *Saturnalia* — A festival held on December 17 in honor the Roman deity Saturn.
- *Senaculum* — a meeting area for senators outside of the senate house, where they would gather before a meeting began.
- *Scutum(a)* — Standard shield issued to Roman legionaries.
- *Subura* — a rough neighborhood near the Viminal and Quirinal hills. It was known for violence and thievery, as well as for the fires that spread because of the close proximity of its insulae.
- *Taberna(e)* — Could be translated as "tavern," but tabernae served several different functions in Ancient Rome. They served as hostels for travelers, occasionally operated as brothels, and offered a place for people to congregate and enjoy food and wine.
- *Tablinum* — A form of study or office for the head of a household. This is where he would generally greet his clients at his morning levy.
- *Tarpeian Rock* — a place where executions were held. Criminals of the highest degree and political threats were thrown from this cliff to their inevitable deaths.
- *Tata* — Roman term for father, closer to the modern "daddy".
- *Tecombre* — The military order to break from the testudo formation and revert to their previous formation.
- *Temple of Ascelpius* — located on the Tiber island, it was a temple of healing. The sick and ailing made pilgrimages here in hope of healing.
- *Temple of Bellona* — dedicated to the consort of Mars and goddess of war, this was a temple often used for meetings of the Senate when they needed to host foreign emissaries or

meet with returning generals awaiting a triumph. It lay outside the city limits, but close to the Servian wall.

- Temple of Castor and Pollux—often times referred simply to "Temple of Castor", it remained at the entrance of the Forum by the via sacra. It was often used for meetings of the senate, as it was actually larger than the Curia. Speeches were often given from the temple steps as well.
- Temple of Concordia (Concord)—a temple devoted to peace and reunification in the Roman Forum. It often held meetings of the senate.
- Temple of Jupiter Capitolinus (Optimus Maximus)—a temple devoted to Rome's patron God, which resided on the Capitoline hill. It was sometimes referred to as the "Capitol".
- Temple of Saturn—a temple of deep religious significance which lay at the foot of the Capitoline hill in the Roman Forum. Sacrifices were often held here following a triumph, if the generals didn't surpass it to sacrifice at the aforementioned Temple of Jupiter.
- Testudo—The "tortoise" formation. The command was used to provide additional protection by linking their scuta together.
- Teutones—a tribe of northern invaders with uncertain origins which fought Rome for over a decade. Along with the Cimbri, they nearly defeated Rome. Sertorius began his career by fighting these tribes.
- Tiber River—a body of water which connected to the Tyrrhenian sea and flowed along the western boarder of Rome. The victims of political assassinations were unceremoniously dumped here rather than receive proper burial.
- Tiberinus—the god of the Tiber river.
- Toga virilis—Literally "toga of manhood." It was a plain white toga worn by adult male citizens who were not

magistrates. The donning of the toga virilis represented the coming of age of a young Roman male.

- Tribe—Political grouping of Roman citizens. By Sertorius's time, there were thirty-six tribes, thirty-two of which were rural, four of which were urban.
- Tribune of plebs—Elected magistrates who were designed to represent the interests of the people.
- Triclinium—The dining room, which often had three couches set up in the shape of a U.
- Triumph—A parade and festival given to celebrate a victorious general and his accomplishments. He must first be hailed as imperator by his legions and then petition the Senate to grant him the Triumph.
- Valetudinarium—a hospital, typically present in Roman military camps.
- Via(e)—"Road," typically a major path large enough to travel on horseback or by carriage.
- Via Appia- (see **Appian Way**).
- Via Latina—"Latin road", led from Rome southeast.
- Via Sacra—the main road of ancient Rome, leading from the Capitoline hill through the forum, with all of the major religious and political buildings on either side.
- Via Salaria—"Salt Road" led northeast from Rome. This was the path Sertorius would have taken to and from his home in Nursia.
- Zeno—The founder of Stoic philosophy. Sertorius was a devoted reader of Zeno's works.

ACKNOWLEDGMENTS

This book is dedicated to my sweet cousin Addison Grace Hutchison. As the youngest in my family, Addison was the first child I spent an extended amount of time with. She quickly became something more akin to a sister or a niece in the years where we were both growing up. She was the light of my world. She made me become the thirteen-year-old who wanted to babysit rather than hang out with his buddies.

Tragically, Addison passed away at 11 years old in her sleep. While words can't express how badly we've hurt, all the questions we've asked, and how deeply we miss her, we know she will live on through all of us.

Addison, you will live on in every word I ever write. This work and every work I ever produced is dedicated to you and your beautiful heart. You're gone, but your legacy will continue to impact lives forever. The kind of love you shared does not expire. And I will see you again.

As some of you may have noticed in previous books, I donate $1 for every review to the Addison Grace Hutchison Foundation, established in her honor. This isn't a marketing tactic to get reviews—whether or not you leave one is completely up to you. It's just one more way I want to give back to the little girl who inspired me to become everything that I am.

There are also many others who I must acknowledge here, as without them this book doesn't exist.

First of all, Conor Franklin. I used to have a principal that I didn't read what I wrote until I was finished with a manuscript. But I was so passionate writing this book that I just had to share with someone... and you were there. After every scene you'd gathered around my desk and listen in as I read through the manuscript in my improvised Latin accents. You'll never know how much that meant to me, let alone all the encouragement, tips, and suggestions. Without you, this book doesn't exist in it's current form. Just remember... whatever this book is able to accomplish, whatever *I* am able to accomplish, you are a part of that.

Next, I have to thank all of my friends and family. It's cliché, and expected of about any author to throw out general praise to loved ones in the acknowledgements of his book. But let me state firmly that this comes from the bottom of my heart. It almost brings me to tears. For everyone who has believed me since I was a toddler running around with a Jar-Jar Binks notebook... to those who have shared blog posts and spread the word... from those who told me to pursue my dreams when it was foolish and risky... for those of you who have never read a word but have loved me for who I am regardless... thank you. You know who you are. I love you all dearly.

I also need to thank (and you should too) my editors. Without them, this story would not be what it is. The prose would be unreadable at some points. There would be errors abounding. For those that still remain, I take full responsibility. When given a manuscript loaded to the brim with imperfections, it's impossible to wipe them all out. Michael and Michelle, there is a reason I keep coming back to you. You are part of my success, and as long as I'm writing, I hope you'll remain part of my "legion".

My cover designer, Dane, should also be acknowledged. Many of you wouldn't be here if it wasn't for his incredible artwork. It can be incredibly difficult to find beautiful, time-appropriate cover images for a book set in Ancient Rome, but you put in the time and dedicated yourself to creating the best cover possible. It will continue to pay dividends, I'm certain, for a very long time. It's the same reason I'll keep coming back to you and sending others to you when they have the need. Thank you, Dane.

My narrator, Joshua Saxon, has been an immense blessing in my career. If you haven't listened to any of my books on audible, I encourage you to do so. Joshua is a master storyteller. Joshua, I didn't think it would be possible to enjoy my own books after going through them a few dozen times in the editorial phase. You have given me that ability with your incredible voice and way with words. Brother, I want you to remain a part of my legion as long as you can. Something tells me before long you'll be so slammed with narrating gigs you'll struggle to fit me in!

Aside from these folks who worked with me on this project, there are a number of individuals who VOLUNTEERED their time to read the book early and give critical advice on how the book should proceed and fixing my numerous mistakes even before my editors had to. My "First Cohort" as I call them are so important to me. This small team is currently made up of Leah Shaver, Allen Dahl, Richard Poska, Adam, and Keith Stringfellow. I thank you all from the bottom of my heart.

On top of that, there have been numerous individuals willing to receive early copies of this book in the hopes that they'll leave honest reviews. My arCenturions, as I call them, are too many to be named directly, but never doubt Centurions, that you are so valuable to me and dear to my heart.

And to all of my subscribers, "The Legion", you are the reason I write. With every word, I think of you. I hope you find entertainment, encouragement, and inspiration for my writing. When I have writer's block, when deadlines are crushing, when I am terrified of my keyboard because of a difficult scene that needs writing… it's you that gives me the courage to write. For all your encouragement, patience, and support I am overflowing with gratitude. You make me glad that I pursued this crazy life of writing. And I will keep pushing forward when things are difficult with you by my side.

And finally, I want to thank *you*. Thank you for reading this book. You have truly made my dream a reality. I started out writing Lord of the Rings and Star Wars fan fiction while I still had baby teeth. I never knew that one day my stories would be able to reach so many people. Whether or not you continue to read my books, let me say in big bold letters: THANK YOU. I cherish each and every one of you, and I pray that you have enjoyed and found some value within these scrolls.

Vincent B. Davis II
   May 5, 2020

ABOUT THE AUTHOR

Vincent B. Davis II is an author, entrepreneur, and soldier.

He is a graduate of East Tennessee State University, and has served in the United States Army since 2014.

He's the author of six books, three of which have become international bestsellers. When he's not researching or writing his next book, you can find him watching Carolina Panthers football or playing with his rescued mutt, Buddy. You can connect with the author on Facebook or Twitter @vbdavisii, vincentbdavisii.com, or at Vincent@thirteenthpress.com.

BB bookbub.com/profile/vincent-b-davis-ii

g goodreads.com/vbdavisii

f facebook.com/vbdavisii

O instagram.com/vbdavisii

Printed in Great Britain
by Amazon

38542518R00192